**Praise for #1 New York Times
bestselling author**

NORA ROBERTS

"Her stories have fueled the dreams
of twenty-five million readers."
—*Entertainment Weekly*

"Roberts is indeed a word artist, painting her story
and her characters with vitality and verve."
—*Los Angeles Daily News*

"Nora Roberts just keeps getting better and better."
—*Milwaukee Journal Sentinal*

"Roberts creates exceptional characters who...
live on in the reader's imagination and heart."
—*Publishers Weekly*

"Roberts has a warm feel for her characters
and an eye for the evocative detail."
—*Chicago Tribune*

"Roberts...is at the top of her game."
—*People Magazine*

"Roberts's bestselling novels are some of the best
in the romance genre."
—*USA Today*

"...an author of extraordinary power."
—*Rave Reviews*

"Nora Roberts's gift...is her ability to pull the reader
into the lives of her characters—we live, love,
anguish and triumph with them."
—*Rendezvous*

"Everything Nora Roberts writes turns to gold."
—*Romantic Times Magazine*

Dear Reader,

Though Mikhail's and Alex's stories were originally published as the second and fourth stories in my series featuring the Stanislaski family, I'm delighted that both books are now available in one volume.

Mikhail and Alex are as different as two brothers can be—one hot-tempered and proud, the other an irresistible ladies' man—but both have a strong love of family and the kind of bonds that only a shared history in a warm, caring home can bring.

In *Luring A Lady,* Mikhail storms into Sidney Hayward's life looking for a villain and discovers a cool beauty he longs to possess. And in *Convincing Alex,* it's Alex's turn to be charmed—and seduced—when he becomes the object of bold and beautiful Bess McNee's affections.

I hope you enjoy reading these stories. Look for *The Stanislaski Sisters: Natasha and Rachel,* which contains books one and three in the series, coming in February 2001 from Silhouette Books. Also in February, from Silhouette Special Edition, *Considering Kate,* a brand-new story in the Stanislaski saga.

All the best,

NORA ROBERTS

The Stanislaski Brothers

Mikhail and Alex

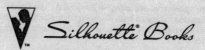

Published by Silhouette Books
America's Publisher of Contemporary Romance

The books contained in *The Stanislaski Brothers: Mikhail and Alex*
and *The Stanislaski Sisters: Natasha and Rachel,* available in
February 2001, were originally published in the following order:

TAMING NATASHA (SSE#583), LURING A LADY (SSE#709),
FALLING FOR RACHEL (SSE#810), CONVINCING ALEX (SSE#872)

 SILHOUETTE BOOKS

THE STANISLASKI BROTHERS: MIKHAIL AND ALEX

Copyright © 2000 by Harlequin Books S.A.

ISBN 0-373-48422-4

The publisher acknowledges the copyright holder
of the individual works as follows:

LURING A LADY
Copyright © 1991 by Nora Roberts

CONVINCING ALEX
Copyright © 1994 by Nora Roberts

Visit Silhouette at www.eHarlequin.com

Printed in U.S.A.

CONTENTS

Book 2

Book 4

THE STANISLASKI BROTHERS: Mikhail and Alex

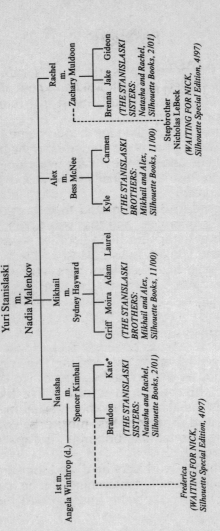

Yuri Stanislaski
m.
Nadia Malenkov

Natasha
m.
Spencer Kimball

1st m.
Angela Winthrop (d.)

Brandon   Kate*

*(THE STANISLASKI
SISTERS:
Natasha and Rachel,
Silhouette Books, 2/01)*

Frederica
*(WAITING FOR NICK,
Silhouette Special Edition, 4/97)*

Mikhail
m.
Sydney Hayward

Griff   Moira   Adam   Laurel

*(THE STANISLASKI
BROTHERS:
Mikhail and Alex,
Silhouette Books, 11/00)*

Alex
m.
Bess McNee

Kyle   Carmen

*(THE STANISLASKI
BROTHERS:
Mikhail and Alex,
Silhouette Books, 11/00)*

Stepbrother
Nicholas LeBeck
*(WAITING FOR NICK,
Silhouette Special Edition, 4/97)*

Rachel
m.
Zachary Muldoon

Brenna   Jake   Gideon

*(THE STANISLASKI
SISTERS:
Natasha and Rachel, 2/01)*

Look for THE STANISLASKI SISTERS: Natasha and Rachel in February 2001.

*And also in February 2001, CONSIDERING KATE, a brand-new book in the
Stanislaski series from Silhouette Special Edition.

Prologue

The playground was full of noise, drama and politics. Even at eight, Mikhail knew about politics. He had, after all, been in America nearly two full years.

He no longer waited for men to come drag his father away, or to wake up one morning back in the Ukraine and find the escape into Hungary, the travel to Austria and finally to New York had all been a dream.

He lived in Brooklyn, and that was good. He was an American, and that was better. He and his big sister, his little brother went to school—and spoke English. Most of the time. His baby sister had been born here, and would never know what it was to shiver in the cold while hiding in a wagon, waiting, waiting for discovery.

Or freedom.

There were times he didn't think of it at all. He liked getting up in the morning and seeing the little houses that looked so much like their house out his bedroom window. He liked smelling the breakfast his mother cooked in the kitchen, and hearing his mother's voice murmuring, his father's booming as Papa got ready for work.

Papa had to work very hard, and sometimes he came home tired in the evening. But he had a smile in his eyes, and the lines around them were fading.

And at night there was hot food and laughter around the dinner table.

School was not so bad, and he was learning—except his teachers said he daydreamed too much and too often.

"The girls are jumping rope." Alexi, Mikhail's little brother, plopped down beside him.

Both had dark hair and golden brown eyes, and the sharp facial bones that would make women swoon in only a few more years. Now, of course, girls were something to be ignored. Unless they were family.

"Natasha," Alex said with smug pride in his older sister, "is the best."

"She is Stanislaski."

Alex acknowledged this with a shrug. It went without saying. His eyes scanned the playground. He liked to watch how people behaved, what they did—and didn't do. His jacket—just a bit too big as his brother's was a bit too small—was open despite the brisk March wind.

Alex nodded toward two boys on the far end of the blacktop. "After school, we have to beat up Will and Charlie Braunstein."

Mikhail pursed his lips, scratched an itch just under his ribs. "Okay. Why?"

"Because Will said we were Russian spies and Charlie laughed and made noises like a pig. So."

"So," Mikhail agreed. And the brothers looked at each other and grinned.

They were late getting home from school, which would probably mean a punishment. Mikhail's pants were ripped at the knee and Alexi's lip was split—which would undoubtedly mean a lecture.

But it had been worth it. The Stanislaski brothers had emerged from the battle victorious. They strolled down the sidewalk, arms slung over each other's shoulders, book bags dragging as they recapped the combat.

"Charlie, he has a good punch," Mikhail said. "So if you fight again, you have to be fast. He has longer arms than you have."

"And he has a black eye," Alex noted with satisfaction.

"Yes." Mikhail swelled with pride over his baby brother's exploits. "This is good. When we go to school tomorrow, we... Uh-oh."

He broke off, and the fearless warrior trembled.

Nadia Stanislaski stood on the stoop outside their front door. His mama's hands were fisted on her hips, and even from half a block away he knew her eagle eye had spotted the rip in his trousers.

"Now we're in for it," Alexi muttered.

"We're not in yet."

"No, it means...in trouble." Alexi tried his best smile, even though it caused his lip to throb. But Nadia's eyes narrowed.

She swaggered down the walk like a gunfighter prepared to draw and fire. "You fight again?"

As the eldest, Mikhail stepped in front of his brother. "Just a little."

Her sharp eyes scanned them, top to bottom and judged the damage minor. "You fight each other again?"

"No, Mama." Alex sent her a hopeful look. "Will Braunstein said—"

"I don't want to hear what Will Braunstein said. Am I Will Braunstein's mama?"

At the tone, both boys dropped their chins to their chests and murmured: "No, Mama."

"Whose mama am I?"

Both boys sighed. Heavily. "Our mama."

"So, this is what I do when my boys make me worry and come late from school and fight like hooligans." It was a word she'd learned from her neighbor Grace MacNamara—and one she thought, sentimentally, suited her sons so well. Her boys yelped when she grabbed each one by the earlobe.

Before she could pull them toward the house, she heard the rattle and thump that could only be her husband Yuri's secondhand pickup truck.

He swung to the curb, wiggled his eyebrows when he saw his wife holding each of his sons by the ear. "What have they done?"

"Fighting the Braunsteins. We go inside now to call Mrs. Braunstein and apologize."

"Aw. Ow!" Mikhail's protest turned into a muffled yip as Nadia expertly twisted his earlobe.

"This can wait, yes? I have something." Yuri

clambered out of the truck, and held up a little gray pup. "This is Sasha, your new brother."

Both boys shouted with delight and, released, sprang forward. Sasha responded with licks and nips and wriggles until Yuri bundled the pup into Mikhail's arms.

"He is for you and Alexi and Tasha and Rachel to take care. Not for your mama," he said even as Nadia rolled her eyes. "This is understood?"

"We'll take good care of him, Papa. Let me hold him, Mik!" Alex demanded and tried to elbow Mikhail aside.

"I'm the oldest. I hold him first."

"Everybody will hold. Go. Go show your sisters." Yuri waved his hands. Before scrambling away, both boys pressed against him.

"Thank you, Papa." Mikhail turned to kiss his mother's cheek. "We'll call Mrs. Braunstein, Mama."

"Yes, you will." Nadia shook her head as they ran into the house, calling for their sisters. "Hooligans," she said, relishing the word.

"Boys will be what boys will be." Yuri lifted her off her feet, laughed long and deep. "We are an American family." He set her down, but kept his arm around her waist as they started into the house. "What's for dinner?"

LURING A LADY

To my nephew Kenni,
my second favorite carpenter

Chapter One

She wasn't a patient woman. Delays and excuses were barely tolerated, and never tolerated well. Waiting—and she was waiting now—had her temper dropping degree by degree toward ice. With Sydney Hayward icy anger was a great deal more dangerous than boiling rage. One frigid glance, one frosty phrase could make the recipient quake. And she knew it.

Now she paced her new office, ten stories up in midtown Manhattan. She swept from corner to corner over the deep oatmeal-colored carpet. Everything was perfectly in place, papers, files, coordinated appointment and address books. Even her brass-and-ebony desk set was perfectly aligned, the pens and pencils marching in a straight row across the polished mahogany, the notepads carefully placed beside the phone.

Her appearance mirrored the meticulous precision and tasteful elegance of the office. Her crisp beige suit was all straight lines and starch, but didn't disguise the fact that there was a great pair of legs striding across the carpet.

With it she wore a single strand of pearls, earrings to match and a slim gold watch, all very discreet and exclusive. As a Hayward, she'd been raised to be both.

Her dark auburn hair was swept off her neck and secured with a gold clip. The pale freckles that went with the hair were nearly invisible after a light dusting of powder. Sydney felt they made her look too young and too vulnerable. At twenty-eight she had a face that reflected her breeding. High, slashing cheekbones, the strong, slightly pointed chin, the small straight nose. An aristocratic face, it was pale as porcelain, with a softly shaped mouth she knew could sulk too easily, and large smoky-blue eyes that people often mistook for guileless.

Sydney glanced at her watch again, let out a little hiss of breath, then marched over to her desk. Before she could pick up the phone, her intercom buzzed.

"Yes."

"Ms. Hayward. There's a man here who insists on seeing the person in charge of the Soho project. And your four-o'clock appointment—"

"It's now four-fifteen," Sydney cut in, her voice low and smooth and final. "Send him in."

"Yes, ma'am, but he's not Mr. Howington."

So Howington had sent an underling. Annoyance hiked Sydney's chin up another fraction. "Send him in," she repeated, and flicked off the intercom with one frosted pink nail. So, they thought she'd be pacified with a junior executive. Sydney took a deep breath and prepared to kill the messenger.

It was years of training that prevented her mouth from dropping open when the man walked in. No, not walked, she corrected. Swaggered. Like a black-patched pirate over the rolling deck of a boarded ship.

She wished she'd had the foresight to have fired a warning shot over his bow.

Her initial shock had nothing to do with the fact that he

was wildly handsome, though the adjective suited perfectly. A mane of thick, curling black hair flowed just beyond the nape of his neck, to be caught by a leather thong in a short ponytail that did nothing to detract from rampant masculinity. His face was rawboned and lean, with skin the color of an old gold coin. Hooded eyes were nearly as black as his hair. His full lips were shadowed by a day or two's growth of beard that gave him a rough and dangerous look.

Though he skimmed under six foot and was leanly built, he made her delicately furnished office resemble a doll's house.

What was worse was the fact that he wore work clothes. Dusty jeans and a sweaty T-shirt with a pair of scarred boots that left a trail of dirt across her pale carpet. They hadn't even bothered with the junior executive, she thought as her lips firmed, but had sent along a common laborer who hadn't had the sense to clean up before the interview.

"You're Hayward?" The insolence in the tone and the slight hint of a Slavic accent had her imagining him striding up to a camp fire with a whip tucked in his belt.

The misty romance of the image made her tone unnecessarily sharp. "Yes, and you're late."

His eyes narrowed fractionally as they studied each other across the desk. "Am I?"

"Yes. You might find it helpful to wear a watch. My time is valuable if yours is not. Mr...."

"Stanislaski," He hooked his thumbs in the belt loops of his jeans, shifting his weight easily, arrogantly onto one hip. "Sydney's a man's name."

She arched a brow. "Obviously you're mistaken."

He skimmed his gaze over her slowly, with as much interest as annoyance. She was pretty as a frosted cake, but he hadn't come straight and sweaty from a job to waste time with a female. "Obviously. I thought Hayward was an old man with a bald head and a white mustache."

"You're thinking of my grandfather."

"Ah, then it's your grandfather I want to see."

"That won't be possible, Mr. Stanislaski, as my grandfather's been dead for nearly two months."

The arrogance in his eyes turned quickly to compassion. "I'm sorry. It hurts to lose family."

She couldn't say why, of all the condolences she had received, these few words from a stranger touched her. "Yes, it does. Now, if you'll take a seat, we can get down to business."

Cold, hard and distant as the moon. Just as well, he thought. It would keep him from thinking of her in more personal ways—at least until he got what he wanted.

"I have sent your grandfather letters," he began as he settled into one of the trim Queen Anne chairs in front of the desk. "Perhaps the last were misplaced during the confusion of death."

An odd way to put it, Sydney thought, but apt. Her life had certainly been turned upside down in the past few months. "Correspondence should be addressed to me." She sat, folding her hands on the desk. "As you know Hayward Enterprises is considering several firms—"

"For what?"

She struggled to shrug off the irritation of being interrupted. "I beg your pardon?"

"For what are you considering several firms?"

If she had been alone, she would have sighed and shut her eyes. Instead, she drummed her fingers on the desk. "What position do you hold, Mr. Stanislaski?"

"Position?"

"Yes, yes, what is it you do?"

The impatience in her voice made him grin. His teeth were very white, and not quite straight. "You mean, what is it I do? I work with wood."

"You're a carpenter?"

"Sometimes."

"Sometimes," she repeated, and sat back. Behind her,

buildings punched into a hard blue sky. "Perhaps you can tell me why Howington Construction sent a sometimes carpenter to represent them in this interview."

The room smelled of lemon and rosemary and only reminded him that he was hot, thirsty and as impatient as she. "I could—if they had sent me."

It took her a moment to realize he wasn't being deliberately obtuse. "You're not from Howington?"

"No. I'm Mikhail Stanislaski, and I live in one of your buildings." He propped a dirty boot on a dusty knee. "If you're thinking of hiring Howington, I would think again. I once worked for them, but they cut too many corners."

"Excuse me." Sydney gave the intercom a sharp jab. "Janine, did Mr. Stanislaski tell you he represented Howington?"

"Oh, no, ma'am. He just asked to see you. Howington called about ten minutes ago to reschedule. If you—"

"Never mind." Sitting back again, she studied the man who was grinning at her. "Apparently I've been laboring under a misconception."

"If you mean you made a mistake, yes. I'm here to talk to you about your apartment building in Soho."

She wanted, badly, to drag her hands through her hair. "You're here with a tenant complaint."

"I'm here with many tenants' complaints," he corrected.

"You should be aware that there's a certain procedure one follows in this kind of matter."

He lifted one black brow. "You own the building, yes?"

"Yes, but—"

"Then it's your responsibility."

She stiffened. "I'm perfectly aware of my responsibilities, Mr. Stanislaski. And now…"

He rose as she did, and didn't budge an inch. "Your grandfather made promises. To honor him, you must keep them."

"What I must do," she said in a frigid voice, "is run

my business." And she was trying desperately to learn how. "You may tell the other tenants that Hayward is at the point of hiring a contractor as we're quite aware that many of our properties are in need of repair or renovation. The apartments in Soho will be dealt with in turn."

His expression didn't change at the dismissal, nor did the tone of his voice or the spread-legged, feet-planted stance. "We're tired of waiting for our turn. We want what was promised to us, now."

"If you'll send me a list of your demands—"

"We have."

She set her teeth. "Then I'll look over the files this evening."

"Files aren't people. You take the rent money every month, but you don't think of the people." He placed his hands on the desk and leaned forward. Sydney caught a wisp of sawdust and sweat that was uncomfortably appealing. "Have you seen the building, or the people who live in it?"

"I have reports," she began.

"Reports." He swore—it wasn't in a language she understood, but she was certain it was an oath. "You have your accountants and your lawyers, and you sit up here in your pretty office and look through papers." With one quick slash of the hand, he dismissed her office and herself. "But you know nothing. It's not you who's cold when the heat doesn't work, or who must climb five flights of stairs when the elevator is broken. You don't worry that the water won't get hot or that the wiring is too old to be safe."

No one spoke to her that way. No one. Her own temper was making her heart beat too fast. It made her forget that she was facing a very dangerous man. "You're wrong. I'm very concerned about all of those things. And I intend to correct them as soon as possible."

His eyes flashed and narrowed, like a sword raised and turned on its edge. "This is a promise we've heard before."

"Now, it's my promise, and you haven't had that before."

"And we're supposed to trust you. You, who are too lazy or too afraid to even go see what she owns."

Her face went dead white, the only outward sign of fury. "I've had enough of your insults for one afternoon, Mr. Stanislaski. Now, you can either find your way out, or I'll call security to help you find it."

"I know my way," he said evenly. "I'll tell you this, Miss Sydney Hayward, you will begin to keep those promises within two days, or we'll go to the building commissioner, and the press."

Sydney waited until he had stalked out before she sat again. Slowly she took a sheet of stationery from the drawer then methodically tore it into shreds. She stared at the smudges his big wide-palmed hands had left on her glossy desk and chose and shredded another sheet. Calmer, she punched the intercom, "Janine, bring me everything you've got on the Soho project."

An hour later, Sydney pushed the files aside and made two calls. The first was to cancel her dinner plans for the evening. The second was to Lloyd Bingham, her grandfather's—now her—executive assistant.

"You just caught me," Lloyd told her as he walked into Sydney's office. "I was on my way out. What can I do for you?"

Sydney shot him a brief glance. He was a handsome, ambitious man who preferred Italian tailors and French food. Not yet forty, he was on his second divorce and liked to escort society women who were attracted to his smooth blond looks and polished manners. Sydney knew that he had worked hard and long to gain his position with Hayward and that he had taken over the reins during her grandfather's illness the past year.

She also knew that he resented her because she was sitting behind a desk he considered rightfully his.

"For starters, you can explain why nothing has been done about the Soho apartments."

"The unit in Soho?" Lloyd took a cigarette from a slim gold case. "It's on the agenda."

"It's been on the agenda for nearly eighteen months. The first letter in the file, signed by the tenants, was dated almost two years ago and lists twenty-seven specific complaints."

"And I believe you'll also see in the file that a number of them were addressed." He blew out a thin stream of smoke as he made himself comfortable on one of the chairs.

"A number of them," Sydney repeated. "Such as the furnace repairs. The tenants seemed to think a new furnace was required."

Lloyd made a vague gesture. "You're new to the game, Sydney. You'll find that tenants always want new, better and more."

"That may be. However, it hardly seems cost-effective to me to repair a thirty-year-old furnace and have it break down again two months later." She held up a finger before he could speak. "Broken railings in stairwells, peeling paint, an insufficient water heater, a defective elevator, cracked porcelain..." She glanced up. "I could go on, but it doesn't seem necessary. There's a memo here, from my grandfather to you, requesting that you take over the repairs and maintenance of this building."

"Which I did," Lloyd said stiffly. "You know very well that your grandfather's health turned this company upside down over the last year. That apartment complex is only one of several buildings he owned."

"You're absolutely right." Her voice was quiet but without warmth. "I also know that we have a responsibility, a legal and a moral responsibility to our tenants, whether the building is in Soho or on Central Park West." She closed the folder, linked her hands over it and, in that gesture, stated ownership. "I don't want to antagonize you, Lloyd, but I want you to understand that I've decided to handle this particular property myself."

"Why?"

She granted him a small smile. "I'm not entirely sure. Let's just say I want to get my feet wet, and I've decided to make this property my pet project. In the meantime, I'd like you to look over the reports on the construction firms, and give me your recommendations." She offered him another file. "I've included a list of the properties, in order of priority. We'll have a meeting Friday, ten o'clock, to finalize."

"All right." He tapped out his cigarette before he rose. "Sydney, I hope you won't take offense, but a woman who's spent most of her life traveling and buying clothes doesn't know much about business, or making a profit."

She did take offense, but she'd be damned if she'd show it. "Then I'd better learn, hadn't I? Good night, Lloyd."

Not until the door closed did she look down at her hands. They were shaking. He was right, absolutely right to point out her inadequacies. But he couldn't know how badly she needed to prove herself here, to make something out of what her grandfather had left her. Nor could he know how terrified she was that she would let down the family name. Again.

Before she could change her mind, she tucked the file into her briefcase and left the office. She walked down the wide pastel corridor with its tasteful watercolors and thriving ficus trees, through the thick glass doors that closed in her suite of offices. She took her private elevator down to the lobby, where she nodded to the guard before she walked outside.

The heat punched like a fist. Though it was only mid-June, New York was in the clutches of a vicious heat wave with temperatures and humidity spiraling gleefully. She had only to cross the sidewalk to be cocooned in the waiting car, sheltered from the dripping air and noise. After giving her driver the address, she settled back for the ride to Soho.

Traffic was miserable, snarling and edgy. But that would only give her more time to think. She wasn't certain what she was going to do when she got there. Nor was she sure what she would do if she ran into Mikhail Stanislaski again.

He'd made quite an impression on her, Sydney mused. Exotic looks, hot eyes, a complete lack of courtesy. The worst part was the file had shown that he'd had a perfect right to be rude and impatient. He'd written letter after letter during the past year, only to be put off with half-baked promises.

Perhaps if her grandfather hadn't been so stubborn about keeping his illness out of the press. Sydney rubbed a finger over her temple and wished she'd taken a couple of aspirin before she'd left the office.

Whatever had happened before, she was in charge now. She intended to respect her inheritance and all the responsibilities that went with it. She closed her eyes and fell into a half doze as her driver fought his way downtown.

Inside his apartment, Mikhail carved a piece of cherrywood. He wasn't sure why he continued. His heart wasn't in it, but he felt it more productive to do something with his hands.

He kept thinking about the woman. Sydney. All ice and pride, he thought. One of the aristocrats it was in his blood to rebel against. Though he and his family had escaped to America when he had still been a child, there was no denying his heritage. His ancestors had been Gypsies in the Ukraine, hot-blooded, hot tempered and with little respect for structured authority.

Mikhail considered himself to be American—except when it suited him to be Russian.

Curls of wood fell on the table or the floor. Most of his

cramped living space was taken up with his work—blocks
and slabs of wood, even an oak burl, knives, chisels, hammers, drills, calipers. There was a small lathe in the corner
and jars that held brushes. The room smelled of linseed oil,
sweat and sawdust.

Mikhail took a pull from the beer at his elbow and sat
back to study the cherry. It wasn't ready, as yet, to let him
see what was inside. He let his fingers roam over it, over
the grain, into the grooves, while the sound of traffic and
music and shouts rose up and through the open window at
his back.

He had had enough success in the past two years that he
could have moved into bigger and more modern dwellings.
He liked it here, in this noisy neighborhood, with the bak-
ery on the corner, the bazaarlike atmosphere on Canal, only
a short walk away, the women who gossiped from their
stoops in the morning, the men who sat there at night.

He didn't need wall-to-wall carpet or a sunken tub or a
big stylish kitchen. All he wanted was a roof that didn't
leak, a shower that offered hot water and a refrigerator that
would keep the beer and cold cuts cold. At the moment, he
didn't have any of those things. And Miss Sydney Hayward
hadn't seen the last of him.

He glanced up at the three brisk knocks on his door, then
grinned as his down-the-hall neighbor burst in. "What's
the story?"

Keely O'Brian slammed the door, leaned dramatically
against it, then did a quick jig. "I got the part." Letting
out a whoop, she raced to the table to throw her arms
around Mikhail's neck. "I got it." She gave him a loud,
smacking kiss on one cheek. "I got it." Then the other.

"I told you you would." He reached back to ruffle her
short cap of dusty blond hair. "Get a beer. We'll celebrate."

"Oh, Mik." She crossed to the tiny refrigerator on long,
slim legs left stunningly revealed by a pair of neon green

shorts. "I was so nervous before the audition I got the hiccups, then I drank a gallon of water and sloshed my way through the reading." She tossed the cap into the trash before toasting herself. "And I still got it. A movie of the week. I'll probably only get like sixth or seventh billing, but I don't get murdered till the third act." She took a sip, then let out a long, bloodcurdling scream. "That's what I have to do when the serial killer corners me in the alley. I really think my scream turned the tide."

"No doubt." As always, her quick, nervous speech amused him. She was twenty-three, with an appealing colt-ish body, lively green eyes and a heart as wide as the Grand Canyon. If Mikhail hadn't felt so much like her brother right from the beginning of their relationship, he would have long since attempted to talk her into bed.

Keely took a sip of beer. "Hey, do you want to order some Chinese or pizza or something? I've got a frozen pizza, but my oven is on the blink again."

The simple statement made his eyes flash and his lips purse. "I went today to see Hayward."

The bottle paused on the way to her lips. "In person? You mean like, face-to-face?"

"Yes." Mikhail set aside his carving tools, afraid he would gouge the wood.

Impressed, Keely walked over to sit on the windowsill. "Wow. So, what's he like?"

"He's dead."

She choked on the beer, watching him wide-eyed as she pounded on her chest. "Dead? You didn't…"

"Kill him?" This time Mikhail smiled. Another thing he enjoyed about Keely was her innate flare for the dramatic. "No, but I considered killing the new Hayward—his grand-daughter."

"The new landlord's a woman? What's she like?"

"Very beautiful, very cold." He was frowning as he skimmed his fingertips over the wood grain. "She has red hair and white skin. Blue eyes like frost on a lake. When she speaks, icicles form.''

Keely grimaced and sipped. "Rich people," she said, "can afford to be cold."

"I told her she has two days before I go to the building commissioner."

This time Keely smiled. As much as she admired Mikhail, she felt he was naive in a lot of ways. "Good luck. Maybe we should take Mrs. Bayford's idea about a rent strike. Of course, then we risk eviction, but...hey." She leaned out the open window. "You should see this car. It's like a Lincoln or something—with a driver. There's a woman getting out of the back." More fascinated than envious, she let out a long, appreciative breath. "*Harper's Bazaar*'s version of the executive woman." Grinning, she shot a glance over her shoulder. "I think your ice princess has come slumming."

Outside, Sydney studied the building. It was really quite lovely, she thought. Like an old woman who had maintained her dignity and a shadow of her youthful beauty. The red brick had faded to a soft pink, smudged here and there by soot and exhaust. The trimming paint was peeling and cracked, but that could be easily remedied. Taking out a legal pad, she began to take notes.

She was aware that the men sitting out on the stoop were watching her, but she ignored them. It was a noisy place, she noted. Most of the windows were open and there was a variety of sound—televisions, radios, babies crying, someone singing "The Desert Song" in a warbling soprano. There were useless little balconies crowded with potted flowers, bicycles, clothes drying in the still, hot air.

Shading her eyes, she let her gaze travel up. Most of the railings were badly rusted and many had spokes missing. She frowned, then spotted Mikhail, leaning out of a window on the top floor, nearly cheek to cheek with a stunning blonde. Since he was bare chested and the blonde was wearing the tiniest excuse for a tank top, Sydney imagined she'd interrupted them. She acknowledged him with a frigid nod, then went back to her notes.

When she started toward the entrance, the men shifted to make a path for her. The small lobby was dim and oppressively hot. On this level the windows were apparently painted shut. The old parquet floor was scarred and scraped, and there was a smell, a very definite smell, of mold. She studied the elevator dubiously. Someone had hand-lettered a sign above the button that read Abandon Hope Ye Who Enter Here.

Curious, Sydney punched the up button and listened to the grinding rattles and wheezes. On an impatient breath, she made more notes. It was deplorable, she thought. The unit should have been inspected, and Hayward should have been slapped with a citation. Well, she was Hayward now.

The doors squeaked open, and Mikhail stepped out.

"Did you come to look over your empire?" he asked her.

Very deliberately she finished her notes before she met his gaze. At least he had pulled on a shirt—if you could call it that. The thin white T-shirt was ripped at the sleeves and mangled at the hem.

"I believe I told you I'd look over the file. Once I did, I thought it best to inspect the building myself." She glanced at the elevator, then back at him. "You're either very brave or very stupid, Mr. Stanislaski."

"A realist," he corrected with a slow shrug. "What happens, happens."

"Perhaps. But I'd prefer that no one use this elevator until it's repaired or replaced."

He slipped his hands into his pockets. "And will it be?"

"Yes, as quickly as possible. I believe you mentioned in your letter that some of the stair railings were broken."

"I've replaced the worst of them."

Her brow lifted. "You?"

"There are children and old people in this building."

The simplicity of his answer made her ashamed. "I see. Since you've taken it on yourself to represent the tenants, perhaps you'd take me through and show me the worst of the problems."

As they started up the stairs, she noted that the railing was obviously new, an unstained line of wood that was sturdy under her hand. She made a note that it had been replaced by a tenant.

He knocked on apartment doors. People greeted him enthusiastically, her warily. There were smells of cooking—meals just finished, meals yet to be eaten. She was offered strudel, brownies, goulash, chicken wings. Some of the complaints were bitter, some were nervous. But Sydney saw for herself that Mikhail's letters hadn't exaggerated.

By the time they reached the third floor, the heat was making her dizzy. On the fourth, she refused the offer of spaghetti and meatballs—wondering how anyone could bear to cook in all this heat—and accepted a glass of water. Dutifully she noted down how the pipes rattled and thumped. When they reached the fifth floor, she was wishing desperately for a cool shower, a chilled glass of chardonnay and the blissful comfort of her air-conditioned apartment.

Mikhail noted that her face was glowing from the heat. On the last flight of stairs, she'd been puffing a bit, which pleased him. It wouldn't hurt the queen to see how her subjects lived. He wondered why she didn't at least peel off her suit jacket or loosen a couple of those prim buttons on her blouse.

He wasn't pleased with the thought that he would enjoy doing both of those things for her.

"I would think that some of these tenants would have window units." Sweat slithered nastily down her back. "Air-conditioning."

"The wiring won't handle it," he told her. "When peo-

ple turn them on, it blows the fuses and we lose power.
The hallways are the worst,'' he went on conversationally.
"Airless. And up here is worst of all. Heat rises.''

"So I've heard.''

She was white as a sheet, he noted, and swore. "Take
off your jacket.''

"I beg your pardon?''

"You're stupid.'' He tugged the linen off her shoulders
and began to pull her arms free.

The combination of heat and his rough, purposeful fingers had spots dancing in front of her eyes. "Stop it.''

"Very stupid. This is not a boardroom.''

His touch wasn't the least bit loverlike, but it was very
disturbing. She batted at his hands the moment one of her
arms was free. Ignoring her, Mikhail pushed her into his
apartment.

"Mr. Stanislaski,'' she said, out of breath but not out of
dignity. "I will not be pawed.''

"I have doubts you've ever been pawed in your life,
Your Highness. What man wants frostbite? Sit.''

"I have no desire to—''

He simply shoved her into a chair, then glanced over
where Keely stood in the kitchen, gaping. "Get her some
water,'' he ordered.

Sydney caught her breath. A fan whirled beside the chair
and cooled her skin. "You are the rudest, most ill-
mannered, most insufferable man I've ever been forced to
deal with.''

He took the glass from Keely and was tempted to toss
the contents into Sydney's beautiful face. Instead he shoved
the glass into her hand. "Drink.''

"Jeez, Mik, have a heart,'' Keely murmured. "She looks
beat. You want a cold cloth?'' Even as she offered, she
couldn't help but admire the ivory silk blouse with its tiny
pearl buttons.

"No, thank you. I'm fine.''

"I'm Keely O'Brian, 502."

"Her oven doesn't work," Mikhail said. "And she gets no hot water. The roof leaks."

"Only when it rains." Keely tried to smile but got no response. "I guess I'll run along. Nice to meet you."

When they were alone, Sydney took slow sips of the tepid water. Mikhail hadn't complained about his own apartment, but she could see from where she sat that the linoleum on the kitchen floor was ripped, and the refrigerator was hopelessly small and out-of-date. She simply didn't have the energy to look at the rest.

His approach had been anything but tactful, still the bottom line was he was right and her company was wrong.

He sat on the edge of the kitchen counter and watched as color seeped slowly back into her cheeks. It relieved him. For a moment in the hall he'd been afraid she would faint. He already felt like a clod.

"Do you want food?" His voice was clipped and unfriendly. "You can have a sandwich."

She remembered that she was supposed to be dining at Le Cirque with the latest eligible bachelor her mother had chosen. "No, thank you. You don't think much of me, do you?"

He moved his shoulders in the way she now recognized as habit. "I think of you quite a bit."

She frowned and set the glass aside. The way he said it left a little too much to the imagination. "You said you were a carpenter?"

"I am sometimes a carpenter."

"You have a license?"

His eyes narrowed. "A contractor's license, yes. For remodeling, renovations."

"Then you'd have a list of other contractors you've worked with—electricians, plumbers, that sort of thing."

"Yes."

"Fine. Work up a bid on repairs, including the finish

work, painting, tile, replacing fixtures, appliances. Have it on my desk in a week.'' She rose, picking up her crumpled jacket.

He stayed where he was as she folded the jacket over her arm, lifted her briefcase. "And then?"

She shot him a cool look. "And then, Mr. Stanislaski, I'm going to put my money where your mouth is. You're hired.''

Chapter Two

"Mother, I really don't have time for this."

"Sydney, dear, one always has time for tea." So saying, Margerite Rothchild Hayward Kinsdale LaRue poured ginseng into a china cup. "I'm afraid you're taking this real estate business too seriously."

"Maybe because I'm in charge," Sydney muttered without looking up from the papers on her desk.

"I can't imagine what your grandfather was thinking of. But then, he always was an unusual man." She sighed a moment, remembering how fond she'd been of the old goat. "Come, darling, have some tea and one of these delightful little sandwiches. Even Madam Executive needs a spot of lunch."

Sydney gave in, hoping to move her mother along more quickly by being agreeable. "This is really very sweet of you. It's just that I'm pressed for time today."

"All this corporate nonsense," Margerite began as Sydney sat beside her. "I don't know why you bother. It would have been so simple to hire a manager or whatever." Margerite added a squirt of lemon to her cup before she sat back. "I realize it might be diverting for a while, but the thought of you with a career. Well, it seems so pointless."

"Does it?" Sydney murmured, struggling to keep the bitterness out of her voice. "I may surprise everyone and be good at it."

"Oh, I'm sure you'd be wonderful at whatever you do, darling." Her hand fluttered absently over Sydney's. The girl had been so little trouble as a child, she thought. Margerite really hadn't a clue how to deal with this sudden and—she was sure—temporary spot of rebellion. She tried placating. "And I was delighted when Grandfather Hayward left you all those nice buildings." She nibbled on a sandwich, a striking woman who looked ten years younger than her fifty years, groomed and polished in a Chanel suit. "But to actually become involved in running things." Baffled, she patted her carefully tinted chestnut hair. "Well, one might think it's just a bit unfeminine. A man is easily put off by what he considers a high-powered woman."

Sydney gave her mother's newly bare ring finger a pointed look. "Not every woman's sole ambition centers around a man."

"Oh, don't be silly." With a gay little laugh, Margerite patted her daughter's hand. "A husband isn't something a woman wants to be without for long. You mustn't be discouraged because you and Peter didn't work things out. First marriages are often just a testing ground."

Reining in her feelings, Sydney set her cup down carefully. "Is that what you consider your marriage to Father? A testing ground?"

"We both learned some valuable lessons from it, I'm sure." Confident and content, she beamed at her daughter. "Now, dear, tell me about your evening with Channing. How was it?"

"Stifling."

Margerite's mild blue eyes flickered with annoyance. "Sydney, really."

"You asked." To fortify herself, Sydney picked up her tea again. Why was it, she asked herself, that she perpetually felt inadequate around the woman who had given birth to her. "I'm sorry, Mother, but we simply don't suit."

"Nonsense. You're perfectly suited. Channing Warfield is an intelligent, successful man from a very fine family."

"So was Peter."

China clinked against china as Margerite set her cup in its saucer. "Sydney, you must not compare every man you meet with Peter."

"I don't." Taking a chance, she laid a hand on her mother's. There was a bond there, there had to be. Why did she always feel as though her fingers were just sliding away from it? "Honestly, I don't compare Channing with anyone. The simple fact is, I find him stilted, boring and pretentious. It could be that I'd find any man the same just now. I'm not interested in men at this point of my life, Mother. I want to make something of myself."

"Make something of yourself," Margerite repeated, more stunned than angry. "You're a Hayward. You don't need to make yourself anything else." She plucked up a napkin to dab at her lips. "For heaven's sake, Sydney, you've been divorced from Peter for four years. It's time you found a suitable husband. It's women who write the invitations," she reminded her daughter. "And they have a policy of excluding beautiful, unattached females. You have a place in society, Sydney. And a responsibility to your name."

The familiar clutching in her stomach had Sydney setting the tea aside. "So you've always told me."

Satisfied that Sydney would be reasonable, she smiled. "If Channing won't do, there are others. But I really think you shouldn't be so quick to dismiss him. If I were twenty years younger...well." She glanced at her watch and gave a little squeak. "Dear me, I'm going to be late for the hairdresser. I'll just run and powder my nose first."

When Margerite slipped into the adjoining bath, Sydney leaned her head back and closed her eyes. Where was she to put all these feelings of guilt and inadequacy? How could she explain herself to her mother when she couldn't explain herself to herself?

Rising, she went back to her desk. She couldn't convince Margerite that her unwillingness to become involved again had nothing to do with Peter when, in fact, it did. They had been friends, damn it. She and Peter had grown up with each other, had cared for each other. They simply hadn't been in love with each other. Family pressure had pushed them down the aisle while they'd been too young to realize the mistake. Then they had spent the best part of two years trying miserably to make the marriage work.

The pity of it wasn't the divorce, but the fact that when they had finally parted, they were no longer friends. If she couldn't make a go of it with someone she'd cared for, someone she'd had so much in common with, someone she'd liked so much, surely the lack was in her.

All she wanted to do now was to feel deserving of her grandfather's faith in her. She'd been offered a different kind of responsibility, a different kind of challenge. This time, she couldn't afford to fail.

Wearily she answered her intercom. "Yes, Janine."

"Mr. Stanislaski's here, Miss Hayward. He doesn't have an appointment, but he says he has some papers you wanted to see."

A full day early, she mused, and straightened her shoulders. "Send him in."

At least he'd shaved, she thought, though this time there were holes in his jeans. Closing the door, he took as long and as thorough a look at her. As if they were two boxers sizing up the competition from neutral corners.

She looked just as starched and prim as before, in one

of her tidy business suits, this time in pale gray, with all those little silver buttons on her blouse done up to her smooth white throat. He glanced down at the tea tray with its delicate cups and tiny sandwiches. His lips curled.

"Interrupting your lunch, Hayward?"

"Not at all." She didn't bother to stand or smile but gestured him across the room. "Do you have the bid, Mr. Stanislaski?"

"Yes."

"You work fast."

He grinned. "Yes." He caught a scent—rather a clash of scents. Something very subtle and cool and another, florid and overly feminine. "You have company?"

Her brow arched. "Why do you ask?"

"There is perfume here that isn't yours." Then with a shrug, he handed her the papers he carried. "The first is what must be done, the second is what should be done."

"I see." She could feel the heat radiating off him. For some reason it felt comforting, life affirming. As if she'd stepped out of a dark cave into the sunlight. Sydney made certain her fingers didn't brush his as she took the papers. "You have estimates from the subcontractors?"

"They are there." While she glanced through his work, he lifted one of the neat triangles of bread, sniffed at it like a wolf. "What is this stuff in here?"

She barely looked up. "Watercress."

With a grunt, he dropped it back onto the plate. "Why would you eat it?"

She looked up again, and this time, she smiled. "Good question."

She shouldn't have done that, he thought as he shifted his hands to his pockets. When she smiled, she changed. Her eyes warmed, her lips softened, and beauty became approachable rather than aloof.

It made him forget he wasn't the least bit interested in her type of woman.

"Then I'll ask you another question."

Her lips pursed as she scanned the list. She liked what she saw. "You seem to be full of them today."

"Why do you wear colors like that? Dull ones, when you should be wearing vivid. Sapphire or emerald."

It was surprise that had her staring at him. As far as she could remember, no one had ever questioned her taste. In some circles, she was thought to be quite elegant. "Are you a carpenter or a fashion consultant, Mr. Stanislaski?"

His shoulders moved. "I'm a man. Is this tea?" He lifted the pot and sniffed at the contents while she continued to gape at him. "It's too hot for tea. You have something cold?"

Shaking her head, she pressed her intercom. "Janine, bring in something cold for Mr. Stanislaski, please." Because she had a nagging urge to get up and inspect herself in a mirror, she cleared her throat. "There's quite a line of demarcation between your must and your should list, Mr.—"

"Mikhail," he said easily. "It's because there are more things you should do than things you must. Like life."

"Now a philosopher," she muttered. "We'll start with the must, and perhaps incorporate some of the should. If we work quickly, we could have a contract by the end of the week."

His nod was slow, considering. "You, too, work fast."

"When necessary. Now first, I'd like you to explain to me why I should replace all the windows."

"Because they're single glazed and not efficient."

"Yes, but—"

"Sydney, dear, the lighting in there is just ghastly. Oh." Margerite stopped at the doorway. "I beg your pardon, I see you're in a meeting." She would have looked down her nose at Mikhail's worn jeans, but she had a difficult time getting past his face. "How do you do?" she said, pleased that he had risen at her entrance.

"You are Sydney's mother?" Mikhail asked before Sydney could shoo Margerite along.

"Why, yes." Margerite's smile was reserved. She didn't approve of her daughter being on a first-name basis in her relationships with the help. Particularly when that help wore stubby ponytails and dirty boots. "How did you know?"

"Real beauty matures well."

"Oh." Charmed, Margerite allowed her smile to warm fractionally. Her lashes fluttered in reflex. "How kind."

"Mother, I'm sorry, but Mr. Stanislaski and I have business to discuss."

"Of course, of course." Margerite walked over to kiss the air an inch from her daughter's cheek. "I'll just be running along. Now, dear, you won't forget we're to have lunch next week? And I wanted to remind you that…Stanislaski," she repeated, turning back to Mikhail. "I thought you looked familiar. Oh, my." Suddenly breathless, she laid a hand on her heart. "You're Mikhail Stanislaski?"

"Yes. Have we met?"

"No. Oh, no, we haven't, but I saw your photo in *Art/World.* I consider myself a patron." Face beaming, she skirted the desk and, under her daughter's astonished gaze, took his hands in hers. To Margerite, the ponytail was now artistic, the tattered jeans eccentric. "Your work, Mr. Stanislaski—magnificent. Truly magnificent. I bought two of your pieces from your last showing. I can't tell you what a pleasure this is."

"You flatter me."

"Not at all," Margerite insisted. "You're already being called one of the top artists of the nineties. And you've commissioned him." She turned to beam at her speechless daughter. "A brilliant move, darling."

"I—actually, I—"

"I'm delighted," Mikhail interrupted, "to be working with your daughter."

"It's wonderful." She gave his hands a final squeeze. "You must come to a little dinner party I'm having on Friday on Long Island. Please, don't tell me you're already engaged for the evening." She slanted a look from under her lashes. "I'll be devastated."

He was careful not to grin over her head at Sydney. "I could never be responsible for devastating a beautiful woman."

"Fabulous. Sydney will bring you. Eight o'clock. Now I must run." She patted her hair, shot an absent wave at Sydney and hurried out just as Janine brought in a soft drink.

Mikhail took the glass with thanks, then sat again. "So," he began, "you were asking about windows."

Sydney very carefully relaxed the hands that were balled into fists under her desk. "You said you were a carpenter."

"Sometimes I am." He took a long, cooling drink. "Sometimes I carve wood instead of hammering it."

If he had set out to make a fool of her—which she wasn't sure he hadn't—he could have succeeded no better. "I've spent the last two years in Europe," she told him, "so I'm a bit out of touch with the American art world."

"You don't have to apologize," he said, enjoying himself.

"I'm not apologizing." She had to force herself to speak calmly, to not stand up and rip his bid into tiny little pieces. "I'd like to know what kind of game you're playing, Stanislaski."

"You offered me work, on a job that has some value for me. I am accepting it."

"You lied to me."

"How?" He lifted one hand, palm up. "I have a contractor's license. I've made my living in construction since

I was sixteen. What difference does it make to you if people now buy my sculpture?''

"None.'' She snatched up the bids again. He probably produced primitive, ugly pieces in any case, she thought. The man was too rough and unmannered to be an artist. All that mattered was that he could do the job she was hiring him to do.

But she hated being duped. To make him pay for it, she forced him to go over every detail of the bid, wasting over an hour of his time and hers.

"All right then.'' She pushed aside her own meticulous notes. "Your contract will be ready for signing on Friday.''

"Good.'' He rose. "You can bring it when you pick me up. We should make it seven.''

"Excuse me?''

"For dinner.'' He leaned forward. For a shocking moment, she thought he was actually going to kiss her. She went rigid as a spear, but he only rubbed the lapel of her suit between his thumb and forefinger. "You must wear something with color.''

She pushed the chair back and stood. "I have no intention of taking you to my mother's home for dinner.''

"You're afraid to be with me.'' He said so with no little amount of pride.

Her chin jutted out. "Certainly not.''

"What else could it be?'' With his eyes on hers, he strolled around the desk until they were face-to-face. "A woman like you could not be so ill-mannered without a reason.''

The breath was backing up in her lungs. Sydney forced it out in one huff. "It's reason enough that I dislike you.''

He only smiled and toyed with the pearls at her throat. "No. Aristocrats are predictable, Hayward. You would be taught to tolerate people you don't like. For them, you would be the most polite.''

"Stop touching me.''

"I'm putting color in your cheeks." He laughed and let the pearls slide out of his fingers. Her skin, he was sure, would be just as smooth, just as cool. "Come now, Sydney, what will you tell your charming mother when you go to her party without me? How will you explain that you refused to bring me?" He could see the war in her eyes, the one fought between pride and manners and temper, and laughed again. "Trapped by your breeding," he murmured. "This is not something I have to worry about myself."

"No doubt," she said between her teeth.

"Friday," he said, and infuriated her by flicking a finger down her cheek. "Seven o'clock."

"Mr. Stanislaski," she murmured when he reached the door. As he turned back, she offered her coolest smile. "Try to find something in your closet without holes in it."

She could hear him laughing at her as he walked down the hallway. If only, she thought as she dropped back into her chair. If only she hadn't been so well-bred, she could have released some of this venom by throwing breakables at the door.

She wore black quite deliberately. Under no circumstances did she want him to believe that she would fuss through her wardrobe, looking for something colorful because he'd suggested it. And she thought the simple tube of a dress was both businesslike, fashionable and appropriate.

On impulse, she had taken her hair down so that it fluffed out to skim her shoulders—only because she'd tired of wearing it pulled back. As always, she had debated her look for the evening carefully and was satisfied that she had achieved an aloof elegance.

She could hear the music blasting through his door before she knocked. It surprised her to hear the passionate strains of *Carmen*. She rapped harder, nearly gave in to the urge to shout over the aria, when the door swung open.

Behind it was the blond knockout in a skimpy T-shirt and skimpier shorts.

"Hi." Keely crunched a piece of ice between her teeth and swallowed. "I was just borrowing an ice tray from Mik—my freezer's set on melt these days." She managed to smile and forced herself not to tug on her clothes. She felt like a peasant caught poaching by the royal princess. "I was just leaving." Before Sydney could speak, she dashed back inside to scoop up a tray of ice. "Mik, your date's here."

Sydney winced at the term *date* as the blond bullet streaked past her. "There's no need for you to rush off—"

"Three's a crowd," Keely told her on the run and, with a quick fleeting grin, kept going.

"Did you call me?" Mikhail came to the bedroom doorway. There was one, very small white towel anchored at his waist. He used another to rub at his wet, unruly hair. He stopped when he spotted Sydney. Something flickered in his eyes as he let his gaze roam down the long, cool lines of the dress. Then he smiled. "I'm late," he said simply.

She was grateful she'd managed not to let her mouth fall open. His body was all lean muscle, long bones and bronzed skin—skin that was gleaming with tiny drops of water that made her feel unbearably thirsty. The towel hung dangerously low on his hips. Dazed, she watched a drop of water slide down his chest, over his stomach and disappear beneath the terry cloth.

The temperature in the room, already steamy, rose several degrees.

"You're..." She knew she could speak coherently—in a minute. "We said seven."

"I was busy." He shrugged. The towel shifted. Sydney swallowed. "I won't be long. Fix a drink." A smile, wicked around the edges, tugged at his mouth. A man would have to be dead not to see her reaction—not to be pleased by it. "You look…hot, Sydney." He took a step forward, watching her eyes widen, watching her mouth tremble open. With his gaze on hers, he turned on a small portable fan. Steamy air stirred. "That will help," he said mildly.

She nodded. It was cooling, but it also brought the scent of his shower, of his skin into the room. Because she could see the knowledge and the amusement in his eyes, she got a grip on herself. "Your contracts." She set the folder down on a table. Mikhail barely glanced at them.

"I'll look and sign later."

"Fine. It would be best if you got dressed." She had to swallow another obstruction in her throat when he smiled at her. Her voice was edgy and annoyed. "We'll be late."

"A little. There's cold drink in the refrigerator," he added as he turned back to the bedroom. "Be at home."

Alone, she managed to take three normal breaths. Degree by degree she felt her system level. Any man who looked like that in a towel should be arrested, she thought, and turned to study the room.

She'd been too annoyed to take stock of it on her other visit. And too preoccupied, she admitted with a slight frown. A man like that had a way of keeping a woman preoccupied. Now she noted the hunks of wood, small and large, the tools, the jars stuffed with brushes. There was a long worktable beneath the living room window. She wandered toward it, seeing that a few of those hunks of wood were works in progress.

Shrugging, she ran a finger over a piece of cherry that was scarred with groves and gouges. Rude and primitive, just as she'd thought. It soothed her ruffled ego to be assured she'd been right about his lack of talent. Obviously a ruffian who'd made a momentary impression on the capricious art world.

Then she turned and saw the shelves.

They were crowded with his work. Long smooth columns of wood, beautifully shaped. A profile of a woman with long, flowing hair, a young child caught in gleeful laughter, lovers trapped endlessly in a first tentative kiss. She couldn't stop herself from touching, nor from feeling. His work ranged from the passionate to the charming, from the bold to the delicate.

Fascinated, she crouched down to get a closer look at the pieces on the lower shelves. Was it possible, she wondered, that a man with such rough manners, with such cocky arrogance possessed the wit, the sensitivity, the compassion to create such lovely things out of blocks of wood?

With a half laugh Sydney reached for a carving of a tiny kangaroo with a baby peeking out of her pouch. It felt as smooth and as delicate as glass. Even as she replaced it with a little sigh, she spotted the miniature figurine. Cinderella, she thought, charmed as she held it in her fingertips. The pretty fairy-tale heroine was still dressed for the ball, but one foot was bare as Mikhail had captured her in her dash before the clock struck twelve. For a moment, Sydney thought she could almost see tears in the painted eyes.

"You like?"

She jolted, then stood up quickly, still nestling the figurine in her hand. "Yes—I'm sorry."

"You don't have to be sorry for liking." Mikhail rested a hip, now more conservatively covered in wheat-colored slacks, on the worktable. His hair had been brushed back and now curled damply nearly to his shoulders.

Still flustered, she set the miniature back on the shelf. "I meant I should apologize for touching your work."

A smile tugged at his lips. It fascinated him that she could go from wide-eyed delight to frosty politeness in the blink of an eye. "Better to be touched than to sit apart, only to be admired. Don't you think?"

It was impossible to miss the implication in the tone of his voice, in the look in his eyes. "That would depend."

As she started by, he shifted, rose. His timing was perfect. She all but collided with him. "On what?"

She didn't flush or stiffen or retreat. She'd become accustomed to taking a stand. "On whether one chooses to be touched."

He grinned. "I thought we were talking about sculpture."

So, she thought on a careful breath, she'd walked into that one. "Yes, we were. Now, we really will be late. If you're ready, Mr. Stanislaski—"

"Mikhail." He lifted a hand casually to flick a finger at the sapphire drop at her ear. "It's easier." Before she could reply, his gaze came back and locked on hers. Trapped in that one long stare, she wasn't certain she could remember her own name. "You smell like an English garden at teatime," he murmured. "Very cool, very appealing. And just a little too formal."

It was too hot, she told herself. Much too hot and close. That was why she had difficulty breathing. It had nothing to do with him. Rather, she wouldn't allow it to have anything to do with him. "You're in my way."

"I know." And for reasons he wasn't entirely sure of, he intended to stay there. "You're used to brushing people aside."

"I don't see what that has to do with—"

"An observation," he interrupted, amusing himself by toying with the ends of her hair. The texture was as rich as the color, he decided, pleased she had left it free for the evening. "Artists observe. You'll find that some people don't brush aside as quickly as others." He heard her breath catch, ignored her defensive jerk as he cupped her chin in his hand. He'd been right about her skin—smooth as polished pearls. Patiently he turned her face from side to side. "Nearly perfect," he decided. "Nearly perfect is better than perfect."

"I beg your pardon?"

"Your eyes are too big, and your mouth is just a bit wider than it should be."

Insulted, she slapped his hand away. It embarrassed and infuriated her that she'd actually expected a compliment. "My eyes and mouth are none of your business."

"Very much mine," he corrected. "I'm doing your face."

When she frowned, a faint line etched between her brows. He liked it. "You're doing what?"

"Your face. In rosewood, I think. And with your hair down like this."

Again she pushed his hand away. "If you're asking me to model for you, I'm afraid I'm not interested."

"It doesn't matter whether you are. I am." He took her arm to lead her to the door.

"If you think I'm flattered—"

"Why should you be?" He opened the door, then stood just inside, studying her with apparent curiosity. "You were born with your face. You didn't earn it. If I said you sang well, or danced well, or kissed well, you could be flattered."

He eased her out, then closed the door. "Do you?" he asked, almost in afterthought.

Ruffled and irritated, she snapped back. "Do I what?"

"Kiss well?"

Her brows lifted. Haughty arches over frosty eyes. "The day you find out, you can be flattered." Rather pleased with the line, she started down the hall ahead of him.

His fingers barely touched her—she would have sworn it. But in the space of a heartbeat her back was to the wall and she was caged between his arms, with his hands planted on either side of her head. Both shock and a trembling river of fear came before she could even think to be insulted.

Knowing he was being obnoxious, enjoying it, he kept his lips a few scant inches from hers. He recognized the curling in his gut as desire. And by God, he could deal with that. And her. Their breath met and tangled, and he smiled. Hers had come out in a quick, surprised puff.

"I think," he said slowly, consideringly, "you have yet to learn how to kiss well. You have the mouth for it." His gaze lowered, lingered there. "But a man would have to be patient enough to warm that blood up first. A pity I'm not patient."

He was close enough to see her quick wince before her eyes went icy. "I think," she said, borrowing his tone, "that you probably kiss very well. But a woman would have to be tolerant enough to hack through your ego first. Fortunately, I'm not tolerant."

For a moment he stood where he was, close enough to swoop down and test both their theories. Then the smile worked over his face, curving his lips, brightening his eyes. Yes, he could deal with her. When he was ready.

"A man can learn patience, *milaya,* and seduce a woman to tolerance."

She pressed against the wall, but like a cat backed into a corner, she was ready to swipe and spit. He only stepped back and cupped a hand over her elbow.

"We should go now, yes?"

"Yes." Not at all sure if she was relieved or disappointed, she walked with him toward the stairs.

Chapter Three

Margerite had pulled out all the stops. She knew it was a coup to have a rising and mysterious artist such as Stanislaski at her dinner party. Like a general girding for battle, she had inspected the floral arrangements, the kitchens, the dining room and the terraces. Before she was done, the caterers were cursing her, but Margerite was satisfied.

She wasn't pleased when her daughter, along with her most important guest, was late.

Laughing and lilting, she swirled among her guests in a frothy gown of robin's-egg blue. There was a sprinkling of politicians, theater people and the idle rich. But the Ukrainian artist was her coup de grace, and she was fretting to show him off.

And, remembering that wild sexuality, she was fretting to flirt.

The moment she spotted him, Margerite swooped.

"Mr. Stanislaski, how marvelous!" After shooting her daughter a veiled censorious look, she beamed.

"Mikhail, please." Because he knew the game and

played it at his will, Mikhail brought her hand to his lips
and lingered over it. "You must forgive me for being late.
I kept your daughter waiting."

"Oh." She fluttered, her hand resting lightly, possessively on his arm. "A smart woman will always wait for
the right man."

"Then I'm forgiven."

"Absolutely." Her fingers gave his an intimate squeeze.
"This time. Now, you must let me introduce you around,
Mikhail." Linked with him, she glanced absently at her
daughter. "Sydney, do mingle, darling."

Mikhail shot a quick, wicked grin over his shoulder as
he let Margerite haul him away.

He made small talk easily, sliding into the upper crust
of New York society as seamlessly as he slid into the working class in Soho or his parents' close-knit neighborhood
in Brooklyn. They had no idea he might have preferred a
beer with friends or coffee at his mother's kitchen table.

He sipped champagne, admired the house with its cool
white walls and towering windows, and complimented
Margerite on her art collection.

And all the while he chatted, sipped and smiled, he
watched Sydney.

Odd, he thought. He would have said that the sprawling
elegance of the Long Island enclave was the perfect setting
for her. Her looks, her demeanor, reminded him of glistening shaved ice in a rare porcelain bowl. Yet she didn't quite
fit. Oh, she smiled and worked the room as skillfully as her
mother. Her simple black dress was as exclusive as any of
the more colorful choices in the room. Her sapphires
winked as brilliantly as any of the diamonds or emeralds.

But...it was her eyes, Mikhail realized. There wasn't
laughter in them, but impatience. It was as though she were
thinking—let's get this done and over with so I can get on
to something important.

It made him smile. Remembering that he'd have the long

drive back to Manhattan to tease her made the smile widen. It faded abruptly as he watched a tall blond man with football shoulders tucked into a silk dinner jacket kiss Sydney on the mouth.

Sydney smiled into a pair of light blue eyes under golden brows. "Hello, Channing."

"Hello, yourself." He offered a fresh glass of wine. "Where did Margerite find the wild horses?"

"I'm sorry?"

"To drag you out of that office." His smile dispensed charm like penny candy. Sydney couldn't help but respond.

"It wasn't quite that drastic. I have been busy."

"So you've told me." He approved of her in the sleek black dress in much the same way he would have approved of a tasteful accessory for his home. "You missed a wonderful play the other night. It looks like Sondheim's got another hit on his hands." Never doubting her acquiescence, he took her arm to lead her into dinner. "Tell me, darling, when are you going to stop playing the career woman and take a break? I'm going up to the Hamptons for the weekend, and I'd love your company."

Dutifully she forced her clamped teeth apart. There was no use resenting the fact he thought she was playing. Everyone did. "I'm afraid I can't get away just now." She took her seat beside him at the long glass table in the airy dining room. The drapes were thrown wide so that the garden seemed to spill inside with the pastel hues of early roses, late tulips and nodding columbine.

She wished the dinner had been alfresco so she could have sat among the blossoms and scented the sea air.

"I hope you don't mind a little advice."

Sydney nearly dropped her head into her hand. The chatter around them was convivial, glasses were clinking, and the first course of stuffed mushrooms was being served. She felt she'd just been clamped into a cell. "Of course not, Channing."

"You can run a business or let the business run you."

"Hmm." He had a habit of stating his advice in clichés. Sydney reminded herself she should be used to it.

"Take it from someone with more experience in these matters."

She fixed a smile on her face and let her mind wander.

"I hate to see you crushed under the heel of responsibility," he went on. "And after all, we know you're a novice in the dog-eat-dog world of real estate." Gold cuff links, monogrammed, winked as he laid a hand on hers. His eyes were sincere, his mouth quirked in that I'm-only-looking-out-for-you smile. "Naturally, your initial enthusiasm will push you to take on more than is good for you. I'm sure you agree."

Her mind flicked back. "Actually, Channing, I enjoy the work."

"For the moment," he said, his voice so patronizing she nearly stabbed him with her salad fork. "But when reality rushes in you may find yourself trampled under it. Delegate, Sydney. Hand the responsibilities over to those who understand them."

If her spine had been any straighter, it would have snapped her neck. "My grandfather entrusted Hayward to me."

"The elderly become sentimental. But I can't believe he expected you to take it all so seriously." His smooth, lightly tanned brow wrinkled briefly in what she understood was genuine if misguided concern. "Why, you've hardly attended a party in weeks. Everyone's talking about it."

"Are they?" She forced her lips to curve over her clenched teeth. If he offered one more shred of advice, she would have to upend the water goblet in his lap. "Channing, why don't you tell me about the play?"

At the other end of the table, tucked between Margerite and Mrs. Anthony Lowell of the Boston Lowells, Mikhail kept a weather eye on Sydney. He didn't like the way she had her head together with pretty boy. No, by God, he didn't. The man was always touching her. Her hand, her shoulder. Her soft, white, bare shoulder. And she was just smiling and nodding, as though his words were a fascination in themselves.

Apparently the ice queen didn't mind being pawed if the hands doing the pawing were as lily-white as her own.

Mikhail swore under his breath.

"I beg your pardon, Mikhail?"

With an effort, he turned his attention and a smile toward Margerite. "Nothing. The pheasant is excellent."

"Thank you. I wonder if I might ask what Sydney's commissioned you to sculpt."

He flicked a black look down the length of the table. "I'll be working on the project in Soho."

"Ah." Margerite hadn't a clue what Hayward might own in Soho. "Will it be an indoor or outdoor piece?"

"Both. Who is the man beside Sydney? I don't think I met him."

"Oh, that's Channing, Channing Warfield. The Warfields are old friends."

"Friends," he repeated, slightly mollified.

Conspiratorily Margerite leaned closer. "If I can confide, Wilhemina Warfield and I are hoping they'll make an announcement this summer. They're such a lovely couple, so suitable. And since Sydney's first marriage is well behind her—"

"First marriage?" He swooped down on that tidbit of information like a hawk on a dove. "Sydney was married before?"

"Yes, but I'm afraid she and Peter were too young and impetuous," she told him, conveniently overlooking the family pressure that had brought the marriage about. "Now, Sydney and Channing are mature, responsible people. We're looking forward to a spring wedding."

Mikhail picked up his wine. There was an odd and annoying scratching in his throat. "What does this Channing Warfield do?"

"Do?" The question baffled her. "Why, the Warfields are in banking, so I suppose Channing does whatever one does in banking. He's a devil on the polo field."

"Polo," Mikhail repeated with a scowl so dark Helena Lowell choked on her pheasant. Helpfully Mikhail gave her a sharp slap between the shoulder blades, then offered her her water goblet.

"You're, ah, Russian, aren't you, Mr. Stanislaski?" Helena asked. Images of cossacks danced in her head.

"I was born in the Ukraine."

"The Ukraine, yes. I believe I read something about your family escaping over the border when you were just a child."

"We escaped in a wagon, over the mountains into Hungary, then into Austria and finally settled in New York."

"A wagon." Margerite sighed into her wine. "How romantic."

Mikhail remembered the cold, the fear, the hunger. But he only shrugged. He doubted romance was always pretty, or comfortable.

Relieved that he looked approachable again, Helena Lowell began to ask him questions about art.

After an hour, he was glad to escape from the pretensions of the society matron's art school jargon. Guests were treated to violin music, breezy terraces and moon-kissed gardens. His hostess fluttered around him like a butterfly, lashes batting, laughter trilling.

Margerite's flirtations were patently obvious and didn't bother him. She was a pretty, vivacious woman currently between men. Though he had privately deduced she shared little with her daughter other than looks, he considered him harmless, even entertaining. So when she offered to show him the rooftop patio, he went along.

The wind off the sound was playful and fragrant. And it

was blessedly quiet following the ceaseless after-dinner chatter. From the rail, Mikhail could see the water, the curve of beach, the serene elegance of other homes tucked behind walls and circling gardens.

And he could see Sydney as she strolled to the shadowy corner of the terrace below with her arm tucked through Channing's.

"My third husband built this house," Margerite was saying. "He's an architect. When we divorced, I had my choice between this house and the little villa in Nice. Naturally, with so many of my friends here, I chose this." With a sigh, she turned to face him, leaning prettily on the rail. "I must say, I love this spot. When I give house parties people are spread out on every level, so it's both cozy and private. Perhaps you'll join us some weekend this summer."

"Perhaps." The answer was absent as he stared down at Sydney. The moonlight made her hair gleam like polished mahogany.

Margerite shifted, just enough so that their thighs brushed. Mikhail wasn't sure if he was more surprised or more amused. But to save her pride, he smiled, easing away slowly. "You have a lovely home. It suits you."

"I'd love to see your studio." Margerite let the invitation melt into her eyes. "Where you create."

"I'm afraid you'd find it cramped, hot and boring."

"Impossible." Smiling, she traced a fingertip over the back of his hand. "I'm sure I'd find nothing about you boring."

Good God, the woman was old enough to be his mother, and she was coming on to him like a misty-eyed virgin primed for her first tumble. Mikhail nearly sighed, then reminded himself it was only a moment out of his life. He took her hand between both of his hands.

"Margerite, you're charming. And I'm—" he kissed her fingers lightly "—unsuitable."

She lifted a finger and brushed it over his cheek. ''You underestimate yourself, Mikhail.''

No, but he realized how he'd underestimated her.

On the terrace below, Sydney was trying to find a graceful way to discourage Channing. He was attentive, dignified, solicitous, and he was boring her senseless.

It was her lack, she was sure. Any woman with half a soul would be melting under the attraction of a man like Channing. There was moonlight, music, flowers. The breeze in the leafy trees smelled of the sea and murmured of romance. Channing was talking about Paris, and his hand was skimming lightly over her bare back.

She wished she was home, alone, with her eyes crossing over a fat file of quarterly reports.

Taking a deep breath, she turned. She would have to tell him firmly, simply and straight out that he needed to look elsewhere for companionship. It was Sydney's bad luck that she happened to glance up to see Mikhail on the rooftop with her mother just when he took Margerite's hand to his lips.

Why the…she couldn't think of anything vile enough to call him. Slime was too simple. Gigolo too slick. He was nuzzling up to her mother. *Her mother.* When only hours before he'd been…

Nothing, Sydney reminded herself and dismissed the tense scene in the Soho hallway from her mind. He'd been posturing and preening, that was all.

And she could have killed him for it.

As she watched, Mikhail backed away from Margerite, laughing. Then he looked down. The instant their eyes met, Sydney declared war.

She whirled on Channing, her face so fierce he nearly babbled. ''Kiss me,'' she demanded.

''Why, Sydney.''

''I said kiss me.'' She grabbed him by the lapels and hauled him against her.

"Of course, darling." Pleased with her change of heart, he cupped her shoulders in his hands and leaned down to her.

His lips were soft, warm, eager. They slanted over hers with practiced precision while his hands slid down her back. He tasted of after-dinner mints. Her body fit well against his.

And she felt nothing, nothing but an empty inner rage. Then a chill that was both fear and despair.

"You're not trying, darling," he whispered. "You know I won't hurt you."

No, he wouldn't. There was nothing at all to fear from Channing. Miserable, she let him deepen the kiss, ordered herself to feel and respond. She felt his withdrawal even before his lips left hers. The twinges of annoyance and puzzlement.

"Sydney, dear, I'm not sure what the problem is." He smoothed down his crinkled lapels. Marginally frustrated, he lifted his eyes. "That was like kissing my sister."

"I'm tired, Channing," she said to the air between them. "I should go in and get ready to go."

Twenty minutes later, the driver turned the car toward Manhattan. In the back seat Sydney sat ramrod straight well over in her corner, while Mikhail sprawled in his. They didn't bother to speak, not even the polite nonentities of two people who had attended the same function.

He was boiling with rage.

She was frigid with disdain.

She'd done it to annoy him, Mikhail decided. She'd let that silk-suited jerk all but swallow her whole just to make him suffer.

Why was he suffering? he asked himself. She was nothing to him.

No, she was something, he corrected, and brooded into

the dark. His only problem was figuring out exactly what that something was.

Obviously, Sydney reflected, the man had no ethics, no morals, no shame. Here he was, just sitting there, all innocence and quiet reflection, after his disgraceful behavior. She frowned at the pale image of her own face in the window glass and tried to listen to the Chopin prelude on the stereo. Flirting so blatantly with a woman twenty years older. Sneering, yes positively sneering down from the rooftop.

And she'd hired him. Sydney let out a quiet, hissing breath from between her teeth. Oh, that was something she regretted. She'd let her concern, her determination to do the right thing, blind her into hiring some oversexed, amoral Russian carpenter.

Well, if he thought he was going to start playing patty-cake with her mother, he was very much mistaken.

She drew a breath, turned and aimed one steady glare. Mikhail would have sworn the temperature in the car dropped fifty degrees in a snap.

"You stay away from my mother."

He slanted her a look from under his lashes and gracefully crossed his legs. "Excuse me?"

"You heard me, Boris. If you think I'm going to stand by and watch you put the moves on my mother, think again. She's lonely and vulnerable. Her last divorce upset her and she isn't over it."

He said something short and sharp in his native tongue and closed his eyes.

Temper had Sydney sliding across the seat until she could poke his arm. "What the hell does that mean?"

"You want translation? The simplest is bullshit. Now shut up. I'm going to sleep."

"You're not going anywhere until we settle this. You keep your big, grimy hands off my mother, or I'll turn that building you're so fond of into a parking lot."

His eyes slitted open. She found the glitter of angry eyes immensely satisfying. "A big threat from a small woman," he said in a deceptively lazy voice. She was entirely too close for his comfort, and her scent was swimming in his senses, tangling his temper with something more basic. "You should concentrate on the suit, and let your mother handle her own."

"Suit? What suit?"

"The banker who spent the evening sniffing your ankles."

Her face flooded with color. "He certainly was not. He's entirely too well mannered to sniff at my ankles or anything else. And Channing is my business."

"So. You have your business, and I have mine. Now, let's see what we have together." One moment he was stretched out, and the next he had her twisted over his lap. Stunned, Sydney pressed her hands against his chest and tried to struggle out of his hold. He tightened it. "As you see, I have no manners."

"Oh, I know it." She tossed her head back, chin jutting. "What do you think you're doing?"

He wished to hell he knew. She was rigid as an ice floe, but there was something incredible, and Lord, inevitable, about the way she fit into his arms. Though he was cursing himself, he held her close, close enough that he felt the uneven rise and fall of her breasts against his chest, tasted the sweet, wine-tipped flavor of her breath on his lips.

There was a lesson here, he thought grimly, and she was going to learn it.

"I've decided to teach you how to kiss. From what I saw from the roof, you did a poor job of it with the polo player."

Shock and fury had her going still. She would not squirm or scream or give him the satisfaction of frightening her. His eyes were close and challenging. She thought she understood exactly how Lucifer would have looked as he walked through the gates of his own dark paradise.

"You conceited jerk." Because she wanted to slug him, badly, she fisted her hands closed and looked haughtily down her small, straight nose. "There's nothing you can teach me."

"No?" He wondered if he'd be better off just strangling her and having done with it. "Let's see then. Your Channing put his hands here. Yes?" He slid them over her shoulders. The quick, involuntary shudder chilled her skin. "You afraid of me, *milaya?*"

"Don't be ridiculous." But she was, suddenly and deeply. She swallowed the fear as his thumbs caressed her bare skin.

"Tremble is good. It makes a man feel strong. I don't think you trembled for this Channing."

She said nothing and wondered if he knew his accent had thickened. It sounded exotic, erotic. He wondered he could speak at all with her watching him and waiting.

"His way isn't mine," he muttered. "I'll show you."

His fingers clamped around the back of her neck, pulled her face toward his. He heard her breath catch then shudder out when he paused only a fraction before their lips touched. Her eyes filled his vision, that wide, wary blue. Ignoring the twist in his gut, he smiled, turned his head just an inch and skimmed his lips over her jawline.

She bit back only part of the moan. Instinctively she tipped her head back, giving him access to the long, sensitive column of her throat.

What was he doing to her? Her mind raced frantically to catch up with her soaring body. Why didn't he just get it over with so she could escape with her pride intact?

She'd kill him for this. Crush him. Destroy him.

And oh, it felt wonderful, delicious. Wicked.

He could only think she tasted of morning—cool, spring mornings when the dew slicked over green, green grass and new flowers. She shivered against him, her body still held stiffly away even as her head fell back in surrender.

Who was she? He nibbled lazily over to her ear and burned for her to show him.

A thousand, a million pinpricks of pleasure danced along her skin. Shaken by them, she started to pull away. But his hands slid down her back and melted her spine. All the while his lips teased and tormented, never, never coming against hers to relieve the aching pressure.

She wanted.

The slow, flickering heat kindling in the pit of her stomach.

She yearned.

Spreading, spreading through her blood and bone.

She needed.

Wave after wave of liquid fire lapping, cruising, flowing over her skin.

She took.

In a fire flash her system exploded. Mouth to mouth she strained against him, pressing ice to heat and letting it steam until the air was so thick with it, it clogged in her throat. Her fingers speared through his hair and fisted as she fed greedily on the stunning flavor of her own passion.

This. At last this. He was rough and restless and smelled of man instead of expensive colognes. The words he muttered were incomprehensible against her mouth. But they didn't sound like endearments, reassurances, promises. They sounded like threats.

His mouth wasn't soft and warm and eager, but hot and hard and ruthless. She wanted that, how she wanted the heedless and hasty meeting of lips and tongues.

His hands weren't hesitant or practiced, but strong and impatient. It ran giddily through her brain that he would take what he wanted, when and where it suited him. The pleasure and power of it burst through her like sunlight.

She choked out his name when he tugged her bodice down and filled his calloused hands with her breasts.

He was drowning in her. The ice had melted and he was over his head, too dazed to know if he should dive deeper or scrabble for the surface. The scent, the taste, oh Lord, the texture. Alabaster and silk and rose petals. Every fine thing a man could want to touch, to steal, to claim as his own. His hands raced over her as he fought for more.

On an oath he shifted, and she was under him on the long plush seat of the car, her hair spread out like melted copper, her body moving, moving under his, her white breasts spilling out above the stark black dress and tormenting him into tasting.

She arched, and her fingers dug into his back as he suckled. A deep and delicious ache tugged at the center of her body. And she wanted him there, there where the heat was most intense. There where she felt so soft, so needy.

"Please." She could hear the whimper in her voice but felt no embarrassment. Only desperation. "Mikhail, please."

The throaty purr of her voice burst in his blood. He came back to her mouth, assaulting it, devouring it. Crazed, he hooked one hand in the top of her dress, on the verge of ripping it from her. And he looked, looked at her face, the huge eyes, the trembling lips. Light and shadow washed over it, leaving her pale as a ghost. She was shaking like a leaf beneath his hands.

And he heard the drum of traffic from outside.

He surfaced abruptly, shaking his head to clear it and gulping in air like a diver down too long. They were driving through the city, their privacy as thin as the panel of smoked glass that separated them from her chauffeur. And he was mauling her, yes, mauling her as if he were a reckless teenager with none of the sense God had given him.

The apology stuck in his throat. An "I beg your pardon" would hardly do the trick. Eyes grim, loins aching, he tugged her dress back into place. She only stared at him and made him feel like a drooling heathen over a virgin sacrifice. And Lord help him, he wanted to plunder.

Swearing, he pushed away and yanked her upright. He leaned back in the shadows and stared out of the dark window. They were only blocks from his apartment. Blocks, and he'd very nearly…it wouldn't do to think about what he'd nearly.

"We're almost there." Strain had his voice coming out clipped and hard. Sydney winced away as though it had been a slap.

What had she done wrong this time? She'd felt, and she'd wanted. Felt and wanted more than she ever had before. Yet she had still failed. For that one timeless moment she'd been willing to toss aside pride and fear. There had been passion in her, real and ready. And, she'd thought, he'd felt passion for her.

But not enough. She closed her eyes. It never seemed to be enough. Now she was cold, freezing, and wrapped her arms tight to try to hold in some remnant of heat.

Damn it, why didn't she say something? Mikhail dragged an unsteady hand through his hair. He deserved to be slapped. Shot was more like it. And she just sat there.

As he brooded out the window, he reminded himself that it hadn't been all his doing. She'd been as rash, pressing that wonderful body against his, letting that wide, mobile mouth make him crazy. Squirting that damnable perfume all over that soft skin until he'd been drunk with it.

He started to feel better.

Yes, there had been two people grappling in the back seat. She was every bit as guilty as he.

"Look, Sydney." He turned and she jerked back like an overwound spring.

"Don't touch me." He heard only the venom and none of the tears.

"Fine." Guilt hammered away at him as the car cruised

to the curb. "I'll keep my big, grimy hands off you, Hayward. Call someone else when you want a little romp in the back seat."

Her fisted hands held on to pride and composure. "I meant what I said about my mother."

He shoved the door open. Light spilled in, splashing over his face, turning it frosty white. "So did I. Thanks for the ride."

When the door slammed, she closed her eyes tight. She would not cry. A single tear slipped past her guard and was dashed away. She would not cry. And she would not forget.

Chapter Four

She'd put in a long day. Actually she'd put in a long week that was edging toward sixty hours between office time, luncheon meetings and evenings at home with files. This particular day had a few hours yet to run, but Sydney recognized the new feeling of relief and satisfaction that came with Friday afternoons when the work force began to anticipate Saturday mornings.

Throughout her adult life one day of the week had been the same as the next; all of them a scattershot of charity functions, shopping and lunch dates. There had been no work schedule, and weekends had simply been a time when the parties had lasted longer.

Things had changed. As she read over a new contract, she was glad they had. She was beginning to understand why her grandfather had always been so lusty and full of life. He'd had a purpose, a place, a goal.

Now they were hers.

True, she still had to ask advice on the more technical wordings of contracts and depended heavily on her board when it came to making deals. But she was starting to appreciate—more, she was starting to relish the grand chess game of buying and selling buildings.

She circled what she considered a badly worded clause then answered her intercom.

"Mr. Bingham to see you, Ms. Hayward."

"Send him in, Janine. Oh, and see if you can reach Frank Marlowe at Marlowe, Radcliffe and Smyth."

"Yes, ma'am."

When Lloyd strode in a moment later, Sydney was still huddled over the contract. She held up one finger to give herself a minute to finish.

"Lloyd. I'm sorry, if I lose my concentration on all these *whereas*es, I have to start over." She scrawled a note to herself, set it and the contract aside, then smiled at him. "What can I do for you?"

"This Soho project. It's gotten entirely out of hand."

Her lips tightened. Thinking of Soho made her think of Mikhail. Mikhail reminded her of the turbulent ride from Long Island and her latest failure as a woman. She didn't care for it.

"In what way?"

"In every way." With fury barely leashed, he began to pace her office. "A quarter of a million. You earmarked a quarter of a million to rehab that building."

Sydney stayed where she was and quietly folded her hands on the desk. "I'm aware of that, Lloyd. Considering the condition of the building, Mr. Stanislaski's bid was very reasonable."

"How would you know?" he shot back. "Did you get competing bids?"

"No." Her fingers flexed, then relaxed again. It was difficult, but she reminded herself that he'd earned his way up the ladder while she'd been hoisted to the top rung. "I went with my instincts."

"Instincts?" Eyes narrowed, he spun back to her. The

derision in his voice was as thick as the pile of her carpet. "You've been in the business for a matter of months, and you have instincts."

"That's right. I'm also aware that the estimate for rewiring, the plumbing and the carpentry were well in line with other, similar rehabs."

"Damn it, Sydney, we didn't put much more than that into this building last year."

One slim finger began to tap on the desk. "What we did here in the Hayward Building was little more than decorating. A good many of the repairs in Soho are a matter of safety and bringing the facilities up to code."

"A quarter of a million in repairs." He slapped his palms on the desk and leaned forward. Sydney was reminded of Mikhail making a similar gesture. But of course Lloyd's hands would leave no smudge of dirt. "Do you know what our annual income is from those apartments?"

"As a matter of fact I do." She rattled off a figure, surprising him. It was accurate to the penny. "On one hand, it will certainly take more than a year of full occupancy to recoup the principal on this investment. On the other, when people pay rent in good faith, they deserve decent housing."

"Decent, certainly," Lloyd said stiffly. "You're mixing morals with business."

"Oh, I hope so. I certainly hope so."

He drew back, infuriated that she would sit so smug and righteous behind a desk that should have been his. "You're naive, Sydney."

"That may be. But as long as I run this company, it will be run by my standards."

"You think you run it because you sign a few contracts and make phone calls. You've put a quarter million into what you yourself termed your pet project, and you don't have a clue what this Stanislaski's up to. How do you know he isn't buying inferior grades and pocketing the excess?"

"That's absurd."

"As I said, you're naive. You put some Russian artist in charge of a major project, then don't even bother to check the work."

"I intend to inspect the project myself. I've been tied up. And I have Mr. Stanislaski's weekly report."

He sneered. Before Sydney's temper could fray, she realized Lloyd was right. She'd hired Mikhail on impulse and instinct, then because of personal feelings, had neglected to follow through with her involvement on the project.

That wasn't naive. It was gutless.

"You're absolutely right, Lloyd, and I'll correct it." She leaned back in her chair. "Was there anything else?"

"You've made a mistake," he said. "A costly one in this case. The board won't tolerate another."

With her hands laid lightly on the arms of her chair, she nodded. "And you're hoping to convince them that you belong at this desk."

"They're businessmen, Sydney. And though sentiment might prefer a Hayward at the head of the table, profit and loss will turn the tide."

Her expression remained placid, her voice steady. "I'm sure you're right again. And if the board continues to back me, I want one of two things from you. Your resignation or your loyalty. I won't accept anything in between. Now, if you'll excuse me?"

When the door slammed behind him, she reached for the phone. But her hand was trembling, and she drew it back. She plucked up a paper clip and mangled it. Then another, then a third. Between that and the two sheets of stationery she shredded, she felt the worst of the rage subside.

Clearheaded, she faced the facts.

Lloyd Bingham was an enemy, and he was an enemy with experience and influence. She had acted in haste with Soho. Not that she'd been wrong; she didn't believe she'd been wrong. But if there were mistakes, Lloyd would capitalize on them and drop them right in her lap.

Was it possible that she was risking everything her grandfather had given her with one project? Could she be forced to step down if she couldn't prove the worth and right of what she had done?

She wasn't sure, and that was the worst of it.

One step at a time. That was the only way to go on. And the first step was to get down to Soho and do her job.

The sky was the color of drywall. Over the past few days, the heat had ebbed, but it had flowed back into the city that morning like a river, flooding Manhattan with humidity. The pedestrian traffic surged through it, streaming across the intersections in hot little packs.

Girls in shorts and men in wilted business suits crowded around the sidewalk vendors in hopes that an ice-cream bar or a soft drink would help them beat the heat.

When Sydney stepped out of her car, the sticky oppression of the air punched like a fist. She thought of her driver sitting in the enclosed car and dismissed him for the day. Shielding her eyes, she turned to study her building.

Scaffolding crept up the walls like metal ivy. Windows glittered, their manufacturer stickers slashed across the glass. She thought she saw a pair of arthritic hands scraping away at a label at a third-floor window.

There were signs in the doorway, warning of construction in progress. She could hear the sounds of it, booming hammers, buzzing saws, the clang of metal and the tinny sound of rock and roll through portable speakers.

At the curb she saw the plumber's van, a dented pickup and a scattering of interested onlookers. Since they were all peering up, she followed their direction. And saw Mikhail.

For an instant, her heart stopped dead. He stood outside

the top floor, five stories up, moving nimbly on what seemed to Sydney to be a very narrow board.

"Man, get a load of those buns," a woman beside her sighed. "They are class A."

Sydney swallowed. She supposed they were. And his naked back wasn't anything to sneeze at, either. The trouble was, it was hard to enjoy it when she had a hideous flash of him plummeting off the scaffolding and breaking that beautiful back on the concrete below.

Panicked, she rushed inside. The elevator doors were open, and a couple of mechanics were either loading or unloading their tools inside it. She didn't stop to ask but bolted up the steps.

Sweaty men were replastering the stairwell between two and three. They took the time to whistle and wink, but she kept climbing. Someone had the television up too loud, probably to drown out the sound of construction. A baby was crying fitfully. She smelled chicken frying.

Without pausing for breath, she dashed from four to five. There was music playing here. Tough and gritty rock, poorly accompanied by a laborer in an off-key tenor.

Mikhail's door was open, and Sydney streaked through. She nearly tumbled over a graying man with arms like tree trunks. He rose gracefully from his crouched position where he'd been sorting tools and steadied her.

"I'm sorry. I didn't see you."

"Is all right. I like women to fall at my feet."

She registered the Slavic accent even as she glanced desperately around the room for Mikhail. Maybe everybody in the building was Russian, she thought frantically. Maybe he'd imported plumbers from the mother country.

"Can I help you?"

"No. Yes." She pressed a hand to her heart when she realized she was completely out of breath. "Mikhail."

"He is just outside." Intrigued, he watched her as he jerked a thumb toward the window.

She could see him there—at least she could see the flat, tanned torso. "Outside. But, but—"

"We are finishing for the day. You will sit?"

"Get him in," Sydney whispered. "Please, get him in."

Before he could respond, the window was sliding up, and Mikhail was tossing one long, muscled leg inside. He said something in his native tongue, laughter in his voice as the rest of his body followed. When he saw Sydney, the laughter vanished.

"Hayward." He tapped his caulking gun against his palm.

"What were you doing out there?" The question came out in an accusing rush.

"Replacing windows." He set the caulking gun aside. "Is there a problem?"

"No, I..." She couldn't remember ever feeling more of a fool. "I came by to check the progress."

"So. I'll take you around in a minute." He walked into the kitchen, stuck his head into the sink and turned the faucet on full cold.

"He's a hothead," the man behind her said, chuckling at his own humor. When Sydney only managed a weak smile, he called out to Mikhail, speaking rapidly in that exotic foreign tongue.

"*Tak*" was all he said. Mikhail came up dripping, hair streaming over the bandanna he'd tied around it. He shook it back, splattering water, then shrugged and hooked his thumbs in his belt loops. He was wet, sweaty and half-naked. Sydney had to fold her tongue inside her mouth to keep it from hanging out.

"My son is rude." Yuri Stanislaski shook his head. "I raised him better."

"Your—oh." Sydney looked back at the man with the broad face and beautiful hands. Mikhail's hands. "How do you do, Mr. Stanislaski."

"I do well. I am Yuri. I ask my son if you are the Hay-

ward who owns this business. He only says yes and
scowls.''

"Yes, well, I am."

"It's a good building. Only a little sick. And we are the
doctors.'' He grinned at his son, then boomed out something else in Ukrainian.

This time an answering smile tugged at Mikhail's mouth.
"No, you haven't lost a patient yet, Papa. Go home and
have your dinner."

Yuri hauled up his tool chest. "You come and bring the
pretty lady. Your mama makes enough."

"Oh, well, thank you, but—"

"I'm busy tonight, Papa." Mikhail cut off Sydney's polite refusal.

Yuri raised a bushy brow. "You're stupid tonight," he
said in Ukrainian. "Is this the one who makes you sulk all
week?''

Annoyed, Mikhail picked up a kitchen towel and wiped
his face. "Women don't make me sulk."

Yuri only smiled. "This one would." Then he turned to
Sydney. "Now I am rude, too, talking so you don't understand. He is bad influence.'' He lifted her hand and kissed
it with considerable charm. "I am glad to meet you."

"I'm glad to meet you, too."

"Put on a shirt," Yuri ordered his son, then left, whis-
tling.

"He's very nice," Sydney said.

"Yes." Mikhail picked up the T-shirt he'd peeled off
hours before, but only held it. "So, you want to see the
work?''

"Yes, I thought—"

"The windows are done," he interrupted. "The wiring
is almost done. That and the plumbing will take another
week. Come."

He moved out, skirting her by a good two feet, then
walked into the apartment next door without knocking.

"Keely's," he told her. "She is out."

The room was a clash of sharp colors and scents. The furniture was old and sagging but covered with vivid pillows and various articles of female attire.

The adjoining kitchen was a mess—not with dishes or pots and pans—but with walls torn down to studs and thick wires snaked through.

"It must be inconvenient for her, for everyone, during the construction."

"Better than plugging in a cake mixer and shorting out the building. The old wire was tube and knob, forty years old or more, and frayed. This is Romex. More efficient, safer."

She bent over his arm, studying the wiring. "Well. Hmm."

He nearly smiled. Perhaps he would have if she hadn't smelled so good. Instead, he moved a deliberate foot away. "After the inspection, we will put up new walls. Come."

It was a trial for both of them, but he took her through every stage of the work, moving from floor to floor, showing her elbows of plastic pipe and yards of copper tubing.

"Most of the flooring can be saved with sanding and refinishing. But some must be replaced." He kicked at a square of plywood he'd nailed to a hole in the second-floor landing.

Sydney merely nodded, asking questions only when they seemed intelligent. Most of the workers were gone, off to cash their week's paychecks. The noise level had lowered so that she could hear muted voices behind closed doors, snatches of music or televised car chases. She lifted a brow at the sound of a tenor sax swinging into "Rhapsody in Blue."

"That's Will Metcalf," Mikhail told her. "He's good. Plays in a band."

"Yes, he's good." The rail felt smooth and sturdy under her hand as they went down. Mikhail had done that, she thought. He'd fixed, repaired, replaced, as needed because he cared about the people who lived in the building. He knew who was playing the sax or eating the fried chicken, whose baby was laughing.

"Are you happy with the progress?" she asked quietly.

The tone of her voice made him look at her, something he'd been trying to avoid. A few tendrils of hair had escaped their pins to curl at her temples. He could see a pale dusting of freckles across her nose. "Happy enough. It's you who should answer. It's your building."

"No, it's not." Her eyes were very serious, very sad. "It's yours. I only write the checks."

"Sydney—"

"I've seen enough to know you've made a good start." She was hurrying down the steps as she spoke. "Be sure to contact my office when it's time for the next draw."

"Damn it. Slow down." He caught up with her at the bottom of the steps and grabbed her arm. "What's wrong with you? First you stand in my room pale and out of breath. Now you run away, and your eyes are miserable."

It had hit her, hard, that she had no community of people who cared. Her circle of friends was so narrow, so self-involved. Her best friend had been Peter, and that had been horribly spoiled. Her life was on the sidelines, and she envied the involvement, the closeness she felt in this place. The building wasn't hers, she thought again. She only owned it.

"I'm not running away, and nothing's wrong with me." She had to get out, get away, but she had to do it with dignity. "I take this job very seriously. It's my first major project since taking over Hayward. I want it done right. And I took a chance by…" She trailed off, glancing toward the door just to her right. She could have sworn she'd heard someone call for help. Television, she thought, but before she could continue, she heard the thin, pitiful call again. "Mikhail, do you hear that?"

"Hear what?" How could he hear anything when he was trying not to kiss her again?

"In here." She turned toward the door, straining her ears. "Yes, in here, I heard—"

That time he'd heard it, too. Lifting a fist, he pounded on the door. "Mrs. Wolburg. Mrs. Wolburg, it's Mik."

The shaky voice barely penetrated the wood. "Hurt. Help me."

"Oh, God, she's—"

Before Sydney could finish, Mikhail rammed his shoulder against the door. With the second thud, it crashed open to lean drunkenly on its hinges.

"In the kitchen," Mrs. Wolburg called weakly. "Mik, thank God."

He bolted through the apartment with its starched doilies and paper flowers to find her on the kitchen floor. She was a tiny woman, mostly bone and thin flesh. Her usually neat cap of white hair was matted with sweat.

"Can't see," she said. "Dropped my glasses."

"Don't worry." He knelt beside her, automatically checking her pulse as he studied her pain-filled eyes. "Call an ambulance," he ordered Sydney, but she was already on the phone. "I'm not going to help you up, because I don't know how you're hurt."

"Hip." She gritted her teeth at the awful, radiating pain. "I think I busted my hip. Fell, caught my foot. Couldn't move. All the noise, nobody could hear me calling. Been here two, three hours. Got so weak."

"It's all right now." He tried to chafe some heat into her hands. "Sydney, get a blanket and pillow."

She had them in her arms and was already crouching beside Mrs. Wolburg before he'd finished the order. "Here now. I'm just going to lift your head a little." Gently she set the woman's limp head on the pillow. Despite the raging heat, Mrs. Wolburg was shivering with cold. As she continued to speak in quiet, soothing tones, Sydney tucked the blanket around her. "Just a few more minutes," Sydney murmured, and stroked the clammy forehead.

A crowd was forming at the door. Though he didn't like leaving Sydney with the injured woman, he rose. "I want to keep the neighbors away. Send someone to keep an eye for the ambulance."

"Fine." While fear pumped hard in her heart, she continued to smile down at Mrs. Wolburg. "You have a lovely apartment. Do you crochet the doilies yourself?"

"Been doing needlework for sixty years, since I was pregnant with my first daughter."

"They're beautiful. Do you have other children?"

"Six, three of each. And twenty grandchildren. Five great…" She shut her eyes on a flood of pain, then opened them again and managed a smile. "Been after me for living alone, but I like my own place and my own way."

"Of course."

"And my daughter, Lizzy? Moved clear out to Phoenix, Arizona. Now what would I want to live out there for?"

Sydney smiled and stroked. "I couldn't say."

"They'll be on me now," she muttered, and let her eyes close again. "Wouldn't have happened if I hadn't dropped my glasses. Terrible nearsighted. Getting old's hell, girl, and don't let anyone tell you different. Couldn't see where I was going and snagged my foot in that torn linoleum. Mik told me to keep it taped down, but I wanted to give it a good scrub." She managed a wavery smile. "Least I've been lying here on a clean floor."

"Paramedics are coming up," Mikhail said from behind her. Sydney only nodded, filled with a terrible guilt and anger she was afraid to voice.

"You call my grandson, Mik? He lives up on Eighty-first. He'll take care of the rest of the family."

"Don't worry about it, Mrs. Wolburg."

Fifteen efficient minutes later, Sydney stood on the sidewalk watching as the stretcher was lifted into the back of the ambulance.

"Did you reach her grandson?" she asked Mikhail.

"I left a message on his machine."

Nodding, she walked to the curb and tried to hail a cab. "Where's your car?"

"I sent him home. I didn't know how long I'd be and it was too hot to leave him sitting there. Maybe I should go back in and call a cab."

"In a hurry?"

She winced as the siren shrieked. "I want to get to the hospital."

Nonplussed, he jammed his hands into his pockets. "There's no need for you to go."

She turned, and her eyes, in the brief moment they held his, were ripe with emotion. Saying nothing, she faced away until a cab finally swung to the curb. Nor did she speak when Mikhail climbed in behind her.

She hated the smell of hospitals. Layers of illness, antiseptics, fear and heavy cleaners. The memory of the last days her grandfather had lain dying were still too fresh in her mind. The Emergency Room of the downtown hospital added one more layer. Fresh blood.

Sydney steeled herself against it and walked through the crowds of the sick and injured to the admitting window.

"You had a Mrs. Wolburg just come in."

"That's right." The clerk stabbed keys on her computer. "You family?"

"No, I—"

"We're going to need some family to fill out these forms. Patient said she wasn't insured."

Mikhail was already leaning over, eyes dangerous, when Sydney snapped out her answer. "Hayward Industries will be responsible for Mrs. Wolburg's medical expenses." She reached into her bag for identification and slapped it onto the counter. "I'm Sydney Hayward. Where is Mrs. Wolburg?"

"In X ray." The frost in Sydney's eyes had the clerk shifting in her chair. "Dr. Cohen's attending."

So they waited, drinking bad coffee among the moans and tears of inner city ER. Sometimes Sydney would lay her head back against the wall and shut her eyes. She appeared to be dozing, but all the while she was thinking what it would be like to be old, and alone and helpless.

He wanted to think she was only there to cover her butt. Oh yes, he wanted to think that of her. It was so much more comfortable to think of her as the head of some bloodless company than as a woman.

But he remembered how quickly she had acted in the Wolburg apartment, how gentle she had been with the old woman. And most of all, he remembered the look in her eyes out on the street. All that misery and compassion and guilt welling up in those big eyes.

"She tripped on the linoleum," Sydney murmured.

It was the first time she'd spoken in nearly an hour, and Mikhail turned his head to study her. Her eyes were still closed, her face pale and in repose.

"She was only walking in her own kitchen and fell because the floor was old and unsafe."

"You're making it safe."

Sydney continued as if she hadn't heard. "Then she could only lie there, hurt and alone. Her voice was so weak. I nearly walked right by."

"You didn't walk by." His hand hesitated over hers. Then, with an oath, he pressed his palm to the back of her hand. "You're only one Hayward, Sydney. Your grandfather—"

"He was ill." Her hand clenched under Mikhail's, and her eyes squeezed more tightly closed. "He was sick nearly two years, and I was in Europe. I didn't know. He didn't want to disrupt my life. My father was dead, and there was only me, and he didn't want to worry me. When he finally called me, it was almost over. He was a good man. He wouldn't have let things get so bad, but he couldn't...he just couldn't.''

She let out a short, shuddering breath. Mikhail turned her hand over and linked his fingers with hers.

"When I got to New York, he was in the hospital. He looked so small, so tired. He told me I was the only Hayward left. Then he died,'' she said wearily. "And I was.''

"You're doing what needs to be done. No one can ask for more than that.''

She opened her eyes again, met his. "I don't know.''

They waited again, in silence.

It was nearly two hours before Mrs. Wolburg's frantic grandson rushed in. The entire story had to be told again before he hurried off to call the rest of his family.

Four hours after they'd walked into Emergency, the doctor came out to fill them in.

A fractured hip, a mild concussion. She would be moved to a room right after she'd finished in Recovery. Her age made the break serious, but her health helped balance that. Sydney left both her office and home numbers with the doctor and the grandson, requesting to be kept informed of Mrs. Wolburg's condition.

Unbearably weary in body and mind, Sydney walked out of the hospital.

"You need food,'' Mikhail said.

"What? No, really, I'm just tired.''

Ignoring that, he grabbed her arm and pulled her down the street. "Why do you always say the opposite of what I say?''

"I don't.''

"See, you did it again. You need meat.''

If she kept trying to drag her heels, he was going to pull her arm right out of the socket. Annoyed, she scrambled to keep pace. "What makes you think you know what I need?"

"Because I do." He pulled up short at a light and she bumped into him. Before he could stop it, his hand had lifted to touch her face. "God, you're so beautiful."

While she blinked in surprise, he swore, scowled then dragged her into the street seconds before the light turned.

"Maybe I'm not happy with you," he went on, muttering to himself. "Maybe I think you're a nuisance, and a snob, and—"

"I am not a snob."

He said something vaguely familiar in his native language. Sydney's chin set when she recalled the translation. "It is not bull. You're the snob if you think I am just because I come from a different background."

He stopped, eyeing her with a mixture of distrust and interest. "Fine then, you won't mind eating in here." He yanked her into a noisy bar and grill. She found herself plopped down in a narrow booth with him, hip to hip.

There were scents of meat cooking, onions frying, spilled beer, all overlaid with grease. Her mouth watered. "I said I wasn't hungry."

"And I say you're a snob, and a liar."

The color that stung her cheeks pleased him, but it didn't last long enough. She leaned forward. "And would you like to know what I think of you?"

Again he lifted a hand to touch her cheek. It was irresistible. "Yes, I would."

She was saved from finding a description in her suddenly murky brain by the waitress.

"Two steaks, medium rare, and two of what you've got on tap."

"I don't like men to order for me," Sydney said tightly.

"Then you can order for me next time and we'll be even." Making himself comfortable, he tossed his arm over the back of the booth and stretched out his legs. "Why don't you take off your jacket, Hayward? You're hot."

"Stop telling me what I am. And stop that, too."

"What?"

"Playing with my hair."

He grinned. "I was playing with your neck. I like your neck." To prove it, he skimmed a finger down it again.

She clamped her teeth on the delicious shudder that followed it down her spine. "I wish you'd move over."

"Okay." He shifted closer. "Better?"

Calm, she told herself. She would be calm. After a cleansing breath, she turned her head. "If you don't..." And his lips brushed over hers, stopping the words and the thought behind them.

"I want you to kiss me back."

She started to shake her head, but couldn't manage it.

"I want to watch you when you do," he murmured. "I want to know what's there."

"There's nothing there."

But his mouth closed over hers and proved her a liar. She fell into the kiss, one hand lost in his hair, the other clamped on his shoulder.

She felt everything. Everything. And it all moved too fast. Her mind seemed to dim until she could barely hear the clatter and bustle of the bar. But she felt his mouth angle over hers, his teeth nip, his tongue seduce.

Whatever she was doing to him, he was doing to her. He knew it. He saw it in the way her eyes glazed before they closed, felt it in the hot, ready passion of her lips. It was supposed to soothe his ego, prove a point. But it did neither.

It only left him aching.

"Sorry to break this up." The waitress slapped two frosted mugs on the table. "Steak's on its way."

Sydney jerked her head back. His arms were still around her, though his grip had loosened. And she, she was plas-

tered against him. Her body molded to his as they sat in a
booth in a public place. Shame and fury battled for suprem-
acy as she yanked herself away.

"That was a despicable thing to do."

He shrugged and picked up his beer. "I didn't do it
alone." Over the foam, his eyes sharpened. "Not this time,
or last time."

"Last time, you…"

"What?"

Sydney lifted her mug and sipped gingerly. "I don't
want to discuss it."

He wanted to argue, even started to, but there was a
sheen of hurt in her eyes that baffled him. He didn't mind
making her angry. Hell, he enjoyed it. But he didn't know
what he'd done to make her hurt. He waited until the waitress had set the steaks in front of them.

"You've had a rough day," he said so kindly Sydney
gasped. "I don't mean to make it worse."

"It's…" She struggled with a response. "It's been a
rough day all around. Let's just put it behind us."

"Done." Smiling, he handed her a knife and fork. "Eat
your dinner. We'll have a truce."

"Good." She discovered she had an appetite after all.

Chapter Five

Sydney didn't know how Mildred Wolburg's accident had leaked to the press, but by Tuesday afternoon her office was flooded with calls from reporters. A few of the more enterprising staked out the lobby of the Hayward Building and cornered her when she left for the day.

By Wednesday rumors were flying around the offices that Hayward was facing a multimillion-dollar suit, and Sydney had several unhappy board members on her hands. The consensus was that by assuming responsibility for Mrs. Wolburg's medical expenses, Sydney had admitted Hayward's neglect and had set the company up for a large public settlement.

It was bad press, and bad business.

Knowing no route but the direct one, Sydney prepared a statement for the press and agreed to an emergency board meeting. By Friday, she thought as she walked into the hospital, she would know if she would remain in charge of Hayward or whether her position would be whittled down to figurehead.

Carrying a stack of paperbacks in one hand and a potted plant in the other, Sydney paused outside of Mrs. Wolburg's room. Because it was Sydney's third visit since the accident, she knew the widow wasn't likely to be alone. Invariably, friends and family streamed in and out during visiting hours. This time she saw Mikhail, Keely and two of Mrs. Wolburg's children.

Mikhail spotted her as Sydney was debating whether to slip out again and leave the books and plant she'd brought at the nurse's station.

"You have more company, Mrs. Wolburg."

"Sydney." The widow's eyes brightened behind her thick lenses. "More books."

"Your grandson told me you liked to read." Feeling awkward, she set the books on the table beside the bed and took Mrs. Wolburg's outstretched hand.

"My Harry used to say I'd rather read than eat." The thin, bony fingers squeezed Sydney's. "That's a beautiful plant."

"I noticed you have several in your apartment." She smiled, feeling slightly more relaxed as the conversation in the room picked up again to flow around them. "And the last time I was here the room looked like a florist's shop." She glanced around at the banks of cut flowers in vases, pots, baskets, even in a ceramic shoe. "So I settled on an African violet."

"I do have a weakness for flowers and growing things. Set it right there on the dresser, will you, dear? Between the roses and the carnations."

"She's getting spoiled." As Sydney moved to comply, the visiting daughter winked at her brother. "Flowers, presents, pampering. We'll be lucky to ever get home-baked cookies again."

"Oh, I might have a batch or two left in me." Mrs. Wolburg preened in her new crocheted bed jacket. "Mik tells me I'm getting a brand-new oven. Eye level, so I won't have to bend and stoop.''

"So I think I should get the first batch," Mikhail said as he sniffed the roses. "The chocolate chip."

"Please." Keely pressed a hand to her stomach. "I'm dieting. I'm getting murdered next week, and I have to look my best." She noted Sydney's stunned expression and grinned. *"Death Stalk,"* she explained. "My first TV movie. I'm the third victim of the maniacal psychopath. I get strangled in this really terrific negligee."

"You shouldn't have left your windows unlocked," Mrs. Wolburg told her, and Keely grinned again.

"Well, that's show biz."

Sydney waited until a break in the conversation, then made her excuses. Mikhail gave her a ten-second lead before he slipped a yellow rose out of a vase. "See you later, beautiful." He kissed Mrs. Wolburg on the cheek and left her chuckling.

In a few long strides, he caught up with Sydney at the elevators. "Hey. You look like you could use this." He offered the flower.

"It couldn't hurt." After sniffing the bloom, she worked up a smile. "Thanks."

"You want to tell me why you're upset?"

"I'm not upset." She jabbed the down button again.

"Never argue with an artist about your feelings." Insistently he tipped back her chin with one finger. "I see fatigue and distress, worry and annoyance."

The ding of the elevator relieved her, though she knew he would step inside the crowded car with her. She frowned a little when she found herself pressed between Mikhail and a large woman carrying a suitcase-sized purse. Someone on the elevator had used an excess of expensive perfume. Fleetingly Sydney wondered if that shouldn't be as illegal as smoking in a closed car.

"Any Gypsies in your family?" she asked Mikhail on impulse.

"Naturally."

"I'd rather you use a crystal ball to figure out the future than analyze my feelings at the moment."

"We'll see what we can do."

The car stopped on each floor. People shuffled off or squeezed in. By the time they reached the lobby, Sydney was hard up against Mikhail's side, with his arm casually around her waist. He didn't bother to remove it after they'd stepped off. She didn't bother to mention it.

"The work's going well," he told her.

"Good." She didn't care to think how much longer she'd be directly involved with the project.

"The electrical inspection is done. Plumbing will perhaps take another week." He studied her abstracted expression. "And we have decided to make the new roof out of blue cheese."

"Hmm." She stepped outside, stopped and looked back at him. With a quick laugh, she shook her head. "That might look very distinctive—but risky with this heat."

"You were listening."

"Almost." Absently she pressed fingers to her throbbing temple as her driver pulled up to the curb. "I'm sorry. I've got a lot on my mind."

"Tell me."

It surprised her that she wanted to. She hadn't been able to talk to her mother. Margerite would only be baffled. Channing—that was a joke. Sydney doubted that any of her friends would understand how she had become so attached to Hayward in such a short time.

"There really isn't any point," she decided, and started toward her waiting car and driver.

Did she think he would let her walk away, with that worry line between her brows and the tension knotted tight in her shoulders?

"How about a lift home?"

She glanced back. The ride home from her mother's party was still a raw memory. But he was smiling at her in an easy, friendly fashion. Nonthreatening? No, he would never be that with those dark looks and untamed aura. But they had agreed on a truce, and it was only a few blocks.

"Sure. We'll drop Mr. Stanislaski off in Soho, Donald."

"Yes, ma'am."

She took the precaution of sliding, casually, she hoped, all the way over to the far window. "Mrs. Wolburg looks amazingly well, considering," she began.

"She's strong." It was Mozart this time, he noted, low and sweet through the car speakers.

"The doctor says she'll be able to go home with her son soon."

"And you've arranged for the therapist to visit." Sydney stopped passing the rose from hand to hand and looked at him. "She told me," he explained. "Also that when she is ready to go home again, there will be a nurse to stay with her, until she is well enough to be on her own."

"I'm not playing Samaritan," Sydney mumbled. "I'm just trying to do what's right."

"I realize that. I realize, too, that you're concerned for her. But there's something more on your mind. Is it the papers and the television news?"

Her eyes went from troubled to frigid. "I didn't assume responsibility for Mrs. Wolburg's medical expenses for publicity, good or bad. And I don't—"

"I know you didn't." He cupped a hand over one of her clenched ones. "Remember, I was there. I saw you with her."

Sydney drew a deep breath. She had to. She'd very nearly had a tirade, and a lost temper was hardly the answer. "The point is," she said more calmly, "an elderly woman was seriously injured. Her pain shouldn't become company politics or journalistic fodder. What I did, I did because I knew it was right. I just want to make sure the right thing continues to be done.''

"You are president of Hayward.''

"For the moment.'' She turned to look out the window as they pulled up in front of the apartment building. ''I see we're making progress on the roof.''

"Among other things.'' Because he was far from finished, he leaned over her and opened the door on her side. For a moment, they were so close, his body pressed lightly to hers. She had an urge, almost desperate, to rub her fingers over his cheek, to feel the rough stubble he'd neglected to shave away. ''I'd like you to come up,'' he told her. ''I have something for you.''

Sydney caught her fingers creeping up and snatched them back. ''It's nearly six. I really should—''

"Come up for an hour,'' he finished. ''Your driver can come back for you, yes?''

"Yes.'' She shifted away, not sure whether she wanted to get out or simply create some distance between them. ''You can messenger your report over.''

"I could.''

He moved another inch. In defense, Sydney swung her legs out of the car. ''All right then, but I don't think it'll take an hour.''

"But it will.''

She relented because she preferred spending an hour going over a report than sitting in her empty apartment thinking about the scheduled board meeting. After giving her driver instructions, she walked with Mikhail toward the building.

"You've repaired the stoop.''

"Tuesday. It wasn't easy getting the men to stop sitting on it long enough.'' He exchanged greetings with the three who were ranged across it now as Sydney passed through the aroma of beer and tobacco. ''We can take the elevator. The inspection certificate is hardly dry.''

She thought of the five long flights up. "I can't tell you how glad I am to hear that." She stepped in with him, waited while he pulled the open iron doors closed.

"It has character now," he said as they began the assent. "And you don't worry that you'll get in to get downstairs and spend the night inside."

"There's good news."

He pulled the doors open again as the car slid to a smooth, quiet stop. In the hallway, the ceiling was gone, leaving bare joists and new wiring exposed.

"The water damage from leaking was bad," Mikhail said conversationally. "Once the roof is finished, we'll replace."

"I've expected some complaints from the tenants, but we haven't received a single one. Isn't it difficult for everyone, living in a construction zone?"

Mikhail jingled his keys. "Inconvenient. But everyone is excited and watches the progress. Mr. Stuben from the third floor comes up every morning before he leaves for work. Every day he says, 'Mikhail, you have your work cut out for you.'" He grinned as he opened the door. "Some days I'd like to throw my hammer at him." He stepped back and nudged her inside. "Sit."

Lips pursed, Sydney studied the room. The furniture had been pushed together in the center—to make it easier to work, she imagined. Tables were stacked on top of chairs, the rug had been rolled up. Under the sheet he'd tossed over his worktable were a variety of interesting shapes that were his sculptures, his tools, and blocks of wood yet to be carved.

It smelled like sawdust, she thought, and turpentine.

"Where?"

He stopped on his way to the kitchen and looked back. After a quick study, he leaned into the jumble and lifted out an old oak rocker. One-handed, Sydney noted, and felt foolish and impressed.

"Here." After setting it on a clear spot, he headed back into the kitchen.

The surface of the rocker was smooth as satin. When Sydney sat, she found the chair slipped around her like comforting arms. Ten seconds after she'd settled, she was moving it gently to and fro.

"This is beautiful."

He could hear the faint creak as the rocker moved and didn't bother to turn. "I made it for my sister years ago when she had a baby." His voice changed subtly as he turned on the kitchen tap. "She lost the baby, Lily, after only a few months, and it was painful for Natasha to keep the chair."

"I'm sorry." The creaking stopped. "I can't think of anything worse for a parent to face."

"Because there is nothing." He came back in, carrying a glass of water and a bottle. "Lily will always leave a little scar on the heart. But Tash has three children now. So pain is balanced with joy. Here." He put the glass in her hand, then shook two aspirin out of the bottle. "You have a headache."

She frowned down at the pills he dropped into her palm. True, her head was splitting, but she hadn't mentioned it. "I might have a little one," she muttered. "How do you know?"

"I can see it in your eyes." He waited until she'd sipped and swallowed, then walked behind the chair to circle her temples with his fingers. "It's not such a little one, either."

There was no doubt she should tell him to stop. And she would. Any minute. Unable to resist, she leaned back, letting her eyes close as his fingers stroked away the worst of the pain.

"Is this what you had for me? Headache remedies?"

Her voice was so quiet, so tired that his heart twisted a little. "No, I have something else for you. But it can wait until you're feeling better. Talk to me, Sydney. Tell me what's wrong. Maybe I can help.''

"It's something I have to take care of myself."

"Okay. Will that change if you talk to me?"

No, she thought. It was her problem, her future. But what harm would it do to talk it out, to say it all out loud and hear someone else's viewpoint?

"Office politics." She sighed as he began to massage the base of her neck. His rough, calloused fingers were as gentle as a mother's. "I imagine they can be tricky enough when you have experience. All I have is the family name and my grandfather's last wishes. The publicity on Mrs. Wolburg has left my position in the company very shaky. I assumed responsibility without going through channels or consulting legal. The board isn't pleased with me."

His eyes had darkened, but his hands remained gentle. "Because you have integrity?"

"Because I jumped the gun, so to speak. The resulting publicity only made things worse. The consensus is that someone with more savvy could have handled the Wolburg matter—that's how it's referred to at Hayward. The Wolburg matter in a quiet, tidy fashion. There's a board meeting at noon on Friday, and they could very well request that I step down as president."

"And will you?"

"I don't know." He was working on her shoulders now, competently, thoroughly. "I'd like to fight, draw the whole thing out. Then again, the company's been in upheaval for over a year, and having the president and the board as adversaries won't help Hayward. Added to that, my executive vice president and I are already on poor terms. He feels, perhaps justifiably, that he should be in the number one slot." She laughed softly. "There are times I wish he had it."

"No, you don't." He resisted the urge to bend down and press his lips to the long, slender column of her neck.

Barely. "You like being in charge, and I think you're good at it."

She stopped rocking to turn her head and stare at him. "You're the first person who's ever said that to me. Most of the people who know me think I'm playing at this, or that I'm experiencing a kind of temporary insanity."

His hand slid lightly down her arm as he came around to crouch in front of her. "Then they don't know you, do they?"

There were so many emotions popping through her as she kept her eyes on his. But pleasure, the simple pleasure of being understood was paramount. "Maybe they don't," she murmured. "Maybe they don't."

"I won't give you advice." He picked up one of her hands because he enjoyed examining it, the long, ringless fingers, the slender wrist, the smooth, cool skin. "I don't know about office politics or board meetings. But I think you'll do what's right. You have a good brain and a good heart."

Hardly aware that she'd turned her hand over under his and linked them, she smiled. The connection was more complete than joined fingers, and she couldn't understand it. This was support, a belief in her, and an encouragement she'd never expected to find.

"Odd that I'd have to come to a Ukrainian carpenter for a pep talk. Thanks."

"You're welcome." He looked back into her eyes. "Your headache's gone."

Surprised, she touched her fingers to her temple. "Yes, yes it is." In fact, she couldn't remember ever feeling more relaxed. "You could make a fortune with those hands."

He grinned and slid them up her arms, pushing the sleeves of her jacket along so he could feel the bare flesh beneath. "It's only a matter of knowing what to do with them, and when." And he knew exactly how he wanted to use those hands on her. Unfortunately, the timing was wrong.

"Yes, well…" It was happening again, those little licks of fire in the pit of her stomach, the trembling heat along her skin. "I really am grateful, for everything. I should be going."

"You have time yet." His fingers glided back down her arms to link with hers. "I haven't given you your present."

"Present?" He was drawing her slowly to her feet. Now they were thigh to thigh, her eyes level with his mouth. It was curved and close, sending her system into overdrive.

He had only to lean down. Inches, bare inches. Imagining it nearly drove him crazy. Not an altogether unpleasant feeling, he discovered, this anticipation, this wondering. If she offered, and only when she offered, would he take.

"Don't you like presents, *milaya?*"

His voice was like hot cream, pouring richly over her. "I…the report," she said, remembering. "Weren't you going to give me your report?"

His thumbs skimmed over her wrist and felt the erratic beat of her pulse. It was tempting, very tempting. "I can send the report. I had something else in mind."

"Something…" Her own mind quite simply shut down.

He laughed, so delighted with her he wanted to kiss her breathless. Instead he released her hands and walked away. She didn't move, not an inch as he strolled over to the shelves and tossed up the drop cloth. In a moment he was back, pressing the little Cinderella into her hand.

"I'd like you to have this."

"Oh, but…" She tried, really tried to form a proper refusal. The words wouldn't come.

"You don't like?"

"No. I mean, yes, of course I like it, it's exquisite. But why?" Her fingers were already curving possessively around it when she lifted her eyes to his. "Why would you give it to me?"

"Because she reminds me of you. She's lovely, fragile, unsure of herself."

The description had Sydney's pleasure dimming. "Most people would term her romantic."

"I'm not most. Here, as she runs away, she doesn't believe enough." He stroked a finger down the delicate folds of the ball gown. "She follows the rules, without question. It's midnight, and she was in the arms of her prince, but she breaks away and runs. Because that was the rule. And she is afraid, afraid to let him see beneath the illusion to the woman."

"She had to leave. She'd promised. Besides, she'd have been humiliated to have been caught there in rags and bare feet."

Tilting his head, Mikhail studied her. "Do you think he cared about her dress?"

"Well, no, I don't suppose it would have mattered to him." Sydney let out an impatient breath as he grinned at her. It was ridiculous, standing here debating the psychology of a fairy-tale character. "In any case, it ended happily, and though I've nothing in common with Cinderella, the figurine's beautiful. I'll treasure it."

"Good. Now, I'll walk you downstairs. You don't want to be late for dinner with your mother."

"She won't be there until eight-thirty. She's always late." Halfway through the door, Sydney stopped. "How did you know I was meeting my mother?"

"She told me, ah, two days ago. We had a drink uptown."

Sydney turned completely around so that he was standing on one side of the threshold, she on the other. "You had drinks with my mother?" she asked, spacing each word carefully.

"Yes." Lazily he leaned on the jamb. "Before you try to turn me into an iceberg, understand that I have no sexual interest in Margerite."

"That's lovely. Just lovely." If she hadn't already put the figurine into her purse, she might have thrown it in his face. "We agreed you'd leave my mother alone."

"We agreed nothing," he corrected. "And I don't bother your mother." There was little to be gained by telling her that Margerite had called him three times before he'd given in and met her. "It was a friendly drink, and after it was done, I think Margerite understood we are unsuitable for anything but friendship. Particularly," he said, holding up a finger to block her interruption, "since I am very sexually interested in her daughter."

That stopped her words cold. She swallowed, struggled for composure and failed. "You are not, all you're interested in is scoring a few macho points."

Something flickered in his eyes. "Would you like to come back inside so that I can show you exactly what I'm interested in?"

"No." Before she could stop herself, she'd taken a retreating step. "But I would like you to have the decency not to play games with my mother."

He wondered if Margerite would leap so quickly to her daughter's defense, or if Sydney would understand that her mother was only interested in a brief affair with a younger man—something he'd made very clear he wanted no part in.

"Since I would hate for your headache to come back after I went to the trouble to rid you of it, I will make myself as clear as I can. I have no intention of becoming romantically, physically or emotionally involved with your mother. Does that suit you?"

"It would if I could believe you."

He didn't move, not a muscle, but she sensed he had cocked, like the hammer on a gun. His voice was low and deadly. "I don't lie."

She nodded, cool as an ice slick. "Just stick to hammering nails, Mikhail. We'll get along fine. And I can find my own way down." She didn't whirl away, but turned slowly and walked to the elevator. Though she didn't look back as she stepped inside, she was well aware that he watched her go.

At noon sharp, Sydney sat at the head of the long walnut table of the boardroom. Ten men and two women were ranged down either side with crystal tumblers at their elbows, pads and pens at the ready. Heavy brocade drapes were drawn back to reveal a wall of window, tinted to cut the glare of sunlight—had there been any. Instead there was a thick curtain of rain, gray as soot. She could just make out the silhouette of the Times Building. Occasionally a murmur of thunder sneaked in through the stone and glass.

The gloom suited her. Sydney felt exactly like the reckless child summoned to the principal's office.

She scanned the rows of faces, some of whom had belonged in this office, at this very table, since before she'd been born. Perhaps they would be the toughest to sway, those who thought of her as the little girl who had come to Hayward to bounce on Grandfather's knee.

Then there was Lloyd, halfway down the gleaming surface, his face so smug, so confident, she wanted to snarl. No, she realized as his gaze flicked to hers and held. She wanted to win.

"Ladies, gentlemen." The moment the meeting was called to order she rose. "Before we begin discussion of the matter so much on our minds, I'd like to make a statement."

"You've already made your statement to the press, Sydney," Lloyd pointed out. "I believe everyone here is aware of your position."

There was a rippling murmur, some agreement, some dissent. She let it fade before she spoke again. "Nonetheless, as the president, and the major stockholder of Hayward, I will have my say, then the meeting will open for discussion.''

Her throat froze as all eyes fixed on her. Some were patient, some indulgent, some speculative.

''I understand the board's unease with the amount of money allocated to the Soho project. Of Hayward's holdings, this building represents a relatively small annual income. However, this small income has been steady. Over the last ten years, this complex has needed—or I should say received—little or no maintenance. You know, of course, from the quarterly reports just how much this property has increased in value in this space of time. I believe, from a purely practical standpoint, that the money I allocated is insurance to protect our investment.''

She wanted to stop, to pick up her glass and drain it, but knew the gesture would make her seem as nervous as she was.

''In addition, I believe Hayward has a moral, an ethical and a legal obligation to insure that our tenants receive safe and decent housing.''

''That property could have been made safe and decent for half of the money budgeted,'' Lloyd put in.

Sydney barely glanced at him. ''You're quite right. I believe my grandfather wanted more than the minimum required for Hayward. He wanted it to be the best, the finest. I know I do. I won't stand here and quote you figures. They're in your folders and can be discussed at length in a few moments. Yes, the budget for the Soho project is high, and so are Hayward standards.''

''Sydney.'' Howard Keller, one of her grandfather's oldest associates spoke gently. ''None of us here doubt your motives or your enthusiasm. Your judgment, however, in this, and in the Wolburg matter, is something we must consider. The publicity over the past few days has been extremely detrimental. Hayward stock is down a full three percent. That's in addition to the drop we suffered when you took your position as head of the company. Our stock-holders are, understandably, concerned.''

"The Wolburg matter," Sydney said with steel in her voice, "is an eighty-year-old woman with a fractured hip. She fell because the floor in her kitchen, a floor we ne-glected to replace, was unsafe."

"It's precisely that kind of reckless statement that will open Hayward up to a major lawsuit," Lloyd put in. He kept his tone the quiet sound of calm reason. "Isn't it the function of insurance investigators and legal to come to a decision on this, after a careful, thoughtful overview of the situation? We can't run our company on emotion and im-pulse. Miss Hayward's heart might have been touched by the Wolburg matter, but there are procedures, channels to be used. Now that the press has jumped on this—"

"Yes," she broke in. "It's very interesting how quickly the press learned about the accident. It's hard to believe that only days after an unknown, unimportant old lady falls in her downtown apartment, the press is slapping Hayward in the headlines."

"I would imagine she called them herself," Lloyd said.

Her smile was icy. "Would you?"

"I don't think the issue is how the press got wind of this," Mavis Trelane commented. "The point is they did, and the resulting publicity has been shaded heavily against us, putting Hayward in a very vulnerable position. The stockholders want a solution quickly."

"Does anyone here believe Hayward is not culpable for Mrs. Wolburg's injuries?"

"It's not what we believe," Mavis corrected. "And none of us could make a decision on that until a full investigation into the incident. What is relevant is how such matters are handled."

She frowned when a knock interrupted her.

"I'm sorry," Sydney said, and moved away from the

table to walk stiffly to the door. "Janine, I explained we weren't to be interrupted."

"Yes, ma'am." The secretary, who had thrown her loyalty to Sydney five minutes after hearing the story, kept her voice low. "This is important. I just got a call from a friend of mine. He works on Channel 6. Mrs. Wolburg's going to make a statement on the Noon News. Any minute now."

After a moment's hesitation, Sydney nodded. "Thank you, Janine."

"Good luck, Ms. Hayward."

Sydney smiled and shut the door. She was going to need it. Face composed, she turned back to the room. "I've just been told that Mrs. Wolburg is about to make a televised statement. I'm sure we're all interested in what she has to say. So with your permission, I'll turn on the set." Rather than waiting for the debate to settle it, Sydney picked up the remote and aimed it at the console in the corner.

While Lloyd was stating that the board needed to concern themselves with the facts and not a publicity maneuver, Channel 6 cut from commercial to Mrs. Wolburg's hospital bed.

The reporter, a pretty woman in her early twenties with eyes as sharp as nails, began the interview by asking the patient to explain how she came by her injury.

Several members of the board shook their heads and muttered among themselves as she explained about tripping on the ripped linoleum and how the noise of the construction had masked her calls for help.

Lloyd had to stop his lips from curving as he imagined Sydney's ship springing another leak.

"And this floor," the reporter continued. "Had the condition of it been reported to Hayward?"

"Oh, sure. Mik—that's Mikhail Stanislaski, the sweet boy up on the fifth floor wrote letters about the whole building."

"And nothing was done?"

"Nope, not a thing. Why Mr. and Mrs. Kowalski, the young couple in 101, had a piece of plaster as big as a pie plate fall out of their ceiling. Mik fixed it."

"So the tenants were forced to take on the repairs themselves, due to Hayward's neglect."

"I guess you could say that. Up until the last few weeks."

"Oh, and what happened in the last few weeks?"

"That would be when Sydney—that's Miss Hayward—took over the company. She's the granddaughter of old man Hayward. Heard he'd been real sick the last couple years. Guess things got away from him. Anyway, Mik went to see her, and she came out herself that very day to take a look. Not two weeks later, and the building was crawling with construction workers. We got new windows. Got a new roof going on right this minute. All the plumbing's being fixed, too. Every single thing Mik put on the list is going to be taken care of."

"Really? And did all this happen before or after your injury?"

"Before," Mrs. Wolburg said, a bit impatient with the sarcasm. "I told you all that hammering and sawing was the reason nobody heard me when I fell. And I want you to know that Miss Hayward was there checking the place out again that day. She and Mik found me. She sat right there on the floor and talked to me, brought me a pillow and a blanket and stayed with me until the ambulance came. Came to the hospital, too, and took care of all my medical bills. Been to visit me three times since I've been here."

"Wouldn't you say that Hayward, and therefore Sydney Hayward, is responsible for you being here?"

"Bad eyes and a hole in the floor's responsible," she said evenly. "And I'll tell you just what I told those ambulance chasers who've been calling my family. I've got no reason to sue Hayward. They've been taking care of me since the minute I was hurt. Now maybe if they'd dallied around and tried to make like it wasn't any of their doing, I'd feel differently. But they did what was right, and you can't ask for better than that. Sydney's got ethics, and as long as she's in charge I figure Hayward has ethics, too. I'm pleased to live in a building owned by a company with a conscience.''

Sydney stayed where she was after the interview ended. Saying nothing, she switched off the set and waited.

"You can't buy that kind of goodwill," Mavis decided. "Your method may have been unorthodox, Sydney, and I don't doubt there will still be some backwash to deal with, but all in all, I think the stockholders will be pleased.''

The discussion labored on another thirty minutes, but the crisis had passed.

The moment Sydney was back in her own office, she picked up the phone. The receiver rang in her ear twelve times, frustrating her, before it was finally picked up on the other end.

"Yeah?"

"Mikhail?"

"Nope, he's down the hall."

"Oh, well then, I—"

"Hang on." The phone rattled, clanged then clattered as the male voice boomed out Mikhail's name. Feeling like a fool, Sydney stayed on the line.

"Hello?"

"Mikhail, it's Sydney."

He grinned and grabbed the jug of ice water out of the refrigerator. "Hello, anyway."

"I just saw the news. I suppose you knew."

"Caught it on my lunch break. So?"

"You asked her to do it?"

"No, I didn't." He paused long enough to gulp down

about a pint of water. "I told her how things were, and she came up with the idea herself. It was a good one."

"Yes, it was a good one. And I owe you."

"Yeah?" He thought about it. "Okay. Pay up."

Why she'd expected him to politely refuse to take credit was beyond her. "Excuse me?"

"Pay up, Hayward. You can have dinner with me on Sunday."

"Really, I don't see how one has to do with the other."

"You owe me," he reminded her, "and that's what I want. Nothing fancy, okay? I'll pick you up around four."

"Four? Four in the afternoon for dinner?"

"Right." He pulled a carpenter's pencil out of his pocket. "What's your address?"

He let out a low whistle as she reluctantly rattled it off. "Nice." He finished writing it on the wall. "Got a phone number? In case something comes up."

She was scowling, but she gave it to him. "I want to make it clear that—"

"Make it clear when I pick you up. I'm on the clock, and you're paying." On impulse he outlined her address and phone number with a heart. "See you Sunday. Boss."

Chapter Six

Sydney studied her reflection in the cheval glass critically and cautiously. It wasn't as if it were a date. She'd reminded herself of that several hundred times over the weekend. It was more of a payment, and no matter how she felt about Mikhail, she owed him. Haywards paid their debts.

Nothing formal. She'd taken him at his word there. The little dress was simple, its scooped neck and thin straps a concession to the heat. The nipped in waist was flattering, the flared skirt comfortable. The thin, nearly weightless material was teal blue. Not that she'd paid any attention to his suggestion she wear brighter colors.

Maybe the dress was new, purchased after a frantic two hours of searching—but that was only because she'd wanted something new.

The short gold chain with its tiny links and the hoops at her ears were plain but elegant. She'd spent longer than usual on her makeup, but that was only because she'd been experimenting with some new shades of eyeshadow.

After much debate, she'd opted to leave her hair down.

Then, of course, she'd had to fool with it until the style
suited her. Fluffed out, skimming just above her shoulders
seemed casual enough to her. And sexy. Not that she cared
about being sexy tonight, but a woman was entitled to a
certain amount of vanity.

She hesitated over the cut-glass decanter of perfume, remembering how Mikhail had described her scent. With a
shrug, she touched it to pulse points. It hardly mattered if
it appealed to him. She was wearing it for herself.

Satisfied, she checked the contents of her purse, then her
watch. She was a full hour early. Blowing out a long breath,
she sat down on the bed. For the first time in her life, she
actively wished for a drink.

An hour and fifteen minutes later, after she had wandered
through the apartment, plumping pillows, rearranging stat-
uary then putting it back where it had been in the first place,
he knocked on the door. She stopped in the foyer, found
she had to fuss with her hair another moment, then pressed
a hand to her nervous stomach. Outwardly composed, she
opened the door.

It didn't appear he'd worried overmuch about his attire.
The jeans were clean but faded, the high-tops only slightly
less scuffed than his usual work boots. His shirt was tucked
in—a definite change—and was a plain, working man's
cotton the color of smoke. His hair flowed over the collar,
so black, so untamed no woman alive could help but fantasize about letting her fingers dive in.

He looked earthy, a little wild, and more than a little
dangerous.

And he'd brought her a tulip.

"I'm late." He held out the flower, thinking she looked
as cool and delicious as a sherbert parfait in a crystal dish.
"I was working on your face."

"You were—what?"

"Your face." He slid a hand under her chin, his eyes
narrowing in concentration. "I found the right piece of

rosewood and lost track of time.'' As he studied, his fingers moved over her face as they had the wood, searching for answers. ''You will ask me in?''

Her mind, empty as a leaky bucket, struggled to fill again. ''Of course. For a minute.'' She stepped back, breaking contact. ''I'll just put this in water.''

When she left him, Mikhail let his gaze sweep the room. It pleased him. This was not the formal, professionally decorated home some might have expected of her. She really lived here, among the soft colors and quiet comfort. Style was added by a scattering of Art Nouveau, in the bronzed lamp shaped like a long, slim woman, and the sinuous etched flowers on the glass doors of a curio cabinet displaying a collection of antique beaded bags.

He noted his sculpture stood alone in a glossy old shadow box, and was flattered.

She came back, carrying the tulip in a slim silver vase.

''I admire your taste.''

She set the vase atop the curio. ''Thank you.''

''Nouveau is sensuous.'' He traced a finger down the flowing lines of the lamp. ''And rebellious.''

She nearly frowned before she caught herself. ''I find it attractive. Graceful.''

''Graceful, yes. Also powerful.''

She didn't care for the way he was smiling at her, as if he knew a secret she didn't. And that the secret was her. ''Yes, well, I'm sure as an artist you'd agree art should have power. Would you like a drink before we go?''

''No, not before I drive.''

''Drive?''

''Yes. Do you like Sunday drives, Sydney?''

''I...'' She picked up her purse to give her hands something to do. There was no reason, none at all, for her to allow him to make her feel as awkward as a teenager on a first date. ''I don't get much opportunity for them in the city.'' It seemed wise to get started. She moved to the door, wondering what it would be like to be in a car with him. Alone. "I didn't realize you kept a car."

His grin was quick and a tad self-mocking as they moved out into the hall. "A couple of years ago, after my art had some success, I bought one. It was a little fantasy of mine. I think I pay more to keep it parked than I did for the car. But fantasies are rarely free."

In the elevator, he pushed the button for the garage. "I think about it myself," she admitted. "I miss driving, the independence of it, I suppose. In Europe, I could hop in and zoom off whenever I chose. But it seems more practical to keep a driver here than to go to war every time you need a parking space."

"Sometime we'll go up north, along the river, and you can drive."

The image was almost too appealing, whipping along the roads toward the mountains upstate. She thought it was best not to comment. "Your report came in on Friday," she began.

"Not today." He reached down to take her hand as they stepped into the echoing garage. "Talking reports can wait till Monday. Here." He opened the door of a glossy red-and-cream MG. The canvas top was lowered. "You don't mind the top down?" he asked as she settled inside.

Sydney thought of the time and trouble she'd taken with her hair. And she thought of the freedom of having even a hot breeze blow through it. "No, I don't mind."

He climbed into the driver's seat, adjusting long legs, then gunned the engine. After taking a pair of mirrored sunglasses off the dash, he pulled out. The radio was set on rock. Sydney found herself smiling as they cruised around Central Park.

"You didn't mention where we were going."

"I know this little place. The food is good." He noted her foot was tapping along in time with the music. "Tell me where you lived in Europe."

"Oh, I didn't live in any one place. I moved around. Paris, Saint Tropez, Venice, London, Monte Carlo."

"Perhaps you have Gypsies in your blood, too."

"Perhaps." Not Gypsies, she thought. There had been nothing so romantic as wanderlust in her hopscotching travels through Europe. Only dissatisfaction, and a need to hide until wounds had healed. "Have you ever been?"

"When I was very young. But I would like to go back now that I am old enough to appreciate it. The art, you see, and the atmosphere, the architecture. What places did you like best?"

"A little village in the countryside of France where they milked cows by hand and grew fat purple grapes. There was a courtyard at the inn where I stayed, and the flowers were so big and bright. In the late afternoon you could sit and drink the most wonderful white wine and listen to the doves coo." She stopped, faintly embarrassed. "And of course, Paris," she said quickly. "The food, the shopping, the ballet. I knew several people, and enjoyed the parties."

Not so much, he thought, as she enjoyed sitting alone and listening to cooing doves.

"Do you ever think about going back to the Soviet Union?" she asked him.

"Often. To see the place where I was born, the house we lived in. It may not be there now. The hills where I played as a child. They would be."

His glasses only tossed her own reflection back at her. But she thought, behind them, his eyes would be sad. His voice was. "Things have changed so much, so quickly in the last few years. Glasnost, the Berlin Wall. You could go back."

"Sometimes I think I will, then I wonder if it's better to leave it a memory—part bitter, part sweet, but colored through the eyes of a child. I was very young when we left."

"It was difficult."

"Yes. More for my parents who knew the risks better than we. They had the courage to give up everything they had ever known to give their children the one thing they had never had. Freedom."

Moved, she laid a hand over his on the gearshift. Margerite had told her the story of escaping into Hungary in a wagon, making it seem like some sort of romantic adventure. It didn't seem romantic to Sydney. It seemed terrifying. "You must have been frightened."

"More than I ever hope to be again. At night I would lie awake, always cold, always hungry, and listen to my parents talk. One would reassure the other, and they would plan how far we might travel the next day—and the next. When we came to America, my father wept. And I understood it was over. I wasn't afraid anymore."

Her own eyes had filled. She turned away to let the wind dry them. "But coming here must have been frightening, too. A different place, different language, different culture."

He heard the emotion in her voice. Though touched, he didn't want to make her sad. Not today. "The young adjust quickly. I had only to give the boy in the next house a bloody nose to feel at home."

She turned back, saw the grin and responded with a laugh. "Then, I suppose, you became inseparable friends."

"I was best man at his wedding only two years ago."

With a shake of her head, she settled back. It was then she noticed they were crossing the bridge over to Brooklyn. "You couldn't find a place to have dinner in Manhattan?"

His grin widened. "Not like this one."

A few minutes later, he was cruising through one of the old neighborhoods with its faded brick row houses and big, shady trees. Children scrambled along the sidewalks, riding bikes, jumping rope. At the curb where Mikhail stopped, two boys were having a deep and serious transaction with baseball cards.

"Hey, Mik!" Both of them jumped up before he'd even climbed out of the car. "You missed the game. We finished an hour ago."

"I'll catch the next one." He glanced over to see that Sydney had already gotten out and was standing in the street, studying the neighborhood with baffled and wary eyes. He leaned over and winked. "I got a hot date."

"Oh, man." Twelve-year-old disgust prevented either of them from further comment.

Laughing, Mikhail walked over to grab Sydney's hand and pull her to the sidewalk. "I don't understand," she began as he led her across the concrete heaved up by the roots of a huge old oak. "This is a restaurant?"

"No." He had to tug to make her keep up with him as he climbed the steps. "It's a house."

"But you said—"

"That we were going to dinner." He shoved the door open and took a deep sniff. "Smells like Mama made Chicken Kiev. You'll like."

"Your mother?" She nearly stumbled into the narrow entrance way. Scattered emotions flew inside her stomach like a bevy of birds. "You bought me to your parents' house?"

"Yes, for Sunday dinner."

"Oh, good Lord."

He lifted a brow. "You don't like Chicken Kiev?"

"No. Yes. That isn't the point. I wasn't expecting—"

"You're late," Yuri boomed. "Are you going to bring the woman in or stand in the doorway?"

Mikhail kept his eyes on Sydney's. "She doesn't want to come in," he called back.

"That's not it," she whispered, mortified. "You might have told me about this so I could have...oh, never mind." She brushed past him to take the couple of steps necessary to bring her into the living room. Yuri was just hauling himself out of a chair.

"Mr. Stanislaski, it's so nice of you to have me." She offered a hand and had it swallowed whole by his.

"You are welcome here. You will call me Yuri."

"Thank you."

"We are happy Mikhail shows good taste." Grinning, he used a stage whisper. "His mama, she didn't like the dancer with the blond hair."

"Thanks, Papa." Casually Mikhail draped an arm over Sydney's shoulders—felt her resist the urge to shrug it off. "Where is everyone?"

"Mama and Rachel are in the kitchen. Alex is later than you. Alex sees all the girls, at the same time," Yuri told Sydney. "It should confuse him, but it does not."

"Yuri, you have not taken the trash out yet." A small woman with an exotic face and graying hair came out of the kitchen, carrying silverware in the skirt of her apron.

Yuri gave his son an affectionate thump on the back that nearly had Sydney pitching forward. "I wait for Mikhail to come and take it."

"And Mikhail will wait for Alex." She set the flatware down on a heavy table at the other end of the room, then came to Sydney. Her dark eyes were shrewd, not unfriendly, but quietly probing. She smelled of spice and melted butter. "I am Nadia, Mikhail's mother." She offered a hand. "We are happy to have you with us."

"Thank you. You have a lovely home."

She had said it automatically, meaningless politeness. But the moment the words were out, Sydney realized they were true. The entire house would probably fit into one wing of her mother's Long Island estate, and the furniture was old rather than antique. Doilies as charming and intricate as those she had seen at Mrs. Wolburg's covered the arms of chairs. The wallpaper was faded, but that only made the tiny rosebuds scattered over it seem more lovely. The strong sunlight burst through the window and showed every scar, every mend. Just as it showed how lovingly the woodwork and table surfaces had been polished.

Out of the corner of her eye she caught a movement. As she glanced over, she watched a plump ball of gray fur struggling, whimpering from under a chair.

"That is Ivan," Yuri said, clucking to the puppy. "He is only a baby." He sighed a little for his old mutt Sasha who had died peacefully at the age of fifteen six months before. "Alex brings him home from pound."

"Saved you from walking the last mile, right, Ivan?" Mikhail bent down to ruffle fur. Ivan thumped his tail while giving Sydney nervous looks. "He is named for Ivan the Terrible, but he's a coward."

"He's just shy," Sydney corrected, then gave in to need and crouched down. She'd always wanted a pet, but boarding schools didn't permit them. "There, aren't you sweet?" The dog trembled visibly for a moment when she stroked him, then began to lick the toes that peeked out through her sandals.

Mikhail began to think the pup had potential.

"What kind is he?" she asked.

"He is part Russian wolfhound," Yuri declared.

"With plenty of traveling salesmen thrown in." The voice came from the kitchen doorway. Sydney looked over her shoulder and saw a striking woman with a sleek cap of raven hair and tawny eyes. "I'm Mikhail's sister, Rachel. You must be Sydney."

"Yes, hello." Sydney straightened, and wondered what miracles in the gene pool had made all the Stanislaskis so blindingly beautiful.

"Dinner'll be ready in ten minutes." Rachel's voice carried only the faintest wisp of an accent and was as dark and smooth as black velvet. "Mikhail, you can set the table."

"I have to take out the trash," he told her, instantly choosing the lesser of two evils.

"I'll do it." Sydney's impulsive offer was greeted with casual acceptance. She was nearly finished when Alex, as dark, exotic and gorgeous as the rest of the family, strolled in.

"Sorry I'm late, Papa. Just finished a double shift. I barely had time to…" He trailed off when he spotted Sydney. His mouth curved and his eyes flickered with definite interest. "Now I'm really sorry I'm late. Hi."

"Hello." Her lips curved in response. That kind of romantic charm could have raised the blood pressure on a corpse. Providing it was female.

"Mine," Mikhail said mildly as he strolled back out of the kitchen.

Alex merely grinned and continued walking toward Sydney. He took her hand, kissed the knuckles. "Just so you know, of the two of us, I'm less moody and have a steadier job."

She had to laugh. "I'll certainly take that into account."

"He thinks he's a cop." Mikhail sent his brother an amused look. "Mama says to wash your hands. Dinner's ready."

Sydney was certain she'd never seen more food at one table. There were mounds of chicken stuffed with rich, herbed butter. It was served with an enormous bowl of lightly browned potatoes and a platter heaped with slices of grilled vegetables that Nadia had picked from her own kitchen garden that morning. There was a tower of biscuits along with a mountain of some flaky stuffed pastries that was Alex's favorite dish.

Sydney sipped the crisp wine that was offered along with vodka and wondered. The amount and variety of food was nothing compared to the conversation.

Rachel and Alex argued over someone named Goose. After a winding explanation, Sydney learned that while Alex was a rookie cop, Rachel was in her first year with the public defender's office. And Goose was a petty thief Rachel was defending.

Yuri and Mikhail argued about baseball. Sydney didn't need Nadia's affectionate translation to realize that while Yuri was a diehard Yankee fan, Mikhail stood behind the Mets.

There was much gesturing with silverware and Russian exclamations mixed with English. Then laughter, a shouted question, and more arguing.

"Rachel is an idealist," Alex stated. With his elbows on the table and his chin rested on his joined hands, he smiled at Sydney. "What are you?"

She smiled back. "Too smart to be put between a lawyer and a cop."

"Elbows off," Nadia said, and gave her son a quick rap. "Mikhail says you are a businesswoman. And that you are very smart. And fair."

The description surprised her enough that she nearly fumbled. "I try to be."

"Your company was in a sticky situation last week." Rachel downed the last of her vodka with a panache Sydney admired. "You handled it well. It seemed to me that rather than trying to be fair you simply were. Have you known Mikhail long?"

She segued into the question so neatly, Sydney only blinked. "No, actually. We met last month when he barged into my office ready to crush any available Hayward under his work boot."

"I was polite," he corrected.

"You were not polite." Because she could see Yuri was amused, she continued. "He was dirty, angry and ready to fight."

"His temper comes from his mama," Yuri informed Sydney. "She is fierce."

"Only once," Nadia said with a shake of her head.

"Only once did I hit him over the head with a pot. He never forgets."

"I still have the scar. And here." Yuri pointed to his shoulder. "Where you threw the hairbrush at me."

"You should not have said my new dress was ugly."

"It was ugly," he said with a shrug, then tapped a hand on his chest. "And here, where you—"

"Enough." All dignity, she rose. "Or our guest will think I am tyrant."

"She is a tyrant," Yuri told Sydney with a grin.

"And this tyrant says we will clear the table and have dessert."

Sydney was still chuckling over it as Mikhail crossed the bridge back into Manhattan. Sometime during the long, comfortable meal she'd forgotten to be annoyed with him. Perhaps she'd had a half a glass too much wine. Certainly she'd eaten entirely too much kissel—the heavenly apricot pudding Nadia had served with cold, rich cream. But she was relaxed and couldn't remember ever having spent a more enjoyable Sunday evening.

"Did your father make that up?" Snuggled back in her seat, Sydney turned her head to study Mikhail's profile. "About your mother throwing things?"

"No, she throws things." He downshifted and cruised into traffic. "Once a whole plate of spaghetti and meatballs at me because my mouth was too quick."

Her laughter came out in a burst of enjoyment. "Oh, I would have loved to have seen that. Did you duck?"

He flicked her a grin. "Not fast enough."

"I've never thrown anything in my life." Her sigh was part wistful, part envious. "I think it must be very liberating. They're wonderful," she said after another moment. "Your family. You're very lucky."

"So you don't mind eating in Brooklyn?"

Frowning, she straightened a bit. "It wasn't that. I told

you, I'm not a snob. I just wasn't prepared. You should have told me you were taking me there."

"Would you have gone?"

She opened her mouth then closed it again. After a moment, she let her shoulders rise and fall. "I don't know. Why did you take me?"

"I wanted to see you there. Maybe I wanted you to see me there, too."

Puzzled, she turned to look at him again. They were nearly back now. In a few more minutes he would go his way and she hers. "I don't understand why that should matter to you."

"Then you understand much too little, Sydney."

"I might understand if you'd be more clear." It was suddenly important, vital, that she know. The tips of her fingers were beginning to tingle so that she had to rub them together to stop the sensation.

"I'm better with my hands than with words." Impatient with her, with himself, he pulled into the garage beneath her building. When he yanked off his sunglasses, his eyes were dark and turbulent.

Didn't she know that her damn perfume had his nerve ends sizzling? The way she laughed, the way her hair lifted in the wind. How her eyes had softened and yearned as she'd looked at the silly little mutt of his father's.

It was worse, much worse now that he'd seen her with his family. Now that he'd watched how her initial stiffness melted away under a few kind words. He'd worried that he'd made a mistake, that she would be cold to his family, disdainful of the old house and simple meal.

Instead she'd laughed with his father, dried dishes with his mother. Alex's blatant flirting hadn't offended but rather had amused her. And when Rachel had praised her handling of the accident with Mrs. Wolburg, she'd flushed like a schoolgirl.

How the hell was he supposed to know he'd fall in love with her?

And now that she was alone with him again, all that cool reserve was seeping back. He could see it in the way her spine straightened when she stepped out of the car.

Hell, he could feel it—it surprised him that frost didn't form on his windshield.

"I'll walk you up." He slammed the door of the car.

"That isn't necessary." She didn't know what had spoiled the evening, but was ready to place the blame squarely on his shoulders.

"I'll walk you up," he repeated, and pulled her over to the elevator.

"Fine." She folded her arms and waited.

The moment the doors opened, they entered without speaking. Both of them were sure it was the longest elevator ride on record. Sydney swept out in front of him when they reached her floor. She had her keys out and ready two steps before they hit her door.

"I enjoyed your family," she said, carefully polite. "Be sure to tell your parents again how much I appreciated their hospitality." The lock snapped open. "You can reach me in the office if there are any problems this week."

He slapped his hand on the door before she could shut it in his face. "I'm coming in."

Chapter Seven

Sydney considered the chances of shoving the door closed while he had his weight against it, found them slim and opted for shivery reserve.

"It's a bit early for a nightcap and a bit late for coffee."

"I don't want a drink." Mikhail rapped the door closed with enough force to make the foyer mirror rattle.

Though she refused to back up, Sydney felt her stomach muscles experience the same helpless shaking. "Some people might consider it poor manners for a man to bully his way into a woman's apartment."

"I have poor manners," he told her, and, jamming his hands into his pockets, paced into the living room.

"It must be a trial for your parents. Obviously they worked hard to instill a certain code of behavior in their children. It didn't stick with you."

He swung back, and she was reminded of some compact and muscled cat on the prowl. Definitely a man-eater. "You liked them?"

Baffled, she pushed a hand through her disordered hair. "Of course I like them. I've already said so."

While his hands bunched and unbunched in his pockets, he lifted a brow. "I thought perhaps it was just your very perfect manners that made you say so."

As an insult, it was a well-aimed shot. Indignation shivered through the ice. "Well, you were wrong. Now if we've settled everything, you can go."

"We've settled nothing. You tell me why you are so different now from the way you were an hour ago."

She caught herself, tightening her lips before they could move into a pout. "I don't know what you're talking about."

"With my family you were warm and sweet. You smiled so easily. Now with me, you're cold and far away. You don't smile at all."

"That's absurd." Though it was little more than a baring of teeth, she forced her lips to curve. "There, I've smiled at you. Satisfied?"

Temper flickered into his eyes as he began to pace again. "I haven't been satisfied since I walk into your office. You make me suffer and I don't like it."

"Artists are supposed to suffer," she shot back. "And I don't see how I've had anything to do with it. I've given in to every single demand you made. Replaced windows, ripped out plumbing, gotten rid of that tool-and-knot wiring."

"Tube and knob," he corrected, nearly amused.

"Well, it's gone, isn't it? Have you any idea just how much lumber I've authorized?"

"To last two-by-four, I know. This is not point."

She studied him owlishly. "Do you know you drop your articles when you're angry?"

His eyes narrowed. "I drop nothing."

"Your *the*'s and *an*'s and *a*'s," she pointed out. "And your sentence structure suffers. You mix your tenses."

That wounded. "I'd like to hear you speak my language."

She set the purse she still carried onto a table with a snap. "Baryshnikov, glasnost."

His lips curled. "This is Russian. I am Ukrainian. This is a mistake you make, but I overlook."

"It. You overlook *it,*" she corrected. "In any case, it's close enough." He took a step forward, she took one back. "I'm sure we can have a fascinating discussion on the subtleties of language, but it will have to wait." He came closer, and she—casually, she hoped—edged away. "As I said before, I enjoyed the evening. Now—" he maneuvered her around a chair "—stop stalking me."

"You imagine things. You're not *a* rabbit, you're *a* woman."

But she felt like a rabbit, one of those poor, frozen creatures caught in a beam of headlights. "I don't know what's put you in this mood—"

"I have many moods. You put me in this one every time I see you, or think about you."

She shifted so that a table was between them. Because she well knew if she kept retreating her back would be against the wall, she took a stand. "All right, damn it. What do you want?"

"You. You know I want you."

Her heart leaped into her throat, then plummeted to her stomach. "You do not." The tremble in her voice irritated her enough to make her force ice into it. "I don't appreciate this game you're playing."

"I play? What is a man to think when a woman blows hot, then cold? When she looks at him with passion one minute and frost the next?" His hands lifted in frustration, then slapped down on the table. "I tell you straight out when you are so upset that I don't want your mama, I want you. And you call me a liar."

"I don't..." She could hardly get her breath. Deliber-

ately she walked away, moving behind a chair and gripping
the back hard. It had been a mistake to look into his eyes.
There was a ruthlessness there that brought a terrible pitch
of excitement to her blood. "You didn't want me before."

"Before? I think I wanted you before I met you. What
is this before?"

"In the car." Humiliation washed her cheeks of color.
"When I—when we were driving back from Long Island.
We were…" Her fingers dug into the back of the chair. "It
doesn't matter."

In two strides he was in front of the chair, his hands
gripped over hers. "You tell me what you mean."

Pride, she told herself. She would damn well keep her
pride. "All right then, to clarify, and to see that we don't
have this conversation again. You started something in the
car that night. I didn't ask for it, I didn't encourage it, but
you started it." She took a deep breath to be certain her
voice remained steady. "And you just stopped because…well, because I wasn't what you wanted after all."

For a moment he could only stare, too stunned for
speech. Then his face changed, so quickly, Sydney could
only blink at the surge of rage. When he acted, she gave a
yip of surprise. The chair he yanked from between them
landed on its side two feet away.

He swore at her. She didn't need to understand the words
to appreciate the sentiment behind them. Before she could
make an undignified retreat, his hands were clamped hard
on her arms. For an instant she was afraid she was about
to take the same flight as the chair. He was strong enough
and certainly angry enough. But he only continued to shout.

It took her nearly a full minute to realize her feet were
an inch above the floor and that he'd started using English
again.

"Idiot. How can so smart a woman have no brains?"

"I'm not going to stand here and be insulted." Of

course, she wasn't standing at all, she thought, fighting panic. She was dangling.

"It is not insult to speak truth. For weeks I have tried to be gentleman."

"*A* gentleman," she said furiously. "You've tried to be *a* gentleman. And you've failed miserably."

"I think you need time, you need me to show you how I feel. And I am sorry to have treated you as I did in the car that night. It makes me think you will have…" He trailed off, frustrated that the proper word wasn't in him. "That you will think me…"

"A heathen," she tossed out, with relish. "Barbarian."

"No, that's not so bad. But a man who abuses a woman for pleasure. Who forces and hurts her."

"It wasn't a matter of force," Sydney said coldly. "Now put me down."

He hiked her up another inch. "Do you think I stopped because I don't want you?"

"I'm well aware that my sexuality is under par."

He didn't have a clue what she was talking about, and plowed on. "We were in a car, in the middle of the city, with your driver in the front. And I was ready to rip your clothes away and take you, there. It made me angry with myself, and with you because you could make me forget."

She tried to think of a response. But he had set her back on her feet, and his hands were no longer gripping but caressing. The rage in his eyes had become something else, and it took her breath away.

"Every day since," he murmured. "Every night, I remember how you looked, how you felt. So I want more. And I wait for you to offer what I saw in your eyes that night. But you don't. I can't wait longer."

His fingers streaked into her hair, then fisted there, drawing her head back as his mouth crushed down on hers. The heat seered through her skin, into blood and bone. Her moan wasn't borne of pain but of tormented pleasure. Willing, desperately willing, her mouth parted under his, inviting him, accepting him. This time when her heart rose to her throat, there was a wild glory in it.

On an oath, he tore his mouth from hers and buried it against her throat. She had not asked, she had not encouraged. Those were her words, and he wouldn't ignore the truth of them. Whatever slippery grip he had on control, he clamped tight now, fighting to catch his breath and hold to sanity.

"Damn me to hell or take me to heaven," he muttered. "But do it now."

Her arms locked around his neck. He would leave, she knew, just as he had left that first time. And if he did she might never feel this frenzied stirring again. "I want you." *I'm afraid, I'm afraid.* "Yes, I want you. Make love to me."

And his mouth was on hers again, hard, hot, hungry, while his hands flowed like molten steel down her body. Not a caress now, but a branding. In one long, possessive stroke he staked a claim. It was too late for choices.

Fears and pleasures battered her, rough waves of emotion that had her trembling even as she absorbed delights. Her fingers dug into his shoulders, took greedy handfuls of his hair. Through the thin layers of cotton, she could feel the urgent drum of his heart and knew it beat for her.

More. He could only think he needed more, even as her scent swam in his head and her taste flooded his mouth. She moved against him, that small, slim body restless and eager. When he touched her, when his artist's hands sculpted her, finding the curves and planes of her already perfect, her low, throaty whimpers pounded in his ears like thunder.

More.

He tugged the straps from her shoulders, snapping one in his hurry to remove even that small obstacle. While his mouth raced over the smooth, bare curve, he dragged at the zipper, yanking and pulling until the dress pooled at her feet.

Beneath it. Oh, Lord, beneath it.

The strapless little fancy frothed over milk-white breasts, flowed down to long, lovely thighs. She lifted a trembling hand as if to cover herself, but he caught it, held it. He didn't see the nerves in her eyes as he filled himself on how she looked, surrounded in the last flames of sunset that warmed the room.

"Mikhail." Because he wasn't quite ready to speak, he only nodded. "I...the bedroom."

He'd been tempted to take her where they stood, or to do no more than drag her to the floor. Checking himself, he had her up in his arms in one glorious sweep. "It better be close."

On an unsteady laugh, she gestured. No man had ever carried her to bed before, and she found it dazzlingly romantic. Unsure of what part she should play, Sydney pressed her lips tentatively to his throat. He trembled. Encouraged, she skimmed them up to his ear. He groaned. On a sigh of pleasure, she continued to nibble while her fingers slipped beneath his shirt to stroke over his shoulder.

His arms tightened around her. When she turned her head, his mouth was there, taking greedily from hers as he tumbled with her onto the bed.

"Shouldn't we close the drapes?" The question ended on a gasp as he began doing things to her, wonderful things, shattering things. There was no room for shyness in this airless, spinning world.

It wasn't supposed to be like this. She'd always thought lovemaking to be either awkwardly mechanical or quietly comforting. It wasn't supposed to be so urgent, so turbulent. So incredible. Those rough, clever hands rushed over flesh, over silk, then back to flesh, leaving her a quivering mass of sensation. His mouth was just as hurried, just as skilled as it made the same erotic journey.

He was lost in her, utterly, irretrievably lost in her. Even the air was full of her, that quiet, restrained, gloriously seductive scent. Her skin seemed to melt, like liquid flowers, under his fingers, his lips. Each quick tremble he brought to her racked through him until he thought he would go mad.

Desire arced and spiked and hummed even as she grew softer, more pliant. More his.

Impatient, he brought his mouth to her breast to suckle through silk while his hands slid up her thighs to find her, wet and burning.

When he touched her, her body arched in shock. Her arm flew back until her fingers locked over one of the rungs of the brass headboard. She shook her head as pleasure shot into her, hot as a bullet. Suddenly fear and desire were so twisted into a single emotion she didn't know whether to beg him to stop or plead with him to go on. On and on.

Helpless, stripped of control, she gasped for breath. It seemed her system had contracted until she was curled into one tight hot ball. Even as she sobbed out his name, the ball imploded and she was left shattered.

A moan shuddered out as her body went limp again.

Unbearably aroused, he watched her, the stunned, glowing pleasure that flushed her cheeks, the dark, dazed desire that turned her eyes to blue smoke. For her, for himself, he took her up again, driving her higher until her breath was ragged and her body on fire.

"Please," she managed when he tugged the silk aside.

"I will please you." He flicked his tongue over her nipple. "And me."

There couldn't be more. But he showed her there was. Even when she began to drag frantically at his clothes, he continued to assault her system and to give her, give her more than she had ever believed she could hold. His hands were never still as he rolled over the bed with her, helping her to rid him of every possible barrier.

He wanted her crazed for him, as crazed as he for her. He could feel the wild need in the way she moved beneath him, in the way her hands searched. And yes, in the way she cried out when he found some secret she'd been keeping just for him.

When he could wait no longer, he plunged inside her, a sword to the hilt.

She was beyond pleasure. There was no name for the edge she trembled on. Her body moved, arching for his, finding their own intimate rhythm as naturally as breath. She knew he was speaking to her, desperate words in a mixture of languages. She understood that wherever she was, he was with her, as much a captive as she.

And when the power pushed her off that last thin edge, he was all there was. All there had to be.

It was dark, and the room was in shadows. Wondering if her mind would ever clear again, Sydney stared at the ceiling and listened to Mikhail breathe. It was foolish, she supposed, but it was such a soothing, intimate sound, that air moving quietly in and out of his lungs. She could have listened for hours.

Perhaps she had.

She had no idea how much time had passed since he'd slapped his hand on her door and barged in after her. It might have been minutes or hours, but it hardly mattered. Her life had been changed. Smiling to herself, she stroked a hand through his hair. He turned his head, just an inch, and pressed his lips to the underside of her jaw.

"I thought you were asleep," she murmured.

"No. I wouldn't fall asleep on top of you." He lifted his head. She could see the gleam of his eyes, the hint of a smile. "There are so many more interesting things to do on top of you."

She felt color rush to her cheeks and was grateful for the

dark. "I was..." How could she ask? "It was all right, then?"

"No." Even with his body pressed into hers, he could feel her quick retreat. "Sydney, I may not have so many good words as you, but I think 'all right' is a poor choice. A walk through the park is all right."

"I only meant—" She shifted. Though he braced on his elbows to ease his weight from her, he made sure she couldn't wiggle away.

"I think we'll have a light now."

"No, that's not—" The bedside lamp clicked on. "Necessary."

"I want to see you, because I think I will make love with you again in a minute. And I like to look at you." Casually he brushed his lips over hers. "Don't."

"Don't what?"

"Tense your shoulders. I'd like to think you could relax with me."

"I am relaxed," she said, then blew out a long breath. No, she wasn't. "It's just that whenever I ask a direct question, you give evasions. I only wanted to know if you were, well, satisfied."

She'd been sure before, but now, as the heat had faded to warmth, she wondered if she'd only wished.

"Ah." Wrapping her close, he rolled over until she lay atop him. "This is like a quiz. Multiple choice. They were my favorite in school. You want to know, A, was it all right, B, was it very good or C, was it very wonderful."

"Forget it."

He clamped his arms around her when she tried to pull away. "I'm not finished with you, Hayward. I still have to answer the question, but I find there are not enough choices." He nudged her down until her lips had no choice but to meet his. And the kiss was long and sweet. "Do you understand now?"

His eyes were dark, still heavy from the pleasure they'd

shared. The look in them said more than hundreds of silky words. "Yes."

"Good. Come back to me." He nestled her head on his shoulder and began to rub his hand gently up and down her back. "This is nice?"

"Yes." She smiled again. "This is nice." Moments passed in easy silence. "Mikhail."

"Hmm?"

"There weren't enough choices for me, either."

She was so beautiful when she slept, he could hardly look away. Her hair, a tangled flow of golden fire, curtained part of her face. One hand, small and delicate, curled on the pillow where his head had lain. The sheet, tangled from hours of loving showed the outline of her body to where the linen ended just at the curve of her breast.

She had been greater than any fantasy: generous, open, stunningly sexy and shy all at once. It had been like initiating a virgin and being seduced by a siren. And afterward, the faint embarrassment, the puzzling self-doubt. Where had that come from?

He would have to coax the answer from her. And if coaxing didn't work, he would bully.

But now, when he watched her in the morning light, he felt such an aching tenderness.

He hated to wake her, but he knew women enough to be sure she would be hurt if he left her sleeping.

Gently he brushed the hair from her cheek, bent down and kissed her.

She stirred and so did his desire.

He kissed her again, nibbling a trail to her ear. "Sydney." Her sleepy purr of response had his blood heating. "Wake up and kiss me goodbye."

"'S morning?" Her lashes fluttered up to reveal dark, heavy eyes. She stared at him a moment while she struggled to surface. His face was close and shadowed with stubble. To satisfy an old craving, she lifted her hand to it.

"You have a dangerous face." When he grinned, she propped herself up on an elbow. "You're dressed," she realized.

"I thought it the best way to go downtown."

"Go?"

Amused, he sat on the edge of the bed. "To work. It's nearly seven. I made coffee with your machine and used your shower."

She nodded. She could smell both—the coffee and the scent of her soap on his skin. "You should have waked me."

He twined a lock of her hair around his finger, enjoying the way its subtle fire seemed to lick at his flesh. "I didn't let you sleep very long last night. You will come downtown after work? I will fix you dinner."

Relieved, she smiled. "Yes."

"And you'll stay the night with me, sleep in my bed?"

She sat up so they were face-to-face. "Yes."

"Good." He tugged on the lock of hair. "Now kiss me goodbye."

"All right." Testing herself, she sat up, linked her hands around his neck. The sheet slid away to her waist. Pleased, she watched his gaze skim down, felt the tensing of muscles, saw the heat flash. Slowly, waiting until his eyes had come back to hers, she leaned forward. Her lips brushed his and retreated, brushed and retreated until she felt his quick groan. Satisfied she had his full attention, she flicked open the buttons of his shirt.

"Sydney." On a half laugh, he caught at her hands. "You'll make me late."

"That's the idea." She was smiling as she pushed the shirt off his shoulders. "Don't worry, I'll put in a good word for you with the boss."

* * *

Two hours later, Sydney strolled into her offices with an armful of flowers she'd bought on the street. She'd left her hair down, had chosen a sunny yellow suit to match her mood. And she was humming.

Janine looked up from her work station, prepared to offer her usual morning greeting. The formal words stuck. "Wow. Ms. Hayward, you look fabulous."

"Thank you, Janine. I feel that way. These are for you."

Confused, Janine gathered up the armful of summer blossoms. "Thank you. I…thank you."

"When's my first appointment?"

"Nine-thirty. With Ms. Brinkman, Mr. Lowe and Mr. Keller, to finalize the buy on the housing project in New Jersey."

"That gives me about twenty minutes. I'd like to see you in my office."

"Yes, ma'am." Janine was already reaching for her pad.

"You won't need that," Sydney told her, and strode through the double doors. She seated herself, then gestured for Janine to take a chair.

"How long have you worked for Hayward?"

"Five years last March."

Sydney tipped back in her chair and looked at her secretary, really looked. Janine was attractive, neat, had direct gray eyes that were a trifle puzzled at the moment. Her dark blond hair was worn short and sleek. She held herself well, Sydney noted. Appearance was important, not the most important, but it certainly counted for what she was thinking.

"You must have been very young when you started here."

"Twenty-one," Janine answered with a small smile. "Right out of business college."

"Are you doing what you want to do, Janine?"

"Excuse me?"

"Is secretarial work what you want to do with your life or do you have other ambitions?"

Janine resisted the urge to squirm in her chair. "I hope to work my way up to department manager. But I enjoy working for you, Miss Hayward."

"You have five years experience with the company nearly five more than I do, yet you enjoy working for me Why?"

"Why?" Janine stopped being nervous and went to flat-out baffled. "Being secretary to the president of Hayward is an important job, and I think I'm good at it."

"I agree with both statements." Rising, Sydney walked around the desk to perch on the front corner. "Let's be frank, Janine, no one here at Hayward expected me to stay more than a token month or two, and I'm sure it was generally agreed I'd spend most of that time filing my nails or chatting with friends on the phone." She saw by the faint flush that crept up Janine's cheeks that she'd hit very close to the mark. "They gave me an efficient secretary, not an assistant or an office manager, or executive aide, whatever we choose to call them at Hayward, because it wasn't thought I'd require one. True?"

"That's the office gossip." Janine straightened in her chair and met Sydney's eyes levelly. If she was about to be fired, she'd take it on the chin. "I took the job because it was a good position, a promotion and a raise."

"And I think you were very wise. The door opened, and you walked in. Since you've been working for me, you've been excellent. I can't claim to have a lot of experience in having a secretary, but I know that you're at your desk when I arrive in the morning and often stay after I leave at night. When I ask you for information you have it, or you get it. When I ask, you explain, and when I order, you get the job done."

"I don't believe in doing things half way, Ms. Hayward."

Sydney smiled, that was exactly what she wanted to hear. "And you want to move up. Contrarily, when my position was tenuous at best last week, you stood behind me. Breaking into that board meeting was a risk, and putting yourself in my corner at that point certainly lessened your chances of moving up at Hayward had I been asked to step down. And it most certainly earned you a powerful enemy."

"I work for you, not for Mr. Bingham. And even if it wasn't a matter of loyalty, you were doing what was right."

"I feel very strongly about loyalty, Janine, just as strongly as I feel about giving someone who's trying to make something of herself the chance to do so. The flowers were a thank-you for that loyalty, from me to you, personally."

"Thank you, Ms. Hayward." Janine's face relaxed in a smile.

"You're welcome. I consider your promotion to my executive assistant, with the appropriate salary and benefits, to be a good business decision."

Janine's mouth dropped open. "I beg your pardon?"

"I hope you'll accept the position, Janine. I need someone I trust, someone I respect, and someone who knows how the hell to run an office. Agreed?" Sydney offered a hand. Janine stared at it before she managed to rise and grip it firmly in hers.

"Ms. Hayward—"

"Sydney. We're going to be in this together."

Janine gave a quick, dazzled laugh. "Sydney. I hope I'm not dreaming."

"You're wide-awake, and the flak's going to fall before the day's over. Your first job in your new position is to arrange a meeting with Lloyd. Make it a formal request, here in my office before the close of business hours today."

He put her off until four-fifteen, but Sydney was patient. If anything, the extra time gave her the opportunity to ex-

amine her feelings and make certain her decision wasn'
based on emotion.

When Janine buzzed him in, Sydney was ready, and she
was sure.

"You picked a busy day for this," he began.

"Sit down, Lloyd."

He did, and she waited again while he took out a cigarette. "I won't take up much of your time," she told him
"I felt it best to discuss this matter as quickly as possible."

His gaze flicked up, and he smiled confidently through
the haze of smoke. "Having problems on one of the projects?"

"No." Her lips curved in a wintry smile. "There's nothing I can't handle. It's the internal strife at Hayward that
concerns me, and I've decided to remedy it."

"Office reorganization is a tricky business." He crossed
his legs and leaned back. "Do you really think you've been
around long enough to attempt it?"

"I'm not going to attempt it, I'm going to do it. I'd like
your resignation on my desk by five o'clock tomorrow."

He bolted up. "What the hell are you talking about?"

"Your resignation, Lloyd. Or if necessary, your termi-
nation at Hayward. That distinction will be up to you."

He crushed the cigarette into pulp in the ashtray. "You
think you can fire me? Walk in here with barely three
months under your belt and fire me when I've been at Hayward for twelve years?"

"Here's the point," she said evenly. "Whether it's been
three months or three days, I am Hayward. I will not tolerate one of my top executives undermining my position.
It's obvious you're not happy with the current status at
Hayward, and I can guarantee you, I'm going to remain in
charge of this company for a long time. Therefore, I believe
it's in your own interest, and certainly in mine, for you to
resign."

"The hell I will."

"That's your choice, of course. I will, however, take the matter before the board, and use all the power at my disposal to limit yours."

Going with instinct, she pushed the next button. "Leaking Mrs. Wolburg's accident to the press didn't just put me in a difficult position. It put Hayward in a difficult position. As an executive vice president, your first duty is to the company, not to go off on some vindictive tangent because you dislike working for me."

He stiffened, and she knew she'd guessed correctly. "You have no way of proving the leak came from my office."

"You'd be surprised what I can prove," she bluffed. "I told you I wanted your loyalty or your resignation if the board stood behind me in the Soho project. We both know your loyalty is out of the question."

"I'll tell you what you'll get." There was a sneer in his voice, but beneath the neat gray suit, he was sweating. "I'll be sitting behind that desk when you're back in Europe dancing from shop to shop."

"No, Lloyd. You'll never sit behind this desk. As the major stockholder of Hayward, I'll see to that. Now," she continued quietly, "it wasn't necessary for me to document to the board the many cases in which you've ignored my requests, overlooked complaints from clients, tenants and other associates at the meeting on Friday. I will do so, however, at the next. In the current climate, I believe my wishes will be met."

His fingers curled. He imagined the satisfaction of hooking them around her throat. "You think because you skidded through one mess, because your senile grandfather plopped you down at that desk, you can shoehorn me out? Lady, I'll bury you."

Coolly she inclined her head. "You're welcome to try. If you don't manage it, it may be difficult for you to find a similar position with another company." Her eyes iced over. "If you don't think I have any influence, or the basic guts to carry this off, you're making a mistake. You have twenty-four hours to consider your options. This meeting is over."

"Why you cold-blooded bitch."

She stood, and this time it was she who leaned over her desk. "Take me on," she said in a quiet voice. "Do it."

"This isn't over." Turning on his heel, he marched to the door to swing it open hard enough that it banged against the wall.

After three deep breaths, Sydney sank into her chair. Okay, she was shaking—but only a little. And it was temper, she realized as she pressed a testing hand against her stomach. Not fear. Good, solid temper. She found she didn't need to vent any anger by mangling paper clips or shredding stationery. In fact, she found she felt just wonderful.

Chapter Eight

Mikhail stirred the mixture of meats and spices and tomatoes in the old cast-iron skillet and watched the street below through his kitchen window. After a sniff and a taste, he added another splash of red wine to the mixture. Behind him in the living room *The Marriage of Figaro* soared from the stereo.

He wondered how soon Sydney would arrive.

Leaving the meal to simmer, he walked into the living room to study the rosewood block that was slowly becoming her face.

Her mouth. There was a softness about it that was just emerging. Testing, he measured it between his index finger and thumb. And remembered how it had tasted, moving eagerly under his. Hot candy, coated with cool, white wine. Addictive.

Those cheekbones, so aristocratic, so elegant. They could add a regal, haughty look one moment, or that of an ice-blooded warrior the next. That firm, proud jawline—he traced a fingertip along it and thought of how sensitive and smooth her skin was there.

Her eyes, he'd wondered if he'd have problems with her eyes. Oh, not the shape of them—that was basic to craft, but the feeling in them, the mysteries behind them.

There was still so much he needed to know.

He leaned closer until he was eye to eye with the half-formed bust. "You will let me in," he whispered. At the knock on the door, he stayed where he was, peering into Sydney's emerging face. "Is open."

"Hey, Mik." Keely breezed in wearing a polka-dotted T-shirt and shorts in neon green. "Got anything cold? My fridge finally gave up the ghost."

"Help yourself," he said absently, "I'll put you on top of the list for the new ones."

"My hero." She paused in the kitchen to sniff at the skillet. "God, this smells sinful." She tipped the spoon in and took a sample. "It is sinful. Looks like a lot for one."

"It's for two."

"Oh." She gave the word three ascending syllables as she pulled a soft drink out of the refrigerator. The smell was making her mouth water, and she glanced wistfully at the skillet again. "Looks like a lot for two, too."

He glanced over his shoulder and grinned. "Put some in a bowl. Simmer it a little longer."

"You're a prince, Mik." She rattled in his cupboards. "So who's the lucky lady?"

"Sydney Hayward."

"Sydney." Her eyes widened. The spoon she held halted in midair above the pan of bubbling goulash. "Hayward," she finished. "You mean the rich and beautiful Hayward who wears silk to work and carries a six-hundred-dollar purse, which I personally priced at Saks. She's coming here, to have dinner and everything?"

He was counting on the everything. "Yes."

"Gee." She couldn't think of anything more profound.

But she wasn't sure she liked it. No, she wasn't sure at all,
Keely thought as she scooped her impromptu dinner into a
bowl.

The rich were different. She firmly believed it. And this
lady was rich in capital letters. Keely knew Mikhail had
earned some pretty big bucks with his art, but she couldn't
think of him as rich. He was just Mik, the sexy guy next
door who was always willing to unclog a sink or kill a
spider or share a beer.

Carrying the bowl, she walked over to him and noticed
his latest work in progress. "Oh," she said, but this time
it was only a sigh. She would have killed for cheekbones
like that.

"You like?"

"Sure, I always like your stuff." But she shifted from
foot to foot. She didn't like the way he was looking at the
face in the wood. "I, ah, guess you two have more than a
business thing going."

"Yes." He hooked his thumbs in his pockets as he
looked into Keely's troubled eyes. "This is a problem?"

"Problem? No, no problem." She worried her lower lip.
"Well, it's just—boy, Mik, she's so uptown."

He knew she was talking about more than an address,
but smiled and ran a hand over her hair. "You're worried
for me."

"Well, we're pals, aren't we? I can't stand to see a pal
get hurt."

Touched, he kissed her nose. "Like you did with the
actor with the skinny legs?"

She moved her shoulders. "Yeah, I guess. But I wasn't
in love with him or anything. Or only a little."

"You cried."

"Sure, but I'm a wienie. I tear up during greeting card
commercials." Dissatisfied, she looked back at the bust.
Definitely uptown. "A woman who looks like that, I figure

she could drive a guy to joining the Foreign Legion or
something."

He laughed and ruffled her hair. "Don't worry. I'
write."

Before she could think of anything else, there was an
other knock. Giving Keely a pat on the shoulder, he wer
to answer it.

"Hi." Sydney's face brightened the moment she sa
him. She carried a garment bag in one hand and a bottl
of champagne in the other. "Something smells wonderfu
My mouth started watering on the third floor, and…" Sh
spotted Keely standing near the worktable with a bow
cupped in her hands. "Hello." After clearing her throa
Sydney told herself she would not be embarrassed to hav
Mikhail's neighbor see her coming into his apartment wit
a suitcase.

"Hi. I was just going." Every bit as uncomfortable a
Sydney, Keely darted back into the kitchen to grab her so
drink.

"It's nice to see you again." Sydney stood awkwardl
beside the open door. "How did your murder go?"

"He strangled me in three takes." With a fleeting smile
she dashed through the door. "Enjoy your dinner. Thanks
Mik."

When the door down the hall slammed shut, Sydney le
out a long breath. "Does she always move so fast?"

"Mostly." He circled Sydney's waist with his hands
"She is worried you will seduce me, use me, then toss m
aside."

"Oh, well, really."

Chuckling, he nipped at her bottom lip. "I don't min
the first two." As his mouth settled more truly on hers, h
slipped the garment bag out of her lax fingers and tosse
it aside. Taking the bottle of wine, he used it to push th
door closed at her back. "I like your dress. You look lik
a rose in sunshine."

Freed, her hands could roam along his back, slip under the chambray work shirt he hadn't tucked into his jeans. "I like the way you look, all the time."

His lips were curved as they pressed to her throat. "You're hungry?"

"Mmm. Past hungry. I had to skip lunch."

"Ten minutes," he promised, and reluctantly released her. If he didn't, dinner would be much, much later. "What have you brought us?" He twisted the bottle in his hand to study the label. One dark brow lifted. "This will humble my goulash."

With her eyes shut, Sydney took a long, appreciative sniff. "No, I don't think so." Then she laughed and took the bottle from him. "I wanted to celebrate. I had a really good day."

"You will tell me?"

"Yes."

"Good. Let's find some glasses that won't embarrass this champagne."

She didn't know when she'd been more charmed. He had set a small table and two chairs on the tiny balcony off the bedroom. A single pink peony graced an old green bottle in the center, and music drifted from his radio to lull the sounds of traffic. Thick blue bowls held the spicy stew, and rich black bread was heaped in a wicker basket.

While they ate, she told him about her decision to promote Janine, and her altercation with Lloyd.

"You ask for his resignation. You should fire him."

"It's a little more complicated than that." Flushed with success, Sydney lifted her glass to study the wine in the evening sunlight. "But the result's the same. If he pushes me, I'll have to go before the board. I have memos, other documentation. Take this building, for example." She tapped a finger on the old brick. "My grandfather turned it over to Lloyd more than a year ago with a request that he see to tenant demands and maintenance. You know the rest.''

"Then perhaps I am grateful to him." He reached up to tuck her hair behind her ear, placing his lips just beneath the jet drops she wore. "If he had been honest and efficient I wouldn't have had to be rude in your office. You might not be here with me tonight."

Taking his hand, she pressed it to her cheek. "Maybe I should have given him a raise." She turned her lips into his palm, amazed at how easy it had become for her to show her feelings.

"No. Instead, we'll think this was destiny. I don't like someone that close who would like to hurt you."

"I know he leaked Mrs. Wolburg's story to the press." Worked up again, Sydney broke off a hunk of bread. "His anger toward me caused him to put Hayward in a very unstable position. I won't tolerate that, and neither will the board."

"You'll fix it." He split the last of the champagne between them.

"Yes, I will." She was looking out over the neighborhood, seeing the clothes hung on lines to dry in the sun, the open windows where people could be seen walking by or sitting in front of televisions. There were children on the sidewalk taking advantage of a long summer day. When Mikhail's hand reached for hers, she gripped it tightly.

"Today, for the first time," she said quietly, "I felt in charge. My whole life I went along with what I was told was best or proper or expected." Catching herself, she shook her head. "That doesn't matter. What matters is that sometime over the last few months I started to realize that to be in charge meant you had to take charge. I finally did. I don't know if you can understand how that feels."

"I know what I see. And this is a woman who is beginning to trust herself, and take what is right for her." Smiling, he skimmed a finger down her cheek. "Take me."

She turned to him. He was less than an arm's length away. Those dark, untamed looks would have set any woman's heart leaping. But there was more happening to her than an excited pulse. She was afraid to consider it. There was only now, she reminded herself, and reached for him. He held her, rubbing his cheek against her hair, murmuring lovely words she couldn't understand.

"I'll have to get a phrase book." Her eyes closed on a sigh as his mouth roamed over her face.

"This one is easy." He repeated a phrase between kisses.

She laughed, moving willingly when he drew her to her feet. "Easy for you to say. What does it mean?"

His lips touched hers again. "I love you."

He watched her eyes fly open, saw the race of emotion in them run from shock to hope to panic. "Mikhail, I—"

"Why do the words frighten you?" he interrupted. "Love doesn't threaten."

"I didn't expect this." She put a hand to his chest to insure some distance. Eyes darkening, Mikhail looked down at it, then stepped back.

"What did you expect?"

"I thought you were…" Was there no delicate way? "I assumed that you…"

"Wanted only your body," he finished for her, and his voice heated. He had shown her so much, and she saw so little. "I do want it, but not only. Will you tell me there was nothing last night?"

"Of course not. It was beautiful." She had to sit down, really had to. It felt as though she'd jumped off a cliff and landed on her head. But he was looking at her in such a way that made her realize she'd better stay on her feet.

"The sex was good." He picked up his glass. Though he was tempted to fling it off the balcony, he only sipped. "Good sex is necessary for the body and for the state of mind. But it isn't enough for the heart. The heart needs love, and there was love last night. For both of us."

Her arms fell uselessly to her sides. "I don't know. I've never had good sex before."

He considered her over the rim of his glass. "You were not a virgin. You were married before."

"Yes, I was married before." And the taste of that was still bitter on her tongue. "I don't want to talk about that, Mikhail. Isn't it enough that we're good together, that I feel for you something I've never felt before? I don't want to analyze it. I just can't yet."

"You don't want to know what you feel?" That baffled him. "How can you live without knowing what's inside you?"

"It's different for me. I haven't had what you've had or done what you've done. And your emotions—they're always right there. You can see them in the way you move, the way you talk, in your eyes, in your work. Mine are…mine aren't as volatile. I need time."

He nearly smiled. "Do you think I'm a patient man?"

"No," she said, with feeling.

"Good. Then you'll understand that your time will be very short." He began to gather dishes. "Did this husband of yours hurt you?"

"A failed marriage hurts. Please, don't push me on that now."

"For tonight I won't." With the sky just beginning to deepen at his back, he looked at her. "Because tonight I want you only to think of me." He walked through the door, leaving her to gather the rest of the meal.

He loved her. The words swam in Sydney's mind as she picked up the basket and the flower. It wasn't possible to doubt it. She'd come to understand he was a man who said no more than he meant, and rarely less. But she couldn't know what love meant to him.

To her, it was something sweet and colorful and lasting that happened to other people. Her father had cared for her, in his erratic way. But they had only spent snatches of time together in her early childhood. After the divorce, when she'd been six, they had rarely seen each other.

And her mother. She didn't doubt her mother's affection. But she always realized it ran no deeper than any of Margerite's interests.

There had been Peter, and that had been strong and true and important. Until they had tried to love as husband and wife.

But it wasn't the love of a friend that Mikhail was offering her. Knowing it, feeling it, she was torn by twin forces of giddy happiness and utter terror.

With her mind still whirling, she walked into the kitchen to find him elbow deep in soapsuds. She set basket and bottle aside to pick up a dish towel.

"Are you angry with me?" she ventured after a moment.

"Some. More I'm puzzled by you." And hurt, but he didn't want her guilt or pity. "To be loved should make you happy, warm."

"Part of me is. The other half is afraid of moving too fast and risking spoiling what we've begun." He needed honesty, she thought. Deserved it. She tried to give him what she had. "All day today I looked forward to being here with you, being able to talk to you, to be able to share with you what had happened. To listen to you. I knew you'd make me laugh, that my heart would speed up when you kissed me." She set a dry bowl aside. "Why are you looking at me like that?"

He only shook his head. "You don't even know you're in love with me. But it's all right," he decided, and offered her the next bowl. "You will."

"You're so arrogant," she said, only half-annoyed. "I'm never sure if I admire or detest that."

"You like it very much because it makes you want to fight back."

"I suppose you think I should be flattered because you love me."

"Of course." He grinned at her. "Are you?"

Thinking it over, she stacked the second bowl in the first, then took the skillet. "I suppose. It's human nature. And you're…"

"I'm what?"

She looked up at him again, the cocky grin, the dark amused eyes, the tumble of wild hair. "You're so gorgeous."

His grin vanished when his mouth dropped open. When he managed to close it again, he pulled his hands out of the water and began to mutter.

"Are you swearing at me?" Instead of answering her, he yanked the dishcloth away from her to dry his hands. "I think I embarrassed you." Delighted, she laughed and cupped his face in her hands. "Yes, I did."

"Stop." Thoroughly frazzled, he pushed her hands away. "I can't think of the word for what I am."

"But you are gorgeous." Before he could shake her off, she wound her arms around his neck. "When I first saw you, I thought you looked like a pirate, all dark and dashing."

This time he swore in English and she only smiled.

"Maybe it's the hair," she considered, combing her fingers through it. "I used to imagine what it would be like to get my hands in it. Or the eyes. So moody, so dangerous."

His hands lowered to her hips. "I'm beginning to feel dangerous."

"Hmm. Or the mouth. It just might be the mouth." She touched hers to it, then slowly, her eyes on his, outlined its shape with her tongue. "I can't imagine there's a woman still breathing who could resist it."

"You're trying to seduce me."

She let her hands slide down, her fingers toying with his buttons. "Somebody has to." She only hoped she could do it right. "Then, of course, there's this wonderful body. The first time I saw you without a shirt, I nearly swallowed my tongue.'' She parted his shirt to let her hands roam over his chest. His knees nearly buckled. ''Your skin was wet and glistening, and there were all these muscles.'' She forgot the game, seducing herself as completely as him. ''So hard, and the skin so smooth. I wanted to touch, like this.''

Her breath shuddered out as she pressed her fingers into his shoulders, kneading her way down his arms. When her eyes focused on his again, she saw that they were fiercely intense. Beneath her fingers, his arms were taut as steel. The words dried up in her mouth.

''Do you know what you do to me?'' he asked. He reached for the tiny black buttons on her jacket, and his fingers trembled. Beneath the sunny cap-sleeved suit, she wore lace the color of midnight. He could feel the fast dull thud of his heart in his head. ''Or how much I need you?''

She could only shake her head. ''Just show me. It's enough to show me.''

She was caught fast and hard, her mouth fused to his, their bodies molded. When her arms locked around his neck, he lifted her an inch off the floor, circling slowly, his lips tangling with hers.

Dizzy and desperate, she clung to him as he wound his way into the bedroom. She kicked her shoes off, heedless of where they flew. There was such freedom in the simple gesture, she laughed, then held tight as they fell to the bed.

The mattress groaned and sagged, cupping them in the center. He was muttering her name, and she his, when their mouths met again.

It was as hot and reckless as before. Now she knew where they would go and strained to match his speed. The need to have him was as urgent as breath, and she struggled with his jeans, tugging at denim while he peeled away lace.

She could feel the nubs of the bedspread beneath her bare back, and him, hard and restless above her. Through the open window, the heat poured in. And there was a rum-

ble, low and distant, of thunder. She felt the answering
power echo in her blood.

He wanted the storm, outside, in her. Never before had
he understood what it was to truly crave. He remembered
hunger and a miserable wish for warmth. He remembered
wanting the curves and softness of a woman. But all that
was nothing, nothing like the violent need he felt for her.

His hands hurried over her, wanting to touch every inch,
and everywhere he touched she burned. If she trembled, he
drove her further until she shuddered. When she moaned,
he took and tormented until she cried out.

And still he hungered.

Thunder stalked closer, like a threat. Following it
through the window came the passionate wail of the sax.
The sun plunged down in the sky, tossing flame and shadows.

Inside the hot, darkening room, they were aware of no
time or sound. Reality had been whittled down to one man
and one woman and the ruthless quest to mate.

He filled. She surrounded.

Crazed, he lifted her up until her legs circled his waist
and her back arched like a bow. Shuddering from the power
they made, he pressed his face to her shoulder and let it
take him.

The rain held off until the next afternoon, then came with
a full chorus of thunder and lightning. With her phone on
speaker, Sydney handled a tricky conference call. Though
Janine sat across from her, she took notes of her own.
Thanks to a morning of intense work between herself and
her new assistant, she had the information needed at her
fingertips.

''Yes, Mr. Bernstein, I think the adjustments will be to
everyone's benefit.'' She waited for the confirmation to run
from Bernstein, to his lawyer, to his West Coast partner.
''We'll have the revised draft faxed to all of you by five,

East Coast time, tomorrow.'' She smiled to herself. ''Yes, Hayward Industries believes in moving quickly. Thank you, gentlemen. Goodbye.''

After disengaging the speaker, she glanced at Janine. ''Well?''

''You never even broke a sweat. Look at me.'' Janine held out a hand. ''My palms are wet. Those three were hoping to bulldoze you under and you came out dead even. Congratulations.''

''I think that transaction should please the board.'' Seven million, she thought. She'd just completed a seven-million-dollar deal. And Janine was right. She was steady as a rock. ''Let's get busy on the fine print, Janine.''

''Yes, ma'am.'' Even as she rose, the phone rang. Moving on automatic, she plucked up Sydney's receiver. ''Ms. Hayward's office. One moment, please.'' She clicked to hold. ''Mr. Warfield.''

The faintest wisp of fatigue clouded her eyes as she nodded. ''I'll take it. Thank you, Janine.''

She waited until her door closed again before bringing him back on the line. ''Hello, Channing.''

''Sydney, I've been trying to reach you for a couple of days. Where have you been hiding?''

She thought of Mikhail's lumpy bed and smiled. ''I'm sorry, Channing. I've been...involved.''

''All work and no play, darling,'' he said, and set her teeth on edge. ''I'm going to take you away from all that. How about lunch tomorrow? Lutece.''

As a matter of course, she checked her calendar. ''I have a meeting.''

''Meetings were made to be rescheduled.''

''No, I really can't. As it is, I have a couple of projects coming to a head, and I won't be out of the office much all week.''

''Now, Sydney, I promised Margerite I wouldn't let you bury yourself under the desk. I'm a man of my word.''

Why was it, she thought, she could handle a multimillion-dollar deal with a cool head, but this personal pressure
was making her shoulders tense? "My mother worries unnecessarily. I'm really sorry, Channing, but I can't chat
now. I've got—I'm late for an appointment," she impro-
vised.

"Beautiful women are entitled to be late. If I can't get
you out to lunch, I have to insist that you come with us on
Friday. We have a group going to the theater. Drinks first,
of course, and a light supper after."

"I'm booked, Channing. Have a lovely time though.
Now, I really must ring off. Ciao." Cursing herself, she
settled the receiver on his pipe of protest.

Why hadn't she simply told him she was involved with
someone?

Simple question, she thought, simple answer. Channing
would go to Margerite, and Sydney didn't want her mother
to know. What she had with Mikhail was hers, only hers,
and she wanted to keep it that way for a little while longer.

He loved her.

Closing her eyes, she experienced the same quick trickle
of pleasure and alarm. Maybe, in time, she would be able
to love him back fully, totally, in the full-blooded way she
was so afraid she was incapable of.

She'd thought she'd been frigid, too. She'd certainly
been wrong there. But that was only one step.

Time, she thought again. She needed time to organize
her emotions. And then…then they'd see.

The knock on her office door brought her back to earth.
"Yes?"

"Sorry, Sydney." Janine came in carrying a sheet of
Hayward stationery. "This just came in from Mr. Bingham's office. I thought you'd want to see it right away."

"Yes, thank you." Sydney scanned the letter. It was
carefully worded to disguise the rage and bitterness, but it
was a resignation. Effective immediately. Carefully she set

the letter aside. It took only a marginal ability to read between the lines to know it wasn't over. "Janine, I'll need some personnel files. We'll want to fill Mr. Bingham's position, and I want to see if we can do it in-house."

"Yes, ma'am." She started toward the door, then stopped. "Sydney, does being your executive assistant mean I can offer advice?"

"It certainly does."

"Watch your back. There's a man who would love to stick a knife in it."

"I know. I don't intend to let him get behind me." She rubbed at the pressure at the back of her neck. "Janine, before we deal with the files, how about some coffee? For both of us."

"Coming right up." She turned and nearly collided with Mikhail as he strode through the door. "Excuse me." The man was soaking wet and wore a plain white T-shirt that clung to every ridge of muscle. Janine entertained a brief fantasy of drying him off herself. "I'm sorry, Ms. Hayward is—"

"It's all right." Sydney was already coming around the desk. "I'll see Mr. Stanislaski."

Noting the look in her boss's eye, Janine managed to fight back the worst of the envy. "Shall I hold your calls?"

"Hmm?"

Mikhail grinned. "Please. You're Janine, with the promotion?"

"Why, yes."

"Sydney tells me you are excellent in your work."

"Thank you." Who would have thought the smell of wet male could be so terrific? "Would you like some coffee?"

"No, thank you."

"Hold mine, too, Janine. And take a break yourself."

"Yes, ma'am." With only a small envious sigh, she shut the door.

"Don't you have an umbrella?" Sydney asked him, and leaned forward for a kiss. He kept his hands to himself.

"I can't touch you, I'll mess up your suit. Do you have a towel?"

"Just a minute." She walked into the adjoining bath. "What are you doing uptown at this time of day?"

"The rain slows things up. I did paperwork and knocked off at four." He took the towel she offered and rubbed it over his head.

"Is it that late?" She glanced at the clock and saw it was nearly five.

"You're busy."

She thought of the resignation on her desk and the files she had to study. "A little."

"When you're not busy, maybe you'd like to go with me to the movies."

"I'd love to." She took the towel back. "I need an hour."

"I'll come back." He reached out to toy with the pearls at her throat. "There's something else."

"What?"

"My family goes to visit my sister this weekend. To have a barbecue. Will you go with me?"

"I'd love to go to a barbecue. When?"

"They leave Friday, after work." He wanted to sketch her in those pearls. Just those pearls. Though he rarely worked in anything but wood, he thought he might carve her in alabaster. "We can go when you're ready."

"I should be able to get home and changed by six. Six-thirty," she corrected. "All right?"

"All right." He took her shoulders, holding her a few inches away from his damp clothes as he kissed her. "Natasha will like you."

"I hope so."

He kissed her again. "I love you."

Emotion shuddered through her. "I know."

"And you love me," he murmured. "You're just stubborn." He toyed with her lips another moment. "But soon you'll pose for me."

"I...what?"

"Pose for me. I have a show in the fall, and I think I'll use several pieces of you."

"You never told me you had a show coming up." The rest of it hit her. "Of me?"

"Yes, we'll have to work very hard very soon. So now I leave you alone so you can work."

"Oh." She'd forgotten all about files and phone calls. "Yes, I'll see you in an hour."

"And this weekend there will be no work. But next..." He nodded, his mind made up. Definitely in alabaster.

She ran the damp towel through her hands as he walked to the door. "Mikhail."

With the door open, he stood with his hand on the knob. "Yes?"

"Where does your sister live?"

"West Virginia." He grinned and shut the door behind her. Sydney stared at the blank panel for a full ten seconds.

"West Virginia?"

Chapter Nine

She'd never be ready in time. Always decisive about her wardrobe, Sydney had packed and unpacked twice. What did one wear for a weekend in West Virginia? A few days in Martinique—no problem. A quick trip to Rome would have been easy. But a weekend, a family weekend in West Virginia, had her searching frantically through her closet.

As she fastened her suitcase a third time, she promised herself she wouldn't open it again. To help herself resist temptation, she carried the bag into the living room, then hurried back to the bedroom to change out of her business suit.

She'd just pulled on thin cotton slacks and a sleeveless top in mint green—and was preparing to tear them off again—when the knock sounded at her door.

It would have to do. It would do, she assured herself as she went to answer. They would be arriving so late at his sister's home, it hardly mattered what she was wearing. With a restless hand she brushed her hair back, wondered if she should secure it with a scarf for the drive, then opened the door.

Sequined and sleek, Margerite stood on the other side.

"Sydney, darling." As she glided inside, she kissed her daughter's cheek.

"Mother. I didn't know you were coming into the city today."

"Of course you did." She settled into a chair, crossed her legs. "Channing told you about our little theater party."

"Yes, he did. I'd forgotten."

"Sydney." The name was a sigh. "You're making me worry about you."

Automatically Sydney crossed to the liquor cabinet to pour Margerite a glass of her favored brand of sherry. "There's no need. I'm fine."

"No need?" Margerite's pretty coral-tipped fingers fluttered. "You turn down dozens of invitations, couldn't even spare an afternoon to shop with your mother last week, bury yourself in that office for positively hours on end. And there's no need for me to worry." She smiled indulgently and she accepted the glass. "Well, we're going to fix all of that. I want you to go in and change into something dashing. We'll meet Channing and the rest of the party at Doubles for a drink before curtain."

The odd thing was, Sydney realized, she'd very nearly murmured an agreement, so ingrained was her habit of doing what was expected of her. Instead, she perched on the arm of the sofa and hoped she could do this without hurting Margerite's feelings.

"Mother, I'm sorry. If I've been turning down invitations, it's because the transition at Hayward is taking up most of my time and energy."

"Darling." Margerite gestured with the glass before she sipped. "That's exactly my point."

But Sydney only shook her head. "And the simple fact is, I don't feel the need to have my social calendar filled every night any longer. As for tonight, I appreciate, I really do, the fact that you'd like me to join you. But, as I explained to Channing, I have plans.''

Irritation sparked in Margerite's eyes, but she only tapped a nail on the arm of the chair. "If you think I'm going to leave you here to spend the evening cooped up with some sort of nasty paperwork—''

"I'm not working this weekend," Sydney interrupted. "Actually, I'm going out of town for—'' The quick rap at the door relieved her. "Excuse me a minute." The moment she'd opened the door, Sydney reached out a hand for him. "Mikhail, my—''

Obviously he didn't want to talk until he'd kissed her, which he did, thoroughly, in the open doorway. Pale and rigid, Margerite pushed herself to her feet. She understood, as a woman would, that the kiss she was witnessing was the kind exchanged by lovers.

"Mikhail." Sydney managed to draw back an inch.

"I'm not finished yet."

One hand braced against his chest as she gestured helplessly with the other. "My mother…''

He glanced over, caught the white-faced fury and shifted Sydney easily to his side. A subtle gesture of protection. "Margerite."

"Isn't there a rule," she said stiffly, "about mixing business and pleasure?" She lifted her brows as her gaze skimmed over him. "But then, you wouldn't be a rule follower, would you, Mikhail?''

"Some rules are important, some are not." His voice was gentle, but without regret and without apology. "Honesty is important, Margerite. I was honest with you.''

She turned away, refusing to acknowledge the truth of that. "I'd prefer a moment with you, alone, Sydney.''

There was a pounding at the base of her skull as she looked at her mother's rigid back. "Mikhail, would you take my bag to the car? I'll be down in a few minutes.''

He cupped her chin, troubled by what he read in her eyes. "I'll stay with you."

"No." She put a hand to his wrist. "It would be best if you left us alone. Just a few minutes." Her fingers tightened. "Please."

She left him no choice. Muttering to himself, he picked up her suitcase. The moment the door closed behind him, Margerite whirled. Sydney was already braced. It was rare, very rare for Margerite to go on a tirade. But when she did, it was always an ugly scene with vicious words.

"You fool. You've been sleeping with him."

"I don't see that as your concern. But, yes, I have."

"Do you think you have the sense or skill to handle a man like that?" There was the crack of glass against wood as she slapped the little crystal goblet onto the table. "This sordid little liaison could ruin you, ruin everything I've worked for. God knows you did enough damage by divorcing Peter, but I managed to put that right. Now this. Sneaking off for a weekend at some motel."

Sydney's fists balled at her sides. "There is nothing sordid about my relationship with Mikhail, and I'm not sneaking anywhere. As for Peter, I will not discuss him with you."

Eyes hard, Margerite stepped forward. "From the day you were born, I used everything at my disposal to be certain you had what you deserved as a Hayward. The finest schools, the proper friends, even the right husband. Now, you're tossing it all back at me, all the planning, all the sacrificing. And for what?"

She whirled around the room as Sydney remained stiff and silent.

"Oh, believe me, I understand that man's appeal. I'd even toyed with the idea of having a discreet affair with him myself." The wound to her vanity was raw and throbbing. "A woman's entitled to a wild fling with a magnificent animal now and again. And his artistic talents and reputation are certainly in his favor. But his background is nothing, less than nothing. Gypsies and farmers and peasants. I have the experience to handle him—had I chosen to. I also have no ties at the moment to make an affair awkward. You, however, are on the verge of making a commitment to Channing. Do you think he'd have you if he ever learned you'd been taking that magnificent brute to bed?''

''That's enough.'' Sydney moved forward to take her mother's arm. ''That's past enough. For someone who's so proud of the Hayward lineage, you certainly made no attempt to keep the name yourself. It was always my burden to be a proper Hayward, to do nothing to damage the Hayward name. Well, I've been a proper Hayward, and right now I'm working day and night to be certain the Hayward name remains above reproach. But my personal time, and whom I decide to spend that personal time with, is my business.''

Pale with shock, Margerite jerked her hand away. Not once, from the day she'd been born, had Sydney spoken to her in such a manner. ''Don't you dare use that tone with me. Are you so blinded with lust that you've forgotten where your loyalties lie?''

''I've never forgotten my loyalties,'' Sydney tossed back. ''And at the moment, this is the most reasonable tone I can summon.'' It surprised her as well, this fast, torrid venom, but she couldn't stop it. ''Listen to me, Mother, as far as Channing goes, I have never been on the verge of making a commitment to him, nor do I ever intend to do so. That's what you intended. And I will never, never, be pressured into making that kind of commitment again. If it would help disabuse Channing of the notion, I'd gladly take out a full-page ad in the *Times* announcing my relationship with Mikhail. As to that, you know nothing about Mikhail's family, you know nothing about him, as a man. You never got beyond his looks.''

Margerite's chin lifted. "And you have?"

"Yes, I have, and he's a caring, compassionate man. An honest man who knows what he wants out of life and goes after it. You'd understand that, but the difference is he'd never use or hurt anyone to get it. He loves me. And I..." It flashed through her like light, clear, warm and utterly simple. "I love him."

"Love?" Stunned, Margerite reared back. "Now I know you've taken leave of your senses. My God, Sydney, do you believe everything a man says in bed?"

"I believe what Mikhail says. Now, I'm keeping him waiting, and we have a long trip to make."

Head high, chin set, Margerite streamed toward the door, then tossed a last look over her shoulder. "He'll break your heart, and make a fool of you in the bargain. But perhaps that's what you need to remind you of your responsibilities."

When the door snapped shut, Sydney lowered onto the arm of the sofa. Mikhail would have to wait another moment.

He wasn't waiting; he was prowling. Back and forth in front of the garage elevators he paced, hands jammed into his pockets, thoughts as black as smoke. When the elevator doors slid open, he was on Sydney in a heartbeat.

"Are you all right?" He had her face in his hands. "No, I can see you are not."

"I am, really. It was unpleasant. Family arguments always are."

For him, family arguments were fierce and furious and inventive. They could either leave him enraged or laughing, but never drained as she was now. "Come, we can go upstairs, leave in the morning when you're feeling better."

"No, I'd like to go now."

"I'm sorry." He kissed both of her hands. "I don't like to cause bad feelings between you and your mama."

"It wasn't you. Really." Because she needed it, she rested her head on his chest, soothed when his arms came around her. "It was old business, Mikhail, buried too long. I don't want to talk about it."

"You keep too much from me, Sydney."

"I know. I'm sorry." She closed her eyes, feeling her stomach muscles dance, her throat drying up. It couldn't be so hard to say the words. "I love you, Mikhail."

The hand stroking her back went still, then dived into her hair to draw her head back. His eyes were intense, like two dark suns searching hers. He saw what he wanted to see, what he needed desperately to see. "So, you've stopped being stubborn." His voice was thick with emotion, and his mouth, when it met hers, gave her more than dozens of soft endearments. "You can tell me again while we drive. I like to hear it."

Laughing, she linked an arm through his as they walked to the car. "All right."

"And while you drive, I tell you."

Eyes wide, she stopped. "I drive?"

"Yes." He opened the passenger door for her. "I start, then you have a turn. You have license, yes?"

She glanced dubiously at the gauges on the dash. "Yes."

"You aren't afraid?"

She looked back up to see him grinning. "Not tonight, I'm not."

It was after midnight when Mikhail pulled up at the big brick house in Shepherdstown. It was cooler now. There wasn't a cloud in the star-scattered sky to hold in the heat. Beside him, Sydney slept with her head resting on a curled fist. He remembered that she had taken the wheel on the turnpike, driving from New Jersey into Delaware with verve and enthusiasm. Soon after they'd crossed the border into Maryland and she'd snuggled into the passenger seat again, she'd drifted off.

Always he had known he would love like this. That he would find the one woman who would change the zigzagging course of his life into a smooth circle. She was with him now, dreaming in an open car on a quiet road.

When he looked at her, he could envision how their lives would be. Not perfectly. To see perfectly meant there would be no surprises. But he could imagine waking beside her in the morning, in the big bedroom of the old house they would buy and make into a home together. He could see her coming home at night, wearing one of those pretty suits, her face reflecting the annoyance or the success of the day. And they would sit together and talk, of her work, of his.

One day, her body would grow ripe with child. He would feel their son or daughter move inside her. And they would fill their home with children and watch them grow.

But he was moving too quickly. They had come far already, and he wanted to treasure each moment.

He leaned over to nuzzle his lips over her throat. "I've crossed the states with you, *milaya*." She stirred, murmuring sleepily. "Over rivers and mountains. Kiss me."

She came awake with his mouth warm on hers and her hand resting against his cheek. She felt the flutter of a night breeze on her skin and smelled the fragrance of roses and honeysuckle. And the stir of desire was just as warm, just as sweet.

"Where are we?"

"The sign said, Wild, Wonderful West Virginia." He nipped at her lip. "You will tell me if you think it is so."

Any place, any place at all was wild and wonderful, when he was there, she thought as her arms came around him. He gave a quiet groan, then a grunt as the gearshift pressed into a particularly sensitive portion of his anatomy. "I must be getting old. It is not so easy as it was to seduce a woman in a car."

"I thought you were doing a pretty good job."

He felt the quick excitement stir his blood, fantasized briefly, then shook his head. "I'm intimidated because my mama may peek out the window any minute. Come. We'll find your bed, then I'll sneak into it."

She laughed as he unfolded his long legs out of the open door. "Now I'm intimidated." Pushing her hair back, she turned to look at the house. It was big and brick, with lights glowing gold in the windows of the first floor. Huge leafy trees shaded it, pretty box hedges shielded it from the street.

When Mikhail joined her with their bags, they started up the stone steps that cut through the slope of lawn. And here were the flowers, the roses she had smelled, and dozens of others. No formal garden this, but a splashy display that seemed to grow wild and willfully. She saw the shadow of a tricycle near the porch. In the spill of light from the windows, she noted that a bed of petunias had been recently and ruthlessly dug up.

"I think Ivan has been to work," Mikhail commented, noting the direction of Sydney's gaze. "If he is smart, he hides until it's time to go home again."

Before they had crossed the porch, she heard the laughter and music.

"It sounds as though they're up," Sydney said. "I thought they might have gone to bed."

"We have only two days together. We won't spend much of it sleeping." He opened the screen door and entered without knocking. After setting the bags near the stairs, then taking Sydney's hand, he dragged her down the hall toward the party sounds.

Sydney could feel her reserve settling back into place. She couldn't help it. All the early training, all the years of schooling had drummed into her the proper way to greet strangers. Politely, coolly, giving no more of yourself than a firm handshake and a quiet "how do you do."

She'd hardly made the adjustment when Mikhail burst into the music room, tugging her with him.

"Ha," he said, and swooped down on a small, gorgeous woman in a purple sundress. She laughed when he scooped her up, her black mane of curling hair flying out as he swung her in a circle.

"You're always late," Natasha said. She kissed her brother on both cheeks then the lips. "What did you bring me?"

"Maybe I have something in my bag for you." He set her on her feet, then turned to the man at the piano. "You take good care of her?"

"When she lets me." Spence Kimball rose to clasp hands with Mikhail. "She's been fretting for you for an hour."

"I don't fret," Natasha corrected, turning to Sydney. She smiled—the warmth was automatic—though what she saw concerned her. This cool, distant woman was the one her family insisted Mikhail was in love with? "You haven't introduced me to your friend."

"Sydney Hayward." A little impatient by the way Sydney hung back, he nudged her forward. "My sister, Natasha."

"It's nice to meet you." Sydney offered a hand. "I'm sorry about being so late. It's really my fault."

"I was only teasing. You're welcome here. You already know my family." They were gathering around Mikhail as if it had been years since the last meeting. "And this is my husband, Spence."

But he was stepping forward, puzzlement and pleasure in his eyes. "Sydney? Sydney Hayward?"

She turned, the practiced smile in place. It turned to surprise and genuine delight. "Spence Kimball. I had no idea." Offering both hands, she gripped his. "Mother told me you'd moved south and remarried."

"You've met," Natasha observed, exchanging looks with her own mother as Nadia brought over fresh glasses of wine.

"I've known Sydney since she was Freddie's age," Spence answered, referring to his eldest daughter. "I haven't seen her since…" He trailed off, remembering the last time had been at her wedding. Spence may have been out of touch with New York society in recent years, but he was well aware the marriage hadn't worked out.

"It's been a long time," Sydney murmured, understanding perfectly.

"Is small world," Yuri put in, slapping Spence on the back with fierce affection. "Sydney is owner of building where Mikhail lives. Until she pays attention to him, he sulks."

"I don't sulk." Grumbling a bit, Mikhail took his father's glass and tossed back the remaining vodka in it. "I convince. Now she is crazy for me."

"Back up, everyone," Rachel put in, "his ego's expanding again."

Mikhail merely reached over and twisted his sister's nose. "Tell them you're crazy for me," he ordered Sydney, "so this one eats her words."

Sydney lifted a brow. "How do you manage to speak when your mouth's so full of arrogance?"

Alex hooted and sprawled onto the couch. "She has your number, Mikhail. Come over here, Sydney, and sit beside me. I'm humble."

"You tease her enough for tonight." Nadia shot Alex a daunting look. "You are tired after your drive?" she asked Sydney.

"A little. I—"

"I'm sorry." Instantly Natasha was at her side. "Of course you're tired. I'll show you your room." She was already leading Sydney out. "If you like you can rest, or come back down. We want you to be at home while you're here."

"Thank you," Sydney replied. Before she could reach

for her bag, Natasha had hefted it. "It's kind of you to have me."

Natasha merely glanced over her shoulder. "You're my brother's friend, so you're mine." But she certainly intended to grill Spence before the night was over.

At the end of the hall, she took Sydney into a small room with a narrow four-poster. Faded rugs were tossed over a gleaming oak floor. Snapdragons spiked out of an old milk bottle on a table by the window where gauzy Priscillas fluttered in the breeze.

"I hope you're comfortable here." Natasha set the suitcase on a cherrywood trunk at the foot of the bed.

"It's charming." The room smelled of the cedar wardrobe against the wall and the rose petals scattered in a bowl on the nightstand. "I'm very happy to meet Mikhail's sister, and the wife of an old friend. I'd heard Spence was teaching music at a university."

"He teaches at Shepherd College. And he composes again."

"That's wonderful. He's tremendously talented." Feeling awkward, she traced a finger over the wedding ring quilt. "I remember his little girl, Freddie."

"She is ten now." Natasha's smile warmed. "She tried to wait up for Mikhail, but fell asleep on the couch." Her chin angled. "She took Ivan with her to bed, thinking I would not strangle him there. He dug up my petunias. Tomorrow, I think…"

She trailed off, head cocked.

"Is something wrong?"

"No, it's Katie, our baby." Automatically Natasha laid a hand on her breast where her milk waited. "She wakes for a midnight snack. If you'll excuse me."

"Of course."

At the door, Natasha hesitated. She could go with her instincts or her observations. She'd always trusted her instincts. "Would you like to see her?"

After only an instant's hesitation, Sydney's lips curved. "Yes, very much."

Across the hall and three doors down, the sound of the child's restless crying was louder. The room was softly lit by a nightlight in the shape of a pink sea horse.

"There, sweetheart." Natasha murmured in two languages as she lifted her baby from the crib. "Mama's here now." As the crying turned to a soft whimpering, Natasha turned to see Spence at the doorway. "I have her. She's wet and hungry, that's all."

But he had to come in. He never tired of looking at his youngest child, that perfect and beautiful replica of the woman he'd fallen in love with. Bending close, his cheek brushing his wife's, he stroked a finger over Katie's. The whimpering stopped completely, and the gurgling began.

"You're just showing off for Sydney," Natasha said with a laugh.

While Sydney watched, they cuddled the baby. There was a look exchanged over the small dark head, a look of such intimacy and love and power that it brought tears burning in her throat. Unbearably moved, she slipped out silently and left them alone.

She was awakened shortly past seven by high, excited barking, maniacal laughter and giggling shouts coming from outside her window. Moaning a bit, she turned over and found the bed empty.

Mikhail had lived up to his promise to sneak into her room, and she doubted either of them found sleep in the narrow bed much before dawn.

But he was gone now.

Rolling over, she put the pillow over her head to smother the sounds from the yard below. Since it also smothered her, she gave it up. Resigned, she climbed out of bed and pulled on her robe. She just managed to find the doorknob and open the door, when Rachel opened the one across the hall.

The two disheveled women gave each other bleary-eyed stares. Rachel yawned first.

"When I have kids," she began, "they're not going to be allowed out of bed until ten on Saturday mornings. Noon on Sunday. And only if they're bringing me breakfast in bed."

Sydney ran her tongue over her teeth, propping herself on the doorjamb. "Good luck."

"I wish I wasn't such a sucker for them." She yawned again. "Got a quarter?"

Because she was still half-asleep, Sydney automatically searched the pockets of her robe. "No, I'm sorry."

"Hold on." Rachel disappeared into her room, then came back out with a coin. "Call it."

"Excuse me?"

"Heads or tails. Winner gets the shower first. Loser has to go down and get the coffee."

"Oh." Her first inclination was to be polite and offer to get the coffee, then she thought of a nice hot shower. "Tails."

Rachel flipped, caught the coin and held it out. "Damn. Cream and sugar?"

"Black."

"Ten minutes," Rachel promised, then started down the hall. She stopped, glanced around to make sure they were alone. "Since it's just you and me, are you really crazy about Mikhail?"

"Since it's just you and me, yes."

Rachel's grin was quick and she rocked back on her heels. "I guess there's no accounting for taste."

Thirty minutes later, refreshed by the shower and coffee, Sydney wandered downstairs. Following the sounds of activity, she found most of the family had centered in the kitchen for the morning.

Natasha stood at the stove in a pair of shorts and a T-shirt. Yuri sat at the table, shoveling in pancakes and making faces at the giggling baby who was strapped into one of those clever swings that rocked and played music. Alex slouched with his head in his hands, barely murmuring when his mother shoved a mug of coffee under his nose.

"Ah, Sydney."

Alex winced at his father's booming greeting. "Papa, have some respect for the dying."

He only gave Alex an affectionate punch on the arm. "You come sit beside me," Yuri instructed Sydney. "And try Tash's pancakes."

"Good morning," Natasha said even as her mother refilled Sydney's coffee cup. "I apologize for my barbaric children and the mongrel who woke the entire house so early."

"Children make noise," Yuri said indulgently. Katie expressed agreement by squealing and slamming a rattle onto the tray of the swing.

"Everyone's up then?" Sydney took her seat.

"Spence is showing Mikhail the barbecue pit he built," Natasha told her and set a heaping platter of pancakes on the table. "They'll stand and study and make men noises. You were comfortable in the night?"

Sydney thought of Mikhail and struggled not to blush. "Yes, thank you. Oh, please," she started to protest when Yuri piled pancakes on her plate.

"For energy," he said, and winked.

Before she could think how to respond, a small curly-haired bullet shot through the back door. Yuri caught him on the fly and hauled the wriggling bundle into his arms.

"This is my grandson, Brandon. He is monster. And I eat monsters for breakfast. Chomp, chomp."

The boy of about three was wiry and tough, squirming and squealing on Yuri's lap. "Papa, come watch me ride my bike. Come watch me!"

"You have a guest," Nadia said mildly, "and no manners."

Resting his head against Yuri's chest, Brandon gave Sydney a long, owlish stare. "You can come watch me, too," he invited. "You have pretty hair. Like Lucy."

"That's a very high compliment," Natasha told her. "Lucy is a cat. Miss Hayward can watch you later. She hasn't finished her breakfast."

"You watch, Mama."

Unable to resist, Natasha rubbed a hand over her son's curls. "Soon. Go tell your daddy he has to go to the store for me."

"Papa has to come."

Knowing the game, Yuri huffed and puffed and stuck Brandon on his shoulders. The boy gave a shout of laughter and gripped tight to Yuri's hair as his grandfather rose to his feet.

"Daddy, look! Look how tall I am," Brandon was shouting as they slammed out of the screen door.

"Does the kid ever stop yelling?" Alex wanted to know.

"You didn't stop yelling until you were twelve," Nadia told him, and added a flick with her dishcloth.

Feeling a little sorry for him, Sydney rose to pour more coffee into his mug herself. He snatched her hand and brought it to his lips for a smacking kiss. "You're a queen among women, Sydney. Run away with me."

"Do I have to kill you?" Mikhail asked as he strolled into the kitchen.

Alex only grinned. "We can arm wrestle for her."

"God, men are such pigs," Rachel observed as she walked in from the opposite direction.

"Why?" The question came from a pretty, golden-haired girl who popped through the doorway, behind Mikhail.

"Because, Freddie, they think they can solve everything with muscles and sweat instead of their tiny little brains."

Ignoring his sister, Mikhail pushed plates aside, sat down

and braced an elbow on the table. Alex grinned at the muttered Ukrainian challenge. Palms slapped together.

"What are they doing?" Freddie wanted to know.

"Being silly." Natasha sighed and swung an arm around Freddie's shoulder. "Sydney, this is my oldest, Freddie. Freddie, this is Miss Hayward, Mikhail's friend."

Disconcerted, Sydney smiled at Freddie over Mikhail's head. "It's nice to see you again, Freddie. I met you a long time ago when you were just a baby."

"Really?" Intrigued, Freddie was torn between studying Sydney or watching Mikhail and Alex. They were knee to knee, hands clasped, and the muscles in their arms were bulging.

"Yes, I, ah..." Sydney was having a problem herself. Mikhail's eyes flicked up and over her before returning to his brother's. "I knew your father when you lived in New York."

There were a couple of grunts from the men at the table. Rachel sat at the other end and helped herself to pancakes. "Pass me the syrup."

With his free hand, Mikhail shoved it at her.

Smothering a grin, Rachel poured lavishly. "Mama, do you want to take a walk into town after I eat?"

"That would be nice." Ignoring her sons, Nadia began to load the dishwasher. She preferred the arm wrestling to the rolling and kicking they'd treated each other to as boys. "We can take Katie in the stroller if you like, Natasha."

"I'll walk in with you, and check on the shop." Natasha washed her hands. "I own a toy store in town," she told Sydney.

"Oh." Sydney couldn't take her eyes off the two men. Natasha could very well have told her she owned a missile site. "That's nice."

The three Stanislaski women grinned at each other. Sentimental, Nadia began to imagine a fall wedding. "Would you like more coffee?" she asked Sydney.

"Oh, I—"

Mikhail gave a grunt of triumph as he slapped his brother's arm on the table. Dishes jumped. Caught up in the moment, Freddie clapped and had her baby sister mimicking the gesture.

Grinning, Alex flexed his numbed fingers. "Two out of three."

"Get your own woman." Before Sydney could react, Mikhail scooped her up, planted a hard kiss on her mouth that tasted faintly and erotically of sweat, then carried her out the door.

Chapter Ten

"You might have lost, you know."

Amused by the lingering annoyance in her voice, Mikhail slid an arm around Sydney's waist and continued to walk down the sloping sidewalk. "I didn't."

"The point——" She sucked in her breath. She'd been trying to get the point through that thick Slavic skull off and on for more than an hour. "The point is that you and Alex arm wrestled for me as if I were a six-pack of beer."

His grin only widened, a six-pack would make him a little drunk, but that was nothing to what he'd felt when he'd looked up and seen the fascination in her eyes as she'd stared at his biceps. He flexed them a little, believing a man had a right to vanity.

"And then," she continued, making sure her voice was low, as his family was wandering along in front and behind them. "You manhandled me—in front of your mother."

"You liked it."

"I certainly——"

"Did," he finished, remembering the hot, helpless way

she'd responded to the kiss he'd given her on his sister's back porch. "So did I."

She would not smile. She would not admit for a moment to the spinning excitement she'd felt when he'd scooped her up like some sweaty barbarian carrying off the spoils of war.

"Maybe I was rooting for Alex. It seems to me he got the lion's share of your father's charm."

"All the Stanislaskis have charm," he said, unoffended. He stopped and, bending down, plucked a painted daisy from the slope of the lawn they passed. "See?"

"Hmm." Sydney twirled the flower under her nose. Perhaps it was time to change the subject before she was tempted to try to carry him off. "It's good seeing Spence again. When I was fifteen or so, I had a terrible crush on him."

Narrow eyed, Mikhail studied his brother-in-law's back. "Yes?"

"Yes. Your sister's a lucky woman."

Family pride came first. "He's lucky to have her."

This time she did smile. "I think we're both right."

Brandon, tired of holding his mother's hand, bolted back toward them. "You have to carry me," he told his uncle.

"Have to?"

With an enthusiastic nod, Brandon began to shimmy up Mikhail's leg like a monkey up a tree. "Like Papa does."

Mikhail hauled him up, then to the boy's delight, carried him for a while upside down.

"He'll lose his breakfast," Nadia called out.

"Then we fill him up again." But Mikhail flipped him over so Brandon could cling to his back. Pink cheeked, the boy grinned over at Sydney.

"I'm three years old," he told her loftily. "And I can dress my own self."

"And very well, too." Amused, she tapped his sneakered

foot. "Are you going to be a famous composer like your father?"

"Nah. I'm going to be a water tower. They're the biggest."

"I see." It was the first time she'd heard quite so grand an ambition.

"Do you live with Uncle Mikhail?"

"No," she said quickly.

"Not yet," Mikhail said simultaneously, and grinned at her.

"You were kissing him," Brandon pointed out. "How come you don't have any kids?"

"That's enough questions." Natasha came to the rescue, plucking her son from Mikhail's back as her brother roared with laughter.

"I just wanna know—"

"Everything," Natasha supplied, and gave him a smacking kiss. "But for now it's enough you know you can have one new car from the shop."

He forgot all about babies. His chocolate-brown eyes turned shrewd. "Any car?"

"Any *little* car."

"You did kiss me," Mikhail reminded Sydney as Brandon began to badger his mother about how little was little. Sydney settled the discussion by ramming her elbow into Mikhail's ribs.

She found the town charming, with its sloping streets and little shops. Natasha's toy store, The Fun House, was impressive, its stock running the range from tiny plastic cars to exquisite porcelain dolls and music boxes.

Mikhail proved to be cooperative when Sydney wandered in and out of antique shops, craft stores and boutiques. Somewhere along the line they'd lost the rest of the family. Or the family had lost them. It wasn't until they'd started back, uphill, with his arms loaded with purchases that he began to complain.

"Why did I think you were a sensible woman?"

"Because I am."

He muttered one of the few Ukrainian phrases she understood. "If you're so sensible, why did you buy all this? How do you expect to get it back to New York?"

Pleased with herself, she fiddled with the new earrings she wore. The pretty enameled stars swung jauntily. "You're so clever, I knew you'd find a way."

"Now you're trying to flatter me, and make me stupid."

She smiled. "You were the one who bought me the porcelain box."

Trapped, he shook his head. She'd studied the oval box, its top decorated with a woman's serene face in bas-relief for ten minutes, obviously in love and just as obviously wondering if she should be extravagant. "You were mooning over it."

"I know." She rose on her toes to kiss his cheek. "Thank you."

"You won't thank me when you have to ride for five hours with all this on your lap."

They climbed to the top of the steps into the yard just as Ivan, tail tucked securely between his legs streaked across the grass. In hot pursuit were a pair of long, lean cats. Mikhail let out a manful sigh.

"He is an embarrassment to the family."

"Poor little thing." Sydney shoved the package she carried at Mikhail. "Ivan!" She clapped her hands and crouched down. "Here, boy."

Spotting salvation, he swung about, scrambled for footing and shot back in her direction. Sydney caught him up, and he buried his trembling head against her neck. The cats, sinuous and smug, sat down a few feet away and began to wash.

"Hiding behind a woman," Mikhail said in disgust.

"He's just a baby. Go arm wrestle with your brother."

Chuckling, he left her to soothe the traumatized pup. A

moment later, panting, Freddie rounded the side of the house. "There he is."

"The cats frightened him," Sydney explained, as Freddie came up to stroke Ivan's fur.

"They were just playing. Do you like puppies?" Freddie asked.

"Yes." Unable to resist, Sydney nuzzled. "Yes, I do."

"Me, too. And cats. We've had Lucy and Desi for a long time. Now I'm trying to talk Mama into a puppy." Petting Ivan, she looked back at the mangled petunias. "I thought maybe if I fixed the flowers."

Sydney knew what it was to be a little girl yearning for a pet. "It's a good start. Want some help?"

She spent the next thirty minutes saving what flowers she could or—since she'd never done any gardening—following Freddie's instructions. The pup stayed nearby, shivering when the cats strolled up to wind around legs or be scratched between the ears.

When the job was done, Sydney left Ivan to Freddie's care and went inside to wash up. It occurred to her that it was barely noon and she'd done several things that day for the first time.

She'd been the grand prize in an arm wrestling contest. She'd played with children, been kissed by the man she loved on a public street. She'd gardened and had sat on a sunny lawn with a puppy on her lap.

If the weekend kept going this way, there was no telling what she might experience next.

Attracted by shouts and laughter, she slipped into the music room and looked out the window. A softball game, she realized. Rachel was pitching, one long leg cocking back as she whizzed one by Alex. Obviously displeased by the call, he turned to argue with his mother. She continued to shake her head at him, bouncing Brandon on her knee as she held firm to her authority as umpire.

Mikhail stood spread legged, his hands on his hips, and

one heel touching a ripped seat cushion that stood in as second base. He tossed in his own opinion, and Rachel threw him a withering glance over her shoulder, still displeased that he'd caught a piece of her curve ball.

Yuri and Spence stood in the outfield, catcalling as Alex fanned for a second strike. Intrigued, Sydney leaned on the windowsill. How beautiful they were, she thought. She watched as Brandon turned to give Nadia what looked like a very sloppy kiss before he bounded off on sturdy little legs toward a blue-and-white swing set. A screen door slammed, then Freddie zoomed into view, detouring to the swing to give her brother a couple of starter pushes before taking her place in the game.

Alex caught the next pitch, and the ball flew high and wide. Voices erupted into shouts. Surprisingly spry, Yuri danced a few steps to the left and snagged the ball out of the air. Mikhail tagged up, streaked past third and headed for home, where Rachel had raced to wait for the throw.

His long strides ate up the ground, those wonderful muscles bunching as he went into a slide. Rachel crowded the plate, apparently undisturbed by the thought of nearly six feet of solid male hurtling toward her. There was a collision, a tangle of limbs and a great deal of swearing.

"Out." Nadia's voice rang clearly over the din.

In the majors, they called it clearing the benches.

Every member of the family rushed toward the plate— not to fuss over the two forms still nursing bruises, but to shout and gesture. Rachel punched Mikhail in the chest. He responded by covering her face with his hand and shoving her back onto the grass. With a happy shout, Brandon jumped into the fray to climb up his father's back.

Sydney had never envied anything more.

"We can never play without fighting," Natasha said from behind her. She was smiling, looking over Sydney's shoulder at the chaos in her backyard. Her arms still felt the slight weight of the baby she'd just rocked to sleep. "You're wise to watch from a distance."

But when Sydney turned, Natasha saw that her eyes were wet.

"Oh, please." Quickly she moved to Sydney's side to take her hand. "Don't be upset. They don't mean it."

"No. I know." Desperately embarrassed, she blinked the tears back. "I wasn't upset. It was just—it was silly. Watching them was something like looking at a really beautiful painting or hearing some incredibly lovely music. I got carried away."

She didn't need to say more. Natasha understood after Spence's explanation of Sydney's background that there had never been softball games, horseplay or the fun of passionate arguments in her life.

"You love him very much."

Sydney fumbled. That quiet statement wasn't as easy to respond to as Rachel's cocky question had been.

"It's not my business," Natasha continued. "But he is special to me. And I see that you're special to him. You don't find him an easy man."

"No. No, I don't."

Natasha glanced outside again, and her gaze rested on her husband, who was currently wrestling both Freddie and Brandon on the grass. Not so many years before, she thought, she'd been afraid to hope for such things.

"Does he frighten you?"

Sydney started to deny it, then found herself speaking slowly, thoughtfully. "The hugeness of his emotions sometimes frightens me. He has so many, and he finds it so easy to feel them, understand them, express them. I've never been the type to be led by mine, or swept away by them. Sometimes he just overwhelms me, and that's unnerving."

"He is what he feels," Natasha said simply. "Would you like to see some of it?" Without waiting for an answer, she walked over to a wall of shelves.

Lovely carved and painted figures danced across the shelves, some of them so tiny and exquisite it seemed impossible that any hand could have created them.

A miniature house with a gingerbread roof and candy-cane shutters, a high silver tower where a beautiful woman's golden hair streamed from the topmost window, a palm-sized canopy bed where a handsome prince knelt beside a lovely, sleeping princess.

"He brought me this one yesterday." Natasha picked up the painted figure of a woman at a spinning wheel. It sat on a tiny platform scattered with wisps of straw and specks of gold. "The miller's daughter from Rumpelstiltskin." She smiled, tracing the delicate fingertips that rode the spindle.

"They're lovely, all of them. Like a magical world of their own."

"Mikhail has magic," Natasha said. "For me, he carves fairy tales, because I learned English by reading them. Some of his work is more powerful, tragic, erotic, bold, even frightening. But it's always real, because it comes from inside him as much as from the wood or stone."

"I know. What you're trying to show me here is his sensitivity. It's not necessary. I've never known anyone more capable of kindness or compassion."

"I thought perhaps you were afraid he would hurt you."

"No," Sydney said quietly. She thought of the richness of heart it would take to create something as beautiful, as fanciful as the diminutive woman spinning straw into gold. "I'm afraid I'll hurt him."

"Sydney—" But the back door slammed and feet clambered down the hall.

The interruption relieved Sydney. Confiding her feelings was new and far from comfortable. It amazed her that she had done so with a woman she'd known less than a day.

There was something about this family, she realized. Something as magical as the fairy-tale figures Mikhail carved for his sister. Perhaps the magic was as simple as happiness.

As the afternoon wore on, they ebbed and flowed out of the house, noisy, demanding and very often dirty. Nadia eventually cleared the decks by ordering all of the men outside.

"How come they get to go out and sit in the shade with a bottle of beer while we do the cooking," Rachel grumbled as her hands worked quickly, expertly with potatoes and a peeler.

"Because…" Nadia put two dozen eggs on boil. "In here they will pick at the food, get big feet in my way and make a mess."

"Good point. Still—"

"They'll have to clean the mess we make," Natasha told her.

Satisfied, Rachel attacked another potato. Her complaints were only tokens. She was a woman who loved to cook as much as she loved trying a case. "If Vera was here, they wouldn't even do that."

"Our housekeeper," Natasha explained to Sydney while she sliced and chopped a mountain of vegetables. "She's been with us for years. We gave her the month off to take a trip with her sister. Could you wash those grapes?"

Obediently Sydney followed instructions, scrubbing fruit, fetching ingredients, stirring the occasional pot. But she knew very well that three efficient women were working around her.

"You can make deviled eggs," Nadia said kindly when she noted Sydney was at a loss. "They will be cool soon."

"I, ah…" She stared, marginally horrified, at the shiny white orbs she'd rinsed in the sink. "I don't know how."

"Your mama didn't teach you to cook?" It wasn't annoyance in Nadia's voice, just disbelief. Nadia had considered it her duty to teach every one of her children—whether they'd wanted to learn or not.

As far as Sydney knew, Margerite had never boiled an egg much less deviled one. Sydney offered a weak smile. "No, she taught me how to order in restaurants."

Nadia patted her cheek. "When they cool, I show you how to make them the way Mikhail likes best." She murmured in Ukrainian when Katie's waking wail came through the kitchen intercom. On impulse, Natasha shook her head before Nadia could dry her hands and go up to fetch her granddaughter.

"Sydney, would you mind?" With a guileless smile, Natasha turned to her. "My hands are full."

Sydney blinked and stared. "You want me to go get the baby?"

"Please."

More than a little uneasy, Sydney started out of the kitchen.

"What are you up to, Tash?" Rachel wanted to know.

"She wants family."

With a hoot of laughter, Rachel swung an arm around her sister and mother. "She'll get more than her share with this one."

The baby sounded very upset, Sydney thought as she hurried down the hall. She might be sick. What in the world had Natasha been thinking of not coming up to get Katie herself? Maybe when you were the mother of three, you became casual about such things. Taking a deep breath, she walked into the nursery.

Katie, her hair curling damply around her face, was hanging on to the side of the crib and howling. Unsteady legs dipped and straightened as she struggled to keep her balance. One look at Sydney had her tear-drenched face crumpling. She flung out her arms, tilted and landed on her bottom on the bright pink sheet.

"Oh, poor baby," Sydney crooned, too touched to be nervous. "Did you think no one was coming?" She picked the sniffling baby up, and Katie compensated for Sydney's

awkwardness by cuddling trustingly against her body.
"You're so little. Such a pretty little thing." On a shuddering sigh, Katie tipped her head back. "You look like
your uncle, don't you? He got embarrassed when I said he
was gorgeous, but you are."

Downstairs, three women chuckled as Sydney's voice
came clearly through the intercom.

"Oh-oh." After giving the little bottom an affectionate
pat, Sydney discovered a definite problem. "You're wet,
right? Look, I figure your mother could handle this in about
thirty seconds flat—that goes for everybody else downstairs. But everybody else isn't here. So what do we do?"

Katie had stopped sniffling and was blowing bubbles
with her mouth while she tugged on Sydney's hair. "I
guess we'll give it a try. I've never changed a diaper in my
life," she began as she glanced around the room. "Or deviled an egg or played softball, or any damn thing. Whoops.
No swearing in front of the baby. Here we go." She spotted
a diaper bag in bold green stripes. "Oh, God, Katie, they're
real ones."

Blowing out a breath, she took one of the neatly folded
cotton diapers. "Okay, in for a penny, in for a pound. We'll
just put you down on here." Gently she laid Katie on the
changing table and prepared to give the operation her best
shot.

"Hey." Mikhail bounded into the kitchen and was
greeted by three hissing "shhs!"

"What?"

"Sydney's changing Katie," Natasha murmured and
smiled at the sounds flowing through the intercom.

"Sydney?" Mikhail forgot the beer he'd been sent to
fetch and stayed to listen.

"Okay, we're halfway there." Katie's little butt was dry
and powdered. Perhaps a little over powdered, but better to
err on the side of caution, Sydney'd figured. Her brow
creased as she attempted to make the fresh diaper look like

the one she'd removed, sans dampness. "This looks pretty close. What do you think?" Katie kicked her feet and giggled. "You'd be the expert. Okay, this is the tricky part. No wriggling."

Of course, she did. The more she wriggled and kicked, the more Sydney laughed and cuddled. When she'd managed to secure the diaper, Katie looked so cute, smelled so fresh, felt so soft, she had to cuddle some more. Then it seemed only right that she hold Katie up high so the baby could squeal and kick and blow more bubbles.

The diaper sagged but stayed generally where it belonged.

"Okay, gorgeous, now we're set. Want to go down and see Mama?"

"Mama," Katie gurgled, and bounced in Sydney's arms. "Mama."

In the kitchen, four people scattered and tried to look busy or casual.

"Sorry it took so long," she began as she came in. "She was wet." She saw Mikhail and stopped, her cheek pressed against Katie's.

When their eyes met, color washed to her cheeks. The muscles in her thighs went lax. It was no way, no way at all, she thought, for him to be looking at her with his mother and sisters in the room.

"I'll take her." Stepping forward, he held out his arms. Katie stretched into them. Still watching Sydney, he rubbed his cheek over the baby's head and settled her with a natural ease on his hip. "Come here." Before Sydney could respond, he cupped a hand behind her head and pulled her against him for a long, blood-thumping kiss. Well used to such behavior, Katie only bounced and gurgled.

Slowly he slid away, then smiled at her. "I'll come back for the beer." Juggling Katie, he swaggered out, slamming the screen door behind him.

"Now." Nadia took a dazed Sydney by the hands. "You make deviled eggs."

The sun was just setting on the weekend when Sydney unlocked the door of her apartment. She was laughing—and she was sure she'd laughed more in two days than she had in her entire life. She set the packages she carried on the sofa as Mikhail kicked the door closed.

"You put more in here to come back than you had when you left," he accused, and set her suitcase down.

"One or two things." Smiling, she walked over to slip her arms around his waist. It felt good, wonderfully good, especially knowing that his would circle her in response. *"Dyakuyu,"* she said, sampling *thank you* in his language.

"You mangle it, but you're welcome." He kissed both her cheeks. *"This* is the traditional greeting or farewell."

She had to bite the tip of her tongue to hold back the grin. "I know." She also knew why he was telling her—again. She'd been kissed warmly by each member of the family. Not the careless touch of cheek to cheek she was accustomed to, but a firm pressure of lips, accompanied by a full-blooded embrace. Only Alex hadn't settled for her cheeks.

"Your brother kisses very well." Eyes as solemn as she could manage, Sydney touched her lips to Mikhail's cheeks in turn. "It must run in the family."

"You liked it?"

"Well..." She shot Mikhail a look from under her lashes. "He did have a certain style."

"He's a boy," Mikhail muttered, though Alex was less than two years his junior.

"Oh, no." This time a quick laugh bubbled out. "He's definitely not a boy. But I think you have a marginal advantage."

"Marginal."

She linked her hands comfortably behind his neck. "As

a carpenter, you'd know that even a fraction of an inch can
be vital—for fit.''

His hands snagged her hips to settle her against him.
"So, I fit you, Hayward?"

"Yes." She smiled as he touched his lips to her brow.
"It seems you do."

"And you like my kisses better than Alex's?"

She sighed, enjoying the way his mouth felt skimming
down her temples, over her jaw. "Marginally." Her eyes
flew open when he pinched her. "Well, really—"

But that was all she managed to get out before his mouth
closed over hers. She thought of flash fires, ball lightning
and electrical overloads. With a murmur of approval, she
tossed heat back at him.

"Now." Instantly aroused, he scooped her up in his
arms. "I suppose I must prove myself."

Sydney hooked her arms around his neck. "If you insist."

A dozen long strides and he was in the bedroom, where
he dropped her unceremoniously onto the bed. By the time
she had her breath back, he'd yanked off his shirt and
shoes.

"What are you grinning at?" he demanded.

"It's that pirate look again." Still smiling, she brushed
hair out of her eyes. "All you need is a saber and a black
patch."

He hooked his thumbs in frayed belt loops. "So, you
think I'm a barbarian."

She let her gaze slide up his naked torso, over the wild
mane of hair, the stubble that proved he hadn't bothered to
pack a razor for the weekend. To his eyes, those dark, dramatic, dangerous eyes. "I think you're dazzling."

He would have winced but she looked so small and
pretty, sitting on the bed, her hair tumbled from the wind,
her face still flushed from his rough, impatient kiss.

He remembered how she'd looked, walking into the

kitchen, carrying Katie. Her eyes had been full of delight and wonder and shyness. She'd flushed when his mother had announced that Sydney had made the eggs herself. And again, when his father had wrapped her in a bear hug. But Mikhail had seen that she'd hung on, that her fingers had curled into Yuri's shirt, just for an instant.

There were dozens of other flashes of memory. How she'd snuggled the puppy or taken Brandon's hand or stroked Freddie's hair.

She needed love. She was strong and smart and sensible. And she needed love.

Frowning, he sat on the edge of the bed and took her hand. Uneasiness skidded down Sydney's spine.

"What is it? What did I do wrong?"

It wasn't the first time he'd heard that strain of insecurity and doubt in her voice. Biting back the questions and the impatience, he shook his head. "Nothing. It's me." Turning her hand over, he pressed a soft kiss in the center of her palm, then to her wrist where her pulse was beating as quickly from fear as from arousal. "I forget to be gentle with you. To be tender."

She'd hurt his feelings. His ego. She hadn't been responsive enough. Too responsive. Oh, God. "Mikhail, I was only teasing about Alex. I wasn't complaining."

"Maybe you should."

"No." Shifting to her knees, she threw her arms around him and pressed her lips to his. "I want you," she said desperately. "You know how much I want you."

Even as the fire leaped in his gut, he brought his hands lightly to her face, fingers stroking easily. The emotion he poured into the kiss came from the heart only and was filled with sweetness, with kindness, with love.

For a moment, she struggled for the heat, afraid she might never find it. But his mouth was so soft, so patient. As her urgency turned to wonder, his lips rubbed over hers. And the friction sparked not the familiar flash fire, but a warm glow, golden, so quietly beautiful her throat ached with it. Even when he took the kiss deeper, deeper, there was only tenderness. Weakened by it, her body melted like wax. Her hands slid limp and useless from his shoulders in total surrender.

"Beautiful. So beautiful," he murmured as he laid her back on the bed, emptying her mind, stirring her soul with long, drowning kisses. "I should be shot for showing you only one way."

"I can't..." Think, breathe, move.

"Shh." Gently, with an artist's touch, he undressed her. "Tonight is only for you. Only to enjoy." His breath caught as the dying sunlight glowed over her skin. She looked too fragile to touch. Too lovely not to. "Let me show you what you are to me."

Everything. She was everything. After tonight he wanted her to have no doubt of it. With slow, worshipful hands, he showed her that beyond passion, beyond desire, was a merging of spirits. A generosity of the soul.

Love could be peaceful, selfless, enduring.

Her body was a banquet, fragrant, dazzling with erotic flavors. But tonight, he sampled slowly, savoring, sharing. Each sigh, each shudder filled him with gratitude that she was his.

He wouldn't allow her to race. Helpless to resist, she floated down the long, dark river where he guided her through air the essence of silk. Never, not even during their most passionate joining, had she been so aware of her own body. Her own texture and shape and scent. And his. Oh, Lord, and his.

Those rock-hard muscles and brute strength now channeled into unimagined gentleness. The subtlety of movement elicited new longings, fresh knowledge and a symphony of understanding that was exquisite in its harmony.

Let me give you. Let me show you. Let me take.

Sensitive fingertips traced over her, lingering to arouse,

moving on to seek out some new shattering pleasure. And from her pleasure came his own, just as sweet, just as staggering, just as simple.

She could hear her own breathing, a quiet, trembling sound as the room deepened with night. A tribute to beauty, tears dampened her cheeks and thickened her voice when she spoke his name.

His mouth covered hers again as at last he slipped inside her. Enfolded in her, cradled by her, he trembled under the long, sighing sweep of sensation. Her mouth opened beneath his, her arms lifted, circled, held.

More. He remembered that he had once fought desperately for more. Now, with her, he had all.

Even with hot hammers of need pounding at him, he moved slowly, knowing he could take her soaring again and again before that last glorious release.

"I love you, Sydney." His muscles trembled as he felt her rise to meet him. "Only you. Always you."

Chapter Eleven

When the phone rang, it was pitch-dark and they were sleeping, tangled together like wrestling children. Sydney snuggled closer to Mikhail, squeezing her eyes tighter and muttered a single no, determined to ignore it.

With a grunt, Mikhail rolled over her, seriously considered staying just as he was as her body curved deliciously to his.

"Milaya," he murmured, then with an oath, snatched the shrilling phone off the hook.

"What?" Because Sydney was pounding on his shoulder, he shifted off her. "Alexi?" The sound of his brother's voice had him sitting straight up, firing off in Ukrainian. Only when Alex assured him there was nothing wrong with the family did the sick panic fade. "You'd better be in the hospital or jail. Neither?" He sat back, rapped his head on the brass poles of the headboard and swore again. "Why are you calling in the middle of the night?" Rubbing his hand over his face, Mikhail gave Sydney's clock a vicious stare. The glowing dial read 4:45. "What?" Struggling to tune in, he shifted the phone to his other ear. "Damn it, when? I'll be there."

He slammed the phone down and was already up searching for his clothes when he realized Sydney has turned on the light. Her face was dead pale.

"Your parents."

"No, no, it's not the family." He sat on the bed again to take her hand. "It's the apartment. Vandals."

The sharp edge of fear dulled to puzzlement. "Vandals?"

"One of the cops who answered the call knows Alex, and that I live there, so he called him. There's been some damage."

"To the building." Her heart was beginning to pound, heavy and slow, in her throat.

"Yes, no one was hurt." He watched her eyes close in relief at that before she nodded. "Spray paint, broken windows." He bit off an oath. "Two of the empty apartments were flooded. I'm going to go see what has to be done."

"Give me ten minutes," Sydney said and sprang out of bed.

It hurt. It was only brick and wood and glass, but it hurt her to see it marred. Filthy obscenities were scrawled in bright red paint across the lovely old brownstone. Three of the lower windows were shattered. Inside, someone had used a knife to gouge the railings and hack at the plaster.

In Mrs. Wolburg's apartment water was three inches deep over the old hardwood floor, ruining her rugs, soaking the skirts of her sofa. Her lacy doilies floated like soggy lily pads.

"They clogged up the sinks," Alex explained. "By the time they broke the windows downstairs and woke anyone up, the damage here was pretty much done."

Yes, the damage was done, Sydney thought. But it wasn't over. "The other unit?"

"Up on two. Empty. They did a lot of painting up there, too." He gave Sydney's arm a squeeze. "I'm sorry. We're getting statements from the tenants, but—"

"It was dark," Sydney finished. "Everyone was asleep, and no one's going to have seen anything."

"Nothing's impossible." Alex turned toward the babble of voices coming from the lobby, where most of the tenants had gathered. "Why don't you go on up to Mikhail's place? It's going to take a while to calm everyone down and clear them out."

"No, it's my building. I'd like to go talk to them."

With a nod, he started to lead her down the hall. "Funny they didn't bother to steal anything—and that they only broke into the two empty apartments."

She slanted him a look. He might not have been wearing his uniform, but he was definitely a cop. "Is this an interrogation, Alex?"

"Just an observation. I guess you'd know who had access to the tenants' list."

"I guess I would," she replied. "I have a pretty fair idea who's responsible, Alex." She touched a hand to the ruined banister. "Oh, not who tossed paint or flooded the rooms, but who arranged it. But I don't know if I'll be able to prove it."

"You leave the proving up to us."

She glanced at the streak of paint along the wall. "Would you?" She shook her head before he could reply. "Once I'm sure, I'll turn everything over to you. That's a promise—if you promise to say nothing to Mikhail."

"That's a tough bargain, Sydney."

"I'm a tough lady," she said steadily, and walked down to talk to her tenants.

By eight o'clock she was in her office poring over every word in Lloyd Bingham's personnel file. By ten, she'd made several phone calls, consumed too many cups of coffee and had a structured plan.

She'd authorized Mikhail to hire more men, had spoken with the insurance investigator personally and was now prepared for a little psychological warfare.

She put the call through to Lloyd Bingham herself and waited three rings.

"Hello."

"Lloyd, Sydney Hayward."

She heard the rasp of a lighter. "Got a problem?"

"Not that can't be fixed. It was really a very pitiful gesture, Lloyd."

"I don't know what you're talking about."

"Of course you don't." The sarcasm was brisk, almost careless. "Next time, I'd suggest you do more thorough research."

"You want to come to the point?"

"The point is my building, my tenants and your mistake."

"It's a little early in the day for puzzles." The smug satisfaction in his voice had her fingers curling.

"It's not a puzzle when the solution is so clear. I don't imagine you were aware of just how many service people live in the building. And how early some of those service people get up in the morning, have their coffee, glance out the window. Or how cooperative those people would be in giving descriptions to the police."

"If something happened to your building, that's your problem." He drew hard on his cigarette. "I haven't been near it."

"I never thought you had been," she said easily. "You've always been good at delegating. But once certain parties are picked up by the police, I think you'll discover how unsettling it is not to have loyal employees."

She could have sworn she heard him sweat. "I don't have to listen to this."

"No, of course you don't. And I won't keep you. Oh,

Lloyd, don't let them talk you into a bonus. They didn't do a very thorough job. Ciao.''

She hung up, immensely satisfied. If she knew her quarry, he wouldn't wait long to meet with his hirelings and pay them off. And since the investigator had been very interested in Sydney's theory, she doubted that meeting would go unobserved.

She flicked her intercom. ''Janine, I need food before we start interviewing the new secretaries. Order anything the deli says looks good today and double it.''

''You got it. I was about to buzz you, Sydney. Your mother's here.''

The little bubble of success burst in her throat. ''Tell her I'm…'' *Coward.* ''No, tell her to come in.'' But she took a deep breath before she rose and walked to the door. ''Mother.''

''Sydney, dear.'' Lovely in ivory linen and smelling of Paris, she strolled in and bussed Sydney's cheek. ''I'm so sorry.''

''I—what?''

''I've had to wait all weekend to contact you and apologize.'' Margerite took a steadying breath herself, twisting her envelope bag in her hands. ''May I sit?''

''Of course. I'm sorry. Would you like anything?''

''To completely erase Friday evening from my life.'' Seated, Margerite gave her daughter an embarrassed glance. ''This isn't easy for me, Sydney. The simple fact is, I was jealous.''

''Oh, Mother.''

''No, please.'' Margerite waved her daughter to the chair beside her. ''I don't enjoy the taste of crow and hope you'll let me get it done in one large swallow.''

As embarrassed as her mother, Sydney sat and reached for her hand. ''It isn't necessary that you swallow at all. We'll just forget it.''

Margerite shook her head. ''I hope I'm big enough to

admit my failings. I like thinking I'm still an attractive and desirable woman.''

"You are."

Margerite smiled fleetingly. ''But certainly not an admirable one when I find myself eaten up with envy to see that a man I'd hoped to, well, enchant, was instead enchanted by my daughter. I regret, very much, my behavior and my words. There,'' she said on a puff of breath. ''Will you forgive me?''

"Of course I will. And I'll apologize, too, for speaking to you the way I did.''

Margerite took a little square of lace from her bag and dabbed at her eyes. ''You surprised me, I admit. I've never seen you so passionate about anything. He's a beautiful man, dear. I won't say I approve of a relationship between you, but I can certainly understand it.'' She sighed as she tucked the handkerchief back into her bag. ''Your happiness is important to me, Sydney.''

"I know that.''

Her eyes still glistened when she looked at her daughter. ''I'm so glad we cleared the air. And I want to do something for you, something to make up for all of this.''

"You don't have to do anything.''

"I want to, really. Have dinner with me tonight.''

Sydney thought of the dozens of things she had to do, of the quiet meal she'd hoped for at the end of it all with Mikhail. Then she looked at her mother's anxious eyes. ''I'd love to.''

"Wonderful.'' The spring was back in her step as Margerite got to her feet. ''Eight o'clock. Le Cirque.'' She gave Sydney a quick and genuine hug before she strolled out.

By eight, Sydney would have preferred a long, solitary nap, but stepped from her car dressed for the evening in a sleeveless silk jumpsuit of icy blue.

"My mother's driver will take me home, Donald.''

"Very good, Ms. Hayward. Enjoy your evening."

"Thank you."

The maître d' recognized her the moment she walked in d gracefully led her to her table himself. As she passed rough the elegant restaurant filled with sparkling people d exotic scents, she imagined Mikhail, sitting at his arred workbench with a bottle of beer and a bowl of ulash.

She tried not to sigh in envy.

When she spotted her mother—with Channing—at the rner table, she tried not to grit her teeth.

"There you are, darling." So certain her surprise was st what her daughter needed, Margerite didn't notice the ghts of war in Sydney's eyes. "Isn't this lovely?"

"Lovely." Sydney's voice was flat as Channing rose to ll out her chair. She said nothing when he bent close to ss her cheek.

"You look beautiful tonight, Sydney."

The champagne was already chilled and open. She aited while hers was poured, but the first sip did nothing clear the anger from her throat. "Mother didn't mention u'd be joining us tonight."

"That was my surprise," Margerite bubbled like the ine in her glass. "My little make-up present." Following prearranged signal, she set her napkin aside and rose. I'm sure you two will excuse me while I powder my se."

Knowing he only had fifteen minutes to complete his ission, Channing immediately took Sydney's hand. "I've issed you, darling. It seems like weeks since I've had a oment alone with you."

Skillfully Sydney slipped her hand from him. "It has en weeks. How have you been, Channing?"

"Desolate without you." He skimmed a fingertip up her are arm. She really had exquisite skin. "When are we ing to stop playing these games, Sydney?"

"I haven't been playing." She took a sip of wine. "I'
been working."

A trace of annoyance clouded his eyes then cleared. I
was sure Margerite was right. Once they were married, s
would be too busy with him to bother with a career. It w
best to get right to the point. "Darling, we've been seein
each other for months now. And of course, we've know
each other for years. But things have changed."

She met his eyes. "Yes, they have."

Encouraged, he took her hand again. "I haven't wante
to rush you, but I feel it's time we take the next step. I ca
for you very much, Sydney. I find you lovely and amusin
and sweet."

"And suitable," she muttered.

"Of course. I want you to be my wife." He slipped
box from his pocket, opened the lid so that the round i
diamond could flash in the candlelight.

"Channing—"

"It reminded me of you," he interrupted. "Regal an
elegant."

"It's beautiful, Channing," she said carefully. And col
she thought. So very cold. "And I'm sorry, but I car
accept it. Or you."

Shock came first, then a trickle of annoyance. "Sydne
we're both adults. There's no need to be coy."

"What I'm trying to be is honest." She shifted in h
chair, and this time it was she who took his hands. "I can
tell you how sorry I am that my mother led you to believ
I'd feel differently. By doing so, she's put us both in a
embarrassing position. Let's be candid, Channing. Yo
don't love me, and I don't love you."

Insulted, he pokered up. "I hardly think I'd be offerin
marriage otherwise."

"You're offering it because you find me attractive, yo
think I'd make an excellent hostess, and because I con
from the same circle as you. Those are reasons for

merger, not a marriage." She closed the lid on the diamond and pressed the box into his hands. "I make a poor wife, Channing, that much I know. And I have no intention of becoming one again."

He relaxed a little. "I understand you might still be a bit raw over what happened between you and Peter."

"No, you don't understand at all what happened between me and Peter. To be honest, that has nothing to do with my refusing you. I don't love you, Channing, and I'm very much in love with someone else."

His fair skin flushed dark red. "Then I find it worse than insulting that you would pretend an affection for me."

"I do have an affection for you," she said wearily. "But that's all I have. I can only apologize if I failed to make that clear before this."

"I don't believe an apology covers it, Sydney." Stiffly he rose to his feet. "Please give my regrets to your mother."

Straight as a poker, he strode out, leaving Sydney alone with a miserable mix of temper and guilt. Five minutes later, Margerite came out of the ladies' room, beaming. "Well now." She leaned conspiratorially toward her daughter, pleased to see that Channing had given them a few moments alone. "Tell me everything."

"Channing's gone, Mother."

"Gone?" Bright eyed, Margerite glanced around. "What do you mean gone?"

"I mean he's left, furious, I might add, because I declined his proposal of marriage."

"Declined?" Margerite blinked. "You— Sydney, how could you?"

"How could I?" Her voice rose and, catching herself, she lowered it to a whisper. "How could you? You set this entire evening up."

"Of course I did." Frazzled, Margerite waved the on-coming waiter away and reached for her wine. "I've

planned for months to see you and Channing together. An
since it was obvious that Mikhail had brought you out c
your shell, the timing was perfect. Channing is exactly wha
you need. He's eligible, his family is above reproach, h
has a beautiful home and excellent bearing.''

''I don't love him.''

''Sydney, for heaven's sake, be sensible.''

''I've never been anything else, and perhaps that's bee
the problem. I believed you when you came to see me thi
morning. I believed you were sorry, that you cared, an
that you wanted something more than polite words betwee
us.''

Margerite's eyes filled. ''Everything I said this mornin
was true. I'd been miserable all weekend, thinking I'
driven you away. You're my daughter, I do care. I war
what's best for you.''

''You mean it,'' Sydney murmured, suddenly, unbear
ably weary. ''But you also believe that you know what'
best for me. I don't mean to hurt you, but I've come t
understand you've never known what's best for me. B
doing this tonight, you caused me to hurt Channing in
way I never meant to.''

A tear spilled over. ''Sydney, I only thought—''

''Don't think for me.'' She was perilously close to tear
herself. ''Don't ever think for me again. I let you do tha
before, and I ruined someone's life.''

''I don't want you to be alone,'' Margerite choked out
''It's hateful being alone.''

''Mother.'' Though she was afraid she might weaken too
much, too soon, she took Margerite's hands. ''Listen to me
listen carefully. I love you, but I can't be you. I want t
know that we can have an honest, caring relationship. It'l
take time. But it can't ever happen unless you try to un
derstand me, unless you respect me for who I am, and no
for what you want me to be. I can't marry Channing t
please you. I can't marry anyone.''

"Oh, Sydney."

"There are things you don't know. Things I don't want to talk about. Just please trust me. I know what I'm doing. I've been happier in the last few weeks than I've ever been."

"Stanislaski," Margerite said on a sigh.

"Yes, Stanislaski. And Hayward," she added. "And me. I'm doing something with my life, Mother. It's making a difference. Now let's go fix your makeup and start over."

At his workbench, Mikhail polished the rosewood bust. He hadn't meant to work so late, but Sydney had simply emerged in his hands. There was no way to explain the way it felt to have her come to life there. It wasn't powerful. It was humbling. He'd barely had to think. Though his fingers were cramped, proving how long he had carved and sanded and polished, he could barely remember the technique he'd used.

The tools didn't matter, only the result. Now she was here with him, beautiful, warm, alive. And he knew it was a piece he would never part with.

Sitting back, he circled his shoulders to relieve the stiffness. It had been a viciously long day, starting before dawn. He'd had to channel the edge of his rage into organizing the cleaning up and repair the worst of the damage. Now that the impetus that had driven him to complete the bust was passed, he was punchy with fatigue. But he didn't want to go to bed. An empty bed.

How could he miss her so much after only hours? Why did it feel as though she were a world away when she was only at the other end of the city? He wasn't going to go through another night without her, he vowed as he stood up to pace. She was going to have to understand that. He would make her understand that. A woman had no right to make herself vital to a man's existence then leave him restless and alone at midnight.

Dragging a hand through his hair, he considered his options. He could go to bed and will himself to sleep. He could call her and satisfy himself with the sound of her voice. Or he could go uptown and beat on her door until she let him in.

He grinned, liking the third choice best. Snatching up shirt, he tugged it on as he headed for the door. Sydney gave a surprised gasp as he yanked it open just as her hand was poised to knock.

"Oh. What instincts." She pressed the hand to her heart. "I'm sorry to come by so late, but I saw your light was on, so I—"

He didn't let her finish, but pulled her inside and held her until she wondered her ribs didn't crack. "I was coming for you," he muttered.

"Coming for me? I just left the restaurant."

"I wanted you. I wanted to—" He broke off and snapped her back. "It's after midnight. What are you doing coming all the way downtown after midnight?"

"For heaven's sake—"

"It's not safe for a woman alone."

"I was perfectly safe."

He shook his head, cupping her chin. "Next time, you call. I'll come to you." Then his eyes narrowed. An artist's eyes, a lover's eyes saw beyond carefully repaired makeup. "You've been crying."

There was such fury in the accusation, she had to laugh. "No, not really. Mother got a bit emotional, and there was a chain reaction."

"I thought you said you'd made up with her."

"I did. I have. At least I think we've come to a better understanding."

He smiled a little, tracing a finger over Sydney's lips. "She does not approve of me for her daughter."

"That's not really the problem. I'm afraid she's feeling

little worn down. She had her plans blow up in her face onight.''

"You'll tell me."

"Yes." She walked over, intending to collapse on his adly sprung couch. But she saw the bust. Slowly she moved closer to study it. When she spoke, her voice was ow and thick. "You have an incredible talent."

"I carve what I see, what I know, what I feel."

"Is this how you see me?"

"It's how you are." He laid his hands lightly on her houlders. "For me."

Then she was beautiful for him, Sydney thought. And he was trembling with life and love, for him. "I didn't even pose for you."

"You will." He brushed his lips over her hair. "Talk to me."

"When I met Mother at the restaurant, Channing was with her."

Over Sydney's head, Mikhail's eyes darkened dangerously. "The banker with the silk suits. You let him kiss you before you let me."

"I knew him before I knew you." Amused, Sydney urned and looked jealousy in the eye. "And I didn't let you kiss me, as I recall. You just did."

He did so again, ruthlessly. "You won't let him again."

"No."

"Good." He drew her to the sofa. "Then he can live."

With a laugh, she threw her arms around him for a hug, hen settled her head on his shoulder. "None of it's his fault, really. Or my mother's, either. It's more a matter of habit and circumstance. She'd set up the evening after persuading Channing that the time was ripe to propose."

"Propose?" Mikhail spun her around to face him. "He wants to marry you?"

"Not really. He thought he did. He certainly doesn't want to marry me anymore." But he was shoving her out

of the way so he could get up and pace. "There's no reaso
to be angry," Sydney said as she smoothed down her jump
suit. "I was the one in the awkward position. As it is
doubt he'll speak to me again."

"If he does, I'll cut out his tongue." Slowly, Mikhai
thought, working up the rage. "No one marries you bu
me."

"I've already explained..." She trailed off as breat
lodged in a hard ball in her throat. "There's really no nee
to go into this," she managed as she rose. "It's late."

"You wait," Mikhail ordered and strode into the bed
room. When he came back carrying a small box, Sydney'
blood turned to ice. "Sit."

"No, Mikhail, please—"

"Then stand." He flipped open the top of the box t
reveal a ring of hammered gold with a small center ston
of fiery red. "The grandfather of my father made this fo
his wife. He was a goldsmith so the work is fine, even
though the stone is small. It comes to me because I am th
oldest son. If it doesn't please you, I buy you somethin
else."

"No, it's beautiful. Please, don't. I can't." She held he
fisted hands behind her back. "Don't ask me."

"I am asking you," he said impatiently. "Give me you
hand."

She took a step back. "I can't wear the ring. I can'
marry you."

With a shake of his head, he pulled her hand free and
pushed the ring on her finger. "See, you can wear it. It'
too big, but we'll fix it."

"No." She would have pulled it off again, but he closed
his hand over hers. "I don't want to marry you."

His fingers tightened on hers, and a fire darted into hi
eyes, more brilliant than the shine of the ruby. "Why?"

"I don't want to get married," she said as clearly as sh
could. "I won't have what we started together spoiled."

"Marriage doesn't spoil love, it nurtures it."

"You don't know," she snapped back. "You've never been married. I have. And I won't go through it again."

"So." Struggling with temper, he rocked back on his heels. "This husband of yours hurt you, makes you unhappy, so you think I'll do the same."

"Damn it, I loved him." Her voice broke, and she covered her face with her hand as the tears began to fall.

Torn between jealousy and misery, he gathered her close, murmuring endearments as he stroked her hair. "I'm sorry."

"You don't understand."

"Let me understand." He tilted her face up to kiss the tears. "I'm sorry," he repeated. "I won't yell at you anymore."

"It's not that." She let out a shuddering breath. "I don't want to hurt you. Please, let this go."

"I can't let this go. Or you. I love you, Sydney. I need you. For my life I need you. Explain to me why you won't take me."

"If there was anyone," she began in a rush, then shook her head before she could even wish it. "Mikhail, I can't consider marriage. Hayward is too much of a responsibility, and I need to focus on my career."

"This is smoke, to hide the real answer."

"All right." Bracing herself, she stepped away from him. "I don't think I could handle failing again, and losing someone I love. Marriage changes people."

"How did it change you?"

"I loved Peter, Mikhail. Not the way I love you, but more than anyone else. He was my best friend. We grew up together. When my parents divorced, he was the only one I could talk to. He cared, really cared, about how I felt, what I thought, what I wanted. We could sit for hours on the beach up at the Hamptons and watch the water, tell each other secrets."

She turned away. Saying it all out loud brought the pain spearing back.

"And you fell in love."

"No," she said miserably. "We just loved each other. I can hardly remember a time without him. And I can't remember when it started to become a given that we'd marry someday. Not that we talked about it ourselves. Everyone else did. Sydney and Peter, what a lovely couple they make. Isn't it nice how well they suit? I suppose we heard it so much, we started to believe it. Anyway, it was expected, and we'd both been raised to do what was expected of us."

She brushed at tears and wandered over to his shelves. "You were right when you gave me that figure of Cinderella. I've always followed the rules. I was expected to go to boarding school and get top grades. So I did. I was expected to behave presentably, never to show unacceptable emotions. So I did. I was expected to marry Peter. So I did."

She whirled back. "There we were, both of us just turned twenty-two—quite an acceptable age for marriage. I suppose we both thought it would be fine. After all, we'd known each other forever, we liked the same things, understood each other. Loved each other. But it wasn't fine. Almost from the beginning. Honeymooning in Greece. We both loved the country. And we both pretended that the physical part of marriage was fine. Of course, it was anything but fine, and the more we pretended, the further apart we became. We moved back to New York so he could take his place in the family business. I decorated the house, gave parties. And dreaded watching the sun go down."

"It was a mistake," Mikhail said gently.

"Yes, it was. One I made, one I was responsible for. I lost my closest friend, and before it was over, all the love was gone. There were only arguments and accusations. I was frigid, why shouldn't he have turned to someone else for a little warmth? But we kept up appearances. That was expected. And when we divorced, we did so in a very cold, very controlled, very civilized manner. I couldn't be a wife to him, Mikhail.''

"It's not the same for us." He went to her.

"No, it's not. And I won't let it be."

"You're hurt because of something that happened to you, not something you did." He caught her face in his hands when she shook her head. "Yes. You need to let go of it, and trust what we have. I'll give you time."

"No." Desperate, she clamped her hands on his wrists. "Don't you see it's the same thing? You love me, so you expect me to marry you, because that's what you want—what you think is best."

"Not best," he said, giving her a quick shake. "Right. I need to share my life with you. I want to live with you, make babies with you. Watch them grow. There's a family inside us, Sydney."

She jerked away. He wouldn't listen, she thought. He wouldn't understand. "Marriage and family aren't in my plans," she said, suddenly cold. "You're going to have to accept that."

"Accept? You love me. I'm good enough for that. Good enough for you to take to your bed, but not for changing plans. All because you once followed rules instead of your heart."

"What I'm following now is my common sense." She walked by him to the door. "I'm sorry, I can't give you what you want."

"You will not go home alone."

"I think it'll be better if I leave."

"You want to leave, you leave." He stalked over to wrench the door open. "But I'll take you."

It wasn't until she lay teary and fretful in her bed that she realized she still wore his ring.

Chapter Twelve

It wasn't that she buried herself in work over the next two days, it was that work buried her. Sydney only wished it had helped. Keeping busy was supposed to be good for the morale. So why was hers flat on its face?

She closed the biggest deal of her career at Hayward, hired a new secretary to take the clerical weight off Janine and handled a full-staff meeting. Hayward stock had climbed three full points in the past ten days. The board was thrilled with her.

And she was miserable.

"An Officer Stanislaski on two, Ms. Hayward," her new secretary said through the intercom.

"Stan—oh." Her spirits did a jig, then settled. *Officer.* "Yes, I'll take it. Thank you." Sydney pasted on a smile for her own peace of mind. "Alex?"

"Hey, pretty lady. Thought you'd want to be the first to know. They just brought your old pal Lloyd Bingham in for questioning."

Her smiled faded. "I see."

"The insurance investigator took your advice and kept an eye on him. He met with a couple of bad numbers yesterday, passed some bills. Once they were picked up, they sang better than Springsteen."

"Then Lloyd did hire someone to vandalize the building."

"So they say. I don't think you're going to have any trouble from him for a while."

"I'm glad to hear it."

"You were pretty sharp, homing in on him. Brains and beauty," he said with a sigh that nearly made her smile again. "Why don't we take off to Jamaica for a couple of days? Drive Mikhail crazy?"

"I think he's already mad enough."

"Hey, he's giving you a hard time? Just come to Uncle Alex." When she didn't respond, the teasing note dropped out of his voice. "Don't mind Mik, Sydney. He's got moods, that's all. It's the artist. He's nuts about you."

"I know." Her fingers worried the files on her desk. "Maybe you could give him a call, tell him the news."

"Sure. Anything else you want me to pass on?"

"Tell him...no," she decided. "No, I've already told him. Thanks for calling, Alex."

"No problem. Let me know if you change your mind about Jamaica."

She hung up, wishing she felt as young as Alex had sounded. As happy. As easy. But then Alex wasn't in love. And he hadn't punched a hole in his own dreams.

Is that what she'd done? Sydney wondered as she pushed away from her desk. Had she sabotaged her own yearnings? No, she'd stopped herself, and the man she loved from making a mistake. Marriage wasn't always the answer. She had her own example to prove it. And her mother's. Once Mikhail had cooled off, he'd accept her position, and they could go on as they had before.

Who was she kidding?

He was too stubborn, too bullheaded, too damn sure his way was the right way to back down for an instant.

And what if he said all or nothing? What would she do then? Snatching up a paper clip, she began to twist it as she paced the office. If it was a matter of giving him up and losing him, or giving in and risking losing him...

God, she needed someone to talk to. Since it couldn't be Mikhail, she was left with pitifully few choices. Once she would have taken her problems to Peter, but that was...

She stopped, snapping the mangled metal in her fingers. That was the source of the problem. And maybe, just maybe, the solution.

Without giving herself time to think, she rushed out of her office and into Janine's. "I have to leave town for a couple of days," she said without preamble.

Janine was already rising from behind her new desk. "But—"

"I know it's sudden, and inconvenient, but it can't be helped. There's nothing vital pending at the moment, so you should be able to handle whatever comes in. If you can't, then it has to wait."

"Sydney, you have three appointments tomorrow."

"You take them. You have the files, you have my viewpoint. As soon as I get to where I'm going, I'll call in."

"But, Sydney." Janine scurried to the door as Sydney strode away. "Where are you going?"

"To see an old friend."

Less than an hour after Sydney had rushed from her office, Mikhail stormed in. He'd had it. He'd given the woman two days to come to her senses, and she was out of time. They were going to have this out and have it out now.

He breezed by the new secretary with a curt nod and pushed open Sydney's door.

"Excuse me. Sir, excuse me."

Mikhail whirled on the hapless woman. "Where the hell is she?"

"Ms. Hayward is not in the office," she said primly. "I'm afraid you'll have to—"

"If not here, where?"

"I'll handle this, Carla," Janine murmured from the doorway.

"Yes, ma'am." Carla made her exit quickly and with relief.

"Ms. Hayward's not here, Mr. Stanislaski. Is there something I can do for you?"

"Tell me where she is."

"I'm afraid I can't." The look in his eyes had her backing up a step. "I only know she's out of town for a day or two. She left suddenly and didn't tell me where she was going."

"Out of town?" He scowled at the empty desk, then back at Janine. "She doesn't leave her work like this."

"I admit it's unusual. But I got the impression it was important. I'm sure she'll call in. I'll be happy to give her a message for you."

He said something short and hard in Ukrainian and stormed out again.

"I think I'd better let you tell her that yourself," Janine murmured to the empty room.

Twenty-four hours after leaving her office, Sydney stood on a shady sidewalk in Georgetown, Washington, D.C. A headlong rush of adrenaline had brought her this far, far enough to have her looking at the home where Peter had settled when he'd relocated after the divorce.

The impulsive drive to the airport, the quick shuttle from city to city had been easy enough. Even the phone call to request an hour of Peter's time hadn't been so difficult. But this, this last step was nearly impossible.

She hadn't seen him in over three years, and then it had

been across a wide table in a lawyer's office. Civilized, God, yes, they'd been civilized. And strangers.

It was foolish, ridiculous, taking off on this kind of tangent. Talking to Peter wouldn't change anything. Nothing could. Yet she found herself climbing the stairs to the porch of the lovely old row house, lifting the brass knocker and letting it rap on the door.

He answered himself, looking so much the same that she nearly threw out her hands to him as she would have done once. He was tall and leanly built, elegantly casual in khakis and a linen shirt. His sandy hair was attractively rumpled. But the green eyes didn't light with pleasure, instead remaining steady and cool.

"Sydney," he said, backing up to let her inside.

The foyer was cool and light, speaking subtly in its furnishings and artwork of discreet old money. "I appreciate you seeing me like this, Peter."

"You said it was important."

"To me."

"Well, then." Knowing nothing else to say, he ushered her down the hall and into a sitting room. Manners sat seamlessly on both of them, causing her to make the right comments about the house, and him to parry them while offering her a seat and a drink.

"You're enjoying Washington, then."

"Very much." He sipped his own wine while she simply turned her glass around and around in her hand. She was nervous. He knew her too well not to recognize the signs. And she was as lovely as ever. It hurt. He hated the fact that it hurt just to look at her. And the best way to get past the pain was to get to the point.

"What is it I can do for you, Sydney?"

Strangers, she thought again as she looked down at her glass. They had known each other all of their lives, had been married for nearly three years, and were strangers. "It's difficult to know where to start."

He leaned back in his chair and gestured. "Pick a spot."

"Peter, why did you marry me?"

"I beg your pardon."

"I want to know why you married me."

Whatever he'd been expecting, it hadn't been this. Shifting, he drank again. "For several of the usual reasons, I suppose."

"You loved me?"

His eyes flashed to hers. "You know I loved you."

"I know we loved each other. You were my friend." She pressed her lips together. "My best friend."

He got up to pour more wine. "We were children."

"Not when we married. We were young, but we weren't children. And we were still friends. I don't know how it all went so wrong, Peter, or what I did to ruin it so completely, but—"

"You?" He stared, the bottle in one hand, the glass in the other. "What do you mean *you* ruined it?"

"I made you unhappy, miserably unhappy. I know I failed in bed, and it all spilled over into the rest until you couldn't even bear to be around me."

"You didn't want me to touch you," he shot back. "Damn it, it was like making love to—"

"An iceberg," she finished flatly. "So you said."

Fighting guilt, he set his glass down. "I said a lot of things, so did you. I thought I'd gotten past most of it until I heard your voice this afternoon."

"I'm sorry." She rose, her body and voice stiff to compensate for shattered pride. "I've just made it worse coming here. I am sorry, Peter, I'll go."

"It was like making love with my sister." The words burst out and stopped her before she crossed the room. "My pal. Damn, Sydney, I couldn't…" The humiliation of it clawed at him again. "I could never get beyond that, and make you, well, a wife. It unmanned me. And I took it out on you."

"I thought you hated me."

He slapped the bottle back on the table. "It was easier to try to hate you than admit I couldn't arouse either one of us. That I was inadequate."

"But I was." Baffled, she took a step toward him. "I know I was useless to you in bed—before you told me, I knew it. And you had to go elsewhere for what I couldn't give you."

"I cheated on you," he said flatly. "I lied and cheated my closest friend. I hated the way you'd started to look at me, the way I started to look at myself. So I went out to prove my manhood elsewhere, and hurt you. When you found out, I did the manly thing and turned the blame on you. Hell, Sydney, we were barely speaking to each other by that time. Except in public."

"I know. And I remember how I reacted, the hateful things I said to you. I let pride cost me a friend."

"I lost a friend, too. I've never been sorrier for anything in my life." It cost him to walk to her, to take her hand. "You didn't ruin anything, Syd. At least not alone."

"I need a friend, Peter. I very badly need a friend."

He brushed a tear away with his thumb. "Willing to give me another shot?" Smiling a little, he took out his handkerchief. "Here. Blow your nose and sit down."

She did, clinging to his hand. "Was that the only reason it didn't work. Because we couldn't handle the bedroom?"

"That was a big one. Other than that, we're too much alike. It's too easy for us to step behind breeding and let a wound bleed us dry. Hell, Syd, what were we doing getting married?"

"Doing what everyone told us."

"There you go."

Comforted, she brought his hand to her cheek. "Are you happy, Peter?"

"I'm getting there. How about you? President Hayward."

She laughed. "Were you surprised?"

"Flabbergasted. I was so proud of you."

"Don't. You'll make me cry again."

"I've got a better idea." He kissed her forehead. "Come out in the kitchen. I'll fix us a sandwich and you can tell me what you've been up to besides big business."

It was almost easy. There was some awkwardness, little patches of caution, but the bond that had once held them together had stretched instead of broken. Slowly, carefully, they were easing the tension on it.

Over rye bread and coffee, she tried to tell him the rest. "Have you ever been in love, Peter?"

"Marsha Rosenbloom."

"That was when we were fourteen."

"And she'd already given up a training bra," he said with his mouth full. "I was deeply in love." Then he smiled at her. "No, I've escaped that particular madness."

"If you were, if you found yourself in love with someone, would you consider marriage again?"

"I don't know. I'd like to think I'd do a better job of it, but I don't know. Who is he?"

Stalling, she poured more coffee. "He's an artist. A carpenter."

"Which?"

"Both. He sculpts, and he builds. I've only known him a little while, just since June."

"Moving quick, Sydney?"

"I know. That's part of the problem. Everything moves fast with Mikhail. He's so bold and sure and full of emotion. Like his work, I suppose."

As two and two began to make four, his brows shot up. "The Russian?"

"Ukrainian," she corrected automatically.

"Good God, Stanislaski, right? There's a piece of his in the White House."

"Is there?" She gave Peter a bemused smile. "He didn't

mention it. He took me home to meet his family, this wonderful family, but he didn't tell me his work's in the White House. It shows you where his priorities lie."

"And you're in love with him."

"Yes. He wants to marry me." She shook her head. "I got two proposals in the same night. One from Mikhail, and one from Channing Warfield."

"Lord, Sydney, not Channing. He's not your type."

She shoved the coffee aside to lean closer. "Why?"

"In the first place he's nearly humorless. He'd bore you mindless. The only thing he knows about Daddy's business is how to take clients to lunch. And his only true love is his tailor."

She really smiled. "I've missed you, Peter."

He took her hand again. "What about your big, bold artist?"

"He doesn't have a tailor, or take clients to lunch. And he makes me laugh. Peter, I couldn't bear to marry him and have it fall apart on me again."

"I can't tell you if it's right. And if I were you, I wouldn't listen to anyone's good-intentioned advice this time around."

"But you'll give me some anyway?"

"But I'll give you some anyway," he agreed, and felt years drop away. "Don't judge whatever you have with him by the mess we made. Just ask yourself a couple of questions. Does he make you happy? Do you trust him? How do you imagine your life with him? How do you imagine it without him?"

"And when I have the answers?"

"You'll know what to do." He kissed the hand joined with his. "I love you, Sydney."

"I love you, too."

Answer the questions, she thought as she pushed the elevator button in Mikhail's lobby. It was twenty-four hours since Peter had listed them, but she hadn't allowed herself to think of them. Hadn't had to, she corrected as she stepped inside the car. She already knew the answers.

Did he make her happy? Yes, wildly happy.

Did she trust him? Without reservation.

Her life with him? A roller coaster of emotions, demands, arguments, laughter, frustration.

Without him? Blank.

She simply couldn't imagine it. She would have her work, her routine, her ambitions. No, she'd never be without a purpose again. But without him, it would all be straight lines.

So she knew what to do. If it wasn't too late.

There was the scent of drywall dust in the hallway when she stepped out of the elevator. She glanced up to see the ceiling had been replaced, the seams taped, mudded and sanded. All that was left to be done here was the paint and trim.

He did good work, she thought, as she ran her hand along the wall. In a short amount of time, he'd taken a sad old building and turned it into something solid and good. There was still work ahead, weeks before the last nail would be hammered. But what he fixed would last.

Pressing a hand to her stomach, she knocked on his door. And hoped.

There wasn't a sound from inside. No blare of music, no click of work boots on wood. Surely he hadn't gone to bed, she told herself. It was barely ten. She knocked again, louder, and wondered if she should call out his name.

A door opened—not his, but the one just down the hall. Keely poked her head out. After one quick glance at Sydney, the friendliness washed out of her face.

"He's not here," she said. Her champagne voice had gone flat. Keely didn't know the details, but she was sure of one thing. This was the woman who had put Mikhail in a miserable mood for the past few days.

"Oh." Sydney's hand dropped to her side. "Do you know where he is?"

"Out." Keely struggled not to notice that there was misery in Sydney's eyes, as well.

"I see." Sydney willed her shoulders not to slump. "I'll just wait."

"Suit yourself," Keely said with a shrug. What did she care if the woman was obviously in love? This was the woman who'd hurt her pal. As an actress Keely prided herself on recognizing the mood beneath the actions. Mikhail might have been fiercely angry over the past few days, but beneath the short temper had been raw, seeping hurt. And she'd put it there. What did it matter if she was suffering, too?

Of course it mattered. Keely's sentimental heart went gooey in her chest.

"Listen, he'll probably be back soon. Do you want a drink or something?"

"No, really. I'm fine. How's, ah, your apartment coming?"

"New stove works like a champ." Unable to be anything but kind, Keely leaned on the jamb. "They've still got a little of this and that—especially with the damage those idiots did." She brightened. "Hey, did you know they arrested a guy?"

"Yes." Janine had told her about Lloyd's arrest when she'd called in. "I'm sorry. He was only trying to get back at me."

"It's not your fault the guy's a jerk. Anyway, they sucked up the water, and Mik mixed up some stuff to get the paint off the brick. They had to tear out the ceiling in the apartment below that empty place. And the floors buckled up pretty bad." She shrugged again. "You know, Mik, he'll fix it up."

Yes, she knew Mik. "Do you know if there was much damage to Mrs. Wolburg's things?"

"The rugs are a loss. A lot of other things were pretty soggy. They'll dry out." More comfortable, Keely took a bite of the banana she'd been holding behind her back. "Her grandson was by. She's doing real good. Using a walker and everything already, and crabbing about coming home. We're planning on throwing her a welcome-back party next month. Maybe you'd like to come."

"I'd—" They both turned at the whine of the elevator.

The doors opened, and deep voices raised in some robust Ukrainian folk song poured out just ahead of the two men. They were both a little drunk, more than a little grubby, and the way their arms were wrapped around each other, it was impossible to say who was supporting whom. Sydney noticed the blood first. It was smeared on Mikhail's white T-shirt, obviously from the cuts on his lip and over his eye.

"My God."

The sound of her voice had Mikhail's head whipping up like a wolf. His grin faded to a surly stare as he and his brother stumbled to a halt.

"What do you want?" The words were thickened with vodka and not at all welcoming.

"What happened to you?" She was already rushing toward them. "Was there an accident?"

"Hey, pretty lady." Alex smiled charmingly though his left eye was puffy with bruises and nearly swollen shut. "We had a hell'va party. Should've been there. Right, bro?"

Mikhail responded by giving him a sluggish punch in the stomach. Sydney decided it was meant as affection as Mikhail then turned, locked his brother in a bear hug, kissed both his cheeks.

While Mikhail searched his pockets for keys, Sydney turned to Alex. "What happened? Who did this to you?"

"Did what?" He tried to wink at Keely and winced. "Oh, this?" He touched ginger fingers to his eye and grinned. "He's always had a sneaky left." He shot his brother a look of bleary admiration while Mikhail fought to fit what seemed like a very tiny key in an even tinier lock. "I got a couple good ones in under his guard. Wouldn't have caught him if he hadn't been drunk. Course I was drunk, too." He weaved toward Keely's door. "Hey, Keely, my beautiful gold-haired dream, got a raw steak?"

"No." But having sympathy for the stupid, she took his arm. "Come on, champ, I'll pour you into a cab."

"Let's go dancing," he suggested as she guided him back to the elevator. "Like to dance?"

"I live for it." She glanced over her shoulder as she shoved him into the elevator. "Good luck," she told Sydney.

She was going to need it, Sydney decided, as she walked up behind Mikhail just as he managed to open his own door. He shoved it back, nearly caught her in the nose, but her reflexes were better than his at the moment.

"You've been fighting with your brother," she accused.

"So?" He thought it was a shame, a damn shame, that the sight of her was sobering him up so quickly. "You would rather I fight with strangers?"

"Oh, sit down." Using her temporary advantage, she shoved him into a chair. She strode off into the bathroom, muttering to herself. When she came back with a wet washcloth and antiseptic, he was up again, leaning out the window, trying to clear his head.

"Are you sick?"

He pulled his head in and turned back, disdain clear on his battered face. "Stanislaskis don't get sick from vodka." Maybe a little queasy, he thought, when the vodka was followed by a couple of solid rights to the gut. Then he grinned. His baby brother had a hell of a punch.

"Just drunk then," she said primly, and pointed to the chair. "Sit down. I'll clean your face."

"I don't need nursing." But he sat, because it felt better that way.

"What you need is a keeper." Bending over, she began to dab at the cut above his eye while he tried to resist the urge to lay his cheek against the soft swell of her breast. "Going out and getting drunk, beating up your brother. Why would you do such a stupid thing?"

He scowled at her. "It felt good."

"Oh, I'm sure it feels marvelous to have a naked fist popped in your eye." She tilted his head as she worked. That eye was going to bruise dramatically before morning. "I can't imagine what your mother would say if she knew."

"She would say nothing. She'd smack us both." His breath hissed when she slopped on the antiseptic. "Even when he starts it she smacks us both." Indignation shimmered. "Explain that."

"I'm sure you both deserved it. Pathetic," she muttered, then looked down at his hands. "Idiot!" The skin on the knuckles was bruised and broken. "You're an artist, damn it. You have no business hurting your hands."

It felt good, incredibly good to have her touching and scolding him. Any minute he was going to pull her into his lap and beg.

"I do what I like with my own hands," he said. And thought about what he'd like to be doing with them right now.

"You do what you like, period," she tossed back as she gently cleaned his knuckles. "Shouting at people, punching people. Drinking until you smell like the inside of a vodka bottle."

He wasn't so drunk he didn't know an insult when he heard one. Nudging her aside, he stood and, staggering only a little, disappeared into the next room. A moment later, she heard the shower running.

This wasn't the way she'd planned it, Sydney thought, wringing the washcloth in her hands. She was supposed to come to him, tell him how much she loved him, ask him to forgive her for being a fool. And he was supposed to be kind and understanding, taking her in his arms, telling her she'd made him the happiest man in the world.

Instead he'd been drunk and surly. And she'd been snappish and critical.

Well, he deserved it. Before she had time to think, she'd heaved the washcloth toward the kitchen, where it slapped wetly against the wall then slid down to the sink. She stared at it for a minute, then down at her own hands.

She'd thrown something. And it felt wonderful. Glancing around, she spotted a paperback book and sent it sailing. A plastic cup gave a nice ring when it hit the wall, but she'd have preferred the crash of glass. Snatching up a battered sneaker, she prepared to heave that, as well. A sound in the doorway had her turning, redirecting aim and shooting it straight into Mikhail's damp, naked chest. His breath woofed out.

"What are you doing?"

"Throwing things." She snatched up the second shoe and let it fly. He caught that one before it beaned him.

"You leave me, go away without a word, and you come to throw things?"

"That's right."

Eyes narrowed, he tested the weight of the shoe he held. It was tempting, very tempting to see if he could land it on the point of that jutting chin. On an oath, he dropped it. However much she deserved it, he just couldn't hit a woman.

"Where did you go?"

She tossed her hair back. "I went to see Peter."

He shoved his bruised hands into the pockets of the jeans he'd tugged on. "You leave me to go see another man, then you come back to throw shoes at my head. Tell me why I shouldn't just toss you out that window and be done with it."

"It was important that I see him, that I talk to him. And I—"

"You hurt me," he blurted out. The words burned on his tongue. He hated to admit it. "Do you think I care about getting a punch in the face? You'd already twisted my heart. This I can fight," he said, touching the back of his hand to his cut lip. "What you do to me inside leaves me helpless. And I hate it."

"I'm sorry." She took a step toward him but saw she wasn't yet welcome. "I was afraid I'd hurt you more if I tried to give you what you wanted. Mikhail, listen, please. Peter was the only person who cared for me. For *me*. My parents…" She could only shake her head. "They're not like yours. They wanted what was best for me, I'm sure, but their way of giving it was to hire nannies and buy me pretty clothes, send me to the best boarding school. You don't know how lonely it was." Impatient, she rubbed her fingers over her eyes to dry them. "I only had Peter, and then I lost him. What I feel for you is so much bigger, so much more, that I don't know what I'd do if I lost you."

He was softening. She could do that to him, as well. No matter how he tried to harden his heart, she could melt it. "You left me, Sydney. I'm not lost."

"I had to see him. I hurt him terribly, Mikhail. I was convinced that I'd ruined the marriage, the friendship, the love. What if I'd done the same with us?" With a little sigh, she walked to the window. "The funny thing was, he was carrying around the same guilt, the same remorse, the same fears. Talking with him, being friends again, made all the difference."

"I'm not angry that you talked to him, but that you went away. I was afraid you wouldn't come back."

She turned from the window. "I'm finished with running. I only went away because I'd hoped I could come back to you. Really come back."

He stared into her eyes, trying to see inside. "Have you?"

"Yes." She let out a shaky breath. "All the answers are yes. We walked through this building once, and I could hear the voices, all the sounds behind the doors. The smells, the laughing. I envied you belonging here. I need to belong. I want to have the chance to belong. To have that family you said was inside us."

She reached up, drawing a chain from around her neck. At the end, the little ruby flashed its flame.

Shaken, he crossed the room to cup the ring in his hand. "You wear it," he murmured.

"I was afraid to keep it on my finger. That I'd lose it. I need you to tell me if you still want me to have it."

His eyes came back to hers and locked. Even as he touched his lips to hers gently, he watched her. "I didn't ask you right the first time."

"I didn't answer right the first time." She took his face in her hands to kiss him again, to feel again. "You were perfect."

"I was clumsy. Angry that the banker had asked you before me."

Eyes wet, she smiled. "What banker? I don't know any bankers."

Unfastening the chain from around her neck, he set it aside. "It was not how I'd planned it. There was no music."

"I hear music."

"No soft words, no pretty light, no flowers."

"There's a moon. I still have the first rose you gave me."

Touched, he kissed her hands. "I told you only what I wanted, not what I'd give. You have my heart, Sydney. As long as it beats. My life is your life.'' He slipped the ring onto her finger. "Will you belong to me?'

She curled her fingers to keep the ring in place. "I already do.''

* * * * *

CONVINCING ALEX

For Pat Gaffney,
to even things out

Chapter One

The curvy blonde in hot-pink spandex tottered on stiletto heels as she worked her corner. Her eyes, heavily painted with a sunburst of colors, kept a sharp watch on her associates, those spangled shadows of the night. There was a great deal of laughter on the street. After all, it was springtime in New York. But beneath the laughter there was a flat sheen of boredom that no amount of glitter or sex could disguise.

For these ladies, business was business.

After popping in some fresh gum, she adjusted the large canvas bag on her bare shoulder. Thank God it was warm, she thought. It would be hell to strut around half-dressed if the weather was ugly.

A gorgeous black woman in red leather that barely covered the essentials languidly lit a cigarette and cocked her hip. "Come on, baby," she said to no one in particular, in a voice husky from the smoke she exhaled. "Wanna have some fun?"

Some did, Bess noted, her eyes skimming the block.

Some didn't. All in all, she thought, business was pretty brisk on this spring night. She'd observed several transactions, and the varied ways they were contracted. It was too bad boredom was the byword here. Boredom, and a defiant kind of hopelessness.

"You talking to yourself, honey?"

"Huh?" Bess blinked up into the shrewd eyes of the black goddess in red leather who had strolled over. "Was I?"

"You're new?" Studying Bess, she blew out smoke. "Who's your man?"

"My... I don't have one."

"Don't have one?" The woman arched her ruthlessly plucked brows and sneered. "Girl, you can't work this street without a man."

"That's what I'm doing." Since she didn't have a cigarette, Bess blew a bubble with her gum. Then snapped it.

"Bobby or Big Ed find out, they're going to mess you up." She shrugged. After all, it wasn't her problem.

"Free country."

"Girl, ain't nothing free." With a laugh, she ran a hand down her slick, leather-covered hip. "Nothing at all." She flicked her cigarette into the street, where it bounced off the rear fender of a cab.

There were dozens of questions on Bess's lips. It was in her nature to ask them, but she remembered that she had to go slow. "So who's *your* man?"

"Bobby." With her lips pursed, the woman skimmed her gaze up and down Bess. "He'd take you on. A little skinny through the butt, but you'd do. You need protection when you work the streets." And she could use the extra money Bobby would pass her way if she brought him a new girl.

"Nobody protected the two girls who got murdered last month."

The black woman's eyes flickered. Bess considered herself an excellent judge of emotion, and she saw grief, regret and sorrow before the eyes hardened again. "You a cop?"

Bess's mouth fell open before she laughed. That was a good one, she thought. Sort of flattering. "No, I'm not a cop. I'm just trying to make a living. Did you know either of them? The women who were killed?"

"We don't like questions around here." The woman tilted her head. "If you're trying to make a living, let's see you do it."

Bess felt a quick ripple of unease. Not only was the woman gorgeous, she was big. Big and suspicious. Both qualities were going to make it difficult for Bess to hang back on the fringes and observe. But she considered herself an agile thinker and a quick study. After all, she reminded herself, she'd come here tonight to do business.

"Sure." Turning, she strutted slowly along the sidewalk. Her hips—and she didn't for a minute believe that her butt was skinny—swayed seductively.

Maybe her throat was a little dry. Maybe her heart was pounding a bit too quickly. But Bess McNee took a great deal of pride in her work.

She spotted the two men half a block away and licked her lips. The one on the left, the dark one, looked very promising.

"Look, rookie, the idea's to take one, maybe two." Alex scanned the sidewalk ahead. Hookers, drunks, junkies and those unfortunate enough to have to pass through them to get home. "My snitch says that the tall black one—Rosalie—knew both the victims."

"So why don't we just pick her up and take her in for questioning?" Judd Malloy was anxious for action. His detective's shield was only forty-eight hours old. And he was working with Alexi Stanislaski, a cop who had a reputation for moving quickly and getting the job done. "Better yet, why don't we go roust her pimp?"

Rookies, Alex thought. Why were they always teaming him up with rookies? "Because we want her cooperation. We're going to pick her up, book her for solicitation. Then we're going to talk to her, real nice, before Bobby can come along and tell her to clam up."

"If my wife finds out I spent the night picking up hook-ers—"

"A smart cop doesn't tell his family anything they'd don't need to know. And they don't need to know much." Alex's dark brown eyes were cool, very cool, as they flicked over his new partner's face. "Stanislaski's rule number one."

He spotted the blonde. She was staring at him. Alex stared back. Odd face, he thought. Sharp, sexy, despite the makeup she'd troweled on. Beneath all the gunk, her eyes were a vivid green. The face itself was all angles, some of them wrong. Her nose was slightly crooked, as if it had been broken. Some john or pimp, he figured, then skimmed his eyes down to her mouth.

Full, overfull, and a glossy red. It didn't please him at all that he felt a reaction to it. Not knowing what she was, what she did. Her chin came to a slight point, and with her prominent cheekbones it gave her face a triangular, foxlike look.

The clinging tube top and spandex capri pants showed every inch of her curvy, athletic little body. He'd always been a sucker for the athletic type—but he reminded him-self just where this particular number got her exercise.

In any case, she wasn't the one he was looking for.

Now or never, Bess told herself, feeling her new ac-quaintance's eyes on her.

"Hey, baby…" Though she hadn't smoked since she'd been fifteen, her voice was husky. Saying a prayer to what-ever gods were listening, she veered in on Alex. "Want to party?"

"Maybe." He hooked a finger in the top of her tube,

and was surprised when she flinched. "You're not quite what I had it mind, sweetie."

"Oh?" What next? Combining instinct with her observations, she tossed her head and leaned into him. She had the quick impression of pressing against steel—hard, unyielding and very cool. "Just what *did* you have in mind?"

Then, for a moment, she had nothing at all on hers. Not with the way those dark eyes cut into her, through her. His knuckles were brushing her skin, just above the breasts. She felt the heat from them, from him. As she continued to stare, she was struck by a vivid image of the two of them, rolling on a narrow bed in some dark room.

And it had nothing to do with business.

It was the first time Alex had ever seen a hooker blush. It threw him off, made him want to apologize for the fantasy that had just whipped through his brain. Then he remembered himself.

"Just a different type, babe."

In her heels, they were eye-to-eye. It made him want to rub off the powders and paints to see what was beneath.

"I can be a different type," Bess said, delighted with her inspired response.

"Hey, girlfriend." Rosalie strutted over and slipped a friendly arm around Bess's shoulders. "You're not going to be greedy and take both of these boys, are you?"

"I—"

Pay dirt, Alex thought, and shifted his attention to Rosalie. "You two a team?"

"We are tonight." She glanced from Alex to his partner. "How 'bout you two?"

Judd searched for his voice. He'd rather have been facing a gunman in an alley. And he simply couldn't put his hands on this big, beautiful woman, when a picture of his wife's trusting face was flashing in his head like a neon light.

"Sure." He let out a long breath and tried to emulate some of Alex's cocky confidence.

Rosalie threw back her head and laughed before she stepped forward, bumping bodies with Judd. He gave way instinctively as a dark red flush crept up his neck. "I believe you're new at this, honey. Why don't you let Rosalie show you the ropes?"

Because his partner seemed to have developed laryngitis, Alex took over. "How much?"

"Well…" Rosalie didn't bother to look over at Bess, who had gone dead pale. "Special rate tonight. You get both of us for a hundred. That's the first hour." She leaned down and whispered something in Judd's ear that had him babbling. "After that," she continued, "we can negotiate."

"I don't—" Bess began, then felt Rosalie's fingers dig into her bare shoulder like sharp little knives.

"I think that'll do it," Alex said, and pulled out his badge. "Ladies, you're busted."

Cops, Bess realized on a wave of sweet relief. While Rosalie expressed her opinion with a single vicious word, Bess struggled not to burst into wild laughter.

Perfect, Bess thought as she was bumped along into the squad room. She'd been arrested for solicitation, and life couldn't be better. Trying to take everything in at once, she grinned as she scanned the station house. She'd been in one before, of course. As she always said, she took her work seriously. But not in this precinct. Not downtown.

It was dirty—grimy, really, she decided, making mental notes and muttering to herself. Floors, walls, the barred windows. Everything had a nice, picturesque coat of crud.

It smelled, too. She took a deep breath so that she wouldn't forget the ripe stench of human sweat, bitter coffee and strong disinfectant.

And it was noisy. With every nerve on sensory alert, she separated the din into ringing phones, angry curses, weeping, and the clickety-clack of keyboards at work.

Man, oh, man, she thought. Her luck was really in.

"You're not a tourist, sweetheart," Alex reminded her, adding a firm nudge.

"Sorry."

The vibrant excitement in her eyes was so out of place that he stared. Then, with a shake of his head, he jabbed a finger toward a chair. He was letting the rookie get his feet wet getting the vitals from Rosalie. Once they had her booked, he'd take over himself, using charm or threats or whatever seemed most expedient to make her talk to him about her two murdered associates.

"Okay." He took his seat behind his battered and over-crowded desk. "You know the drill."

She'd been staring at a young man of about twenty with a face full of bruises and a torn denim jacket. "Excuse me?"

Alex just sighed as he rolled a form onto his typewriter. "Name?"

"Oh, I'm Bess." She held out her hand in a gesture so natural and friendly he nearly took it.

Instead, he swore softly. "Bess what?"

"McNee. And you're?"

"In charge. Date of birth."

"Why?"

His eyes flicked up, arrowed hers. "Why what?"

"Why do you want to know?"

Patience, never his strong suit, strained. He tapped a finger on the form. "Because I've got this space to fill."

"Okay. I'm twenty-eight. A Gemini. I was born on June the first."

Alex did the math and typed in the year. "Residence."

Natural curiosity had her poking through the folders and papers on his desk until he slapped her hand. "You're awfully tense," she commented. "Is it because you work undercover?"

Damn that smile, he thought. It was sassy, sexy, and far from stupid. That, and those sharp, intelligent green eyes, might have fooled him. But she looked like a hooker, and she smelled like a hooker. Therefore...

"Listen, doll, here's the way this works. I ask the questions, you answer them."

"Tough, cynical, street-smart."

One dark brow lifted. "Excuse me?"

"Just a quick personality check. You want my address, right?" she rattled off an address that made both of Alex's brows raise.

"Let's get serious."

"Okay." Willing to oblige, Bess folded her hands on the edge of his desk.

"Your address," he repeated.

"I just gave it to you."

"I know what real estate goes for in that area. Maybe you're good." Thoughtful, he scanned her attributes one more time. "Maybe you're better than you look. But you don't make enough working the streets to pop for that kind of rent."

Bess knew an insult when it hit her over the head. What made it worse was that she'd spent over an hour on her makeup. And she happened to know that her body was good. Lord knew, she sweated to keep it that way by working out three days a week. "That's where I live, cop." Her temper, which had a habit of flaring quickly, had her upending her enormous canvas tote onto his desk.

Alex watched, fascinated, as she pawed through the pile of contents. There were enough cosmetics to supply a small department store. And they weren't the cheap kind. Six lipsticks, two compacts, several mascara sticks and pots of eye shadow. A rainbow of eyeliner pencils. Scattered with them were two sets of keys, a snowfall of credit-card receipts, rubber bands, paper clips, twelve pens—he counted—a few broken pencils, a steno pad, two paperback books, matches, a leather address book embossed with the initials *ELM,* a stapler—he didn't even pause to wonder why she would carry one—tissues and crumpled papers, a tiny micro-cassette recorder. And a gun.

He whipped it out of the pile and stared at it. A water gun.

"Careful with that," she warned as she found her over-burdened wallet. "It's full of ammonia."

"Ammonia?"

"I used to carry Mace, but this works fine. Here." Pleased with herself, she pushed the open wallet under his nose.

It might have been her in the picture. The hair was short and curly and chic, a deep chestnut rather than a brassy blonde. But that nose, that chin. And those eyes. He frowned over the driver's license. The address was right.

"You got a car?"

She shrugged and began to dump things back into her purse. "So?"

"Women in your position usually don't."

Because it made sense, Bess stalled. "I've got a license. Everybody who has a license doesn't have to have a car, do they?"

"No." He jerked the wallet out of her reach. "Take off the wig."

Pouting a little, she patted it. "How come?"

He reached across the desk and yanked it off himself. She scowled at him while she ran her fingers through short, springy red curls. "I want that back. It's borrowed."

"Sure." He tossed it onto his desk before he leaned back in his squeaky chair for a fresh evaluation. If this lady was a hooker, he was Clark Kent. "What the hell *are* you?"

It was time to come clean. She knew it. But something about him egged her on. "I'm just a woman trying to make a living, Officer." That was how Jade would handle it, Bess was sure. And since Jade was her creation, Bess was determined to do right by her.

He opened the wallet, skimmed through the bills. She

was carrying around what would be for him more than two weeks' pay. "Right."

"Can you do that?" she demanded, more curious than annoyed. "Go through my personal property?"

"Honey, right now *you* are *my* personal property." There were pictures in the wallet, as well. Snapshots of people, some with her, some without her. And the lady was a card-carrying member of dozens of groups, including Greenpeace, the World Wildlife Federation, Amnesty International and the Writers' Guild. The last brought him back to the tape recorder. When he picked up the little toy, he noted that it was running. "Let's have it, Bess."

God, he was cute. The thought passed through her head as she smiled at him. "Have what?"

"What were you doing hanging around with Rosalie and the rest of the girls?"

"My job." When his eyes narrowed that way, Bess thought, he was downright irresistible. Impatient, a little mean, with a flash of recklessness just barely under control. Fabulous.

"Really." All honesty and cheap perfume, she leaned forward. "You see, it all has to do with Jade, and how she's having this problem with a dual personality. By day, she's a dedicated lawyer—a real straight arrow, *you* know—but by night she hits the streets. She's blocking what happened between her and Brock, and coupled with a childhood memory that's begun to resurface, the strain's been too much for her. She's on a path of self-destruction."

The frown in his eyes turned them nearly black. "Who the hell is Jade?"

"Jade Sullivan Carstairs. Don't you watch daytime TV?"

His head was beginning to buzz. "No."

"You don't know what you're missing. You'd probably really enjoy the Jade-Storm-Brock story line. Storm's a cop, you see, and he's falling in love with Jade. Her emotional problems, and the hold Brock has on her, complicate things. Then there was a miscarriage, and the kidnapping. Naturally, Storm has problems of his own.''

''Naturally. What's your point?''

''Oh, sorry. I get offtrack. I write for 'Secret Sins' Daytime drama.''

''You're a soap-opera writer?''

''Yeah.'' Unlike many in the trade, she wasn't bothered by that particular label. ''And I like to get the feel of the situations I put my characters into. Since Jade is a special pet of mine, I—''

''Are you out of your mind?'' Alex barked the question as he leaned over into her face. ''Do you have any idea what you were doing?''

She blinked, at once innocent and amused. ''Research?''

He swore again, and Bess found she liked the way he raked impatient fingers through his thick black hair. ''Lady, just how far were you intending to take your research?''

''How—? Oh.'' Her eyes brightened with laughter. ''Well no, not quite that far.''

''What the hell would you have done if I hadn't been a cop?''

''I'd have thought of something.'' She continued to smile. He had a fascinating face—golden skin, dark eyes, wonderful bones. And that mouth, so beautifully sculpted, even if it did tend to scowl. ''It's my job to think of things. And when I spotted you, I thought you looked safe. What I mean is, you didn't strike me as the kind of man who'd be interested in…'' What was a delicate way of putting it? she wondered. ''Paying for pleasure.''

He was so angry he wanted to yank her up and toss her over his lap. The idea of administering a few good whacks to that cute little butt was tremendously appealing. ''And if you'd guessed wrong?''

''I didn't,'' she pointed out. ''For a minute there, I was worried, but it all worked out. Better than I expected, really, because I had a chance to ride in a— Do you still call them paddy wagons?"

He'd been so sure he'd seen everything. Heard everything. With his temper straining at the bit, he spoke through clenched teeth. "Two hookers are dead. Two who worked that area."

"I know," she said quickly, as if that explained it all. "That was one of the reasons I chose it. You see, I plan to have Jade—"

"I'm talking about you," he interrupted in a voice that had her wincing. "You. Some bubbleheaded hack writer who thinks she can strut around in spandex and a half a ton of makeup, then go home to her nice neighborhood and wash it all off."

"Hack?" It was the only thing she took offense to. "Look, cop—"

"*You* look. You stay out of my territory, and out of those slut clothes. Do your research out of a book."

Her chin shot out. "I can go where I want, wearing what I want."

"You think so?" There was a way to teach her a lesson. A perfect way. "Fine." He rose, tugged the tote out of her hands, then took a firm grip on her arm. "Let's go."

"Where?"

"To holding, babe. You're under arrest, remember?"

She stumbled in the three-inch heels and squawked, "But I just explained—"

"I hear better stories before breakfast every day."

"You're not going to put me in a cell." Bess was sure of it. Positive. Right up until the moment the bars closed in her face.

It took about ten minutes for the shock to wear off. When it did, Bess decided it wasn't such a bad turn. She could be furious with the cop—whoever he was—but she could appreciate and take advantage of the unique opportunity he'd given her. She was in a holding cell with several other women. There was atmosphere to be absorbed, and there were interviews to be conducted.

When one of her cellmates informed her that she was entitled to a phone call, she demanded one. Pleased with the progress she was making, she settled back on her hard cot to talk to her new acquaintances.

It was thirty minutes later when she looked up and spotted her friend and cowriter Lori Banes, standing beside a uniformed policeman.

"Bess, you look so natural here."

With a grin, Bess popped up as the guard unlocked the door. "It's been great."

"Hey!" one of her cellmates called out. "I'm telling you that Vicki's a witch, and Jeffrey should boot her out. Amelia's the right woman for him."

Bess sent back a wink. "I'll see what I can do. 'Bye, girls."

Lori didn't consider herself long-suffering. She didn't consider herself a prude or a stuffed shirt. And she said as much to Bess as they walked through the corridors, up the stairs and back into the lobby area outside the squad room. "But," she added, pressing fingers to her tired eyes. "There's something that puts me off about being woken up at 2:00 a.m. to come bail you out of jail."

"Sorry, but it's been great. Wait until I tell you."

"Do you know what you look like, dear?"

"Yep." Unconcerned, Bess craned her neck. The chair behind Alex's desk was empty. "I had no idea that so many of the working girls watched the show. But they do work nights, mostly. Uh, excuse me…" She caught the sleeve of one of New York's finest as he walked by. "The officer who uses that desk?"

The cop swallowed the best part of a bite of his pastrami sandwich. "Stanislaski?"

"Whew. That's a mouthful. Is he still around?"

"He's in Interrogation."

"Oh. Thanks."

"Come on, Bess, we've got to pick up your things."

Bess had signed for her purse and its contents, still keeping an eye out for Alex. "Stanislaski," she repeated to herself. "Is that Polish, do you think?"

"How the hell do I know?" Out of patience, Lori steered her toward the door. "Let's get out of here. The place is lousy with criminals."

"I know. It's fabulous." With a laugh, she tucked an arm around Lori's waist. "I got ideas for the next three years. If we decide to have Elana arrested for Reed's murder…"

"I don't know about having Reed murdered."

With a sigh, Bess looked around for a cab. "Lori, we both know Jim isn't going to sign another contract. He wants to try the big leagues. Having his character offed is the perfect way to beef up Elana's story line."

"Maybe."

Bess slyly pulled out her ace. "'Our Lives, Our Loves' picked up two points in the ratings last month."

Lori only grunted.

"Word is Dr. Amanda Jamison is going to have twins."

"Twins?" Lori shut her eyes. Soap diva Ariel Kirkwood, who played the long-suffering psychiatrist on the competing soap, was daytime's most popular star. "It had to be twins," Lori muttered. "Okay, Reed dies."

Bess allowed herself one quick victory smile, then hurried on.

"Anyway, while I was in there, I was picturing the elegant, cool Dr. Elana Warfield Stafford Carstairs in prison. Fabulous, Lori. It'd be fabulous. I wish you'd seen the cop."

They'd walked to the corner, and there wasn't a cab in sight. "What cop?"

"The one who arrested me. He was incredibly sexy."

Lori only had the energy to sigh. "Leave it to you to get busted by a sexy cop."

"Really. All this thick black hair. His eyes were nearly black, too. Very intense. He had all those hollows and planes in his face, and this beautiful mouth. Nice build, too. Sort of rough-and-ready. Like a boxer, maybe."

"Don't start, Bess."

"I'm not. I can find a man sexy and attractive without falling in love."

Lori shot her a look. "Since when?"

"Since the last time. I've sworn off, remember?" Her smile perked up when she spotted a cab heading their way. "I'm interested in this Stanislaski for strictly professional reasons."

"Right." Resigned, Lori climbed in when the cab swung to the curb.

"I swear." She lifted her right hand to add impact to the oath. "We want to get into Storm's head more, into his background and stuff. So I pick this cop's brain a little." She gave a cabbie both her address and Lori's. "After Jade gets attacked by the Millbrook Maniac, Storm isn't going to be able to hold back his feelings for her. More has to come out about who and what he is. If we do have Elana arrested for Reed's murder, that's going to complicate his life—you know, family loyalty versus professional ethics. And once he confronts Brock—"

"Hey." At a red light, the cabbie turned, peering at them from under his fading Mets cap. "You talking about 'Secret Sins'?"

"Yeah." Bess brightened. "Do you watch it?"

"The wife tapes it every day. You don't look familiar."

"We're not on it," Bess explained. "We write it."

"Gotcha." Satisfied, he punched the accelerator when the light changed. "Let me tell you what I think about that two-timing Vicki."

As he proceeded to do just that, Bess leaned forward, debating with him. Lori closed her eyes and tried to catch up on lost sleep.

Chapter Two

"My wife went nuts." Judd Malloy munched on his cherry Danish while Alex swung in and out of downtown traffic. "She's a big fan of that soap, you know? Tapes it every day when she's in school."

"Terrific." Alex had been doing his best to forget his little encounter with the soap queen, but his partner wasn't cooperating.

"Holly figures it was just like meeting a celebrity."

"You don't find many celebrities turning tricks."

"Come on, Alex." Judd washed down the Danish with heavily sugared coffee. "She wasn't, really. You said so yourself, or the charges wouldn't have been dropped."

"She was stupid," Alex said between his teeth. "Carrying a damn water pistol in that suitcase of hers. I guess she figured if a john got rough, she'd blat him between the eyes and that would be that."

Judd started to comment on how it might feel to get a blat of ammonia in the eyes, but didn't think his partner wanted to hear it. "Well, Holly was impressed, and we got some fresh juice out of Rosalie, so we didn't waste our time.''

"Malloy, you'd better get used to wasting time. Stanis-laski's rule number four." Alex spotted the building he was looking for and double-parked. He was already out of the car and across the sidewalk before Judd found the NYPD sign and stuck it in the window. "We sure as hell could be wasting it here with this Domingo."

"Rosalie said—''

"Rosalie said what we wanted to hear so we'd spring her," Alex told him. His cop's eyes were already studying the building, noting windows, fire escapes, roof. "Maybe she gave us the straight shot on Domingo, and maybe she pulled it out of a hat. We'll see.''

The place was in good repair. No graffiti, no broken glass or debris. Lower-middle-income, Alex surmised. Established families, mostly blue-collar. He pulled open the heavy entrance door, then scanned the names above the line of mailboxes.

"J. Domingo. 212." Alex pushed the buzzer for 110, waited, then hit 305. The answering buzz released the inner door. "People are so careless," he commented. He could feel Judd's nerves shimmering as they climbed the stairs, but he could tell he was holding it together. He'd damn well better hold it together, Alex thought as he gestured Judd into position, then knocked on the door of 212. He knocked a second time before he heard the cursing answer.

When the door opened a crack, Alex braced his body against it to keep it that way. "How's it going, Jesus?"

"What the hell do you want?"

He fit Rosalie's description, Alex noted. Right down to the natty Clark Gable moustache and the gold incisor. "Conversation, Jesus. Just a little conversation.''

"I don't talk to nobody at this hour.''

When he tried to shove the door to, Alex merely leaned

on it and flipped open his badge. "You don't want to be rude, do you? Why don't you ask us in?"

Swearing in Spanish, Jesús Domingo cracked the door a little wider. "You got a warrant?"

"I can get one, if you want more than conversation. I can take you down for questioning, get the paperwork and do the job before your shyster lawyer can tap-dance you out. Want a team of badges in here, Jesus?"

"I haven't done nothing." He stepped back from the door, a small man with wiry muscles who was wearing nothing but a pair of gym shorts.

"Nobody said you did. Did I say he did, Malloy?"

Enjoying himself, Judd stepped in behind Alex. "Nope."

The building might be lower-middle-class, but Domingo's apartment was a small high-tech palace. State-of-the-art stereo equipment, Alex noted. A big-screen TV with some very classy video toys. The wall of tapes ran mostly to the X-rated.

"Nice place," Alex commented. "You sure know how to make your unemployment check stretch."

"I got a good head for figures." Domingo plucked up a pack of cigarettes from a table, lighted one. "So?"

"So, let's talk about Angie Horowitz."

Domingo blew out smoke and scratched at the hair on his chest. "Never heard of her."

"Funny, we got word you were one of her regulars, and her main supplier."

"You got the wrong word."

"Maybe you don't recognize the name." Alex reached into his inside jacket pocket, and his fingers brushed over his leather shoulder harness as he pulled out a manila envelope. "Why don't you take a look?" He stuck the police shot under Domingo's nose and watched his olive complexion go a sickly gray. "Look familiar?"

"Man." Domingo's fingers shook as he brought his cigarette to his lips.

"Problem?" Alex glanced down at the photo himself. There hadn't been much left of Angie for the camera. "Oh, hey, sorry about that, Jesus. Malloy, didn't I tell you not to put the dead shot in?"

Judd shrugged, feigning casualness. He was thinking he was glad he didn't have to look at it again himself. "Guess I made a mistake."

"Yeah." All the while he spoke, Alex held the photo where Domingo could see it. "Guy's a rookie," he explained. "Always screwing up. You know. Poor little Angie sure got sliced, didn't she? Coroner said the guy put about forty holes in her. You can see most of them. Poor Malloy here took one look and lost his breakfast. I keep telling him not to eat those damned greasy Danishes before we go check out a stiff, but like I said…" Alex grinned to himself as Domingo made a dash for the bathroom.

"That was cold, Stanislaski," Judd said, grinning.

"Yeah, I'm that kind of guy."

"And I didn't throw up my breakfast."

"You wanted to." The sounds coming from the bathroom were as unpleasant as they get. Alex tapped on the door. "Hey, Jesús, you okay, man? I'm really sorry about that." He passed the photo and envelope to Judd. "Tell you what, let me get you some nice cold water, okay?"

The answer was a muffled retch that Alex figured anyone could take for assent. He moved into the kitchen and opened the freezer. The two kilos were exactly where Rosalie had said he'd find them. He took one out just as Domingo rushed in.

"You got no warrant. You got no right."

"I was getting you some ice." Alex turned the frozen cocaine over in his hands. "This doesn't look like a TV dinner to me. What do you think, Malloy?"

By leaning a shoulder against the door jamb, Judd blocked the doorway. "Not the kind my mother used to make."

"You son of a bitch." Domingo wiped his mouth with a clenched fist. "You violated my civil rights. I'll be out before you can blink."

"Could be." Taking an evidence bag out of his pocket, Alex slipped both kilos inside. "Malloy, why don't you read our friend his rights while he's getting dressed? And, Jesús, try some mouthwash."

"Stanislaski," the desk sergeant called out when Alex came up from seeing Domingo into a cell. "You got company."

Alex glanced over toward his desk, seeing that several cops were huddled around it. There was quite a bit of laughter overriding the usual squad room noise. Curiosity had him moving forward even before he saw the legs. Legs he recognized. They were crossed at the knee and covered almost modestly in a canary-yellow skirt.

He recognized the rest of her, too, though the tough little body was clad in a multihued striped blazer and a scoop-necked blouse the same color as the skirt. Half a dozen slim columns of gold danced at her ears as she laughed. She looked better, sexier, he was forced to admit, with her mouth unpainted, her freckles showing, and those big green eyes subtly smudged with color. Her hair was artfully tousled, a rich, deep red that made him think of a mahogany statue his brother had carved for him.

"So I told the mayor we'd try to work it in, and we'd love for him to come on the show and do a cameo." She shifted on the desk and spotted Alex. He was frowning at her, his thumbs tucked into the pockets of a leather bomber jacket. "Officer Stanislaski."

"McNee." He inclined his head, then swept his gaze over his fellow officers. "The boss comes in and finds you here, I might have to tell him how you didn't have enough work and volunteered to take some of mine."

"Just entertaining your guest, Stanislaski." But the use

of the squad room's nickname for their captain had the men drifting reluctantly away.

"What can I do for you?"

"Well, I—"

"You're sitting on a homicide," he told her.

"Oh." She scooted off the desk. Without the stilettos, she was half a head shorter than he. Alex discovered he preferred it that way. "Sorry. I came by to thank you for straightening things out for me."

"That's what they pay me for. Straightening things out." He'd been certain she would rave a bit about being tossed into a cell, but she was smiling, friendly as a kindergarten teacher. Though he couldn't recall ever having a teacher who looked like her. Or smelled like her.

"Regardless, I appreciate it. My producer's very tolerant, but if it had gone much further, she would have been annoyed."

"Annoyed?" Alex repeated. He stripped off his jacket and tossed it onto his chair. "She'd have been annoyed to find out that one of her writers was out soliciting johns down at Twenty-third and Eleventh Avenue."

"Researching," Bess corrected, unoffended. "Darla—that's my producer—she gets these headaches. I gave her a whopper when I went on a job with a cat burglar."

"With a…" He let his words trail off and eased down on the spot on the desk she'd just vacated. "I don't think you want to tell me about that."

"Actually, he was a former cat burglar. Fascinating guy. I just had him show me how he'd break into my apartment." She frowned a little, remembering. "I guess he was a little rusty. The alarm—"

"Don't." Alex held up a hand. He was beginning to feel a headache coming on himself.

"That's old news, anyway." She waved it away with a cheerful gesture of her hands. "Do you have a first name, or do I just call you Officer?"

"It's Detective."

"Your first name is Detective?"

"No, my rank." He let out a sigh. "Alex."

"Alex. That's nice." She ran a fingertip over the strap of his harness. She wasn't being provocative; she wanted to know what it felt like. Once she knew him better, she was sure, she'd talk him into letting her try it on. "Well, Alex, I was wondering if you'd let me use you."

He'd been a cop for more than five years, and until this moment he hadn't thought anything could surprise him. But it took him three seconds to close his mouth. "I beg your pardon?"

"It's just that you're so perfect." She stepped closer. She really wanted to get a better look at his weapon—without being obvious about it.

She smelled like sunshine and sex. As he drew it in, Alex thought that combination would baffle any man. "I'm perfect?"

"Absolutely." She looked straight into his eyes and smiled. Her gaze was frank and assessing. She was studying him, the way a woman might study a dress in a showroom window. "You're exactly what I've been looking for."

Her eyes were pure green. No hint of gray or blue, no flecks of gold. There was a small dimple near her mouth. Only one. Nothing about that odd, sexy face was balanced. "What you're looking for?"

"I know you're busy, but I'd try not to take up too much of your time. An hour now and then."

"An hour?" He caught himself echoing her, and shook himself loose. "Listen, I appreciate—"

"You're not married, are you?"

"Married? No, but—"

"That makes it simpler. It just came to me last night when I was getting into bed."

God. He'd learned to appreciate women early. And he'd learned to juggle them skillfully—if he said so himself. He knew how to dodge, when to evade and when to sit back and enjoy. But with this one, all bets were off.

"Is this heavy?" she asked, fiddling with his harness.

"You get used to it. It's just there."

Her smile warmed, making him think of sunlight again. "Perfect," she murmured. "I'd be willing to compensate you for your time, and your expertise."

"You'd be—" He wasn't certain if he was insulted or embarrassed. "Hold on, babe."

"Just think about it," Bess said quickly. "I know it's a lot to ask, but I have this problem with Matthew."

A brand-new emotion snuck in under his guard, and it was as green as her eyes. "Matthew? Who the hell is Matthew?"

"We call him Storm, actually. Lieutenant Storm Warfield, Millbrook PD."

Now he definitely had a headache. Alex rubbed his fingers against his temple. "Millbrook?"

"The fictional town of Millbrook, where the show's set. It's supposed to be somewhere in the Midwest. Storm's a cop. Personally, his life's a mess, but professionally, he's focused and intense and occasionally ruthless. In this new story line I'm working on, I want to concentrate on his police work, the routine, the frustrations."

"Wait." He'd always been quick, but it was taking him a minute to change gears. "You want me to help you with a story line?"

"Exactly. If you could just tell me how you think, how you go about solving a case, working with the system or around it. TV cops have to work around the system quite a bit, you know. It plays better than by-the-book."

He swore under his breath and rubbed his hands over his face. Damn it, his palms were sweaty. "You're a real case, McNee."

"You don't have to decide right now." She was also persistent. And she wondered if he had a spare gun strapped o his calf. One of those sexy-looking little chrome jobs. She'd seen that ploy in several movies. Still, she thought f she asked him that, she'd lose her edge. "I'm having a thing tonight." As she spoke, she dug into her huge bag or her notebook. "Eight o'clock until whenever. Bring a friend, if you like. Your partner, too. He seemed very sweet."

"He's adorable."

"Yeah." She ripped off the page and handed it to him. "I'd really like you to stop by."

He took the sheet, not bothering to remind her he already had her address. "Why?"

"Why not?" She beamed at him again.

Before he could list the reasons, he heard his name called.

"Alexi."

Alexi. Bess was already enchanted with the sound as she rolled the name over in her head. Different, exotic. Sexy. She was certain it suited him much more than the casual *Alex.*

Bess studied the woman bearing down on them. This wasn't one who'd be lost in a crowd, she mused. She was stunning, totally self-assured and very pregnant. Beside Bess, Alex pushed off the desk and sighed.

"Rachel."

"A moment of your time, Detective," Rachel said, flipping a glance over Bess before pinning Alex with a tawny stare. "To reacquaint you with civil rights."

"Your sister?" Bess surmised, beaming at both of them.

Alex sent her a considering frown. "How did you know that?"

"I'm really good with faces. Same bone structure, same coloring, same mouth. You have to be brother and sister, or first cousins."

"Guilty," Rachel admitted. Though she would have liked to know what Alex was doing with the sharp-eyed

redhead, she wasn't about to be swayed from her duties as
a public defender. "Jesús Domingo, Alexi. Illegal search
and seizure."

"Bull." Alex crossed his arms and leaned back against
the desk.

"You had a search warrant?"

"Didn't need one. He invited us in."

"And invited you to poke through his belongings, I suppose."

"Nope." Alex grinned while Bess watched them bounce
the verbal ball as though they were champion tennis players. "Jesús got sick. I offered to get him some water. He
didn't object. I opened the freezer to get the poor guy some
ice, and there it was. Two kilos. It'll all be in my report."

"That's lame, Alexi. You'll never get a conviction."

"Maybe. Maybe not. Talk to the DA."

"I intend to." Rachel shifted her briefcase and began to
rub her belly in circular motions to soothe the baby, who
seemed to be doing aerobics in her womb. "You had no
probable cause."

"Sit down."

"I don't want to sit down."

"The baby does." He yanked over a chair and all but
shoved her into it. "When are you going to knock this
off?"

It did feel better to sit. Indescribably better. But she
wasn't about to admit it. "The baby's not due for two
months. I have plenty of time. We were discussing…"

"Rach." He laid a hand on her cheek, very gently. A
shouted curse wouldn't have stopped her, but the small gesture did. "Don't make me worry about you."

"I'm perfectly fine."

"You shouldn't be here."

"I'm having a baby. It's not contagious. Now, about
Domingo."

Alex gave a brief, pithy opinion on what could be done

with Domingo. "Talk to the DA," he repeated. "Sitting down."

"She looks pretty strong to me," Bess commented. Two pair of eyes turned to her, one furious, the other thoughtful.

"Thank you. The men in my life are coddlers," Rachel explained. "Sweet, but annoying."

"Muldoon should take better care of you," Alex insisted.

"I don't need Zack to take care of me. And the fact is, between him and Nick, I'm barely allowed to brush my own teeth." She held out a hand to Bess. "Since my brother is too rude to introduce me, I'm Rachel Muldoon."

"Bess McNee. You're a lawyer?"

"That's right. I work for the public defender's office."

"Really?" Bess's thoughts began to perk. "What's it like to—"

Alex held up a hand. "Don't get her started. She'll pick your brain clean before you know she's had her fingers in it. Look, McNee—" he turned to Bess, determined not to be charmed by her easy smile "—we're a little busy here."

"Of course you are. I'm sorry." Obligingly she swung her huge purse onto her shoulder. "We'll talk tonight. Nice to meet you, Rachel."

"Same here." Rachel ran her tongue over her teeth, and both she and Alex watched Bess weave her way out of the squad room. "Well, that was rude."

"It's the only way to handle her. Believe me."

"Hmm... She seems like an interesting woman. How did you meet her?"

"Don't ask." He sat back down on his desk, irked that the scent of sunshine and sex still lingered in the air.

"I can't believe we're doing this." Holly, Judd's pretty wife of eight months, was all but hopping out of her party shoes. "Wait until I tell everyone in the teachers' lounge where I spent the evening."

"Take it easy, honey." Judd tugged at the tie she'd insisted he wear. "It's just a party."

"Just a party?" As the elevator rode up, she fussed with her honey-brown hair. "I don't know about you two, but it isn't every day I get to eat canapés with celebrities."

Ominously silent, Alex stayed hunched in his leather jacket. He didn't know what the hell he was doing here. His first mistake had been mentioning the invitation to Judd. No matter how insouciant Judd pretended to be, he'd been bursting at the seams when he called his wife. Alex had been swept along in their enthusiasm.

But he wasn't going to stay. Holly's sense of decorum might have insisted that she and Judd couldn't attend without him, but he'd already decided just how he'd play it. He'd go in, maybe have a beer and a couple of crackers. Then he'd slip out again. He'd be damned if he'd spend this rare free evening playing soap-opera groupie.

"Oh, my" was all Holly could say when the elevator doors opened.

The walls of the private foyer were splashed with a mural of the city. Times Square, Rockefeller Center, Harlem, Little Italy, Broadway. People seemed to be rushing along the walls, just as they did the streets below. It was as if the woman who lived here didn't want to miss one moment of the action.

The wide door to the main apartment was open, and music, laughter and conversation were pouring out, along with the scents of hot food and burning candles.

"Oh, my," Holly said again, dragging her husband along as she stepped inside.

From behind them, Alex scanned the room. It was huge, and it was packed with people. Draped in silk or cotton, clad in business suits and lush gowns, they stood elbow to elbow on the hardwood floor, lounged hip to hip on the sapphire cushions of the enormous circular conversation pit, sat knee to knee on the steps of a bronze circular staircase that led to an open loft where still more people leaned against a railing decked with naked cherubs.

Two huge windows let the lights of the city in. More partygoers sat on the pillow-plumped window seats, balancing plates and glasses on their laps.

Paintings were scattered over the ivory-toned walls. Vivid, frenetic modern art, mind-bending surrealism. There was enough color to make his head swim. Yet, through the crowd and the clashing tones, he saw her. Dancing seductively with a distinguished-looking man in a gray pin-striped suit.

She wore an excuse for a dress, the color of crushed purple grapes. He wondered, irritated, if she owned anything that covered those legs. This number certainly didn't. Nor did it cover much territory at all, the way it dipped to the waist in the back, skimmed above mid-thigh and left her shoulders bare, but for skinny, glittery straps. Multihued gemstones fell in a rope from her earlobes to those nicely sloped shoulders. Her feet were bare.

She looked, Alex thought as his stomach muscles twisted themselves into nasty knots, outrageously alluring.

"Oh, Lord, there's Jade. Oh, and Storm and Vicki. Dr. Carstairs, too." Holly's fingers dug into her husband's arm. "It's Amelia."

"Who?"

"'Secret Sins,' dummy." She gave Judd a playful punch. "The whole cast's here."

"That's not all." Because he remembered in time he was supposed to be jaded, Judd stopped himself from pointing and inclined his head. "That's Lawrence D. Strater dancing with our hostess. *The* L. D. Strater, of Strater Industries. The *Fortune* 500's darling. The mayor's over in that corner, talking with Hannah Loy, the grand old lady of Broadway." His excitement began to hum in his voice as he continued to scan the room. "Man, there are enough luminaries in this room to light every borough in New York."

But Alex hadn't noticed. Furthermore, he didn't give a damn. His attention was focused on Bess. She'd stopped dancing, and had leaned up to whisper something in her partner's ear that made him laugh before he kissed her. Smack on the lips.

She kissed him back, too, her hands lightly intimate at his waist, before she turned and spotted the new arrivals. She waved, made her excuses, then scooted and dodged her way through the crowd toward them.

"You made it." She gave both Alex and Judd a friendly peck on the cheek before holding out both hands to Holly. "Nice to meet you."

"My wife, Holly, this is Bess McNee."

"Thanks for asking us." Holly caught herself starting to stutter, as she had the first time she faced a classroom of ten-year-olds. She flushed.

"My pleasure." Bess gave her hands a reassuring squeeze. "Let's get you something to eat and drink." She gestured toward a long table by the wall. Instead of the useless finger food and fancy, unrecognizable dishes Alex had expected, it was laden with big pots of spaghetti, mountains of garlic bread, and generous trays of antipasti.

"It's Italian night," she explained, grabbing a plate and heaping it high. "There's plenty of wine and beer, and a full bar." She handed the plate to Holly and began to dish up another. "The desserts are on the other side of the room. They're unbelievable." As she passed Judd a plate, she noted the gleam in Holly's eyes. "Would you like to meet some of the cast?"

"Oh, I..." The hell with sophistication. "Yes. I'd love it."

"Great. Excuse us. Help yourself, Alexi."

"This is really something," Judd said over a mouthful of spaghetti.

"Something," Alex agreed. Deciding to make the best of it, he fixed himself a plate.

He wasn't going to stay. But the food was great. In any
ase, he didn't have anything else to do. It didn't hurt to
ang around and rub elbows with the fast and famous while
e was helping himself to a good hot meal. It certainly
ade a change from his daily routine of wading through
isery and bitterness.

After washing down spaghetti with some good red wine,
e found himself a spot on a window seat where he could
t back and watch the show.

Bess dropped down beside him, clinked her glass against
s. "Best seat in the house."

"Some house."

"Yeah, I like it. I'll show you the rest later, if you
ant." She broke off a tiny piece of the pastry on his plate
nd sampled it. "Great stuff."

"Yeah. You got a little…here." Before his good sense
ould take over, he rubbed a bit of the rich cream from her
p. Watching her, he licked it from the pad of his thumb.
nd tasted her. "It's not bad."

For a moment she wondered if the circuits in her brain
ad crossed. Something certainly had sent out a spark. She
anaged a small sound of agreement as she flicked her
ngue to the corner of her mouth. And tasted him.

"Your, ah, partner's wife. Holly." Small talk, any talk,
ad always come easily to her. She wasn't sure why she
as laboring now.

"What about her?"

"Who? Oh, right. Holly. She's nice. I can't imagine what
would be like to teach fifth-graders."

"I'm sure you'll ask her."

"I already did." At ease again, she smiled at him. Some-
ing about that sarcastic edge to his voice made her relax
nd enjoy. "Come on, Alexi. We may be in different pro-
essions, but both of them require a certain amount of cu-
osity about human nature. Aren't you sitting here right

now wondering about all of these people, and what they'r
doing at my party?''

"Not as much as I'm wondering what *I'm* doing at you
party." He swirled the wine in his glass before sippin;
When he drank, his eyes stayed on hers. Watchful.

She liked that. She liked that very much, the way h
could sit so still, energy humming from every pore, whil
he watched. While he waited. Bess was willing to adm
that one of her biggest failings was being unable to wa
for anything.

"You were curious," she told him.

"Some."

Her skirt hitched up another inch when she curled he
legs up on the seat. "I'd be happy to tell you whatever yo
want to know, in exchange for your help. You see that gu
over there, the gorgeous one with the blonde hanging o
his biceps?"

Alex scanned, homed in. "Yeah. I wouldn't say he wa
gorgeous."

"You're not a woman. That's my detective, Storm Wa
field, the black sheep of the snooty, disgustingly rich Wa
field clan, the rebel, the volatile brother of the long
suffering Elana Warfield Stafford Carstairs. He's recentl
pulled himself out of the destructive affair with the wicke
wily Vicki. The blonde crawling up his chest. They're a
item off-camera, but on, Storm is madly in love with th
tragedy-prone and ethereal Jade, who is, of course, tor
between her feelings for him and her misplaced loyalty t
the maniacally clever and dastardly Brock Carstairs—ha!
brother to Elana's stalwart husband Dr. Maxwell Carstairs
Max was once married to Jade's formerly conniving bu
now repentant sister, Flame, who was killed in a Peruvia
earthquake soon after the birth of her son—who may o
may not be her husband's child. Naturally, the body wa
never recovered."

"Either I've had too much wine, or you're making me dizzy."

Bess smiled and gave him a companionable pat on the thigh that sent his blood pressure soaring. "It's really not that complicated, once you know the players. But I want you for Storm."

Alex sent the actor a considering look. "I don't think he's my type."

"Your professional expertise, Detective. I need an informal technical advisor. My producer'd be happy to compensate you for your time—particularly since we've been number one in the ratings for the past nine months." Someone called her name, and Bess sent a quick wave. "Looks like it's going to start to thin out. Listen, can you hang around until I've finished playing hostess?"

She popped up and was gone before he could answer. After a moment, Alex set the rest of the dessert aside and rose. If he was going to see the party through, he might as well enjoy himself.

As she saw to the rest of her guests, Bess kept an eye on him. Once he decided to relax, she noted, he made the most of it. It didn't surprise her that he knew how to flirt, or that several women in the room made a point of wandering in his direction. Not even Lori—no pushover in the men department—was unaffected.

"So, that's the one who busted you?" Lori asked her, popping a plump olive into her mouth.

"What do you think?"

Lori chewed, savored, swallowed. "Yum-yum."

With a laugh, Bess chose a wedge of cheese. "I assume that's a comment on the man, not my buffet."

"You bet. And the best part is, he's not an actor."

"Still sore?" Bess murmured.

Lori shrugged, but her gaze cut over to Steven Marshall, alias Brock Carstairs. "I never give him, or his weenie little brain, a thought. No sensible woman would spend her life competing with an actor's ego for attention.''

"Sense has nothing to do with it."

Lori looked away, because it hurt, more than she could bear to admit, to watch Steven while he was so busy ignoring her. "This from the queen of the bungled relationships."

"I don't bungle them, I enjoy them."

"I hasten to remind you that two of your former fiancés are in this room."

"It's a big party. Besides, I wasn't engaged to Lawrence."

"He gave you a ring with a rock the size of a Buick."

"A token of his esteem," Bess said blithely. "I never agreed to marry him. And Charlie and I..." She waved to Charles Stutman, esteemed playwright. "We were only engaged for a few months. We both agreed Gabrielle was perfect for him and parted the closest of friends."

"It was the first time I'd heard of a woman being best man at her former fiancé's wedding," Lori admitted. "I don't know how you do it. You don't angst over men, and they never toss blame your way when things fall apart."

"Because I end up being a pal." Bess's lips curved. For the briefest of moments, there was something wistful in the smile. "Not always a position a woman craves, but it seems to suit me."

"Going to be pals with the cop?"

Once again Bess found herself searching the remaining guests for Alex. She found him, dancing slow and close with a sultry brunette. "It would help if he'd bring himself to like me a little. I think it's going to take some work."

"I've never known you to fail. I've got to go. See you Monday."

"Okay." Bess was astute enough to glance over in Steven's direction as Lori left. She was also clear-sighted enough to see the expression of misery in his eyes as he watched Lori walk to the elevator.

People were much too hard on themselves, she thought with a sigh. Love, she was certain, was a complicated and painful process only if you wanted it to be. And she should know, she mused as she took another sip of wine. She had slipped painlessly in and out of love for years.

As she set the glass aside, Alex caught her eye. There was a quick, surprising tremor around her heart. But it was gone quickly as someone swept her up into a dance.

Chapter Three

"How often do you have one of these *things*?" Alex asked when he took Bess up on her offer of a last cup of cappuccino in her now empty and horribly cluttered apartment.

"Oh, when the mood strikes." The after-party wreckage didn't concern her. She and the cleaning team she'd hired would shovel it out sooner or later. Besides, she enjoyed this—the mess and debris, the spilled wine, the lingering scents. It was a testament to the fact that she, and a good many others, had enjoyed themselves.

"Want some cold spaghetti?" she asked him.

"No."

"I do." She unfolded herself from the corner section of the pit and wandered over to the buffet. "I didn't get a chance to eat much earlier—just what I could steal off other people's plates." She came back to stretch out on the cushions and twine pasta on her fork. "What did you think of Bonnie?"

"Who?"

"Bonnie. The brunette you were dancing with. The one who stuck her phone number in your pocket."

Remembering, Alex patted his shirt pocket. "Right. Bonnie. Very nice."

"Mmm...she is." As she agreed, Bess twined more pasta. She propped her feet on the coffee table, where they continued to keep the beat of the low-volume rock playing on the stereo. "I appreciate your staying."

"I've got some time."

"I still appreciate it. Let me run this by you, okay?" She continued to eat, rapidly working her way through a large plate full of food. "Jade's got a split personality due to an early-childhood trauma, which I won't go into."

"Thank God."

"Don't be snide—millions of viewers are panting for more. Anyway, Jade's alter ego, Josie, is the hooker—or will be, once we start taping that story line. Storm's nuts about Jade. It's difficult for him, as he's a very passionate sort of guy, and she's fragile at the moment."

"Because of Brock."

"You catch on. Anyway, he's wildly in love and miserably frustrated, and he's got a hot case to solve. The Millbrook Maniac."

"The—" Alex shut his eyes. "Oh, man."

"Hey, the press is always giving psychotics catchy little labels. Anyway, the Maniac's going around strangling women with a pink silk scarf. It's symbolic, but we won't get into that right now, either."

"I can't tell you how grateful I am."

She offered him a forkful of cold pasta. After a moment, he gave in and leaned closer to take it. "Now, the press is going to start hounding Storm," Bess continued. "And the brass will be on his case, too. His emotional life is a wreck. How does he separate it? How does he go about establishing a connection between the three—so far—victims? And when he realizes Jade may be in danger, how does he keep his personal feelings from clouding his professional judgement?''

''That's the kind of stuff you want?''

''For a start.''

''Okay.'' He propped his feet beside hers. ''First, you don't separate, not like you mean. The minute you have to think like a cop, that's what you are, that's how you think, and you've got no personal life until you can stop thinking like a cop again.''

''Wait.'' Bess shoved the plate into his lap, then bounded up and hunted through a drawer until she came up with a notebook. She dropped onto the sofa again, curling up her legs this time, so that her knee lay against the side of his thigh. ''Okay,'' she said, scribbling. ''You're telling me that when you start on a case, or get a call or whatever, everything else just clicks off.''

Since she seemed to be through eating, he set the plate on the coffee table. ''It better click off.''

''How?''

He shook his head. ''There is no how. It just is. Look, cop work is mostly monotonous. It's routine, but it's the kind of routine you have to keep focused on. Make a mistake in the paperwork, and some slime gets bounced on a technicality.''

''What about when you're on the street?''

''That's a routine, too, and you'd better keep your head on that routine, if you want to go home in one piece. You can't starting thinking about the fight you had with your woman, or the bills you can't pay, or the fact that your mother's sick. You think about now, right now, or you won't be able to fix any of those things later. You'll just be dead.''

Her eyes flashed up to his. He said it so matter-of-factly. When she studied him, she saw that he thought of it that way. ''What about fear?''

"You usually have about ten seconds to be afraid. So you take them."

"But what if the fear's for someone else? Someone you love?"

"Then you'd better put it aside and do what you've been trained to do. If you don't, you're no good to yourself or your partner, and you're a liability."

"So, it's cut-and-dried?"

He smiled a little. "Except on TV. You're asking me for feelings, McNee, intangibles."

"A cop's feelings," she told him. "I'd think they would be very tangible. Maybe a cop wouldn't be allowed to show his emotions on the job. An occasional flare-up, maybe, but then you'd have to suck it in and follow routine. And no matter how good you are, an arrest isn't always going to stick. The bad guy isn't always going to pay. That has to cause immeasurable frustration. And repressing that frustration…" Considering, she tapped her pencil against the pad. "See, I think of people as pressure cookers."

"Sure you do."

"No, really." That quick smile, the flash of the single dimple. "Whatever's inside, good or bad, has to have some means of release, or the lids blows." She shifted again, and her fingers nearly brushed his neck. She talked with them, he'd noted. With her hands, her eyes, her whole body. The woman simply didn't know how to be still. "What do you use to keep the lid on, Alexi?"

"I make sure I kick a couple of small dogs every morning."

She smiled with entirely too much understanding. "Too personal? Okay, we'll come back to it later."

"It's not personal." Damn it, she made him uncomfortable. As if he had an itch in the small of his back that he couldn't quite scratch. "I use the gym. Beat the crap out of a punching bag a few days a week. Lift too many weights. Sweat it out."

"That's great. Perfect." Grinning now, she cupped a hand over his biceps and squeezed. "Not too shabby. I guess it works." She flexed her own arm, inviting him to test the muscle. It was the gesture of a small boy on a playground, but Alex couldn't quite think of her that way. "I work out myself," she told him. "I'm addicted to it. But I can't seem to develop any upper-body strength."

He watched her eyes as he curled a hand over her arm and found a tough little muscle. "Your upper body looks fine."

"A compliment." Surprised that a reaction had leapt straight into her gut at the casual touch, she started to move her arm. He held on. It took some work to keep her smile from faltering. "What? You want to arm-wrestle, Detective?"

Her skin was like rose petals—smooth, fragrant. Experimenting, he skimmed his hand down to the curve of her elbow. She was smiling, he noted, and her eyes were lit with humor, but her pulse was racing. "A few years back I arm-wrestled my brother for his wife. I lost."

The idea was just absurd enough to catch her imagination. "Really? Is that how the Stanislaskis win their women?"

"Whatever works." Because he was tempted to explore more of that silky, exposed skin, he rose. He reminded himself that the uncomplicated Bonnie was more his style than the overinquisitive, oddly packaged Bess McNee. "I have to go."

Whatever had been humming between them was fading now. As Bess walked him to the door, she debated with herself whether she wanted to let those echoes fade or pump up the volume until she recognized the tune. "Stanislaski. Is that Polish, Russian, what?"

"We're Ukrainian."

"Ukrainian?" Intrigued, she watched him pull his jacket

on. "From the southwest of the European Soviet Union, with the Carpathian Mountains in the west."

"Yeah." And through those mountains his family had escaped when he was no more than a baby. He felt a tug, a small one, as he often did when he thought of the country of his blood. "You've been there?"

"Only in spirit." Smiling, she straightened his jacket for him. "I minored in geography in college. I like reading about exotic places." She kept her hands on the front of his jacket, enjoying the feel of leather, the scent of it, and of him. Their bodies were close, more casual than intimate, but close. Looking into his eyes, those dark, uncannily focused eyes, she discovered she wanted to hear that tune again after all.

"Are you going to talk to me again?" she asked him.

His fingers itched to roam along that tantalizingly bare skin on her back. For reasons he couldn't have named, he kept his hands at his side. "You know where to find me. If I've got the time and the answers, we'll talk."

"Thanks." Her lips curved as she rose on her toes so that their eyes and mouths were level. She leaned in slowly, an inch, then two, to touch her mouth to his. The kiss was soft and breezy. Either of his sisters might have said goodbye to him in precisely the same manner. But that cool and fleeting taste of her didn't make him feel brotherly.

She heard the humming in her head. A nice, quiet sound of easy pleasure. He tasted faintly of wine and spices, and his firm lips seemed to accept the gesture as it was meant— as one of affection and curiosity. Her lips were still curved when she dropped back on her heels.

"Good night, Alexi."

He nodded. He was fairly sure he could speak, but there was no point in taking the chance. Turning, he walked into the foyer and punched the elevator button. When he glanced back, she was still standing in the doorway. Smiling, she waved another goodbye and started to close the door.

It surprised them both when he whirled around and slapped a hand on it to keep it open. The fact that she took an automatic step in retreat surprised her further. But it was the look in his eyes, she thought, that made her feel like a rabbit caught in a rifle's cross hairs.

"Did you forget something?"

"Yeah." Very slowly, very deliberately, he slid his arms around her waist, ran his hand up her back, so that her eyes widened and her skin shivered. "I forgot I like to make my own moves."

Bess braced for the kind of wild assault that was in his eyes, and was surprised for the third time in as many minutes. He didn't swoop or crush, but eased her closer, degree by degree, until she was molded to him. His fingers cruised lazily up her back until they reached the nape of her neck, where they cupped and held. Still his mouth hovered above her.

His hand moved low, intimately, where skin gave way to silk. "Stand on your toes," he murmured.

"What?"

"Stand on your toes." This time, it was his lips that curved.

Dazed, she obeyed, then gave a strangled gasp when he increased the pressure on her back and pressed them center to center. His eyes stayed open as he moved his mouth to hers, brushing, nipping, then taking, in a dreamy kind of possession that had her own vision blurring.

The humming in her brain increased until it was a wall of sound, unrecognizable. She was deaf to everything else, even her own throaty moan as he dipped his tongue between her lips to seduce hers.

It was all slow-motion and soft-focus, but that didn't stop the heat from building. She could feel the little flames start to flare where she was pressed most intimately against him, then spread long, patient fingers of fire outward. Everywhere.

He never pushed, he never pressured, he savored, as a man might who had enjoyed a satisfying meal and was content to linger over a tasty dessert. Even knowing she was being sampled, tested, lazily consumed, she couldn't protest. For the first time in her life, Bess understood what it was to be helplessly seduced.

He hadn't meant to do this. He'd been thinking about doing just this for hours. However much pleasure it gave him to feel her curvy body melt against his, to hear those small, vulnerable sounds vibrating in her throat, to taste that dizzy passion on her lips, he knew he'd made a mistake.

She wasn't his type. And he was going to want more.

The instinct he'd been born with and then honed during his years on the force helped him to hold back that part of himself that, if let loose, could turn the evening into a disaster for both of them. Still, he lingered another moment, taking himself to the edge. When his system was churning with her, and his mind was clouded with visions of peeling her out of that swatch of a dress, he stepped back. He supported her by the elbows until her eyes fluttered open.

They were big and dazed. He clenched his teeth to fight back the urge to pull her to him again and finish what he'd started. But, however stunned and fragile she looked at the moment, Alex recognized a dangerous woman. He'd been a cop long enough to know when to face danger, and when to avoid it.

"You, ah…" Where was all her glib repartee? Bess wondered. It was a little difficult to think when she wasn't sure her head was still on her shoulders. "Well," she managed, and settled for that.

"Well." He let her go and added a cocky grin before he walked back to the elevator. Though his stance was relaxed, he was praying the elevator would come quickly, before he lost it and crawled back to her door. She was still there when the elevator rumbled open. Alex let out a quiet, relieved breath as he stepped inside and leaned against the back wall. "See you around, McNee," he said as the doors slid shut.

"Yeah." She stared at the mural-covered walls. "See you around."

"Holly hasn't been able to stop talking about that party." Judd was scarfing down a blueberry muffin as Alex cruised Broadway. "It made her queen of the teachers' lounge."

"I bet." Alex didn't want to think about Bess's party. He especially didn't want to think about what would be after the party. Work was what he needed to concentrate on, and right now work meant following up on the few slim leads they'd hassled out of Domingo.

"If Domingo's given it to us straight, Angie Horowitz was excited about a new john." Alex tapped his fingers against the steering wheel. "He'd hired her two Wednesdays running, dressed good, tipped big."

Judd nodded as he brushed muffin crumbs from his shirt. "And she was killed on a Wednesday. So was Rita Shaw. It's still pretty thin, Alex."

"So we make it thick." It continued to frustrate him that they'd wasted time interrogating the desk clerks at the two fleabag hotels where the bodies had been found. Like most in their profession, the clerks had seen nothing. Heard nothing. Knew nothing.

As for the ladies who worked the streets, however nervous they were, they weren't ready to trust a badge.

"Tomorrow's Wednesday," Judd said helpfully.

"I know what the hell tomorrow is. Do you do anything but eat?"

Judd unwrapped another muffin. "I got low blood sugar. If we're going to go back and look at the crime scene again, I need energy."

"What you need is—" Alex broke off as he glanced past Judd's profile and into the glaring lights of an all-night diner. He knew only one person with hair that shade of red. He began to swear, slowly, steadily, as he searched for a parking place.

"You really write for TV?" Rosalie asked.

Bess finished emptying a third container of nondairy product into her coffee. "That's right."

"I didn't think you were a sister." Interested as much in Bess as in the fifty dollars she'd been paid, Rosalie blew out smoke rings. "And you want to know what it's like to turn tricks."

"I want to know whatever you're comfortable telling me." Bess shoved her untouched coffee aside and leaned forward. "I'm not sitting in judgment or asking for confidences, Rosalie. I'd like your story, if you want to tell it. Or we can stick with generalities."

"You figure you can find out what's going on on the streets by putting on spandex and a wig, like you did the other night?"

"I found out a lot," Bess said with a smile. "I found out it's tough to stand in heels on concrete for hours at a time. That a woman has to lose her sense of self in order to do business. That you don't look at the faces. The faces don't matter—the money does. And what you do isn't a matter of intimacy, not even a matter of sex—for you—but a matter of control." She scooted her coffee back and took a sip. "Am I close?"

For a moment, Rosalie said nothing. "You're not as stupid as you look."

"Thanks. I'm always surprising people that way. Especially men."

"Yeah." For the first time, Rosalie smiled. Beneath the hard-edged cosmetics and the lines life had etched in her face, she was a striking woman, not yet thirty. "I'll tell you

this, girlfriend, the men who pay me see a body. They don't
see a mind. But I got a mind, and I got a plan. I've been
on the streets five years. I ain't going to be on them five
more.''

"What are you going to do? What do you want to do?"

"When I get enough saved up, I'm going South. Going
to get me a trailer in Florida, and a straight job. Maybe
selling clothes. I look real fine in good clothes." She
crushed out her cigarette and lit another. "Lots of us have
plans, but don't make it. I will. I'm clean," she said, and
lifted her arms, turning them over. It took Bess a minute
to realize Rosalie was saying she wasn't a user. "One more
year, I'm gone. Less than that, if I hook on to a regular
john with money. Angie did.''

"Angie?" Bess flipped through her mental file. "Angie
Horowitz? Isn't that the woman who was murdered?"

"Yeah." Rosalie moistened her lips before sucking in
smoke. "She wasn't careful. I'm always careful."

"How can you be careful?"

"You keep yourself ready," Rosalie told her. "Angie,
she liked to drink. She'd talk a john into buying a bottle.
That's not being careful. And this guy, the rich one? He—"

"What the hell do you think you're doing?"

Both Rosalie and Bess looked up. Standing beside the
scarred table was a tall man with thin shoulders. There was
a cheroot clamped between his teeth, and a diamond
winked on his finger. His face was moon-pale, with furious
blue eyes. His hair was nearly as white, and slicked back,
ending in a short ponytail.

"I'm having me a cup of coffee and a smoke, Bobby,"
Rosalie told him. But beneath the defiance, Bess recognized
the trickle of fear.

"You get back on the street where you belong."

"Excuse me." Bess offered her best smile. "Bobby, is
it?"

He cast his icy blue eyes on her. "You looking for work,

sweetheart? I'll tell you right now, I don't tolerate any loafing."

"Thank you, but no, I'm not looking. Rosalie was just helping me with a small problem."

"She doesn't solve anyone's problems but mine." He jerked his head toward the street. "Move it."

Bess slid out of the booth but held her ground. "This is a public place, and we're having a conversation."

"You don't talk to anybody I don't tell you to talk to." Bobby gave Rosalie a hard shove toward the door.

Bess didn't think, simply reacted. If she detested anything, it was a bully. "Now just a damn minute." She grabbed his sleeve. He rounded on her. Other patrons put on their blinders when he pushed her into the table. Bess came up, fists clenched, just as Alex slammed through the door.

"One move, Bobby," he said tightly. "Just one move toward her."

Bobby brushed at his sleeve and shrugged. "I just came in for a cup of coffee. Isn't that right, Rosalie?"

"Yeah." Rosalie closed her hand over the business card Bess had slipped her. "We were just having some coffee."

But Alex's eyes were all for Bess. She didn't look pale and frightened. Her eyes were snapping, and her cheeks were flushed with fury. "Tell me you want to press charges."

"I'm sorry." With an effort, Bess relaxed her hands. "We were just having a conversation. Nice talking to you, Rosalie."

"Sure." She swaggered out, blowing smoke in Alex's face for effect.

"Take off."

Bobby moved his shoulders again, smirked. "The coffee's lousy here, anyway." He flicked a glance at Bess. "Next time, sweetheart."

Alex waited ten humming seconds after the door swung

shut. Without a word, he stalked over to Bess and grabbed her by the arm and hustled her out the door.

"Look, if this is a knight-in-shining-armor routine, I appreciate it, but I don't need rescuing."

"You need a straitjacket."

With murder in his heart, he dragged her half a block.

"In the car," he snapped, opening the back door of the patrol car.

"A cab would be—"

He swore, put a hand on her head and shoved her into the back seat.

Resigned, Bess settled back. "Hi, Judd," she said as he took his place in the passenger seat in front. "How's Holly?"

"Great, thanks." He slanted a look toward his partner. "Ah, she really had a good time at your place."

"I'm glad. We'll have to do it again." Alex whipped out into traffic with enough force to have her slamming back against the seat. Without missing a beat, Bess crossed her legs. "Am I allowed to ask where we're going, or is this another bust?"

"I should be taking you to Bellevue, where you belong," Alex responded. "But I'm taking you home."

"Well, thanks for the lift."

His eyes flashed to hers in the rearview mirror. Her face was still flushed, and her irises were a sharp enough jade to slice to the bone, but she looked more miffed than upset. *Miffed*, he thought with a snort. Stupid word. It fit her perfectly.

"You're an idiot, McNee. And, like most idiots, you're dangerous."

"Oh, really?" She scooted up in the seat so that she could lean between him and Judd. "Just how do you figure that, smart guy?"

"Not only do you go back down to an area you have no business even knowing about—"

"Give me a break."

"But," he continued, "you sit there drinking coffee with a hooker, then pick a fight with her pimp. The kind of guy who'd as soon give a woman a black eye as wish her good-morning."

Bess poked a finger at his shoulder. "I didn't pick a fight with anyone, and if I had, it would be my business."

"That's why you're an idiot."

"Hey, Alex, ease off."

"Keep out of this," Alex and Bess snarled in unison.

"I'm not even here," Judd mumbled, scooting down in his seat.

"It so happens I was conducting an interview." Bess folded her arms on the seat so that she wouldn't give in to the nasty urge to twist Alex's ear. "In a public place," she added. "And you had no right to come bursting in and ruining everything before I'd finished."

"If I hadn't come bursting in, babe, you'd have had your nose broken again."

She scowled, wrinkling her undeniably crooked nose. "I can defend my nose, and anything else, just fine."

"Yeah, anyone can see you're a regular amazon. Ow!" He slapped at her hand and swore the air blue when she gave in and twisted his ear. "The minute I get you out of this car, I'm going to—"

"Uh, Alex?"

"I told you to keep out of it."

"I'm out," Judd assured him. "But you might want to take a look at the liquor store coming up at nine o'clock."

Still steaming, Alex did, then let out a heavy sigh. "Perfect. This makes it perfect. Call it in."

Bess watched, wide-eyed, as Judd radioed in an armed robbery in progress, gave their location and requested backup. Before she could shut her gaping mouth, Alex was swinging to the curb.

"You," he said, stabbing a finger in her face. "Stay in the car, or I swear I'll wring your neck."

"I'm not going anywhere," Bess assured him after she managed to swallow the large ball of fear lodged in her throat. But before the words were out, he and Judd were out of the car and drawing their weapons.

He'd already forgotten her, she realized as she stared at his profile. Before he and Judd had crossed the street, he'd put on his cop's mind and his cop's face. She'd seen hundreds of actors try to emulate that particular look. Some came close, she realized, but this was the real thing. It wasn't grim or fierce, but flat, almost blank.

Except for the eyes, she thought with a quick shudder. She'd had only one glimpse of his eyes, but it had been enough.

Life and death had been in them, and a potential for violence she would never have guessed at.

In the darkened car, she gripped her hands together and prayed.

He hadn't forgotten her. It infuriated him that he had to fight to tuck her into some back corner of his mind. There were innocent people in that store. A man and a woman. He could smell the fear while he was still three yards away.

But he broke his concentration long enough to glance back and make certain she was staying put.

He gestured Judd to one side of the door while he took the other. He didn't have time to worry that the rookie might freeze. Right now they were just two cops, and he had to believe Judd would go with him through the door.

The 9 mm felt warm in his hand. He'd already identified the weapons of the two perpetrators. One had a sawed-off shotgun, the other a wicked-looking .45. He could hear the woman crying, pleading not to be hurt. Alex ignored it. They would wait for backup as long as they could.

He shifted just enough to look inside.

Behind the counter, a woman of approximately sixty

stood with her hands at her throat, weeping. A man of about the same age was emptying the cash register as fast as his trembling hands allowed. One of the gunmen grabbed a bottle off a shelf. He ripped off the top and guzzled. Swearing at the old man, he smashed the bottle on the counter and jabbed the broken glass toward his face.

Alex had seen the look before, and he knew they wouldn't be content with the money. "We're going in," he whispered to Judd. "You go low, go for the one on the right."

Pale, Judd nodded. "Say when."

"Don't fire your weapon unless you have to." Alex sucked in his breath and went through the door. "Police!" In the back of his mind he heard the sirens from the backup as the first gunman swung the shotgun in his direction. "Drop it!" he ordered, knowing it was useless. The woman was already screaming before the first shots were fired.

The shotgun blew out a bank of fluorescent lights as the force of Alex's bullet sent the man slamming backward. Alex was getting the second man in his sights when a bullet from the .45 slammed into a bottle inches above his head, spraying alcohol and glass. Judd fired, and stopped being a rookie.

Slowly, with the same blank look on his face, Alex came out of his crouch and studied his partner. Judd wasn't pale now. He was green. "You okay?"

"Yeah." After replacing his weapon, Judd rubbed the back of his hand over his mouth. There was a greasy knot in his stomach that was threatening to leap into his throat. "It was my first."

"I know. Go outside."

"I'm okay."

Alex gave him a nudge on the shoulder. His hand remained there a moment, surprisingly gentle. "Go outside anyway. Tell the backup to call an ambulance."

* * *

Bess was waiting beside the car when Alex came out some twenty minutes later. He looked the same, she thought. Just the same as he'd looked when he walked in. Then he lifted his head and looked at her, and she saw she was wrong.

His eyes hadn't looked so tired, so terribly tired, twenty minutes before.

"I told you to stay in the car."

"I did."

"Then get back in."

Gently she laid a hand on his arm. "Alexi, you made your point. I'll take a cab. You have things to do."

"I've done them." He skirted the car and yanked open the passenger door. She could almost feel his body vibrating, but when he spoke, his voice was firm, sharp. "Get in the damn car, Bess."

She didn't have the heart to argue, so she crossed over and complied. "What about Judd?"

"He's heading to the cop shop to file the report."

"Oh."

He let the silence hang for three blocks. It hadn't been his first, but he hadn't told Judd that the bright, shaky sickness didn't fade. It only turned inward, becoming anger, disgust, frustration. And you never stopped asking yourself why.

"Aren't you going to ask how it felt? What went through my mind? What happens next?"

"No." She said it quietly. "I don't have to ask when I can see. And it's easy enough to find out what happens next."

It wasn't what he wanted. He didn't want her to be understanding, or quietly agreeable, or to turn those damned sympathetic eyes on him. "Passing up a chance for grist for your mill? McNee, you surprise me. Or can't your TV cop blow away a couple of stoned perps?"

He was trying to hurt her. Well, she understood that,

Bess thought. It often helped to lash out when you were in pain. "I'm not sure I can fit it into any of our scheduled story lines, but who knows?"

His hands clenched on the wheel. "I don't want to see you down there again, understand? If I do, I swear I'll find a way to lock you up for a while."

"Don't threaten me, Detective. You had a rough night, and I'm willing to make allowances, but don't threaten me." Leaning back, she shut her eyes. "In fact, do us both a favor and don't talk to me at all."

He didn't, but when he pulled up at her building, the smoke from his anger was still hanging in the air. Satisfied, she slammed out of the car. She'd taken two steps when he caught up with her.

"Come here," he demanded, and hauled her against him. She tasted it, all the violence and pain and fury of what he'd done that night. What he'd had to do. There was no way for her to comfort. She wouldn't have dared. There was no way for her to protest. She couldn't have tried. Instead, she let the sizzling passion of the kiss sweep over her.

Just as abruptly, he let her go. He'd be trembling in a minute, and he knew it. God, he needed…something from her. Needed, but didn't want.

"Stay off my turf, McNee." He turned on his heel and left her standing on the sidewalk.

Chapter Four

"When it comes to murder," Bess mused, "I like a nice, quick-acting poison. Something exotic, I think."

Lori pursed her lips. "If we're going to do it, I really think he should be shot. Through the heart."

Shifting in her seat at the cluttered table, Bess scooped up a handful of sugared almonds. "Too ordinary. Reed's a sophisticated, sensuous cad. I think he should go out with more than just a bang." She munched and considered. "In fact, we could make it a slow, insidious poison—milk a few weeks of him wasting away."

"Nagging headaches, dizzy spells, loss of appetite," Lori put in.

"And chills. He really should have chills." Bess steepled her hands and imagined. "He gives this big cocktail party, see. You know how he likes to flaunt his power and money in the faces of all the people he's dumped on over the years."

Lori sighed. "That's why I love him."

"And why millions of viewers love to hate him. If we're

going to take him out, let's do it big. They're all there at Reed's mansion.... Jade, who's never forgiven him for using her sister for his own evil ends. Elana, who's agonizing over the fact that Reed will use his secret file, distorting the information to discredit Max.''

"Mmm..." Getting into the spirit, Lori gestured with her watered-down soft drink. "Brock, who's furious that with one phone call Reed can upset the delicate balance of the Tryson deal and cost Brock a fortune. And Miriam, of course.''

"Of course. We haven't seen nearly enough of her lately. Reed's self-destructive ex-wife, who blames him for all her problems.''

"Justifiably," Lori pointed out.

"Then there's Vicki, the woman scorned. Jeffrey, the cuckolded husband.'' She grinned. "And the rest of the usual suspects.''

"Okay. What kind of poison?''

"Something rare," Bess mused. "Maybe Oriental. I'll work on it." She scribbled a reminder on a notepad. "So they all have a motive for killing him. Even the housekeeper, because he seduced her naive, innocent daughter, then cast her aside. Sometime during the party, we see a glass of champagne. The room's in shadows. Close-up on a small black vial. A hand pours a few drops into the glass.''

"We'll see if it's a man or woman.''

"The hand's gloved," Bess decided, then realized how ridiculous it would be to wear gloves at a cocktail party. "Okay, okay, we don't see it at the party. Before. There's this box, see? This ornately carved wooden box.''

"And the gloved hand opens it. Candlelight flickers off the glass vial as the hand removes it from the bed of velvet.''

"That's the ticket. We'll cut to that kind of thing three

or four times during the week of the party. Let the audience know it's bad business for somebody.''

"Meanwhile, Reed's playing everyone like puppets. Handing out his personal brand of misery, building the pressure to the boiling point, until it explodes on the night of the party.''

"It'll be great," Bess assured her. "Throughout the evening, Reed's enjoying himself stirring up old fires, poking at sores. Miriam has too much to drink and gets sloppy and shrill. This provides the perfect distraction for our killer to doctor Reed's champagne. Because it's slow-acting, the symptoms don't begin to show right away. We have some fatigue, a little dizziness, some minor pain. Maybe a rash.''

"I like a good rash," Lori agreed.

"By the time he kicks off, it'll be difficult for the cops to pinpoint the time and place when the poison was administered. We just might have the perfect crime.''

"There is no perfect crime.''

Both Bess and Lori glanced toward the doorway. Alex stood there, his hands tucked in his pockets. There was a half smile on his face, a result of his enjoyment at listening to them plotting a murder. "Besides, if your TV cop didn't figure it out, your viewers would be pretty disappointed.''

"He'll figure it out." Bess reached for another almond as she watched him, her bare feet propped on the chair beside her. Alex discovered that the baggy slacks she wore effectively hid her legs but didn't stop him from thinking about them. "Did somebody call a cop?" she asked Lori.

"Not me." Well aware that three was most definitely a crowd, Lori rose. "Listen, I've got to make a call, and I think I'll run up and peek in on the taping. Nice to see you, Detective.''

"Yeah." He shifted so that Lori could get through the door, but he didn't step inside. Instead, he glanced around, annoyed with himself for feeling so awkward. "Some place," he said at length.

Bess's lips curved. The room was hardly bigger than a closet and windowless. The table where she and Lori worked was covered with books, folders and papers, and dominated by a word processor that was still humming. Besides the table, there was one overstuffed chair, a small couch and two televisions.

"We call it home," Bess said, and tilted her head. "So, what brings you down to the dungeons, Alexi?"

The description was fairly apt. They were in the basement of the building that held the studios and production offices for 'Secret Sins' and its network. He shrugged off her question with one of his own. "How long are you in for?"

"The duration, I hope." Casually she rubbed the ball of one foot over the instep of the other. "After the last Emmy, they did offer us an upstairs office with a view, but Lori and I are creatures of habit. Besides, who's going to come down here and peek over our shoulders while we write?" She recrossed her ankles. "Are you off-duty?"

"I took a couple hours personal time."

"Oh." She drew the word out, thinking he looked very appealing when he was embarrassed. "Should I consider this a personal visit?"

"Yeah." He stepped inside, then regretted it. There wasn't enough room to wander around. "Listen, I just wanted to apologize."

It was probably very small of her, Bess thought, but, oh, she was enjoying this. "Generally or specifically?"

"Specifically." He shook his head when she held out the bowl of almonds. "After the robbery attempt, when I took you home. I was out of line."

"Okay." She set the bowl down and smiled at him. "We're dealing with your behavior during the last half hour of the evening."

His brows drew together. "Everything I said before that

sticks. You had no business doing what you were doing where you were doing it."

"Get back to the apology. I like that better."

"I took what I was feeling out on you, and I'm sorry." Figuring the worst was over, he sat on the edge of the table. "You didn't react the way I expected."

"Which was?"

"Scared, outraged, disgusted." He shrugged again. "I don't usually take women to armed robberies."

Now things were getting interesting. "Where *do* you take them?"

His gaze locked on hers. He knew when he was being teased, and he knew when it was good-natured. "To dinner, to the flicks, dancing. To bed."

"Well, armed robbery is probably more exciting. At least than the first three." She rose, placed her hands on his shoulders and kissed him lightly on the mouth. "No hard feelings." When his hands came to her hips and held her in place, she lifted a brow. "Was there something else?"

"I've been thinking about you."

"That could be good."

His lips twitched. "I haven't decided that yet. Maybe we could start with dinner."

"Start what?"

"Working our way to bed. That's where I want you."

"Oh." Her breath came out a little too quickly and not quite steady. It didn't help that his eyes were calm, amused and very confident. How, she wondered, had their positions been so neatly reversed? "That's certainly cutting to the chase."

"You said once that people in our professions observe people. What I've observed about you, McNee, is that you'd probably see through any flowers and moonbeams I might toss at you."

Slowly she ran her tongue over her teeth. "Depends on your pitching arm. The idea isn't without its appeal, Alexi,

ut I prefer taking certain aspects of my life—sex being
one of them—in a cautious, gradual manner.''

He grinned at her. "That could be good."

She had to laugh. "Meanwhile—" But he didn't let her
scoot back.

"Meanwhile," he echoed, keeping his hands firm.
"Have dinner with me. Just dinner."

Hadn't she told herself she wasn't going to get involved
again, fall in love again? Oh, well. "I often enjoy just dinner."

"Tomorrow. I'm on tonight."

"Tomorrow's fine."

He nudged her an inch closer. "I'm making you nervous."

"No, you're not." Yes, he was.

"You're wriggling." He grinned again, surprised at how
satisfying it was to know he'd unsettled her.

"I've got work, that's all."

"Me too. Why don't I come by about seven-thirty? My
brother-in-law's got this place. I think you'll get a kick out
of it."

"Lady clothes or real clothes?"

"What are you wearing now?"

She glanced down at her sweater and slacks. "Real
ones."

"That'll do." He stood, then tilted her chin with a finger
until they were eye-to-eye. "You have the oddest face,"
he said half to himself. "You should be ugly."

She laughed, unoffended. "I was. I've burned all pictures
of me before the age of eighteen." Her dimple winked out
as she smiled at him. "I imagine you were always gorgeous."

He winced, though he knew he should be used to having
that term applied to him. "My sisters were gorgeous," he
told her. "Are. My brother and I are ruggedly attractive."

"Ah, manly men."

"You got it."

"And you grew up surrounded by flocks of adoring females."

"We started with flocks and moved on to hordes."

Her eyes lit with amusement and curiosity. "What was it like to—"

He cut her off the most sensible way. He liked the quick little jolt her body gave before she settled into him. And the way her mouth softened, accepted. No pretenses here, he thought as she gave a quiet sigh and melted into the kiss. It was simple and easy, as basic as breathing.

If his system threatened to overcharge, he knew how to control it. Perhaps he drew the kiss out longer than he'd intended to, deepened it more than he had planned. But he was still in control. Maybe, for just a moment, he imagined what it would be like to lock the door, to sweep all those papers off the table and take her, fast and hot, on top of it.

But he wasn't a maniac. He reminded himself of that, even as his blood began to swim. A slow and gentle touch brought pleasure to both, and let a woman see that she was appreciated for everything she was.

"Dangerous," he murmured in Ukrainian as he slid his mouth from her. "Very dangerous woman."

"What?" She blinked at him with eyes that were arousingly unfocused and heavy. "What does that mean?"

He had to make a conscious effort to keep his hands gentle at her shoulders. "I said I have to go. Keep off the streets, McNee."

She called to him as he reached the doorway. "Detective." Her heart was thumping, her head was reeling, but she really hated not having the last word. For lack of anything better, she dredged up an old line from "Hill Street Blues." "Let's be careful out there."

Alone, she lowered herself into a chair, as carefully as an elderly aunt. Five minutes later, Lori found her in exactly the same spot, still staring into space.

"Uh-oh." One look had Lori dropping down beside her. With a shake of her head, she handed Bess a fresh soft drink. "I knew it. I knew this was going to happen the minute I saw that gorgeous cop at your party."

"It hasn't happened yet." Bess took a long drink. Funny, she hadn't realized how dry her throat had become. "I'm afraid it's going to, but it hasn't happened yet."

"You had that same look on your face when you fell for Charlie. And for Sean. And Miguel. Not to mention—"

"Then don't." Frowning, she focused on Lori. "Miguel? Are you certain? I was sure I had better taste."

"Miguel," Lori said ruthlessly. "Granted, you came to your senses within forty-eight hours, but the day after he took you to the opera you had the same stupid look on your face."

"We saw *Carmen*," Bess pointed out. "I don't think the look had anything to do with him. Besides, I'm not in love with Alexi, I'm just having dinner with him tomorrow."

"That's what you always say. Like with George."

Bess's shoulders straightened. "George was the sweetest man I've ever known. Being engaged to him taught me a lot about understanding and compassion."

"I know. You were understanding enough to be godmother to his firstborn."

"Well, after all, I did introduce him to Nancy."

"And he promptly dumped you and ran off with her."

"He didn't dump me. I wish you wouldn't hold that against him, Lori. Breaking our engagement was a mutual decision."

"And the best thing to happen to you. George was a wimp. A whiny wimp."

Because it was precisely true, Bess sighed. "He just needed a lot of emotional support."

"At least you never slept with him."

"He was saving himself."

They looked at each other and burst out laughing. Once

she caught her breath, Bess shook her head. "I should never have told you that. It was indiscreet."

"Observation," Lori announced, and Bess gestured a go-ahead. "The cop isn't going to save himself."

"I know." Bess felt the warning flutter in her stomach. Thoughtfully she drew her finger down through the moisture on the bottle. "I'll cross that bridge when I come to it."

"Bess, you don't cross bridges, you burn them." Lori gave her hand a quick squeeze. "Don't get hurt."

There was a touch of regret in Bess's smile. "Do I ever?"

Alex liked the way she looked. It took a certain panache, he supposed, to be able to wear the jade-toned blouse with bright blue slacks, particularly if you were going to add hot-pink high-tops. But Bess pulled it off. Everything about her was vivid. He supposed that was why he'd gone into her office to apologize and ended up asking her out.

It was probably why he hadn't been able to get her, or the idea of taking her to bed, out of his mind since he'd met her.

For herself, Bess took one look at Zackary Muldoon's bar, Lower the Boom, and knew she had a relaxed, enjoyable evening in store. There was music from the juke box, a babble of voices, a medley of good, rich scents. The tangle of pear-shaped gemstones at her ears swung as she turned to Alex. "This is great. Is the food as good as it smells?"

"Better." He gave a wave in the general direction of the bar as he found them a table.

As usual, the bar was cluttered with people and thick with noise. Since his sister had married Zack, Alex had made a habit of dropping in once a week or so, and he knew most of the regulars by name. He grinned at the waitress who stopped at their table. "Hey, Lola. How's it going?"

"It'll do, cutie." Resting her tray on her hip, Lola gave Bess the once-over. Though less than ten years Alex's senior, Lola had taken a maternal interest in him. It wasn't often Alex brought a date into the bar, and Lola made it her business to check out his current lady. "So, what can I get you?"

"Tequila." Bess dropped her bag in the empty chair beside her with a thunk. "Straight up."

Alex only lifted a brow at Bess's choice. "Give me a beer, Lola. Rachel around?"

"Upstairs. And she better have her feet up." She gave the ceiling a scowl. "She'll probably sneak down here before the night's over. Can't keep her away from the boss."

"What's Rio's special tonight?"

"Paella." Her eyes lit with appreciation. She'd sampled some herself. "He's been driving Nick crazy, making him shell shrimp."

"You game for that?" Alex asked Bess.

"You bet." As Lola wandered off, Bess propped her chin on her hands. "So, who's the boss, who's Rio, and who's Nick?"

"Zack's the boss." He gestured toward the tall, broad-shouldered man working the bar. "Rio's the cook, this Jamaican giant who'll fix you the best meal this side of heaven. Nick's Zack's brother."

Bess nodded. She liked to know the players. "And Rachel's married to Zack." After a long study of the man behind the bar, she smiled. "Impressive. How'd she meet him?"

"She was Nick's PD after I busted him for attempted burglary."

Bess didn't blink or look shocked, she simply leaned a little closer. "What was he stealing?"

Alex was vaguely disappointed that he hadn't gotten a

reaction. "Electronics—and doing a poor job of it. He was tangled up with a gang at the time. This was about a year and a half ago." Absently he toyed with the square-cut aquamarine on her finger, watching it catch the light. "Nick had some problems. Actually, he's Zack's stepbrother. Nick was still a kid when Zack went off and joined the navy and his mother died. Anyhow, when Zack came back a few years ago, his father was dying, and the kid was chin-deep in trouble."

"This is great." Bess beamed up at Lola as their drinks were served. "Thanks."

The smile did it. Lola sent Alex a look of approval before she swung by the bar to report to Zack.

"Don't stop now."

Alex lifted his mug of beer. He knew very well that Lola was giving Zack a sotto voce rundown of her impressions and opinions of his choice of companion. "You want to hear the whole thing?"

"Of course I do." Bess sprinkled salt on her wrist, licked it, then tossed back the tequila with all the flair of a Mexican bandit. While she sucked on the lime wedge Lola had brought with the drink, she grinned at Zack. "I like the zing."

"How many times can you do that and live?"

"I haven't tested it that far." The liquor left a nice trail of heat down her throat and into her stomach. "I did ten once, but I was younger then, and stupid. So keep going." She leaned forward again. "Zack came back after sailing the seven seas and found his brother in trouble."

"Well, Nick was tangled up with the Cobras..." Alex began. By the time their paella was served, he was enjoying himself. It always polished a man's ego to have a woman's complete and fascinated attention. "So that's how I ended up on the point of having an Irish-Ukrainian niece or nephew."

"Terrific. You've got a flair for storytelling, Alexi. Must be some Gypsy blood in there."

"Naturally."

She smiled at him. All he needed was a hoop of gold in one ear and a violin, she thought—but she was sure he wouldn't want to hear it. "It doesn't hurt that you have this wisp of an accent that peeks out now and then. Of course, your material's first-rate, too. I'm a sucker for happy endings. I can't have many of them in my field. Once we tie things up, we have to unravel them again, or we lose the audience."

"Why? I thought most people went for the happy ending."

"They do. But in soaps, a character loses the edge if he or she isn't dealing with some crisis or tragedy." She sampled the paella and sighed her satisfaction. "That's why Elana's been married twice, had amnesia, was sexually assaulted, had two miscarriages and a nervous breakdown, went temporarily blind, shot a former lover in self-defense, overcame a gambling addiction, had twins who were kidnapped by a psychotic nurse—and recovered them only after a long, heartrending and perilous search through the South American jungles." She took another glorious bite. "Not necessarily in that order."

Before Alex could ask who Elana was, Lola was setting down fresh drinks. "You watch 'Secret Sins'?" she asked Bess.

"Religiously. You?"

"Well, yeah." She shrugged, knowing there were several patrons in the bar who'd rag her about it. "I got hooked when I was in the hospital having my youngest. He's ten now. That was back when Elana was a first-year resident at Millbrook Memorial and in love with Jack Banner. He was a great character."

"One of the best," Bess agreed. "Brooding and self-destructive."

"I was really sorry when he died in that warehouse fire. I didn't think Elana would ever get over it."

"She's a tough lady," Bess commented.

"Had to be." When someone called her, Lola waved to them to wait. "If it hadn't been for her, Storm would never have gotten himself together and become the man he is today."

"You like Storm?"

"Oh, man, who wouldn't?" With a chuckle, Lola rolled her eyes. "The guy's every woman's fantasy, you know? I'm really pulling for him and Jade. They deserve some happiness, after everything they've been through. Jeez, all right, Harry, I'm on my way. Enjoy your dinner," she said to Bess, and hurried off.

Bess turned to Alex with a smile. "You look confused."

He only shook his head. "You two were talking about those characters as though they were real people."

"But they are," Bess told him, and scooped up some shrimp. "For an hour a day, five days a week. Didn't you ever believe in Batman, or Sam Spade? Scarlett O'Hara, Indiana Jones?"

"It's fiction."

"Good fiction creates its own reality. That's entertainment." Picking up the saltshaker, she grinned. "Come on, Alexi, even a cop needs to fantasize now and then."

He looked at her long enough to make her pulse dance. "I do my share."

Bess swallowed the tequila, but its zing paled beside the one that Alex's quiet statement had streaking through her. "You'll have to tell me about that sometime." She glanced around at the sound of piano music.

Against the far wall was a huge upright. A slimly built, sandy-haired young man was caressing blues out of the keys.

"That's Nick," Alex told her.

"Really?" Bess angled her chair around for a better look. "He's very good."

"Yeah. He talked Zack into putting a piano in the bar about a year ago. Rachel and Muldoon tried to get him to go back to school, get more training, but no dice."

"Some things can't be taught," Bess murmured.

"Looks like. Anyway, he still works in the kitchen with Rio, and comes out and plays when the mood strikes."

"And has every female in the joint mooning over him."

"He's just a kid," Alex said quickly—too quickly.

With her tongue in her cheek, Bess turned back. "Younger men have their own appeal to the experienced woman. In fact, right now Jessica is embroiled in a passionate affair with Tod—who's ten years her junior. The mail is running five to one in favor."

"We were talking about you."

She only smiled. "Were we?"

Zack walked over to slap Alex on the back. "How's the meal?"

"It's terrific." Bess held out a hand. "You're Zack? I'm Bess."

"Nice to see you." Zack kept a hand on Alex's shoulder after giving Bess's a quick squeeze. "You must be the Bess Rachel ran into down at the station."

"I must be. You have a great place here. Now that I've found it, I'll be back."

"That's what we like to hear." His blue eyes sparkled with friendly curiosity. "Alex doesn't bring his ladies around very often. He likes to keep us guessing."

She couldn't help but respond to the humor in Zack's eyes. "Is that so?"

"Ease off, Muldoon," Alex muttered.

"He's still sore at me for stealing his baby sister."

Alex sent him an arched look. "I just figured she had better taste." He lifted his beer. "Speaking of which." He gestured with the mug.

Bess saw Zack's eyes change and, recognizing love, her heart sighed. It didn't surprise her when Rachel came to the table.

"What's this?" Rachel demanded. "A party, and nobody invited me?"

"Sit," Zack and Alex said in unison.

"I'm tired of sitting." Ignoring them both, she turned to Bess. "Nice to see you again." She took a deep, appreciative sniff. "Rio's paella. Incredible, isn't it?"

"Yes, it is. Alex was just telling me how the two of you met."

"Oh?" Rachel's brow lifted.

"Why don't you join us and give me your side of it?"

Twenty minutes later, Alex was forced to admit that Bess's casual friendliness had gotten Rachel to sit down and relax in a way neither he nor Zack would have been able to with their demanding concern.

For a woman who was so full of energy and verve, she had a knack for putting people at ease, he noted.

A gift for listening to details and asking just the right question. And for entertaining, he mused—effortlessly.

It didn't surprise him that she was able to talk music with Nick when he was called over to join them, or food with Rio when she asked to go back into the kitchen to compliment him on the meal. He wasn't surprised when she and Rachel made a date to meet for lunch the following week.

"I like your family," Bess stated as they settled into a cab.

"You've only met a fraction of it."

"Well, I like the one's I've met. How much more do you have?"

"My parents. Another sister, her husband, their three kids. A brother, his wife, and their kid. What about you?"

"Hmm?"

"Family."

"Oh. I was an only child. Do they all live in New York?"

"All but Natasha." He toyed with the curls at the nape of her neck. "You don't talk about yourself."

"Are you kidding?" She laughed, though she wanted to curl like a cat into the fingers brushing her skin. "I never stop talking."

"You ask questions. You talk about things, other people, your characters. But you don't talk about Bess."

She should have known a cop would notice what most people didn't. "We haven't had that many conversations," she pointed out. When she turned her head, her mouth was close to his. She wanted to kiss him, Bess thought. It wasn't merely to distract him. After all, she had nothing to hide. But she didn't speak, only moved her lips to his.

The fingers at the back of her neck tensed as he changed the angle of the kiss and the mood of it. It was light and friendly only for an instant. Then it darkened, deepened, lengthened. Mixed with the taste, the texture, were hints of what was to come.

There's a storm brewing, Bess thought dizzily. And, oh, she'd never been able to resist a storm.

Her heart was knocking by the time his lips moved to her temple. "You know how to change the subject, McNee."

"What subject?"

His hand slid to her throat, cupped there. He felt the pigeon beat of her rapid pulse. The rhythm of it was as seductive as jungle drums. "You. Now I'm only more curious."

"There's not that much to tell." Uneasy and confused by the sensation, she drew back as the cab pulled to the curb. "Looks like we're here." She slid across the seat while Alex paid the driver. Her knees were a little weak, she realized. Another first. Alexi Stanislaski was going to require some thought. "You don't have to walk me up," she said, surprised that it unnerved her to see the cab pull away and leave the two of them alone on the shadowy sidewalk.

"Which means you're not going to ask me in."

"No." She smiled a little, running her fingers up and down the strap of her bag. But she wanted to. It was amazing to her just how much she wanted to. "I think it would be smarter if I didn't."

He accepted that, because the choice had to be hers. And the prospect of changing her mind along the way was tremendously appealing. "We'll do this again."

"Yes."

He closed a hand over her restless one, brought it to his lips. "Soon."

She felt something, a small, vague ache centered in her heart. Confused by it, she slipped her hand away. "All right. Soon. Good night."

"Hold it." Before she could turn away, he took her face in his hands, held it there for a moment before lowering his mouth to hers.

The pressure was whisper-light, persuasive, invasive. Even as she responded, the kiss had that odd ache spreading. Helpless, she brought her hands to his wrists, clinging to them for balance. Though his mouth remained beautifully gentle, the pulse she felt beneath her fingers raced in time with her own.

Then he let her go, stepped back. His eyes stared into hers. "Good night," he said.

She managed a nod before hurrying inside.

There was something about Bess, Alex thought as he waited patiently for the light in her apartment to come on. Something. He'd just have to find out what it was.

Chapter Five

The last person Bess expected to see when she left her office a few days later was Rosalie. Even in the bustling crowds of midtown, the woman stood out. After a moment of blank surprise, Bess smiled and crossed the sidewalk.

"Hi. Were you waiting for me?"

"Yeah."

"You should have come in." Bess adjusted the weight of her bag and briefcase.

"I figured it would be better for you if I waited out here."

"Don't be silly..." Her words trailed off as she tried to see through and around Rosalie's huge tinted glasses. Those sunburst colors around the left eye weren't all cosmetics. Bess's friendly smile faded. "What happened to you?"

Rosalie shrugged. "Bobby. He was a little ticked off about the other night."

"That's despicable."

"I've had worse."

"Bastard." She said it between her teeth, but overlying

her fury was a terrible sense of guilt. "I'm sorry. I'm so sorry. It was my fault."

"Ain't nobody's fault, girlfriend. Just the way things are."

"It's not the way they should be. And if I hadn't..." She let that go, knowing you could only go back and change things in scripts. "Do you want to go to the police? I'll go with you. We could—"

"Hell, no." Rosalie let out what passed for a laugh. "I'd get a lot worse than a sore eye if I tried that. And if you think there's a cop alive who gives a damn about a hooker with a black eye, you *are* as dumb as you look."

Alex would care, Bess thought. She refused to believe otherwise. "We'll do whatever you want."

Rosalie pulled out a cigarette, cocking her hip as she lit it. "Listen, you said you'd pay me to talk. I figure I can use the extra money. And I'm on my own time."

"All right." Ideas were beginning to stir. "How much do you average a night?"

As a matter of course, Rosalie started to inflate it, but found the lie stuck in her throat. "After Bobby takes his cut, about seventy-five. Maybe a hundred. Business isn't as good as it used to be."

"We'll talk." Distracted, Bess searched for a cab. "We'll never get a taxi at this hour," she mumbled. "I live uptown about twenty blocks. Do you mind walking?"

This time Rosalie laughed full and long. "Girl, walking the streets comes natural to me."

Once they reached Bess's apartment, Rosalie tipped down her shaded glasses and whistled. Unable to resist, she walked to one of the wide windows. She could see a swatch of the East River through other buildings. The sound of traffic was so muted, it was almost musical. A far cry from the clatter and roar she lived with every day.

"My, oh, my, you do live high."

"How about dinner?" Automatically Bess stepped out

of her shoes. "We'll order in." Red meat, Bess thought. At the moment, she could have eaten it raw. "Sit down, I'll get us some wine."

Wine, Rosalie thought as she stretched out on the plump cushions of the pit. She figured that sounded just dandy. "You pay for all this just writing stuff?"

"Mostly." On impulse, Bess chose one of the best bottles in her wine rack. "You're not a vegetarian, are you?"

Rosalie snorted. "Get real."

"Good. I want a steak." After handing Rosalie a glass, she picked up the phone to order dinner.

"I can't pay for that."

"I'm buying," Bess assured her, and curled up on the couch. "I need a consultant, Rosalie." It was a risk, but so was breathing, she decided. "I'll give you five hundred a week."

Rosalie choked on the wine. "Five hundred, just to tell you about turning tricks?"

"No. I want more. I want why. I want you to tell me about the other women. What draws them in. What you're afraid of, what you're not. When I ask you a question, I'll want an answer." Her voice was brisk now, all business. "I'll know if you lie."

Rosalie's eyes were shrewd and steady. "You need all that for a TV show?"

"You'd be surprised." It had gone well beyond the show. The bruise on Rosalie's face grated on her. She had caused it, Bess reflected. She would find a way to fix it. "I'm buying a lot of your time for five hundred a week, Rosalie. You might want to take a little vacation from Bobby."

"What I do after I talk to you is for me to say."

"Absolutely. But if you decided you wanted to take a break from the streets, and if you needed a place to stay while you did, I could help you."

"Why?"

Bess smiled. "Why not? It wouldn't cost me any more."

Intrigued, Rosalie considered. "I'll think about it."

"Fine. We can get started right away." She rose to gather up pads, pencils, her tape recorder. "Remember, this is daytime TV, and we can only do so much. I'll have to filter down a great deal of what you tell me. Why don't I fill you in on the story line?"

Rosalie merely shrugged. "It's your nickel."

"Yes, it is." She settled down again, and was weaving the complex and overlapping relationships of Millbrook— to Rosalie's confusion and fascination—when she heard the buzzer for her private elevator. Still talking, she walked over to release the security lock. "So, anyway, the Josie personality is dynamically opposed to Jade. The stronger she gets, the more confused and frightened Jade becomes. She doesn't remember where she's been when Josie comes out. And the lapses are getting longer."

"Sounds like the lady needs a shrink."

"Actually, she'll go to Elana—she's a psychiatrist—but that's down the road a bit. And under hypnosis— Ah, here's the food." At the elevator's ding, Bess opened the door. The smile froze on her face.

"Alexi."

"Don't you bother to ask who it is before you let someone come up?" He shook his head before he caught her chin in his hand and kissed her.

"Yes—that is, not when I'm expecting someone. What are you doing here?"

"Kissing you?" And, at that moment, she wasn't as responsive as he'd come to expect. Then it occurred to him that she'd said she was expecting someone. A man? A date? A lover? His eyes cooled as he stepped back. "I guess I should have called first."

"No. I mean, yes. That is…are you off tonight?"

"I go back on in a couple hours."

"Oh. Well." The buzzer sounded again.

"You could always tell him I'm the plumber."

Baffled, she stepped back inside to release the elevator. "Tell who what?"

"The guy on his way up."

"Why should I tell the delivery boy you're a plumber?"

"Delivery boy?" A sound inside the apartment had him edging closer. He wasn't jealous, damn it, he was just curious. "I guess you've already got company," he began, and pushed the door wider.

"Actually, I do." Giving up, Bess gestured him inside. "We were just about to have some dinner."

He looked over at the couch just as Rosalie stood. Caught between them, Bess felt herself battered by double waves of hostility.

"What the hell is she doing here?"

"You called the cops," Rosalie said accusingly before Bess could answer. "You called the damn cops."

"No. No, I didn't."

Rosalie was already striding across the room. Bess knew that if the woman made it to the door she would have lost her chance. "Rosalie." She grabbed her arm. "I didn't call him."

"And why the hell *didn't* you?" Alex tossed back.

"Because it's none of your business." Still gripping Rosalie, Bess swirled on him. "This is my home, and she's my guest."

"And you're a bigger idiot than I thought."

Sizing up the situation, Rosalie relaxed fractionally. "You two got a thing?"

"Yes," Alex shot back.

"No," Bess snapped, then sighed. "Something in between the two," she mumbled. She snatched her wallet out of her bag as she heard the elevator ding. "Excuse me. That's dinner."

While she herded the delivery boy inside to set up the

meal, Alex and Rosalie stood eyeing each other with mutual dislike and suspicion.

"What's the game, Rosalie?"

"No game." She flashed a smile that was as feral as a shark's. "I'm a paid consultant. Your lady hired me."

"The hell with that." He paused a moment, studying her bruised eye. "Bobby do that?"

Rosalie angled her chin. "I walked into a door."

"Sure you did." He did care. Bess might have been surprised at how much he cared. Rosalie certainly would have been stunned. But he also knew there were things that couldn't be fixed. "You'll want to watch your step."

"I don't make the same mistake twice."

He turned away from her, his hands balled into fists in his pockets. "McNee, I want to talk to you."

"Oh, just shut up." She didn't bother to look up as she counted out bills. "Can't you see I'm trying to figure the tip? There you go."

"Thanks, lady." The delivery boy tucked the bills away. "Enjoy your dinner."

"There's enough for three," Bess stated, turning toward Alex. "But you're not going to stay if you're rude."

"Rude?" The single word bounced off her ceiling. He was beside her in two strides. "You think it's rude for me to ask you if you've lost your mind when I walk in and find you've invited a hooker to dinner?"

Her eyes narrowed. "Out."

"Damn it, Bess…"

"I said out." She gave him a hefty shove toward the door. "We went on one date," she reminded him. "*One.* Maybe I entertained the idea of something more, but that gives you no right to come into my house and tell me what to do and who to talk with."

He grabbed her hand before she could push him again. "One has nothing to do with the other."

"You're right. Absolutely right. What I should have said

is that I run my life, Detective." She snatched her hand away so that she could poke a finger at his chest. "Me. Alone. Get the picture?"

"Yeah." He wondered how she'd like a nice clip on that pointy little chin of hers. "I've got a picture for you." He hauled her up and kissed her hard. No gentle touch, no finesse. All steam heat. It lasted only seconds, but he succeeded in shocking her speechless. "Things change, McNee." Dark, furious eyes pinned her to the spot. "Get used to it."

With that, he stormed out, slamming the door behind him.

"Well." Bess took one breath, then another. Her throat felt scalded. "Of all the incredible nerve. Who the hell does he think he is, marching in here that way?" Hands on her hips, she spun to face Rosalie. "Did you see that?"

"Hard to miss it." Grinning, Rosalie snatched a french fry from a plate.

"If he thinks he's getting away with that—that *attitude*—he's very much mistaken."

"Man's nuts about you."

"Excuse me?"

"Girl, that was one lovesick puppy."

Bess snatched up her wine and gulped. "Don't be ridiculous. He was just showing off."

"Uh-huh. If I had me a man who looked at me like that, I'd do one of two things."

"Which are?"

"I'd either sit back and enjoy, or I'd run for my life."

Frowning, Bess sat down and picked up her fork. "I don't like to be pushed."

"Seems to me it depends on who's doing the pushing." She sat, as well, and dug right into her steak. "He sure is one fine-looking man—for a cop."

Bess stabbed at her salad. "I don't want to talk about him."

"You're paying the tab," Rosalie said agreeably.

With a grunt of assent, Bess tried to eat. Damn cop, she thought. He'd ruined her appetite.

There was something to be said for beating the hell out of inanimate objects. Alex had always found the therapy of a pair of boxing gloves and a punching bag immeasurably rewarding. With those so easily accessible, he could never figure out why so many people felt the need for a psychiatrist's couch.

Until recently.

Twenty minutes of sweating and pounding hadn't relieved his basic frustration. He often used the gym—in the middle of a difficult case, when one went wrong, when a good arrest turned sour in court. The same ingredients had worked equally well for him whenever he'd fought with family, or friends, or had female problems.

Not this time.

Whatever hold Bess McNee had on him, Alex couldn't seem to punch himself out of it.

"So much energy, so early."

The familiar voice had Alex blinking away the sweat that had dripped through his headband into his eyes. His brother Mikhail, and Alex's ten-month-old nephew, Griff, were standing hand in hand, grinning identical grins.

"Got your papa out early, did you, tough guy?" Alex swung Griff up for a smacking kiss.

Griff babbled out happily. The only word Alex could decipher in the odd foreign language of a toddler was *Mama*.

"Sydney's tired," Mikhail explained. "She has some wheeling and dealing keeping her up at night. This one's an early riser." He ruffled his son's hair. "So I thought we'd come down and lift weights. Right?"

Griff grinned and cocked his elbows. "Papa."

"Your muscle's bigger," Alex assured him.

"Hey, it's the Griff-man!" Rocky, the former light-weight who ran the gym, gave a whistle and held out his wiry arms. "Come see me, champ."

With a squeal of pleasure, Griff wiggled out of Alex's arms to toddle off on his almost steady legs. "Better watch out, Rock," Mikhail called out. "He's slippery."

"I can handle him." With the confidence of a four-time grandfather, he hefted Griff. "We got things to do," he told Mikhail. "Why don't you talk to your brother there and find out why this is the third time this week he's come in to pound on my equipment?"

"Nosy," Alex muttered. "He's worse than an old woman."

Mikhail tilted a brow when Alex went back to pounding the bag. "Speaking of women…"

"We weren't."

"Why do men come to such places as this unless it's to talk of women?" The music of the Ukraine flavored Mikhail's voice. Alex wondered if his brother knew how much he sounded like their father.

"To hit things," he retorted. "To talk dirty and to sweat."

"That, too. So, it is a woman, yes?"

"It's always a damn woman," Alex said between gritted teeth.

"This one's named Bess."

Alex's punch stopped in midswing. Turning, he used his forearm to swipe his brow. "How do you know about Bess?"

"Rachel tells me." Pleased, Mikhail grinned. "She also tells me that this Bess is not beautiful so much as unique, and that she's smart. This isn't your usual type, Alexi."

"She's nobody's type." Alex turned back to the bag, feinted with his right, then jabbed with his left. "Unique," he said with a snort. "That's her, all right. Her face. It was like God was distracted that day and mixed up the features for five different women. Her eyes are too big, her chin's pointed, her nose is crooked.'' His gloved fist plowed into the bag. ''And she has skin like an angel. I touch it and my mouth waters.''

''Mmm... I'll have to get a look at this one.''

''I've sworn off,'' Alex told him between grunts. ''I don't need the aggravation. She doesn't have all her circuits working at the same time. Maybe Rachel thinks she's smart because she went to college.''

''Radcliffe,'' Mikhail supplied. ''She had lunch with Rachel, and Rachel asked.''

''Radcliffe?'' Letting out a breath, Alex leaned against the bag. ''It figures.''

''She also told Rachel that the two of you had a... misunderstanding.''

''I understood perfectly. Look, maybe she went to some fancy college, but you couldn't fill up a teaspoon with her common sense. I don't need to get involved with someone that flaky.''

Mikhail's bark of laughter echoed through the gym. ''This from a man who once dated Miss Lug Wrench.''

''It was Miss Carburetor.''

''Ah, that's different.''

A smile twitched, and Alex punched halfheartedly at the bag. Working up a sweat hadn't relaxed him, but five minutes with Mikhail was doing the job. ''Anyway, we're finished before we got started. And both better off.''

''Undoubtedly you're right.''

''I know I'm right. We'd always be coming at things from different angles. Hers is cross-eyed. She doesn't see anything the way she should.''

''A difficult woman.''

''Difficult.'' Alex held out his hands so that Mikhail could unlace his gloves. ''That doesn't begin to describe her. She acts so mild and relaxed, you wouldn't think you could rile her with a cattle prod. Then you point out an obvious mistake, for her own good, and she jumps on you with both feet. Kicks you out of the house.''

Mikhail tucked his tongue in his cheek. ''You're better off without her.''

''You're telling me.'' Alex tossed his gloves aside and flexed his hands. ''Who needs unreasonable women?''

''Men.''

''Yeah.'' With a sigh, Alex sent his brother a miserable look. ''I want her so much I can't breathe.''

''I know the feeling.'' He punched his brother's sweaty shoulder. ''So go get her.''

''Go get her,'' Alex repeated.

''Put her in her place.''

A dangerous light, one Mikhail recognized, flickered in Alex's eyes. ''Her place. Right.''

''Hey!'' Mikhail called out when his brother strode off. ''The showers are that way.''

''I'll catch one at the station. See you later.''

''Later,'' Mikhail agreed. He wandered off to find his son, wondering how soon he would meet this unique, unreasonable woman without common sense.

She sounded perfect for his baby brother.

Bess was never at her best in the morning, and she suspected anyone who was. Her alarm was buzzing when she heard the pounding on her door. She'd been ignoring the first for nearly ten minutes, but the incessant knocking had her dragging herself out of bed.

Bleary-eyed, pulling a skimpy silk robe over an equally skimpy nightshirt, she stumbled to the door. ''What the hell?'' she demanded. ''Is it a fire or what?''

''Or what,'' Alex told her when she yanked open the door.

Struggling to focus, she dragged a hand through her hair. The robe drooped off one shoulder. ''How'd you get up here?''

"Flashed my badge for the security guard." After closing the door behind him, he looked his fill. There was a great deal to be said for a sleepy woman in rumpled white silk. "Get you up, McNee?"

"What time is it?" She turned away, following the scent from her coffeemaker, which was set to brew at 7:20 each morning. "What day is it?"

"Thursday." He followed her weaving progress through the living area and into a big white-and-navy kitchen. There was a huge arrangement of fresh orchids on the center island. Orchids in the kitchen, he thought. Only Bess. "About 7:30."

"In the morning?" Blindly she groped for a mug. "What are you doing here at 7:30 on a Thursday morning?"

"This." He spun her around. The taste of her mouth, warm and soft from sleep, had him groaning. Before she could think—he didn't want either of them to think—he slipped his tongue between her lips to seduce hers. Her body went stiff, then melted, softening against his like candle wax touched by a flame.

Through the roaring of his blood, he heard the crash as the china mug she'd held slipped from her fingers and smashed on the tiles.

Was she still dreaming? Bess wondered. Her dreams had always been very vivid, but this... It wouldn't be possible to feel so much, need so desperately, in a dream.

And she could taste him. Really taste him. A mingling of man and desire and salty sweat. Delicious. His mouth was so hot, so unyielding, just as his hands were through the thin silk she wore.

She could feel the cool tiles beneath her feet, a shivery contrast to the heat roaring around her. Under her palms, his cheeks were rough, arousingly rough. And she heard her own voice, a muffled, confused sound, as she tried to say his name.

"I have to wake up," she managed when his mouth left hers to cruise over her throat. "I really have to."

"You are awake." He had to touch her—just once. However unfair his advantage, he had to. So he cupped her breasts in his hands, molding their firmness through the silk, brushing his thumbs, feather-light, over straining nipples. "See?"

She'd never been the swooning type, but she was afraid this would be a first. "I have to—" She gasped, for as she'd started to step back, he'd swept her up into his arms. A skitter of panic, completely unfamiliar, raced down her spine. "Alexi, don't."

He covered her mouth again, felt her trembling surrender. And knew he could. And could not. "Your feet are bare," he said, and set her on the counter. "I made you drop your cup."

Shaken, she stared down at the shards of broken crockery. "Oh."

"You have a broom?"

"A broom." She was awake now, wide-awake. But her mind was still mush. "Somewhere. Why?"

He was making her stupid, he realized, and grinned. "So I can clean it up before you cut yourself. Stay there." He walked to a likely-looking closet and located a dustpan and broom. Because he was a man whose mother had trained him well in such matters, he went about the sweeping job quickly and competently. "So, have you missed me?"

"I haven't given you a thought." She blew the hair out of her eyes. "Hardly."

"Me either." He dumped the shards into the trash, replaced the broom and dustpan. "How about some coffee?"

"Sure." Maybe that would help her regain her normal composure. As he poured, she caught a whiff of him over the homey morning aroma. "You smell like a locker room."

"Sorry. I was at the gym." When he handed her the

coffee, she sat where she was and sipped. Half a cup later, she was able to take her first clear-eyed look at him.

He looked fabulous. Rough and sweaty and ready for action. The thick tangle of hair was falling over a faded gray sweatband. His face was unshaven, his NYPD T-shirt was ripped and darkened in a vee down the chest, his sweatpants were loose and frayed at the cuffs. When she lifted her gaze back to his, he smiled.

"Good morning, McNee."

"Good morning."

He skimmed a finger over her thigh. She was sensitive there, he noted. He could tell by the way her eyes darkened and the pulse in her throat picked up the beat. "I'm not apologizing this time."

"You should be."

"No. I'm right about this." He put a finger over her lips before she could speak. "Trust me. I'm a cop."

He could have all but seduced her in her own kitchen before her eyes were even open, but she had a point to make. Closing a hand over his wrist, she drew his hand away. "My personal decisions, whether they have to do with my professional or my private life, are just that. Personal. I've been making those decisions, right or wrong, for a long time. I don't intend to stop now."

"I'm not going to see you hurt."

"That's very sweet, Alexi." Softening a bit, she brushed a hand through his hair. "I don't intend to be hurt."

"You don't know what you're dealing with. Oh, you think you do," he continued, recognizing the look in her eyes. "But all you know is the surface. There are things that go on in the streets, every day, every night, that you have no conception of. You never will."

She couldn't argue, not with what she saw in his face. "Maybe not. I don't see what you see, or know what you know. Maybe I don't want to. My friendship with Rosalie—"

"Friendship?"

"Yes." The expression on her face dared him to contradict her. "I feel something for her—about her." With a helpless gesture, Bess set her cup aside. "I can't possibly explain it to you, Alexi. You're not a woman. I can help her. Don't tell me it's a fairy tale to believe I can save her from the streets and what she's chosen to be. I've gotten that advice already."

"From someone with at least half a brain," he surmised. "I had no idea this had gotten so out of hand. You said you wanted to talk to her for background stuff for your story."

"That's true enough." But Bess remembered the bruise on Rosalie's face too well. "Is it so impossible that I might be able to make a difference in her life? Has being a cop made you so hard you aren't willing to give someone a chance to change?"

He gripped her hands, hard. "This isn't about me."

"No," she said, and smiled. "It's not."

He swore and let go of her to pace to the coffee maker. "Okay, point taken. It's none of my business. But I'm going to ask for a promise."

"You can ask."

"Don't go out on the streets with her. Don't go anywhere near Bobby's territory."

She thought of the man with the silver hair and the vicious eyes. "That I can promise. Feel better?"

"I'm not through. Don't let her up here unless you're sure she's alone. Meet her down at your office, or in some public place."

"Really, Alexi…"

"Please."

She said nothing for a moment, and then, because she could see how much it had cost him to use that word, she relented. "All right." Bess scooted away from the counter, then opened the bread drawer. "Want a bagel?"

"Sure."

She popped two into the toaster oven before going to the refrigerator for cream cheese. "There's something I should tell you."

"I'm hoping there's a lot of things."

With a puzzled smile, she turned back. "I'm sorry?"

"I want to know about this personal life of yours, McNee. I want to know all about you, then I want to take you to bed and make love with you until we both forget our own names."

"Ah…" It didn't seem to take more than one of those long, level looks of his to make her forget a great deal more than her name. "Anyway…"

"Anyway?" he repeated helpfully as the toaster oven dinged.

"I was going to tell you about Angie Horowitz."

The lazy smile vanished. His eyes went cool and flat. "What do you know about her?"

"Boy, it really does click off," Bess murmured. "I feel like I just stepped into one of those rooms with the two-way mirror and the rubber hoses."

"Angie Horowitz," he repeated. "What do you know about her?"

"I don't know much of anything, but I thought I should tell you what Rosalie told me." She got out plates, then began to spread the bagels generously. "She said that Angie was really happy to have hooked up with this one guy. He'd hired her a couple of times and slipped her some extra money. Treated her well, promised her some presents. In fact, he gave her this little pendant. A gold heart with a crack down the center."

Alex's face remained impassive. There had been a broken neck chain wrapped in Angie's hand when they found her, just as there had been with the first victim. That little detail had been kept out of the press. There hadn't been a heart, he thought now. But someone had broken the chain for a reason.

"She wore it all the time—according to Rosalie," Bess went on. "Rosalie also told me Mary Rodell had one just like it. She was the other victim, wasn't she?" she asked Alex. "She had it on the last time Rosalie saw her alive."

"Is that it?"

Bess was disappointed that he wasn't more pleased with the information. "There's a little more." Sulking a bit, she bit into her bagel. "Angie called the guy Jack, and she bragged to Rosalie that he was a real gentleman, and was built like…" She trailed off, cleared her throat, but her eyes were bright with humor, rather than embarrassment. "Women have colorful terms for certain things, just like men."

"I get the picture."

"He had a scar."

"What kind?"

"I don't know. A scar, on his hip. Angie told Rosalie he got upset when she asked him about it. That's all she told me, Alexi, but I figured the coincidence of the pendants, you might want to know about this guy."

"It never hurts." He gave her an easy smile, though his instincts were humming. "Probably nothing, but I'll look into it." He tugged on her hair. "Do yourself a favor, and don't tell Rosalie you passed this along to me."

"I'm softhearted, Detective. Not softheaded. She thinks you have a really nice butt—but you're still a cop."

He grimaced. "I don't think I like you discussing my anatomy with a—"

"Friend," she supplied, with a warning lift of her brow. "I also had lunch with your sister. We discussed your nasty temperament."

"I heard." He stole her bagel. "Radcliffe, huh?"

"So?"

"So nothing. Want to go dancing with me?"

She debated with herself for almost a full second. "Okay. Tonight?"

"Can't. Tomorrow?"

It meant canceling dinner at Le Cirque with L. D. Strater. That debate took nearly half a second. "That's fine. Sexy or sedate?"

"Sexy. Definitely."

"Good. Why don't you come by around—" She glanced at the clock, stared, then yelped. "Damn it! Now I'm going to be late. I'll owe Lori twenty dollars if I'm late one more time this month." She began pushing Alex out of the kitchen. "It's all your fault. Now beat it, so I can throw on some clothes and get out of here."

"Since you're already late…" He had some very good moves. Even as she shoved him toward the door, he was turning to catch her close. "I can arrange it so you're a lot later."

"Smooth talker," she said with a laugh. "Take a hike."

"You've already lost twenty. I'm just offering to make it worth your while."

"I don't know how I can resist that incredibly romantic gesture, but somehow I find I have the strength."

"You want romance?" There was a gleam in his eyes as he headed for the door. "Tomorrow night. We'll just see how strong you are."

Chapter Six

After spending most of the morning kicking his heels in court, waiting to testify in an assault case, Alex returned to the station to find his partner hip-deep in paperwork. "The boss wants to see you," Judd said through a mouthful of chocolate bar.

"Right." Alex shrugged out of his jacket and dragged off his court-appearance tie. With his free hand, he picked up his pile of messages.

"I think he meant now," Judd said helpfully.

"I got it." As he passed Judd's desk, Alex peeked over his shoulder at the report in the typewriter. "Two *p*'s in apprehend, Einstein."

Judd backspaced and scowled. "You sure?"

"Trust me." He swung through the squad room and knocked on Captain Trilwalter's glass door.

"Come."

Trilwalter glanced up. If Alex often thought he was swamped in paperwork, it was nothing compared to what surrounded his captain. Trilwalter's desk was heaped with it. The overflowing files, stacks of reports and correspondence gave Trilwalter a bookish, accountantlike look. This was enhanced by the half glasses perched on his long, narrow nose, the slightly balding head and the ruthlessly knotted knit tie.

But Alex knew better. Trilwalter was a cop down to the bone, and he might still be on the street but for the bullet that had damaged his left lung.

"You wanted to see me, Captain?"

"Stanislaski." Trilwalter crooked his finger, then pointed it, gesturing to Alex to come in and shut the door. He leaned back in his chair, folded his hands over his flat belly and scowled.

"What the hell is all this about soap operas?"

"Sir?"

"Soap operas," Trilwalter repeated. "I just had a call from the mayor."

Testing his ground, Alex nodded slowly. "The mayor called you about soap operas?"

"You look confused, Detective." A rare, and not entirely humor-filled, smile curved Trilwalter's mouth. "That makes two of us. The name McNee mean anything to you? Bess McNee?"

Alex closed his eyes a moment. "Oh, boy."

"Rings a bell, does it?"

"Yes, sir." Alex gave himself a brief moment to contemplate murder. "Miss McNee and I have a personal relationship. Sort of."

"I'm not interested in your personal relationship, sort of or otherwise. Unless they come across my desk."

"When I arrested her—"

"Arrested her?" Trilwalter held up one hand while he took off his glasses. Slowly, methodically, he massaged the bridge of his nose. "I don't think I have to know about that. No, I'm sure I don't."

Despite himself, Alex began to see the humor in it. "If

I could say so, Captain, Bess tends to bring that kind of reaction out in a man.''

"She's a writer?''

"Yes, sir. For 'Secret Sins.'''

Trilwalter lifted tired eyes. "'Secret Sins.' Apparently the mayor is quite a fan. Not only a fan, Detective, but an old chum of your Bess McNee's. *Old chum* was just how he put it.''

Finding discretion in silence, Alex said nothing as Trilwalter rose. The captain walked to the watercooler wedged between two file cabinets in the corner of his office. He poured out a paper cupful and drank it down.

"His honor, the mayor, requests that Miss McNee be permitted to observe a day in your life, Detective.''

Alex made a comment normally reserved for locker rooms and pool halls. Trilwalter nodded sagely.

"My sentiments exactly. However, one of the less appealing aspects of working this particular desk is playing politics. You lose, Detective.''

"Captain, we're closing in on that robbery on Lexington. I've got a new lead on the hooker murders and a message on my desk from a snitch who could know something about that stiff we found down on East Twenty-third. How am I supposed to work with some ditzy woman hanging over my shoulder?''

"This is the ditzy woman you have a personal relationship with?''

Alex opened his mouth, then closed it again. How to explain Bess? "Sort of,'' he said at length. "Look, Captain, I already agreed to talk to McNee about police work, in general, now and again. I never agreed to specifics. I sure as hell don't want her riding shotgun while I work.''

"A day in your life, Stanislaski.'' With that same grim smile, Trilwalter crushed his cup and tossed it. "Monday next, to be exact.''

"Captain—''

"Deal with it," Trilwalter said. "And see that she stays out of trouble."

Dismissed, Alex stalked back to his desk. He was still muttering to himself when Judd wandered over with two cups of coffee.

"Problem?"

"Women," Alex said.

"Tell me about it." Because he'd been waiting all morning for the chance, Judd sat on the edge of Alex's desk. "Speaking of women, did you know that Bess was engaged to L. D. Strater?"

Alex's head snapped up. "What?"

"Used to be," Judd explained. "One of the teachers at Holly's school's a real gossip-gatherer. Reads all the tabloids and stuff. She was telling Holly how Strater and Bess were a thing a few months ago."

"Is that so?" Alex remembered how they'd danced together at her party. Kissed. His mouth flattened into a grim line as he lifted the cup.

"A real whirlwind sort of thing—according to my sources. Before that, she was engaged to Charles Stutman."

"Who the hell is that?"

"You know, the writer. He's got that hot play on Broadway now. *Dust to Dust.* Holly really wants to see it. I thought maybe Bess could wangle some tickets."

The sound Alex made was neither agreement nor denial. It was more of a growl.

"Then there was George Collaway—you know, the son of that big publisher? That was about three years ago, but he married someone else."

"The lady gets around," Alex said softly.

"Yeah, and in top circles. And, hey, Holly was really blown away when she found out that Bess was Roger K. McNee's daughter. You know, the camera guy."

"Camera guy?" Alex repeated, feeling a hole spreading in the pit of his stomach. "As in McNee-Holden?"

"Yeah. First camera I ever bought was a Holden 500. Use their film all the time, too. Hell, so does the department. Well." He straightened. "If you get a chance, maybe you could ask Bess about those tickets. It sure would mean a lot to Holly."

McNee-Holden. Alex ran the names over in his head while the noise of the squad room buzzed around him. For God's sake, he had one of their cameras himself. He'd bought their little red packs of film hundreds of times over the years. The department used their developing paper. He was pretty sure NASA did too.

Wasn't Bess just full of secrets!

So she was rich. Filthy rich. He picked up his messages again, telling himself it wasn't such a big deal. Wouldn't have been, he corrected silently, if she'd told him about it herself.

Engaged, he thought with a frown. Three times engaged. Shrugging, he picked up the phone. None of his business, he reminded himself as he punched in numbers. If she'd been married three times, it would be none of his business. He was taking her dancing, not on a honeymoon.

But it was a long time before he was able to shuffle her into a back corner of his mind and get on with his job.

Sexy, the man had said, Bess remembered, turning in front of her cheval glass. It looked as though she were going to oblige him.

Snug teal silk hugged every curve and ended abruptly at midthigh. Over the strapless, unadorned bodice, she wore a short, body jacket of fuchsia. Long, wand-shaped crystals dangled at her ears. After stepping into her heels, she gave her hair a last fluff.

She felt like dancing.

When her buzzer sounded, she grinned at her reflection. Leave it to a cop to be right on time. Grabbing her purse—

a small one that bulged with what she considered the essentials—she hurried to the intercom.

"I'll come down. Hold on."

She found him on the sidewalk, looking perfect in gray slacks and a navy shirt. His hands were tucked in the pockets of his bomber jacket.

"Hi." She kissed him lightly, then tucked an arm through his. "Where are we going?"

It gave him a jolt, the way their eyes and mouths lined up. As they would if they were in bed. "Downtown," he said shortly, and steered her left toward the corner to catch a cab.

He couldn't have pleased her more with his choice of the noisy, crowded club. The moment she stepped inside, Bess's blood started to hum. The music was loud, the dancing in full swing. They squeezed up to the bar to wait for a table.

"Vodka, rocks," Alex ordered, raising his voice over the din.

"Two," Bess decided, and smiled at him. "I think I was here before, a few months ago."

"I wouldn't be surprised." Not his business, Alex reminded himself. Her background, the men in her life. None of it.

The hell it wasn't.

"It doesn't look like the kind of place Strater would bring you."

"L.D.?" Her eyes laughed. "No, not his style." She angled herself around. "I love to watch people dance, don't you? It's one of the few legal forms of exhibitionism in this country." When he handed her her drink, she murmured a thank-you. "Take that guy there." She gestured with the glass at a man who was strutting on the floor, thumbs in his belt loops, hips wiggling. "That's definitely one of the standard urban white male mating dances."

"Did you do a lot of dancing with Stutman?" Alex heard himself ask.

"Charlie?" She sampled the vodka, pursed her lips. "Not really. He was more into sitting in some smoky club listening to esoteric music that he could obsess to." Still scanning the crowd, she caught the eye of a man in black leather. He cocked a brow and started toward her. One hard look from Alex, and he veered away.

Bess chuckled into her glass. "That put him in his place." Rattling her ice, she grinned up at him. "Were you born with that talent, or did you have to develop it?"

Alex plucked the glass out of her hand and set it aside. "Let's dance."

Always willing to dance, Bess let him pull her onto the floor. But instead of bopping to the beat, he wrapped his arms around her. While legs flashed and arms waved around them, and the music rocked, they glided.

"Nice." Smiling into his eyes, she linked her arms around his neck. "I see why you like to make your own moves, Detective."

"I believe I promised you romance." He skimmed his lips over her jaw to her ear.

"Yes." Her breath came out slow and warm as she closed her eyes. "You did."

"I'm not sure what a woman like you considers romantic."

Her skin shivered under his lips. "This is a good start."

"It's tough." He drew away so that their lips were an inch apart. "It's tough for a cop to compete with tycoons and playwrights."

Her eyes were half-closed and dreamy through her lashes. "What are you talking about?"

"A couple of your former fiancés."

The lashes lifted fractionally. "What about them?"

"I wondered when you were going to mention them. Or the fact that your father runs one of the biggest conglomerates known to man. Or the little detail about your chum the mayor calling my captain.''

They continued to dance as he spoke, but Bess could see the anger building in his eyes. ''Do you want to take them as separate issues, or all in one piece?''

She was a cool one, he thought. He was feeling anything but cool. ''Why don't we start with the mayor? You had no right.''

''I didn't ask him to call, Alexi.'' She spoke carefully, feeling the taut strength of his fingers at her waist. ''We were having dinner, and—''

''You often have dinner with the mayor?''

''He's an old family friend,'' she said patiently. ''I was telling him how helpful you'd been, and one thing led to another. I didn't know he'd called your captain until after it was done. I admit I liked the idea, and if it's caused you any trouble, I'm sorry.''

''Great.''

''My work's as important to me as yours is to you,'' she shot back, struggling with her own temper. ''If you'd prefer, I can arrange to spend Monday observing another cop.''

''You'll spend Monday where I can keep my eye on you.''

''Fine. Excuse me.'' She broke away and worked her way through the crowd to the rest room. The music pulsed against the walls as she paced the small room, ignoring the chatter from the two women freshening their lipstick at the mirror. Losing her temper would be unproductive, she reminded herself. Better, much better, to handle this situation calmly, coolly.

When she was almost sure she could, she walked back out.

He was waiting for her. Taking her arm, he led her to a table in the rear, where they could talk without shouting.

''I think we should go. There's no use staying when

you're so angry with me," she began, but he merely scraped back her chair.

"Sit."

She sat.

"When were you going to tell me about your family?"

"I don't see it as an issue." And that was true enough. "Why should it be? This is only the second time we've gone out."

The look he sent her had her jiggling a foot under the table. "You know damn well there's more going on between us than a couple of dates."

"All right, yes, I do." She picked up her drink, then set it down again, untouched. "But that's not the point. You're acting as though I deliberately hid something from you, or lied. That's just not true."

He picked up the fresh drink he'd ordered. "So tell me now."

"What? Didn't you run a make on me?" His narrowed eyes gave her some small sense of satisfaction. "Okay, Detective, I'll fill you in since you're so interested. My family owns McNee-Holden, which, since its inception in 1873, has expanded from still cameras and film to movies, television, satellites, and all manner of things. Shall I have them send you a prospectus?"

"Don't get smart."

"I'm just warming up." She hooked an arm over the back of her chair. "My father heads the company, and my mother entertains and does good works. I'm an only child, who was born rather late in life to them. My father's name is Roger, and he enjoys a racketing good game of polo. My mother's name is Susan—never Sue or Susie—and she prefers a challenging rubber of bridge. What else would you like to know?"

Despite his temper, he wanted to take her hand and soothe her. "Damn it, Bess, it isn't an interrogation."

"Isn't it? Let me make it easy for you, Alexi. I was born

in New York, spent the early part of my childhood on our estate on Long Island, in the care of a very British nanny I was extremely fond of, before going off to boarding school. Which I detested. This, however, left my mother free to pursue her many charitable causes, and my father free to pursue his business. We are not close. From time to time we did travel together, but I was not a pretty child, nor a tractable one, and my parents usually left my care up to the servants.''

"Bess—"

"I'm not finished." Her eyes were hard and bright. "This isn't a poor-little-rich-girl story, Alexi. I wasn't neglected or unhappy. Since I had no more in common with my parents than they had with me, I was content to go my own way. They don't interfere, and we get along very well. Because I prefer making my own way, I don't trumpet the fact that I'm Roger K. McNee's little girl. I don't hide it, either—otherwise, I would have changed my name. It's simply a fact. Satisfied?"

He took her hand before she could rise. His voice was calm again, and too gentle to resist. "I wanted to know who you are. I have feelings for you, so it matters."

Slowly her hand relaxed under his. The hard gleam faded from her eyes. "I understand that someone with your background would feel that their family, who and what they came from, are part of what they are. I don't feel that way about myself."

"Where you come from means something, Bess."

"Where you are means more. What does your father do?"

"He's a carpenter."

"Why aren't you a carpenter?"

"Because it wasn't what I wanted." He drummed his fingers on the table as he studied her. "Your point," he acknowledged. "Look, I'm sorry I pushed. It was just weird hearing all this from Judd."

"From Judd?"

"He got it from Holly, who got it from some other teacher who reads the tabloids." Even as he said it, it struck him as ridiculous. He grinned.

"See?" Relaxed again, she leaned forward. "Life really is a soap opera."

"Yours is. *Three* ex-fiancés?"

"That depends on how you count." She took Alex's hand, because she liked the feel of it in hers. "I wasn't engaged to L.D. He did give me a ring, and I didn't have the heart to tell him it was ostentatious. But marriage wasn't discussed."

"One of the ten richest men in the country gave you an ostentatious ring, but marriage wasn't discussed?"

"That's right. He's a very nice man—a little pompous, sometimes, but who wouldn't be, with so many people ready to grovel? Can we get some chips or something?"

"Sure." He signaled to a waitress. "So you didn't want to marry him."

"I never thought about it." Since he asked, she did so now. "No, I don't think I would have liked it very much. He wouldn't have either. L.D. finds me amusing and a little unconventional. Being a tycoon isn't all fun and games, you know."

"If you say so."

She chuckled. "But he'd prefer a different type for his next wife." She dived in immediately when the waitress set baskets of chips and pretzels on the table. "I enjoyed being in love with him for a few weeks, but it wasn't the romance of the century."

"What about the other one, the writer?"

"Charlie." There was a trace of wistfulness now. "I was really stuck on Charlie. He has this kind of glow about him. He's so interested in people, in emotions, in motivations." She gestured with half a pretzel. "The thing about Charlie is, he's good. Deep-down good. Entirely too good for me."

She finished off the pretzel. "See, I do things like join Greenpeace. Charlie flies to Alaska to help clean up oil spills. He's committed. That's why Gabrielle is perfect for him."

"Gabrielle?"

"His wife. They met at a whale rally. They've been married almost two years now."

Alex was determined to get it right. "You were engaged to a married man?"

"No." Insulted, she poked out her lip. "Of course not. He got married after we were engaged—that is, after we weren't engaged anymore. Charlie would never cheat on Gabrielle. He's too decent."

"Sorry. My mistake." He considered changing the subject, but this one was just too fascinating. "How about George? Was he between Charlie and Strater?"

"No, George was before Charlie and after Troy. Practically in another life."

"Troy? There was another one?"

"Oh, you didn't know about him." She propped her chin on her hand. "I guess your source didn't dig back far enough. Troy was while I was in college, and we weren't engaged for very long. Only a couple of weeks. Hardly counts."

Alex picked up his drink again. "Hardly."

"Anyway, George was a mistake—though I'd never admit it to Lori. She gloats."

"George was a mistake? The others weren't?"

She shook her head. "Learning experiences. But George, well... I was a little rash with him. I felt sorry for him, because he was always sure he was coming down with some terminal illness, and he'd been in therapy since kindergarten. We should never have gotten involved romantically. I was really relieved when he decided to marry Nancy instead."

"Is this like a hobby?" Alex asked after a moment.

''No, people plan hobbies. I never plan to fall in love. It just happens.'' Her smile was amused and tolerant. ''It feels good, and when it's over, no one's hurt. It isn't a sexual thing, like with Vicki. She goes from man to man because of the sense of sexual power it gives her. I know most people think if you have a relationship with a man—particularly if you're engaged to him—you must be sleeping with him. But it's not always true.''

''And if you're not engaged to him?''

Because the question demanded it, she met his eyes levelly. ''Every situation has its own rules. I don't know what they are for this one yet.''

''Things may get serious.''

There was a slight pressure around her heart. ''That's always a possibility.''

''They're serious enough right now for me to ask if you're seeing anyone else.''

She knew it was happening. Bess had never been able to prevent that slow, painless slide into love. ''Are you asking me if I am, or are you asking me not to?''

It wasn't painless for him. It was terrifying. With what strength of will he had left, Alex held himself on that thin, shaky edge. ''I'm asking you not to. And I'm telling you that I don't want anyone else. I can't even think of anyone else.''

Her eyes were warm as she leaned over to touch her lips to his. ''There is no one else.''

He laid a hand on her cheek to keep her mouth on his for another moment. Even as he kissed her, he wondered how many other men had heard her say those same words.

He told himself he was a jealous idiot. With an effort, he managed to smother the feeling. Rising, he took her hands and pulled her to her feet.

''We're supposed to be dancing.''

''So I was told. Alexi.'' Snuggling into love as she

would have into a cozy robe, she cupped his face in her hands.

"What?"

"I'm just looking. I want to make sure you're not mad at me anymore."

"I'm not mad at you." To prove it, he kissed the tip of her crooked nose.

No, not angry, she thought, searching his eyes. But there was something else shadowed there. She couldn't quite identify it. "My middle name's Louisa."

With a half smile on his lips, he tilted his head. "Okay."

"I'm trying to think if there's something else you might want to know that I haven't told you." Needing to be close, she rested her cheek against his. "I really don't have any secrets."

He turned his face into her hair. God, what was she doing to him to tie him up in knots like this? He pulled her against him, wrapping his arms tight around her. "I know all I need to know," he said quietly. "We're going to have to figure out those rules, Bess. We're going to have to figure them out fast."

"Okay." She wasn't sure what was holding her back. It would have been so easy to hurry out of the club with him, to go home and be with him. Her body was straining for him. And yet…

The first tremor of panic shocked her enough to have her pull back and smile, too brightly. She wasn't afraid, she assured herself. And she didn't need to overanalyze. When the time was right to move forward, she'd know it. That was all.

"Come on, Detective." Still smiling, she pulled him away from the table. "Let's see if you can keep up with me on the dance floor."

Chapter Seven

Alex read over a particularly grisly autopsy report on half of a suspected murder-suicide, and tried to ignore the fact that Bess was sitting in a chair to his right, scribbling in her notebook. She was as good as her word, he was forced to admit. Though she did tend to mumble to herself now and again, she was quiet, unobtrusive, and once she'd realized he wouldn't answer her questions—much less acknowledge her presence—she'd directed them to Judd.

He couldn't say she was a problem. But, of course, she *was* a problem. She was there. And because she was there, he thought about her.

She'd even dressed quietly, in bone-colored slacks and a navy blazer. As if, he thought, the conservative clothes would help her fade into the background and make him forget she was bothering him. Fat chance, when he was aware of her in every cell.

He could smell her, couldn't he? he thought, seething with resentment. That fresh and seductive scent had been floating at the edges of his senses all morning. Sneaking into his brain the way a good second-story man sneaks through a window.

And he could sense her, too. He didn't need a cop's instincts to know she was behind him, to picture those big green eyes drawing a bead on his every move. To imagine those never-still hands making notes, or that soft, agile mouth curving when a fresh idea came to her.

She could have dressed in cardboard and made him needy.

He was so damn cute, Bess was thinking, smiling at the back of his head. She enjoyed watching him work—the way he scooped his hand through all that gorgeous black hair when he was trying to think. Or shifted the phone from one ear to the other so that he could take notes. The sound of his voice, clipped and no-nonsense or sly and persuasive, depending on what he wanted from the listener.

And she particularly enjoyed the way he moved his shoulders, restlessly, annoyance in every muscle, when he became too aware of her presence.

She had a terrific urge to press a kiss to the back of his neck—and to see what he was reading.

After a couple of scowls from him, she scooted her chair back and stopped peeking over his shoulder.

She was cooperating fully, Alex was forced to admit. Which only made it worse. He wanted her to go away. How could he explain that it was impossible for him to concentrate on his job when the woman he was falling in love with was watching him read an autopsy report?

"Here you go." Bess gave him a cup of coffee and a friendly smile. "You look like you could use it."

"Thanks." Cream, no sugar, he noted as he sipped. She'd remembered. Was that part of her appeal? he wondered. The fact that she absorbed those little details about people? "You must be getting bored."

Taking a chance, she sat on the edge of his desk. "Why?"

"Nothing much going on." He gestured to indicate the pile of paperwork. Maybe, just maybe, he could convince her she was wasting her time. "If you have your TV cop doing this, it isn't going to up your ratings."

"We'll want to show different aspects of his work." She broke a candy bar in half and offered Alex a share. "Like the fact that he'd have to concentrate and handle this sort of paperwork and detail in the middle of all this chaos."

He took a bite. "What chaos?"

She smiled again, jotting down notes. He didn't even see it any longer, she realized. Or hear it. All the noise, the movement, the rush. Dozens of little dramas had taken place that morning, fascinating her, unnoted by him.

"They brought a drug dealer in over there." She gestured with a nod as she continued to write. "Skinny guy in a white fedora and striped jacket, wearing a heavy dose of designer cologne."

"Pasquale," Alex said, noting the description. "So?"

"You saw him?"

"I smelled him." He shrugged. "Wasn't my collar."

Chuckling to herself, Bess crossed her legs and got comfortable. "A Korean shopkeeper came rushing in shouting about vandalism at his store. He was so excited he lost most of his English. They sent out for an interpreter."

"Yeah, it happens." What was her point? he wondered.

She only smiled and finished her chocolate. "Right after that, they brought in a woman who'd been knocked around by her boyfriend. She was sitting over there—defending him, even while her face was swelling. The detective at the far end had a fight with his wife over the phone. He forgot their anniversary."

"Must have been Rogers. He's always fighting with his wife." Impatience rippled back. "What's that got to do with anything?"

"Atmosphere," she told him. "You've stopped noticing it and become a part of it. It's interesting to see. And you're very organized," she added, licking chocolate from her thumb. "Not like Judd over there, with all his neat little piles, but in the way you spread things out and know just where to find the right piece of paper at the right time."

"I hate having you stare at me when I work." He slapped her hand away from the autopsy report.

"I know." Unoffended, she grinned. She leaned a little closer. There was something in her eyes besides humor, he noted. He wasn't sure if he'd ever seen desire and amusement merged in the same expression before. And he certainly hadn't realized how the combination could make a man's blood hum. "You look very sexy plowing your way through all this, gun strapped to your side, your hair all messed up from raking your fingers through it. That keen, dangerous look in your eyes."

Mortified, he shifted in his chair. "Cut it out, McNee."

"I like the way your eyes get all dark and intense when you're taking down some important tidbit of information over the phone."

"For all you know, that was my dry cleaner."

"Uh-uh." She took his coffee to wash down the last bite of candy bar. "Tell me something, Alexi. Are you annoyed that I'm here, or are you nervous that I'm here?"

"Both." He rose. There must be something he had to do someplace else.

"That's what I thought." She hooked a finger around the strap of his holster. She wasn't afraid of the gun he wore. In fact, she was counting on talking him into letting her hold it one day. So that she could see how it felt. How he felt when he was forced to draw it. "You know, you haven't even kissed me."

"I'm not going to kiss you. Here."

She lifted her eyes, slowly. There was a definite dare in them. "Why not?"

"Because the next time I kiss you—" watching her, he slid a hand around her throat, his thumb caressing her col-

rbone, until her cocky smile faded away "—really kiss
ou, it's just going to be you and me. Alone. And I'm going
 keep right on kissing you, and all sorts of other things,
ntil there aren't any more rules. Any more reasons."

Was that what she wanted? She thought it was. Right
ow, when her skin was humming where his fingers lay,
ne thought it was exactly what she wanted. But there was
omething else, some complex mixture of yearning and
:ar, so unfamiliar it caused her to step back.

"What's wrong, McNee?" Delighted by her reaction, he
:t his hand slide down her shoulder and away. "Who's
aking who nervous now?"

"We're supposed to be working," she reminded him.
'Not making each other nervous."

"Today, when I go off the clock, so do you."

"Stanislaski."

Alex's eyes stayed on hers another moment before flick-
ng behind her. "Captain."

"Sorry to interrupt your social hour," he said sourly. "I
eed that report."

"Right here." Even as Alex was turning to reach for it,
sess was offering her hand to Trilwalter.

"Captain, it's so nice to meet you. I'm Bess McNee. I
vanted to let you know how much I appreciate the depart-
nent's cooperation today."

Trilwalter scowled at her a moment, then, remembering,
tifled a sigh. "Right. You're the writer." A sneer twisted
is mouth. "Soap operas."

"Yes, I am." Her smile made the fluorescents overhead
im. "I wonder…if I can have just a moment of your time?
 know you're very busy, so I won't keep you."

He didn't want any part of her. He knew it, she knew it,
nd so did any of the cops hovering close enough to hear.
ut riding a desk had taught him that diplomacy was often
is only weapon. Besides, once he made his feelings

known, she'd be out of his hair and off finding anothe precinct to haunt.

"Why don't you come into my office, Ms. McNee?"

"Thank you." She shot a grin over her shoulder at Ale as she followed Trilwalter.

"You going to let her go in there alone?" Judd mur mured.

"Yeah." Alex bit back a chuckle as he heard the glas of Trilwalter's door rattle. "Oh, yeah. And I'm going t enjoy it."

Ten minutes later, Alex was surprised by a burst c laughter. Swiveling in his chair, he spotted Trilwalter lead ing Bess out of his office. The two of them were chucklin together like two old friends over a private joke.

"I'm going to remember that one, Bess."

"Just don't tell the mayor where you heard it."

"I know how to respect a source." Still smiling, h glanced over at a slack-jawed Alex. "Detective, you tak care of Ms. McNee. Make sure she gets what she needs.'

"Sir." He cut his eyes over to Bess. She merely batte her lashes, managing to look about as innocent as a smok ing gun. "I have every intention of making certain M McNee gets exactly what she needs."

Bess laid her hand in Trilwalter's. "Thank you agair Donald."

"My pleasure. Don't be a stranger."

"Donald?" Alex said, the moment the captain was ou of earshot.

"Yes." Bess made a production out of brushing dus from her sleeve. "That is his name."

"We use several other names for him around here. Wha the hell did you do in there?"

"Why, we chatted. What else?"

Glancing over her shoulder, Alex noticed money chang ing hands. The odds had been even that Trilwalter woul chew her up, then spit her out, within ten minutes. Sinc he'd lost twenty on the deal himself, Alex wasn't particularly pleased.

"Sit down and be quiet," he told her. "I've got work."

"Of course."

Before she could take her seat, his phone rang. "Stanislaski. Yeah." He listened a moment, then pulled out his notepad to scribble. "I hear you. You know how it works, Boomer. It depends on what it's worth." Nodding to himself, he replaced the pad. "Yeah, we'll talk. I'll be there. In ten."

When Alex hung up the phone and grabbed for his jacket, Bess was right behind him. "What is it?"

"I've got someplace to go. Judd, let's hit it."

"I'm going with you."

Alex didn't even glance back as he started out. He was already working on tucking her in some far corner of his mind. "Forget it."

"I'm going with you," she repeated, and snagged his arm. "That's the deal."

It surprised him when he tried to shake her off and she wouldn't shake. The lady had a good grip, he noted. "I didn't make any deal."

She could be just as tough and cold-blooded as he, she thought. She planted her feet, angled her chin. "Your captain did. I ride with you, Detective, wherever you may be going. A day in the life, remember?"

"Fine." Frustration vibrated through him as he stared her down. "You ride—and you stay in the car. No way you're scaring off my snitch."

"Want me to drive?" Judd offered as they headed down the steps to the garage.

"No." Alex's answer was flat and left no room for argument. Judd sent Bess a good-natured shrug. Then, because Alex made no move to do so, he opened the back door of their nondescript unmarked car for her.

"Where are we going?" Bess asked, determined to be pleasant.

"To talk to the scum of the earth," Alex shot back as he pulled out of the garage.

"Sounds fascinating," Bess said, and meant it.

She didn't think she'd ever been in this part of town before. Many of the shop windows were boarded up. Those still in business were grubbier than usual. People still walked as though they were in a hurry, but it didn't look as if they had anyplace to go.

Funny, she thought, how Alex seemed to blend with the surroundings. It wasn't simply the jeans and battered jacket he wore, or the hair he'd deliberately mussed. It was a look in the eyes, a set of the body, a twist of the mouth. No one would look twice at him, she thought. Or if they bothered, they wouldn't see a cop, they'd see another street tough obviously on the edge of his luck.

Taking her cue from him, she pulled out her bag of cosmetics, darkening her mouth, adding just a little too much eyeliner and shadow. She tried a couple of bored looks in the mirror of her compact and decided to tease up her hair.

Alex glanced back at her and scowled. "What the hell are you doing to your face?"

"Getting into character," she said blithely. "Just like you. Are we going to bust somebody?"

He only turned away and muttered.

Just his luck, he thought. He wanted to slip into Boomer's joint unobtrusively, and he was stuck with a red-head who thought they were playing cops and robbers.

Unoffended, Bess put away her mirror and scanned the area. Parking wasn't a problem here. Bess decided that if anyone left his car unattended in this neighborhood for above ten minutes, he'd come back and be lucky to find a hubcap.

Alex swung over the curb and swore. He couldn't leave

her in the car here, damn it. Any of the hustlers or junkies on the streets would take one look, then eat her alive.

"You listen to me." He turned, leaning over the seat to make his point. "Stay close to me, and keep your mouth shut. No questions, no comments."

"All right, but where—"

"No questions." He slammed out of his door, then waited for her. With his hand firm on her arm, he hauled her to the sidewalk. "If you step out of line, I swear, I'll slap the cuffs on you."

"Romantic, isn't he?" she said to Judd. "Just sends shivers down my spine."

"Keep a lid on it, McNee," Alex told her, refusing to be amused. He pulled her through a grimy door into an airless shop.

It took her a minute to get her bearings in the dim light. There were shelves and shelves crowded with dusty merchandise. Radios, picture frames, kitchenware. A tuba. A huge glass display counter with a diagonal crack across it dominated one wall. Security glass ran to the ceiling. Cutting through it was a window, like a bank teller's, studded with bars.

"A pawnshop," Bess said, with such obvious delight that Alex snarled at her.

"One word about atmosphere, I'll clobber you."

But she was already dragging out her notebook. "Go ahead, do what you have to do. You won't even know I'm here."

Sure, he thought. How would anyone know she was there, simply because that sunshine scent of her cut right through the grime and must? He stepped up to the counter just as a scrawny man in a loose white shirt came through the rear door.

"Stanislaski."

"Boomer. What have you got for me?"

Grinning, Boomer passed a hand over his heavily greased

black hair. "Come on, I got some good stuff, and you know I make a point of cooperating with the law. But a man's got to make a living."

"You make one ripping off every poor slob who walks through the door."

"Aw, now you hurt my feelings." Boomer's pale blue eyes glittered. "Rookie?" he asked, nodding at Judd.

"He used to be."

After an appraising look, Boomer glanced over at Bess. She was busy poking through his merchandise. "Looks like I got me a customer. Hang on."

"She's with me." Alex shot him a knife-edged look that forestalled any questions. "Just forget she's here."

Boomer had already appraised the trio of rings on Bess's right hand, and the blue topaz drops at her ears. He sighed his disappointment. "You're the boss, Stanislaski. But listen, I like to be discreet."

Alex leaned on the counter, like a man ready to shoot the bull for hours. His voice was soft, and deadly. "Jerk my chain, Boomer, and I'm going to have to come down here and take a hard look at what you keep in that back room."

"Stock. Just stock." But he grinned. He didn't have any illusions about Alex. Boomer knew when he was detested, but he also knew they had an agreement of sorts. And, thus far, it had been advantageous to both of them. "I got something on those hookers that got sliced up."

Though his expression didn't change, though he didn't move a muscle, Alex went on alert. "What kind of something?"

Boomer merely smiled and rubbed his thumb and forefinger together. When Alex drew out a twenty, it disappeared quickly through the bars. "Twenty more, if you like what I have to say."

"If it's worth it, you'll get it."

"You know I trust you." Smelling of hair grease and

sweat, Boomer leaned closer. "Word on the street is you're looking for some high roller. Guy's name's Jack."

"So far I'm not impressed."

"Just building up to it, pal. The first one that was wasted? She was one of Big Ed's wives. I recognized her from the newspaper picture. Now, she was fine-looking. Not that I ever used her services."

"Turn the page, Boomer."

"Okay, okay." He shot a grin at Judd. "He don't like conversation. I heard both those unfortunate ladies were in possession of a certain piece of jewelry."

"You've got good ears."

"Man in my position hears things. It so happens I had a young lady come in just yesterday. She had a certain piece of jewelry she wanted to exchange." Opening a drawer, Boomer pulled out a thin gold chain. Dangling from it was a heart, cracked down the center. When Alex held out a hand, Boomer shook his head. "I gave her twenty for it."

Saying nothing, Alex pulled another bill out of his wallet.

"Seems to me I'm entitled to a certain amount of profit."

Eyes steady, Alex pulled the twenty back an inch. "You're entitled to go in and answer a bunch of nasty questions down at the cop shop."

With a shrug, Boomer exchanged the bill for the heart. He'd only given ten for it, in any case. "She wasn't much more than a kid," Boomer added. "Eighteen, maybe twenty at a stretch. Still pretty. Bottle blonde, blue eyes. Little mole right here." He tapped beside his left eyebrow.

"Got an address?"

"Well, now…"

"Twenty for the address, Boomer." Alex's tone told the man to take it. "That's it."

Satisfied, Boomer named a hotel a few blocks away. "Signed her name Crystal," he added, wanting to keep the partnership intact. "Crystal LaRue. Figure she made it up."

"Let's check it out," he said to Judd, then tapped Bess

on the shoulder. She was apparently absorbed in an ugly brass lamp in the shape of a rearing horse. "Let's go."

"In a minute." She turned a smile on Boomer. "How much?"

"Oh, for you—"

"Forget it." Alex was dragging her to the door.

"I want to buy—"

"It's ugly."

Annoyed at the loss, but pleased to have recorded the entire conversation, she sighed. "That's the point." But she climbed meekly into the car and began to scribble her impressions in her book.

> *Cramped shop. Very dirty. Mostly junk. Excellent place for props. Proprietor a complete sleaze. Alexi in complete control of exchange—a kind of game-playing. Quietly disgusted but willing to use the tools at hand.*

By the time she'd finished scribbling, Alex was pulling to the curb again.

"Same rules," he said to Bess as they climbed out of the car.

"Absolutely." Lips pursed, she studied the crumbling hotel. She recognized it as a rent-by-the-hour special. "Is this where she lives?"

"Who?"

"The girl you were talking about." She lifted a brow. "I have ears, too, Alexi."

He should have known. "As long as you keep your mouth shut."

"There's no need to be rude," she told him as they started in. "Tell you what, just to show there's no hard feelings, I'll buy you both lunch."

"Great." Judd gallantly opened the door for her.

"You're so easy," Alex muttered to his partner as they entered the filthy lobby.

"Hey, we gotta eat sometime."

He hated to bring her in here, Alex realized. Into this dirty place that smelled of garbage and moldy dreams. How could she be so unaffected by it? he wondered, then struggled to put thoughts of her aside as he approached the desk clerk.

"You got a Crystal LaRue?"

The clerk peered over his newspaper. There was an unfiltered cigarette dangling from the corner of his mouth and total disinterest in his eyes. "Don't ask for names."

Alex merely pulled out his badge, flashed it. "Blonde, about eighteen. Good-looking. A beauty mark beside her eyebrow. Working girl."

"Don't ask what they do for a living, neither." With a shrug, the clerk went back to his paper. "Two-twelve."

"She in?"

"Haven't seen her go out."

With Bess trailing behind, they started up the steps. To entertain herself, she read the various tenants' suggestions and statements that were scrawled on the walls.

There was a screaming match in progress behind one of the doors on the first floor. Someone was banging on the wall from a neighboring room and demanding—in colorful terms—that the two opponents quiet down.

A bag of garbage had spilled on the stairs between the second and first floors. It had gone very ripe.

Alex rapped on the door of 212, waited. He rapped again and called out. "Crystal. Need to talk to you."

With a glance at Judd, Alex tried the door. The knob turned easily. "In a place like this, you'd think she'd lock it," Judd commented.

"And wire it with explosives," Alex added. He slipped out his gun, and Judd did the same. "Stay in the hall," he ordered Bess without looking at her. They went through the door, guns at the ready.

She did exactly what she was told. But that didn't stop her from seeing. Crystal hadn't gone out, and she wouldn't be walking the streets again. As the door hung open, Bess stared at what was sprawled across the sagging mattress inside. The stench of blood—and worse—streamed through the open doorway.

Death. Violent death. She had written about it, discussed it, watched gleefully as it was acted out for the cameras.

But she'd never seen it face-to-face. Had never known how completely a human being could be turned into a thing.

From far away, she heard Alex swear, over and over, but she could only stare, frozen, until his body blocked her view. He had his hands on her shoulders, squeezing. God, she was cold, Bess thought. She'd never been so cold.

"I want you to go downstairs."

She managed to lift her gaze from his chin to his eyes. The iced fury in them had her shivering. "What?"

He nearly swore again. She was white as a sheet, and her pupils had contracted until they were hardly bigger than the point of a pin. "Go downstairs, Bess." He tried to rub the chill out of her arms, knowing he couldn't. "Are you listening to me?" he said, his voice quiet, gentle.

"Yes." She moistened her lips, pressed them together. "I'm sorry, yes."

"Go down, stay in the lobby. Don't say anything, don't do anything, until Judd or I come down. Okay?" He gave her a little shake, and wondered what he would do if she folded on him. "Okay?"

She took one shaky breath, then nodded. "She's...so young." With an effort, she swallowed the sickness that kept threatening to rise in her throat. "I'm all right. Don't worry about me. I'm all right," she repeated, then turned away to go downstairs.

"She shouldn't have seen this," Judd said. His own stomach was quivering.

"Nobody should see this." Banking down on every emotion, Alex closed the door at his back.

* * *

She stuck it out, refusing to budge when Judd came down to drive her home. After finding an old chair, she settled into a corner while the business of death went on around her. From her vantage point, she watched them come and go—forensics, the police photographer, the morgue.

Detached, she studied the people who crowded in, asking questions, making comments, being shuffled out again by blank-faced cops.

There was grief in her for a girl she hadn't known, a fury at the waste of a life. But she remained. Not because of the job. Because of Alex.

He was angry with her. She understood it, and didn't question it. When they were finished at the scene, she rode in silence in the back of the car. Back at the station, she took the same chair she'd had that morning.

Hours went by, endlessly long. At one point she slipped out and bought Alex and Judd sandwiches from a deli. After a time, he went into another room. She followed, still silent, noted a board with pictures tacked to it. Horrible pictures.

She looked away from them, took a chair and listened while Alex and other detectives discussed the latest murder and the ongoing investigation.

Later, she rode with him back to the pawnshop. Waited patiently while he questioned Boomer again. Waited longer while he and Judd returned to the motel to reinterview the clerk, the tenants.

Like them, she learned little about Crystal LaRue. Her name had been Kathy Segal, and she'd once lived in Wisconsin. It had been hard, terribly hard, for Bess to listen when Alex tracked down and notified her parents. Hard, too, to understand from Alex's end of the conversation that they didn't care. For them, their daughter had already been dead.

She'd been nobody's girl. She'd worked the streets on

her own. Two months after she moved into the tiny little room with the sagging mattress, she had died there. No one had known her. No one had wanted to know her.

No one had cared.

Alex couldn't talk to Bess. It was impossible for him. Intolerable. He shared this part of his life with no one who mattered to him. It was true that his sister Rachel saw some of it as a public defender but as far as Alex was concerned that was too much. Perhaps that was why he kept all the pieces he could away from the rest of his family and loved ones.

He hated remembering the look on Bess's face as she'd stood in that doorway. There should have been a way to protect her from that, to shield her from her own stubbornness.

But he hadn't protected her, he hadn't shielded her, though that was precisely what he had sworn to do for people he'd never met from the first day he'd worn a badge. Yet for her, for the woman he was—God, yes, the woman he was in love with—he'd opened the door himself and let her in.

So he didn't talk to her, not even when it was time to turn it off and go home. And in the silence, his anger built and swelled and clawed at his guts. He found the words when he stepped into her apartment and closed the door.

"Did you get enough?"

Bess was in no mood to fight. Her emotions, always close to the surface, had been wrung dry by what she'd seen and heard that day. She would let him yell, if that was what he needed, but she was tired, she was aching, and her heart went out to him.

"Let me get you a drink," she said quietly, but he snagged her arm and whirled her back.

"Is it all in your notes?" That cold, terribly controlled fury swiped out at her. "Can you find a way to use it to entertain those millions of daytime viewers?"

"I'm sorry." It was all she could think of. "Alexi, I'm so sorry." She took a deep breath. "I want a brandy. I'll get us both one."

"Fine. A nice, civilized brandy is just what we need."

She walked away to choose a bottle from an old lacquered cabinet. "I don't know what you want me to say." Very carefully, very deliberately, she poured two snifters. "I'll apologize for choosing today to do this, if that helps. I'll apologize for making it more difficult for you by being there when this happened." She brought the snifter to him, but he didn't take it. "Right now, I'd be willing to say anything you'd like to hear."

He couldn't get beyond it, no matter what she said. He couldn't get beyond knowing he'd opened the door on the kind of horror she'd never be able to forget. "You had no business being there. You had no business seeing any of that."

With a sigh, she set both snifters aside. Maybe brandy wouldn't help after all. "You were there. You saw it."

His eyes flashed white heat. "It's my damn job."

"I know." She lifted a hand to his cheek, soothing. "I know."

Compelled, he grabbed her wrist, held tight a moment before he turned away. "I don't want you touched by it. I don't want you touched by it ever again."

"I can't promise that." Because it was her way, she wrapped her arms around his waist, rested her cheek against his back. He was rigid as steel, unyielding as granite. "Not if you want something between us."

"It's because I do want something between us."

"Alexi." So many emotions, she thought. Always before it had been easy to sort them out, to drift with them. But this time… It had been a long, hard day, she reminded herself. There would be time to think later. "If what you want is someone you can tuck in a comfortable corner, it isn't me. What you do is part of what you are." When he turned, she brushed her hands over his cheeks again, refusing to let him retreat. "You want me to say I was appalled by what I saw in that room? I was. I was appalled by the cruelty of it, sickened by the terrible, terrible waste."

That sliced at him, a long, thin blade through the heart. "I shouldn't have let you go with me. That part of my life isn't ever going to be part of yours."

"Stop." The sorrow that had paled her face hardened into determination. "Do you think that because I write fantasy I don't know anything about the real world? You're wrong. I know, it just doesn't overwhelm my life. And I know that what you faced today you may face tomorrow. Or worse. I know that every time you walk out the door you may not come back." The quick lick of fear reminded her to slow down and speak carefully. "What you are makes that a very real possibility. But I won't let that overwhelm me, either. Because there's nothing about you I'd change."

For a moment, he simply stared at her, a hundred different feelings fighting for control inside him. Then, slowly, he lowered his brow to hers and shut her eyes. "I don't know what to say to you."

"You don't have to say anything. We don't have to talk at all."

He knew what she was offering, even before she tilted her head and touched her lips to his. He wanted it, and her. More than anything, he wanted to steep himself in her until the rest of the world went away.

He took his hands through her hair, letting his fingers toy with those loose, vivid curls. "We haven't come up with those rules."

Her lips curved, slanted over his. "We'll figure them out later."

He murmured his agreement, drawing her closer. "I want you. I need to be with you. I think I'd go crazy if I couldn't be with you tonight."

"I'm here. Right here."

"Bess." His mouth moved from hers to skim along those sharp cheekbones. "I'm in love with you."

She felt her heart stutter. That was the only way she could describe this sensation she'd never experienced before. "Alexi—"

"Don't." He closed his mouth over hers again. "Don't say it. It comes too easy to you. Just come to bed." He buried his face against her neck. "For God's sake, let me take you to bed."

Chapter Eight

Hurt. Oh, she'd read the stories and the poetry, watched the movies. She'd even written the scenes. But she'd never believed that love and pain existed together, could twine into one clenched fist to batter the soul.

Yet his words had hurt her—immeasurably—even as her heart opened to give and accept.

This time it was different. How could she possibly explain that to him, when she was still groping for the answers herself? And what good were words now, when there was so much need?

A touch would be enough, she promised herself as they swayed toward the steps. Tonight would be enough, and tomorrow all the aches would only be memories.

His mouth came back to hers, restless, insistent, as they began the climb. The first helpless sigh caught in her throat as he pulled her close and aroused her unbearably with a long, sumptuous meeting of lips.

Her fingers trembled when she tugged at his jacket. Had they ever trembled for a man before? she wondered. No.

nd as the leather slid away, leaving her free to grip those agnificent shoulders, she knew that none of this had hap-ened before. Not the trembling, not the raw scrape of erves, not the sting of bright tears, not the sweet, slow rob of her blood.

This was the first time for so many things.

He didn't know how much longer he could perform the mple act of drawing breath in and out of his lungs. Not hen her body was shivering against his. Not when he ould hear those small, desperately needy sounds in her roat. The staircase seemed to stretch interminably. With muffled oath, he swept her up into his arms.

Her eyes met his, and though her heart seemed ready to urst, she managed to smile. She knew he needed smiles onight. "And I said you weren't romantic."

"I have my moments."

Shaky, she nuzzled her face into the curve of his neck. "I'm awfully glad I'm here for this one."

"Keep it up," he said in a strained voice as she ran ibbling kisses from throat to ear, "and I'll do something eally romantic, like falling on my face and dropping you."

"Oh, I trust you, Detective." She caught the lobe of his ar in her teeth and felt the quick jerk of reaction. "Com-letely."

With his heart roaring in his head, he reached the top. he was teasing his jawline now, making little murmurs of pproval as she sampled his flesh. He headed for the first oor. "This better be the bedroom."

"Mmm-hmm..." While she worked her way to his nouth, her fingers were busy unbuttoning his shirt.

He recognized her scent first. Even as he passed through he doorway, it wrapped its alluring woman's fingers round him. That cheerful, sexy fragrance hung in the air, he result, no doubt, of spilled powder and an unstoppered ottle of perfume. Her clothes were a colorful mess of silk louses, bright cotton pants, tangled hose. His quick scan

passed over a life-size stuffed ostrich, a pair of thrivin
ficus trees flanking the wide window, and a collection c
antique bottles, elegant in jewel colors, before he focuse
on the bed.

It was a long, wide ocean of cool blue sheets, topped b
a lush mountain of vivid-toned pillows. All satins and silk.

Because his mouth was beginning to water, he took on
long, slow breath. But the air, so fragrant, burned his lung.
"That looks big enough for six close friends."

"I like a lot of room." Even as his stomach quivered
the images that evoked, she was continuing. "I used to fa
out of bed a lot when I was a kid."

"Is that how you broke your nose?"

"No. But I chipped a tooth once."

He set her down beside the bed, pleased that her arm
stayed linked around his neck. "I think we can probabl
keep from falling out of this one. If we work on it."

She raised up on her toes, just a little, just enough t
bring them eye-to-eye. "I'm willing to risk it."

Determined to steady himself, he kissed her brow, he
cheeks. "Let me take my gun off."

He stripped off the holster, set it on the floor. With fin
gers that were suddenly numb and awkward, she reache
for the buttons of her blazer.

"No." It was that one quick flash of nerves in her eye.
that had settled his own. He closed his hands over hers
"Let me." He unfastened buttons, then took his hand.
slowly up her sides, his thumbs just brushing her breasts
"You're shaking."

"I know."

Watching her, he slid the jacket from her shoulders
"Are you afraid of me?"

"No." She couldn't swallow. "Of this, a little. It's
silly."

He toyed with the first button of her blouse, then the

second. Her skin quivered as his knuckle skimmed over it. "I like it."

"That's good." She tried to laugh, but only managed one trembling breath. "Because I can't seem to stop."

"There's plenty of time to relax." The blouse slipped away, and desire curled its powerful fist in his stomach. Midnight-blue silk shimmered in the dimming light, gleaming against ivory skin. "There's no hurry."

"I—" Her head fell back as he traced a finger over the silk. Gently, so gently, over the swell of her breasts, as though hers was the first body he'd touched. The only one he wanted to touch. "God, Alexi…"

"I've spent a lot of time imagining this. Step out of your shoes," he suggested while he unhooked her slacks. In a daze, she obeyed as the slacks slithered down her legs. "I'm going to spend a lot more time enjoying it. I want all of you." Lazily, testingly, he ran a finger under the lace cut high on her thigh. Ah, the skin there was like rose petals dewed with morning. Her eyes went wide and dark; her body quaked. "All of you," he repeated.

She couldn't move. Every muscle in her body had turned to water. Hot, rushing water. She couldn't speak, not when so many emotions clogged her throat. As she stood swaying, helplessly seduced, he watched her. Touched her. Clever fingers brushing, stroking, exploring. He trailed them up her arms, slid them over her shoulders. Then back to silk, until her body burned like fever.

His eyes never left hers. Even when he kissed her, lightly, tormenting her hungry lips with the barest of tastes, his eyes stayed open and aware.

"You're making me crazy." Her voice hitched out through trembling lips.

"I know. I want to."

He caught her wrists when she reached for him, then ran their tangled fingers over her, so that she felt her own response to him, inside and out, as he touched his mouth to hers again. Patiently, erotically, he deepened the kiss, until her hands went limp and her pulse thundered. Then he brought her hands up, spread them over his chest. Together they spread his open shirt apart. With his mouth still clinging to hers, he tugged it off. His heart gave a quick, hard lurch as her hands, hot and eager, raced over him.

Yanking her close, he took off his shoes. His skin was already damp when he fumbled for the snap of his jeans.

"I want you under me." He tore his mouth from hers to savor her throat. "I want to feel you move under me."

They lowered to the bed, rolled once, then twice, over silk. He used every ounce of control, every degree of will, to keep himself from plunging into her and taking the quick, desperate release his body craved. His mind, his soul, wanted more than that.

She seemed smaller like this. Slighter. It helped him remember that passion could outstrip tenderness. So, while the blood pounded and burned in his veins, he loved her slowly.

She discovered that a woman could drown willingly in sweetness. She knew there was a gun on the floor beside them and that he had used it at least once to kill. But the hands that moved over her were those of a gentle man. One who cared. She rested a palm on his cheek as she floated away on the kiss. One who loved.

Who loved her.

Staggered by the knowledge, she poured everything she had into the kiss, needing to show him that whatever he felt was returned, equally. Then his mouth slid from hers to trail down her throat, over her shoulder. All thought, all reason, skittered away.

In a warm, slippery pool of silk and satin, he showed her what it was to ache for someone. To yearn for the sharp, thin point of pain the poets call ecstasy. Her hips arched under his, desperately offering. But he only continued that ormenting journey over her with teasing lips and gentle hands.

When his tongue flicked under the line of lace that clung tenuously to her breasts, she moaned, pressing an urgent hand to the back of his head. The taste there—honey, dampened by her arousal—nearly unraveled the taut knot of his control. So he pleased them both, closing a greedy mouth over that firm, scented swell.

Gasping out with pleasure, she bucked under him, straining for more, her nails digging heedlessly into his back as she whimpered and struggled for what was just out of reach. Maddened by her response, he brought his mouth to hers again, crushing her lips as he slithered a hand down to cup the heat between her thighs. Prayers and pleas trembled on her tongue, but before she could voice them, he slipped under the silk to stroke.

The unbearable pleasure shattered. Fractured lights, whirling colors, spun behind her eyes to blind her. She heard herself cry out; his name was nearly a sob. Then there was his groan, a sound of sweet satisfaction as her body went limp in release.

Never before. Her hands slid away from him, boneless. Sweet Lord, never like this. She felt weak, wrecked, weepy. As her breath sobbed out, as her eyes fluttered closed, they both knew that her mind, her body, were totally his for the taking.

He'd never felt stronger. Her wild response, her absolute surrender, filled him with a kind of intense power he'd never experienced before. Silk rustled against silk as he drew the teddy down, tossed it aside. Her skin, slick with passion, glowed in the shadows. He touched where he chose, watching, fascinated, as his own hands molded her. Gold against ivory. He tasted wherever he liked, feeling her muscles quiver involuntarily as he traced openmouthed kisses over her rib cage, down to her stomach. Heat to heat. Then, wanting that instant of sheer pleasure again, he

drove her up a second time, shuddering himself as her body
convulsed and flowed with the crest of the wave.

At last, unable to wait a moment longer, he slipped inside
that hot, moist sheath. Her groan of stunned delight echoed
his own.

Slowly, as in a dream, her arms lifted to wrap around
him. She rose to meet him, to take him deep. They moved
gently at first, treasuring the intimacy, willing to prolong
it. But need outpaced them, driving them faster, until, thrust
for thrust, they sprinted toward the final crest.

His hand fisted in her hair as the last link of control
snapped clean. Her name exploded from his lips like an
oath as he emptied himself into her.

She wondered how she could ever have thought herself
experienced. While it was true she hadn't been with as
many men as some thought, she hadn't come to Alexi an
innocent.

Yet things had happened tonight that had never happened
before. And, because she was a woman who understood
herself well, she knew that nothing she had experienced
here would happen again—unless it was with him.

Relaxed now, she rubbed her cheek over his chest, content to remain as she'd been since he rolled over and
dragged her across him. Tucked in the cocoon of his arms,
she felt as cozy as a cat, and she arched lazily as he ran a
hand down her spine.

"Will you tell me again?" she asked.

"What?"

She pressed her lips against him, feeling his heart beating
strong and fast beneath them. "What every woman wants
to hear."

"I love you." When she lifted her head, he laid a hand
gently over her lips. He knew it would hurt to hear her say
it, when she didn't mean it as he did.

Suddenly she was glad it was dark, and he couldn't see

the smile fade away from her face. "Even after this," she said carefully, "you don't want me to love you back."

More than anything, he thought. More than life. "Let's just leave things as they are." He traced her face with a fingertip, enjoying those odd angles. "Tell me how you broke your nose."

She was silent a moment, gathering her composure. She couldn't offer what he didn't want to take. "Fistfight."

He chuckled and drew her back to cuddle, instinctively soothing the tension out of her. "I should have figured."

She made an effort to relax against him. There was time to convince him. Hadn't he said they had plenty of time? "At boarding school," she added. "I was twelve and homely as a duck. Too skinny, funny hair, dumb face."

"I like your face. And your hair." His hand cupped her breast comfortably. "And your body."

"You didn't know me when I was twelve. When you're odd in any way, you're a target."

"I know."

Interested, she lifted her head again. "Do you?"

"I didn't learn English until I was five. Before my father's business got off the ground, times were rough." He turned his face into her hair to breathe in the scent. "I was this little Ukrainian kid, wearing my brother's hand-me-downs. And back then, Soviets weren't particularly popular with Americans."

"Well, you made such great villains." She kissed his cheek, comforting the small boy he'd been. "It must have been difficult for you."

"I had the family. We had each other. School was a little rugged at first. Name-calling, playground scuffles. Even some of the parents weren't too keen on having their kids play with the Russkie. No point in trying to explain we were Ukrainian." He shifted, tangled his legs with hers. "So, after a few black eyes and bloody noses, I earned a reputation for being tough. After a while, we kind of go absorbed into the neighborhood.''

''What neighborhood?''

''Brooklyn. My parents still live there. Same house.'' With a shake of his head, he drew back. He could make her out now in the dark, could see the way her eyes were smiling at him. ''How come we're talking about me, when I asked you about your nose?''

''I like hearing it.''

''There was a fistfight,'' he said, prompting her.

Bess sighed. ''One of those girl cliques,'' she began. ''You know the type. The cool kids, all hair and teeth and attitude. I was the nerd they liked to pick on.''

''You were never a nerd.''

''I was a *champion* nerd. Gawky, top of the class academically, socially inept.''

''You?''

There was such pure disbelief in the tone, she laughed. ''Which of those descriptions don't you buy, Alexi?''

He considered a moment. ''Any of them.''

''I guess I'm two-thirds flattered and one-third insulted. I was tall for my age and skinny. A very late bloomer in the bosom and hips department.''

''You might have bloomed slow,'' he began, proving his point with a sweep of his hand, ''but you bloomed very well.''

''Thank you. My mind, however, had developed quite nicely. Straight *A*'s.''

''No kidding?'' He grinned in the dark. ''And you were the kid who always trashed the grading curve for the rest of us.''

''That's the idea. Added to that, I was more comfortable with a book, or thinking, than I was tittering. Young girls do a lot of tittering. Because I was hardheaded, I automatically took a dislike to anything that was popular or fashionable at the time. As a result, I took a lot of flak. Bess the Mess, that sort of thing.''

She paused long enough to shift some pillows. ''Anyway, we had this history exam coming up. One of the cool kids—her name was Dawn Gallagher… Heart-shaped face, perfect features, long, flowing blond hair. You get the picture.''

''Prom-queen type.''

''Exactly. She was flunking big-time and wanted me to let her copy from my paper. She'd made my life adolescent hell, and she figured if she was nice to me for a couple of days, let me stand within five feet of her, maybe sit at the same lunch table, I'd be so grateful, I'd let her.''

''But you hung tough.''

''I don't cheat for anybody. The upshot was, she flunked the exam, and her parents were called to the school for a conference. Dawn retaliated by pinching me whenever I got too close, getting into my room and breaking my things, stealing my books. Small-time terrorism. One day on the basketball court—''

''You shot hoop?''

''Team captain. I was an athletic nerd,'' she explained. ''Anyway, she tripped me. If that wasn't bad enough, she had a few friends on the other team. They elbowed the hell out of me during the game. I had bruises everywhere.''

An immediate flood of resentment had him tightening his hold. ''Little bitches.''

Pleased with the support, she cuddled closer. ''It was an epiphany for me. Suddenly I saw that pacifism, while morally sound, could get you trampled into dust. I waited for Dawn outside the science lab one day. We started out with words—I've always been good at them. We progressed to pushing and shoving and drew quite a crowd. She swung first. I didn't expect it, and she bopped me right on the nose. Let me tell you, Detective, pain can be a great motivator.''

"Separates the nerds from the toughs."

"You got it. It took three of them to pull me off her, but before they did, I'd blackened her baby-blues, split her Cupid's-bow mouth and loosened several of her pearly-whites."

"Good for you, McNee."

"It was good," she said with a sigh. "In fact, it felt so good, I've had to be careful with my temper ever since. I didn't just want to hurt her, you see. I wanted to mangle her."

He took her hand, curled it into a fist and raised it to his lips. "I'll have to watch my step. Did you take much heat?"

"We both got suspended. My parents were appalled and embarrassed enough by my behavior to cancel my summer plans and switch me to another school."

"But—" He cut himself off. Not every family was as supportive as his.

"It was the best thing that could have happened to me," she told him. "I started off with a clean slate. I was still ugly, but I knew how to handle myself."

Even if she didn't realize she was carrying around some emotional scars, he did. He rolled over her, cupping her face in his hands. "Listen, McNee, you're beautiful."

Amused, she grinned. "Sure I am."

He didn't smile. In the dim light, his eyes were very intense. "I said, you're beautiful. Why else haven't I been able to get you out of my mind since the first time I saw you?"

"Intriguing," she corrected. "Unusual."

"Gorgeous," he murmured, and watched her blink in surprise. "Ivory for skin, fire for hair, jade for eyes. And these." He traced a fingertip over a sprinkling of freckles. "Gold dust."

"You've already gotten me into bed, Alexi," she said lightly. She had to speak lightly, or she'd humiliate herself with tears. "But the flattery is appreciated." With a grin, she linked her arms around his neck. "But haven't you heard the one about actions speaking louder than words?"

He arched a brow. "If you insist."

"Oh, I do," she murmured, as his mouth came down to hers. "I absolutely do."

With her bag slapping hard against her hip, Bess raced into the office, ten minutes late. "I have a good excuse," she called to Lori.

Her perpetually prompt partner was standing by the coffeepot, her back to the door. "It's all right. I'm running behind myself."

"You?" Bess dropped her bag, stretched her shoulders. She might have skipped her workout that morning, but she was feeling as limber as a snake. "What is it, a national holiday?" She crossed to the pot herself, chattering as she poured a cup. "Well, I'd save my excuse for another time, but I can hardly stand not to tell you." She lifted shining eyes, then stopped after one look at Lori's face. "What is it, honey?"

"It's nothing." After giving herself a shake, Lori sipped her coffee. "It's just that Steven caught me on my way in."

"Did he say something to upset you?"

"He said he loved me." She pressed her lips together. She'd be damned if she'd cry over him again. "The sonofabitch."

"Let's sit down." Bess curled a comforting arm around Lori's shoulder. "You might not want to hear this, but I think he means it."

"He doesn't even know what it means." Furious, Lori dashed one rogue tear away. "I'm not going to let him do this to me again. Get me believing, get me all churned up, just so he can back off when things get serious. Let him have the fantasy life. I've got reality."

Because she'd been waiting for an opening just like this, Bess crouched down in front of her. "Which is?"

"A job, paying your bills—"

"Boring," Bess finished, and Lori's brimming eyes flashed.

"Then I'm boring."

"No, you're not." Sighing, Bess set her coffee aside and took one of Lori's hands. "Maybe you're afraid to take risks, but that doesn't make you boring. And I know you want more out of life than a job and a good credit rating."

"What's wrong with those things?"

"Nothing, as long as that's not all you have. Lori, I know you're still in love with him."

"That's my problem."

"His, too. He's miserable without you."

Suddenly weary, Lori rubbed her fingers between her brows. "He's the one who broke things off. He said he didn't want complications, a long-term commitment."

"He was wrong. I'd bet the bank that he knows he's wrong. Why don't you just talk to him?"

"I don't know if I can." She squeezed her eyes tight. "It hurts."

An odd light flickered in Bess's eyes. "Is that how you know it's real? When it hurts?"

"It's one of the top symptoms." She opened her eyes again. This time, there was a trace of hope mixed with the tears. "Do you really think he's unhappy?"

"I know he is. Just talk, Lori. Hear each other out."

"Maybe." She gave Bess's hand a quick squeeze, then reached for her coffee again. "I wasn't going to dump this on you first thing."

"What are pals for?"

"Well, pal, we'd better get to work, or a lot of people will be out of a job."

"Great. I've been playing with the dialogue in that scene

between Storm and Jade. We want to bump up the sexual tension.''

Lori was already nodding and booting up the computer. ''You're the dialogue champ,'' she began, then glanced up. ''So why were you late?''

''It's not important. We've got them running into each other at the station house. The long look first, then—''

''Bess, you're only making me more curious. Get it out of the way, or I won't be able to work.''

''Okay.'' She was all but bursting to tell, in any case. ''I was with Alexi.''

''I thought that was yesterday.''

''It was.'' Bess's smile spread. ''And last night. And this morning. Oh, Lori, it's incredible. I've never felt this way about anyone.''

''Right.'' She started to pick up her reading glasses, then looked up again. For a moment, she did nothing but study Bess's face. ''Say that again.''

''I've never felt this way about anyone.''

''Good grief.'' On a quick huff of breath, Lori sat back. ''I think you mean it.''

''It's different.'' With a half laugh, Bess pressed a hand to her cheek. ''It's scary, and it hurts, and sometimes I look at him and I can't even breathe. I'm so afraid he might take a good look at me and realize his mistake.'' She let her hand drop away. ''It's supposed to be easy.''

''No.'' Slowly Lori shook her head. ''That was always *your* mistake. It's supposed to be hard, and scary and real.''

''There's this clutching around my heart.''

''Yeah.''

''And...and...'' Frustrated, Bess turned, scooting around a chair so that she could pace the length of the table. ''And my stomach's all tied up in knots one minute. The next I feel so happy I can hardly bear it. When we were together last night...'' No way to describe it, she thought. No possible way. ''Lori, I swear, no one's ever made me feel like that. And this morning, when I woke up beside him, I didn't know whether to laugh or cry.''

Lori rose, held out a hand. ''Congratulations, McNee. You've finally made it.''

''Looks that way.'' With a laugh, she threw her arms around Lori and squeezed. ''Why didn't you ever tell me how it feels?''

''It's something you have to experience firsthand. How about him?''

''He loves me.'' She felt foolish and weepy. Digging through her bag she found a tattered tissue. ''He told me. He looked at me, and he told me. But—''

''Oh-oh.''

''He doesn't want me to tell him how I feel.'' Hissing a breath through her teeth, she pressed a hand to her stomach. ''Oh, God, it hurts. It hurts everywhere when I realize he doesn't trust me enough. He thinks it's like all the other times. Why shouldn't he? But I want him to know it's not—and I don't know how.''

''He only has to look at you.''

''It's not enough.'' Calmer now, Bess blew her nose. ''Everything's different this time. I guess I have to prove myself. I do love him, Lori.''

''I can see that. I wasn't sure I ever would.'' Touched, she lifted a hand to Bess's hair. ''You could take your own advice, and talk to him.''

''We have talked. But he doesn't want to hear this, at least not yet. He wants things to stay as they are.''

Lori lifted her brows. ''What do you want?''

''For him to be happy.'' She chuckled and stuffed the mangled tissue back in her purse. ''That makes me sound like a wimp. You know I'm not.''

''Who knows you better? It only makes you sound like a woman in the first dizzy stages of love.''

Bess gave her a watery smile. ''Does it get worse or better?''

"Both."

"That's good news. Well, while it's getting worse and better, I'll have time to show him how I feel." She picked up her coffee, then set it aside again. "Lori, there's one more thing."

"What could be bigger?" Lori demanded.

"Alexi wants me to have dinner with his family on Sunday."

After a quick gurgle of laughter, Lori's eyes widened. "He's taking you home to Mother?"

"And Father," Bess put in. "And brothers and sisters and nieces and nephews. A couple times a month they have a big family dinner on Sunday."

"Obviously the man is crazy about you."

"He is. I know he is." Then she shut her eyes and dropped into a chair. "His family is enormously important to him. You can hear it every time he mentions one of them." She grabbed another tissue and began to tear it to shreds. "I want to meet them. Really. But what if they don't like me?"

"You have got it bad. Take it from me, you just be the Bess McNee we all know and love, and they'll be crazy about you, too."

"But what if—"

"What if you pull yourself together?" This time Lori picked up her glasses, perched them on her nose. "Put some of this angst into Storm and Jade's heartbreak. Millions of viewers will thank you."

After a deep breath, Bess nodded. "Okay, okay. That might work. And if we don't get the morning session out of the way, we won't be ready when Rosalie comes in at noon for a consulting session."

"Your deal, sister." Frowning, Lori gestured with a pencil. "That particular lady makes me nervous."

"Don't worry about Rosalie. I know what I'm doing."

"How many times have I heard that?"

But Bess only smiled and let her mind drift. ''Okay
Storm and Jade.'' She closed her eyes, envisioned the
scene. ''So, they run into each other at the station...''

Chapter Nine

"And then," Bess continued as she zipped through traffic, "Jade turns back, devastated, and says, 'But what you want isn't always what you need.' Music swells, fade out."

"It's not that I'm not fascinated by the twists and turns of those people in Holbrook..."

"Millbrook."

"Right." Alex winced as she cut off a sedan. "I just wish you'd watch the road. It would be really embarrassing if you got a ticket while I was in the car with you."

"I'm not speeding." Frowning, she glanced down at her speedometer. "Hardly."

She handled the five-speed like a seasoned veteran of the Indianapolis 500, Alex thought. And at the moment she was treating the other, innocent drivers on the road like competitors. "Maybe you could find a home in one lane and stay there."

"Killjoy." But she did as he asked. "I hardly ever get to drive. I love it."

He had to smile. The wind whipping in through the open

sunroof was blowing her hair everywhere. "I'd never have guessed."

"The last time I had a chance was when L.D. and I went to some fancy do on Long Island." She checked her mirror and, unable to resist, shot into the next lane. "One trip with me and he insisted on taking his car and driver every damn place." She sent Alex a smile, then sobered instantly when she saw his expression. "I'm sorry."

"For what?"

"For bringing him up."

"I didn't say anything."

No, he hadn't said anything, she admitted. A man didn't have to say a word when his eyes could go that cold. Her hands tightened on the wheel. Now she stared straight ahead.

"He was a friend, Alexi. That's all he ever was. I didn't…" She took a long, careful breath. "I never slept with him."

"I didn't ask one way or the other," he said coolly.

"Maybe you should. One minute you want to know all there is about me, and the next you don't. I think—"

"I think you're driving too fast again." He reached over and brushed his knuckles down her cheek. "And you should relax. Okay?"

"Okay." But her fingers remained tight on the wheel. "I'd like—sometime—for us to talk about it."

"Sometime." Damn it, didn't she realize he didn't want to talk about the other men who'd been part of her life? He didn't want to think about them. Especially now, now that he was in love, and he knew what it was like to be with her.

He knew the sound of that little sigh she made when she turned toward him in the night. The way her eyes stayed unfocused and heavy, long after she awakened in the morning. He knew she liked her showers too hot and too long.

And that she smelled so good because she rubbed some fragrant cream all over before she'd even dried off.

She was always losing things. An earring, a scribbled note, money. She never counted her change, and she always overtipped.

He knew those things, was coming to treasure them. Why should he talk about other men who had come to know them?

"Turn here."

"Hmm?"

"I said turn…" He trailed off with a huff of breath as she breezed by the exit. "Okay, take the next one, and we'll double back."

"The next what?"

"Turn, McNee." He reached over and gave her hair a quick tug. "Take the next turn, which means you have to get over in the right lane."

"Oh." She did, punching the gas and handily cutting off another car. At the rude blast of its horn, she only lifted a hand and waved.

"He wasn't being friendly," Alex pointed out—after he took his hands from in front of his eyes.

"I know. But that's no reason for me to be rude, too."

"Some people consider cutting off another driver rude."

"No. That's an adventure."

Somehow they made it without mishap. But the moment she'd squeezed into a parking place two doors down from his parents' row house, he held out his hand. "Keys."

Sulking, she jingled them in her hand. "I didn't get a ticket."

"Probably because there wasn't a traffic cop brave enough to pull you over. Let's have them, McNee. I've had enough adventure for one day."

"You just want to drive." Her eyes narrowed suspiciously. "It's a man thing."

"It's a survival thing." He plucked them from her hand.

"I just want to live." Not that he was going to object to handling the natty little Mercedes. But he decided against bringing that up as they climbed out of opposite doors.

"Pretty neighborhood," she commented, taking in the trees and freshly painted house trim and flowering plants, the scatter of kids riding over the uneven sidewalk on bikes and skateboards.

A few of them called out to Alex. Bess found herself being given the once-over by a group of teenage boys before they sent hoots and whistles and thumbs-up signs in Alex's direction.

"Ah, the first stamp of approval." But she rubbed her damp palm surreptitiously against her skirt before taking his hand. "Did you used to ride bikes along the sidewalk?"

"Sure."

Battling nerves, she strolled with him toward the house. "And sit on the curb in the summer and lie about girls?"

"I didn't have to lie," he told her with a wicked grin. He glanced up the steps as the door opened and Mikhail came out, Griff on his hip.

"You're late again." He started down, jiggling Griff.

"She missed the turn."

"He's always late." Mikhail smiled. "You're Bess."

"Yes. Hello." She held out a hand and found that his was hard as rock. Griff had already leaned over to give Alex a kiss, and now, still puckered, he leaned toward Bess. Laughing, she pressed her mouth to his. "And hello to you, too, handsome."

"Griff likes the ladies," Mikhail told her. "Takes after his uncle."

"Don't start," Alex muttered.

Mikhail ignored him and continued to study Bess until she was fighting the need to squirm. "Do I have dirt on my face, or what?"

"No, sorry." He shifted his gaze to his brother. "You're

improving, Alexi,'' he said in Ukrainian. "This one is well worth a few sweaty mornings in the gym.''

"Tak." He skimmed a hand down to the nape of Bess's neck. "If you tell her about that, I'll strangle you in your sleep.''

Mikhail's grin flashed. The resemblance was startling, Bess thought. Those wild, dark looks, that simmering sexuality. And the child had the looks, as well, she realized. Lord help the women of the twenty-first century.

"Guy talk?'' she asked.

"Bad manners,'' Mikhail said apologetically, deciding he liked not only her unusual looks, but the intelligence in her eyes, as well. Yes, indeed, he thought, Alex was definitely improving. "I was complimenting my brother on his taste. Take her in, Alex. Griff wants to watch the kids ride awhile.''

"Sydney?'' he asked as he mounted the steps.

"She's here, but she's tired.''

"She works too hard.''

"There is that.'' The grin spread again. "And she's pregnant.''

Alex stopped, turned. "Yeah?'' He went down the steps again to catch Mikhail and Griff in a bear hug. "It's good?''

"It's great. We want our children close, our family big.''

"You're off to the right start.'' He grabbed Bess's hand as Mikhail lifted Griff onto his shoulders and crossed the street. Griff was clapping his hands and shouting toddler gibberish to the other kids. "I'm still trying to get used to him being a papa, and now he's going to have another.''

She'd forgotten her nerves. Perhaps the child's sweet, unaffected kiss had done it. She slipped an arm around Alex's waist. "Come on, Uncle Alex. I want to meet the rest of them.''

"They're loud,'' he warned as they started back up the door.

"I like loud."

"They can be nosy."

"So can I."

At the door, he took both of her hands. He'd brought women into his home before, but it had never been important. This was vital. "I love you, Bess." Before she could speak, he kissed her, then pushed open the door.

They certainly were loud, Bess discovered. No one seemed to mind if everyone talked at once, or if the big, droopy-eared dog barked and raced around the living room to hide behind chairs. And they were nosy, though they were charming with it. She'd hardly had a chance to get her bearings before she was sitting next to Alex's father, Yuri, and being cagily interrogated.

"So you write stories for TV." He nodded his big, shaggy head approvingly. "You have brains."

"A few." She smiled up at Zack when he offered her a glass of wine.

"Rachel says more than a few." He sent his wife a wink as she sat with her hands folded over her enormous belly. "She's been watching your show."

"Oh, yeah?"

"I admit I was curious." Rachel wanted to shift to get comfortable, but she knew it was useless. "After we met, I taped it a couple of times. Then, when I gave in to Zack's hounding me about taking maternity leave, I realized how easy it is to get hooked. I'm not sure I've got all the characters straight yet, but it's amazingly entertaining. Nick's caught it with me." She glanced at her brother-in-law.

To his credit, Nick didn't blush, but he did squirm. "I was just keeping you company." He might have come a long way from trying to prove his manhood with gangs like the Cobras, but even at nearly twenty-one, he wasn't quite secure enough to admit he'd gotten caught up in the "Secret Sins" of Millbrook. He shrugged, shook back his shaggy blond hair, then caught the quick grins of his family. "It wasn't like I was really watching." His green eyes glinted with humor. "Except for the babes."

"That's what they all say." Bess smiled back, enjoying him. Too bad he wasn't an actor, she thought. Those brooding good looks—tough, with just a hint of vulnerability beneath—would shine on-screen. "So, who's your type, Nick? LuAnne, our sensitive ingenue with the big, weepy eyes, who suffers in silence, or the scheming Brooke, who uses her sexuality to destroy any man who crosses her?"

Considering, he ran his tongue around his teeth. "Actually, I go for Jade. I've got this thing for older women."

Zack caught him in a headlock.

"Hey." Nick laughed, not bothering to try to free himself. "We're having a conversation here. I'm trying to make time with Alex's lady."

"Kill him in the other room, will you?" Alex said easily. "We have to eat in here."

"I watch your show many times," Nadia said as she popped in from the kitchen. Alex's mother's handsome face was flushed pink from oven heat. "I like it."

"Well, that Vicki's not hard to watch." Zack stood behind his wife now, rubbing her shoulders.

"Men always go for the cheap floozies," Rachel put in. "How about you, Alex? Caught any 'Secret Sins'?"

"No." Not that he'd admit. "McNee keeps me up on what's happening in Millbrook."

"It must be hard." Sydney, looking pale but blissfully relaxed in her corner of the couch, sipped her ginger ale. "The pace."

"It's murder." Bess grinned. "I love it."

"So, how is it you meet Alexi?" Yuri asked.

"He arrested me."

There was a moment of silence, while Alex aimed a killing look at Bess. Then a burst of laughter that sent the dog careening around the room again.

"Did I miss a joke?" Mikhail demanded as he swung through the door with Griff.

"No." Rachel chuckled again while her brother sat on the arm of the couch, beside his wife. "But I have a feeling it's going to be a good one. Come on, Bess, this I have to hear."

She told them, while Alex interrupted a half-dozen times to disagree or correct or put in his own perspective. Even as they sat at the big old table to enjoy Nadia's pot roast, they were shouting with laughter or calling out questions.

"He put you in a cell, but you still go out with him." This from Mikhail.

"Well." Bess ran her tongue over her teeth. "He is kind of cute."

With a hearty laugh, Yuri slapped his son on the back. "The ladies, they always say so."

Alex scooped up potatoes. "Thanks, Papa."

"Is good to be attractive to women." He wiggled his brows at his wife. "Then, when you pick one, she is helpless to resist."

"I picked you," Nadia told him, passing biscuits to Nick. "You were very slow. Like a bear with, ah..." She struggled for the right word. "Soft brains." She ignored Yuri's snort of objection. "He did not come to court me. So I courted him."

"Every time I turn, there she is. In my way." When he looked at his wife, Bess saw memories and more in his eyes. "There was no prettier girl in the village than Nadia. Then she was mine."

"I liked your big hands and shy eyes," she told him. Her smile was quick and lovely. "Soon you were not so shy. But my boys," she added, turning the smile on Bess, "they were never shy with the girls."

"Why waste time?" On impulse, Alex put a hand on Bess's cheek and turned her face to his. Her smile was puzzled. Then surprise shot into her eyes as he covered her mouth with his. Not a quick, friendly kiss, this, but a searing one that made her head buzz.

She had no way of knowing that he'd never kissed a woman not of his family at his mother's table. Nor that by doing so, he was telling those he loved that this was *the* woman.

As the table erupted with applause, Bess cleared her throat. "No," she managed. "Not a bit shy."

Nadia blinked back tears and raised her glass. She understood what her son had told her and felt the bittersweet pleasure that came from knowing the last of her children had given his heart. "Welcome," she said to Bess.

A little confused, Bess reached for her glass as all the others were lifted. "Thank you." She sipped, relieved when the chattering started again.

How easy to fall in love with them, she realized. All of them were so warm, so open, so comfortable with each other. Her parents would never have had such a sweetly intimate conversation at the table. Nor had they ever embraced her with the verve and passion both Yuri and Nadia showed their children.

Was this what she'd been missing all of those years? Bess wondered. Had lacking something like this caused her to be so socially clumsy as a child, and, making up for it, so socially active as an adult?

Still, what she had had, and what she hadn't, had forged her into what she was, so she couldn't regret it. Well, perhaps a little, she mused, falling unknowingly into the family tradition by sneaking the dog bits of food under the table. It was hard not to regret it a little when you saw how lovely it could be to be part of such a solid whole.

Absorbing everything, she glanced around the table. And found Mikhail's eyes on her. This time she smiled. "You're doing it again," she told him.

"Yes. I want to carve you."

"I beg your pardon?"

"Your face." He reached out to take it in his hand. The conversation continued around them, as if he handled women at the dinner table regularly. "Very fascinating. Mahogany would be best."

Amused, she sat patiently while he turned her face this way and that. "Is this a joke?"

"Mikhail never jokes about his work," Sydney commented, coaxing one more green bean into her son. "I'm just surprised it's taken him so long to demand you sit for him."

"Sit?" She shook her head, and then her eyes widened as it all came together. "Oh, of course. Stanislaski. The artist. I've seen your work. Lusted after it, actually."

"You will sit for me, and I'll give you a piece. You'll choose it."

"I could hardly turn down an offer like that."

"Good." Satisfied, he went back to his meal. "She's very beautiful," he said to Alex, in such an offhand way that Bess laughed.

"I'd say that Stanislaski taste runs to the odd, but your wife proves me wrong."

Mikhail brushed a hand over Sydney's halo of auburn hair, stroked a finger down her classically lovely face. "There are different kinds of beauty. You'll come to the studio next week."

"Don't bother to argue." Sydney caught Mikhail's hand, squeezed it. "It won't do you a bit of good."

At the other end of the table, Rachel winced. Nadia leaned closer, spoke gently. "How far apart?"

Rachel gave a little sigh. "Eight, ten minutes. They're very mild yet."

"What's mild?" Zack glanced at her, and then his mouth all but dropped to his knees. "Oh, God, now? *Now?*"

"Not this very minute." She would be calm, Rachel told herself and took a deep, cleansing breath to prove it. "I think you have time for some of Mama's cream cake."

"She's in labor." He gaped across the table at his equally panicked brother.

"We're not ready here." Nick stumbled to his feet. "We're ready back at home. I'm supposed to call the doctor, but I don't have the number."

"Mama does," Rachel assured her husband's younger brother. Then she lifted a hand to her husband's. "Take it easy, Muldoon. There's plenty of time."

"Time, hell. We're going now. Shouldn't we go now?" Zack demanded of Nadia.

She smiled and nodded. "It would be best for you, Zack."

"But, Mama—"

Rachel's protest was cut off by Nadia's gentle flow of Ukrainian, the gist of which had a great deal to do with placating frightened husbands.

"She should put her feet up," Mikhail announced. "This helped you, yes?"

"Yes," Sydney agreed. "But I think we should wait until she gets to the hospital."

"Nine-one-one." Alex shoved away from the table and sprang to his feet. "I'll call."

"Oh, sit down." Rachel waved an annoyed hand at him. "I don't need a cop."

"An ambulance," he insisted.

"I'm not sick, I'm in labor."

"I take her in the truck." Yuri was already up, prepared to lift his baby girl into his big arms. "We get there very fast."

While the men began to argue in a mixture of languages, Nadia rose quietly and went into the kitchen to call Rachel's obstetrician.

"I've already been through this," Mikhail was saying to Alex. "I know how to handle it."

"Ha." Their father pushed them both aside and pounded

a fist on his broad chest. "Me, four times. You know nothing."

"We don't have the tape recorder or the music." Nick ran a hand through his flow of sandy hair. He was desperately afraid he'd be sick. Though no one was listening to him, he continued to babble. "The video camera. We've got to get the video camera."

"Honey, you want some water? You want some juice?" When she yelped, he turned dead white. "Another one? It hasn't been ten minutes, has it?"

"You're breaking my hand." Rachel shook it free and sent a pleading look to Sydney.

"Okay, guys, back off." The steel under velvet that made Sydney a successful businesswoman snapped into her voice. "Alex, go upstairs and get your sister a pillow for the ride. Yuri, go start the truck. That's a very good idea. Nick, you, Mikhail and Griff go back to your apartment and get what Rachel needs. We'll meet you at the hospital."

"How do you get there?" Mikhail demanded.

"I have a car." Bess was watching the family drama with fascinated eyes. "We can fit three in a pinch."

"Wonderful." Dispersing the troops with all the flair of a general, Sydney gave her husband a kiss and a shove. "Get going. Zack and Nadia will ride with Yuri and Rachel. I'll go with Alex and Bess."

As the next contraction hit, Rachel began to breathe slowly, steadily. "Sorry," she said to Bess in between breaths, "to put you out."

"No problem." She had to bite her tongue to prevent herself asking what it felt like to go into labor at a family dinner. There'd be time for that later.

"I called the doctor, and Natasha." Nadia came back into the room, pleased that Sydney had organized the troops. "Natasha and her family are coming."

"We should go." Zack helped Rachel to her feet and swallowed hard. "Shouldn't we go?"

By the time they arrived at the hospital, Sydney and Bess were the best of friends. It was difficult to be otherwise, when they'd been crammed together in one seat while Alex drove like a madman back to Manhattan.

They talked about clothes, a few mutual friends they'd discovered, and the Stanislaski men. Sydney agreed that it was very forbearing of Bess not to mention the quality of Alex's driving, after he'd been so critical of hers.

By the time they found their way to the maternity level, Rachel was already settled in a birthing room, Zack had gotten over the first stages of panic, and Yuri was patting a pocket full of cigars.

"She's in the early stages," Nadia explained to them in the corridor. "Company is good for her."

Alex strode straight through the door, but Bess hung back. "I don't want to intrude," she said to Nadia.

"This is not intrusion. This is family." Nadia cocked her head. "Are you uneasy with childbirth?"

"Oh, no. I couldn't be, after I've written so many."

Alex poked his head back out. "How'd you research that, McNee?"

"I did rounds with an obstetrician." Her dimple winked out. "And found a few mothers-to-be who didn't object to having me hang around during labor and delivery. Have you ever seen one?"

"No." His eyes changed. Just like a man. "They, ah, show us films, just in case, but I've never been at ground zero."

"It's pretty great." She laughed, perfectly able to read his thoughts. "Don't worry. I'll hold your hand."

They passed the time in the big, airy birthing room telling stories, giving advice, joking with Zack once Mikhail and Nick arrived with Rachel's things. Griff was happily settled in with Zack's cook, Rio, so there was little to do but wait.

When Rachel felt like walking, they took turns leading her around the corridors, rubbing her back, making small talk to take her mind off the discomfort between contractions.

"I can see your mind working," Alex murmured to Bess. "'How can I use this?'"

"It's ingrained." She murmured her thanks when he passed her his cold drink. "Your family," she said, glancing around the room. "I've never known anyone like them. My parents—they'd be appalled to be expected to take part in something like this."

"It's our baby, too."

She smiled and lifted a hand to his cheek. "That's what I mean. You're all very special."

"I'm glad you're here." As he leaned over to kiss her, Yuri slapped him on the back.

"Now all my children make babies but you." He wiggled his brows at Bess. "You start soon, yes?"

"Papa…" Not sure how to take Bess's chuckle, Alex rose and spoke, firmly and quietly, in his mother tongue. "When I decide to make babies, I'll let you know."

"What decide?" Yuri gestured toward Bess. "She's the one you want, isn't she?"

"Yes."

Now Yuri gestured expansively with both hands. "Then?"

"I have my reasons for waiting. They're my reasons."

Though the shake of Yuri's head was a gesture of sadness, there was a twinkle in his eye. "How is it all my children are so stubborn?"

"How is it my papa is so nosy?"

With a laugh, Yuri embraced Alex and kissed both his cheeks. "Go take this pretty girl for a walk, steal some kisses. Your sister will be some time yet."

"That's advice I'll take." He reached for Bess's hand and pulled her to her feet. "Come on, let's get some air."

"Alexi." Bess had to quicken her pace to keep up with him. "Don't be angry with him. He didn't mean to embarrass you."

"Yes, he did, but I'm not angry with him."

"What were you two rattling on about?"

He punched the button for the elevator. "You know, I don't think I'll teach you any Ukrainian. It comes in too handy."

"But it's—"

"Rude," he finished for her, grinning. "I know."

By the time they came back again, Alex had taken his father's advice to heart. Bess's head was still spinning when they walked past the waiting room. It was Alex who spotted Nick, pacing and smoking in the smoking lounge like the cliché expectant daddy.

"How's it going, kid?"

"It's been an awfully long time." Nick's hand shook a bit as he lifted the cigarette to his lips. "I mean, Sydney was only in a couple of hours for Griff. It's getting really intense, and Rachel kicked me and the camera out. How come they don't do something?"

"I don't know a lot about it," Alex mused. "But I think babies come when they're ready."

"It's only been a little more than six hours." Bess moved in to soothe, touched that Nick should have such deep concern for his sister-in-law.

"Feels like six days," Zack commented as he staggered in. He plucked the cigarette from Nick's hand and took a deep drag. "She's swearing at me. I know what some of those names are now, even if they aren't in English."

"That's a good sign," Bess assured him. "It means things are moving along."

"She swore at the doctor, too." With a sigh, he passed

the cigarette back to Nick. "But she didn't take a swing at *him*."

"If she missed," Alex commented, "she must be in really bad shape."

Wincing, Zack rubbed his shoulder. "She didn't. I'd better get back."

"Let's go give him some support," Alex began, but then he spotted a woman rushing off the elevator. "Tash!"

"Oh, Alex!"

Bess watched the woman fly into the waiting room, Gypsy hair flowing. There was concern in her eyes and laughter on her lips as she swung into Alex's arms.

"Alexi, how is Rachel?"

"Swearing at her doctor and punching Zack."

"Ah." She relaxed instantly. "That's good. Nick." She held out a hand for his. "Don't look so worried. Your niece or nephew will be along soon. Spence is parking the car. We were going to leave the children, but they were so disappointed, we brought them. Freddie's looking forward to seeing you."

Nick brightened a bit. "How's she doing?"

"She's taller than me now, and so pretty. Alex, where's Rachel?"

"I'll take you. Oh, this is Bess."

"Bess?" Natasha turned, one hand still on her brother's arm. Of course, she'd heard about Bess. West Virginia might be a fair distance from New York, but family business traveled fast on phone wires. "I'm sorry. I didn't realize."

"That's all right. You've got a lot on your mind." And then Bess said the first thing that came to hers. "What fabulous genes you all have."

Natasha's brows lifted. Then, below them, her eyes lit with laughter. "Rachel said I would like you. I hope we have time to talk before we leave town. I'm sorry to rush off."

"Don't worry about it. I think Nick and I'll go to the cafeteria, rustle up some food for this group."

Three hours later, Bess had delivered sandwiches and coffee, bounced Natasha's youngest daughter, Katie, on her knee and introduced herself to Spence Kimball and helped him entertain his very cranky son. She'd met Freddie and noted that the pretty, pixielike teenager was deep in puppy love with Nick.

As time dragged on, she added her support when Mikhail pressured his very tired wife to rest in the waiting room, took a few minutes to interrogate some nurses to help her beef up some hospital scenes and soothed Alex's nerves as his sister's labor reached the final stages.

"It won't be much longer."

"That's what they said an hour ago."

They were standing in the waiting room. Alex refused to sit. After a yawn and a good stretch, Bess wrapped her arms around him.

"She's fully dilated, and the baby was crowning. The last glance I had of the fetal monitor showed a really strong heartbeat. A fast one. I think it's a girl."

"How do you know so much?"

"Research." She settled her head on his shoulder. "I was figuring earlier that I've delivered twelve babies, including one set of twins. In a matter of speaking."

When her voice slurred, he tipped up her chin. "You're asleep on your feet, McNee. I should have sent you home."

"You couldn't have pried me away."

No, that was true, he realized. It was just one more aspect to her beauty. "I owe you."

"Then pay up." She lifted her mouth, sighing into the kiss.

"Mama." Though he'd enjoyed watching his brother, Mikhail shot to his feet when he spotted his parents in the doorway.

"We have a new member of the family." There were tears in Nadia's eyes and in Yuri's as he stood with his arm tight around his wife.

"What is it?" Nick and Alex demanded together.

"You will come see. They bring the baby to the glass in a moment."

"Rachel is resting." Yuri dashed away a tear. "You will kiss her good night soon."

They trooped out together, to wait by the nursery window for the first glimpse.

"I'm an uncle," Nick said to Freddie. The girl's cheeks turned pink as he gave her a hard hug. "Hey, there's Zack." He kept his arm around her as his brother walked forward, holding a tiny bundle. The bundle was squalling, and Zack was grinning from ear to ear.

He held the baby up. Atop the curling black hair was a bright pink bow.

"It's a girl," Alex murmured, and held Bess hard against him. "She's beautiful."

"Man" was the best Nick could do. "Oh, man." Overcome for a moment, he glanced down and found himself looking at Freddie, who was still tucked under his arm. He drew back, brushed a fingertip along her cheek and caught a tear on the tip. "What's this?"

"It's just so sweet." Freddie's eyelashes were spiky and her eyes swam as she looked up at him. He thought for a moment—an uncomfortable moment—that it would be easy to drown in those eyes.

"Yeah, it's great." He let out a careful breath. She was his cousin, he reminded himself. Well, a kind of cousin. And she was hardly more than a kid. "I, ah, don't have a handkerchief or anything."

"It's all right." Freddie felt a drop roll down her cheek, but she didn't mind. After all, these were the very best kind of tears. "Do *you* ever think about having babies?" she asked with disarming candor.

"Having—" Nick would have stepped back then, way back, but the family was crowding him in. "No," he said firmly, and made himself look away from her damp, glowing face. "No way."

"I do." She sighed and let her head rest against his arm.

Mikhail was whispering something to Sydney that had her nodding and wiping away tears. Behind Freddie, Natasha shifted Katie in her arms and turned to her husband. He had one hand on Freddie's shoulder, and his sleeping son lay curved on his own.

"Every one is a miracle."

He bent his head to kiss her damp cheeks. "Just say the word anytime you decide you'd like another miracle of our own."

"I am a man blessed." Yuri grabbed the closest body. It happened to be Bess's, and she found herself whirled in a circle. "Two grandsons. Now three granddaughters." He tossed Bess up. She came down laughing, gripping his shoulders.

"Congratulations." She pleased him enormously by kissing him firmly on the mouth. "Grandpapa."

"It's a good day." He reached in his pocket. "Have a cigar."

Chapter Ten

Rosalie considered herself an excellent judge of people, and she had already decided Bess was one strange lady. But she kept coming back.

Sure, the money was good, Rosalie thought as she sat drinking a diet soda in Bess's basement office. And for a woman with a retirement plan, that had to be number one. Yet it was more than making an extra buck that kept her taking the trip up and across town several days each week. More, too, that kept her hanging around after they finished what Bess liked to call 'consulting sessions.'

Rosalie was human enough to get a charge out of being connected, however remotely, to the entertainment world. She couldn't deny that she'd been excited, awed and impressed when she watched a couple of tapings.

But there was another factor, a much more basic one. Rosalie enjoyed Bess's company.

Besides being a strange lady, Bess had class. Rosalie didn't figure a person had to possess class to recognize it in another. Class wasn't just a matter of pedigree—though she'd discovered Bess had one. It was more than having an old lady in the DAR, or an old man in *Who's Who*. It was hazier than that. Though Rosalie couldn't quite come up with the terms she wanted, she had recognized in Bess those rare and often nebulous qualities, grace and compassion.

She was procrastinating over taking the trip back downtown by dawdling over her drink. Bess didn't seem to mind if Rosalie hung around while she worked. In the few weeks since they'd hooked up, Rosalie had noted that Bess worked hard and long. Harder, in Rosalie's opinion, than she herself, or any of the other ladies in her profession. Certainly Bess's hours were longer.

It amused Rosalie to compare the two. In fact, she and Bess had gotten into a very interesting discussion on the similarities and differences between Bess's selling her mind and Rosalie her body.

What a kick that had been, Rosalie thought now, while Bess typed and mumbled. Philosophical discussions weren't the norm in Rosalie's world.

The simple term she had not quite grasped for their relationship was *friendship*. They had become friends.

"How late you gonna work?" Rosalie asked, and Bess glanced up absently from the computer screen.

"Oh...not much longer." Her eyes were still slightly unfocused when she blew her hair away from them. Brock was on the verge of seducing Jessica. "I just had this idea for a little twist on a scene for tomorrow." She smiled then. It was quick, and a little wicked. "Of course, several members of the cast are going to want to murder me when I toss this at them in the morning. But that's show biz."

Rosalie took a drag on her cigarette. "What time did you get in here this morning?"

"Today? About nine-thirty. I was..." She thought of Alex. "Running a little late."

Lips pursed, Rosalie looked at the fake designer watch

on her wrist. "And it's after seven now." Her grin flashed. "Girlfriend, you'd only put in half that many hours in my line of work."

"Yeah, but I get to sit down." Bess rubbed at the dull ache in the back of her neck. She really was going to have to work on her posture. "Hungry?" she asked. "Want to order something in?"

With a little tug of regret, Rosalie stabbed out the cigarette. "No. I gotta get to work, too."

"You could take the night off." Casually Bess ran a finger lightly over the keyboard. "Maybe we could catch a movie."

Chuckling, Rosalie dug in her purse for a mirror to check her makeup. "You said you weren't going to try to reform me."

"I lied." Bess sat back in her chair while Rosalie painted her mouth bloodred. She'd tried very hard not to pontificate, not to pressure, not to preach. And thought she had succeeded. But she hadn't tried not to care. That would have been useless. "I really worry about you. Especially since the last murder."

The odd twisting in Rosalie's stomach had her shifting her eyes from her compact mirror to Bess. She couldn't remember if anyone had ever worried about her before. Certainly not in years. "Didn't I tell you I could take care of myself?"

"Yes, but—"

"No buts about it, honey." With a second dip into her purse, Rosalie pulled out a stiletto. One flick of the wrist, and the long, razor-sharp blade zipped out. "What I can't handle, this can."

Bess managed to close her mouth, but her eyes stayed riveted to the knife. In the overhead lights, it gleamed silver, bright as sudden death. She couldn't say it was elegant. But it was fascinating, deathly fascinating. "Can I?"

With a shrug of her shoulders, Rosalie passed the

weapon to her. "Don't mess with the blade," she warned. "It's as sharp as it looks."

Bess took a good grip on the handle, twisting her wrist this way and that, like a fencer. She wondered if Jade/Josie might carry one. She was already imagining a scene where the tormented Jade found the knife—maybe with the blade smeared with blood—in one of her practical handbags. No, her briefcase. Better.

"Have you ever—"

"Not yet." Rosalie held out a hand to take it back. "But there's always a first time." She pressed the button, and the blade whisked away again. "So don't loose any sleep over me." After dropping the weapon back into her bag, she took out an atomizer and sprayed scent generously on her skin. The air bloomed with roses. "Couple more months, I'll have enough put away. I'm going to be spending the winter in the Florida sunshine while you slog through dirty snow." She rose, tugging her tight off-the-shoulder top provocatively down, so that the rise of her breasts swelled invitingly over it. "See you around."

"Wait." Bess scrambled through her own purse and came up with her mini recorder. "If it won't bother your ethics, I thought you might use this." At Rosalie's wry glance, Bess's cheeks heated. "I don't mean to record that part. Just the streets, conversations with the other women, maybe a couple of, ah…transactions."

"You're the boss." Taking the recorder, Rosalie slipped it away.

"Be careful," Bess added, though she knew Rosalie would laugh.

She did, sending a last cocky look over her bare shoulder. "Girlfriend, I'm always careful."

Still chuckling, Rosalie headed down the narrow corridor toward the freight elevator. She was already picturing the way Bess's eyes would pop out when she listened to the tape and discovered that her "consultant" had recorded

everything. The prospect of pulling such a fine joke ha
her grinning as the doors slid open. Her amusement died
quick death when Alex walked off.

While they eyed each other with mutual suspicion, Ale
pressed two fingers to the Door Open button. "How's th
moonlighting going, Rosalie?"

"It passes the time."

When she started past him, he raised an arm to block th
elevator opening. "What do you know about Crysta
LaRue?"

"I know she's dead." Rosalie fisted a hand on her hip
cocked it. "Something else you want?"

Alex let her see that her snide invitation only amuse(
him. "What do you know about her before she was dead?'

"Nothing." She would have given him the same answe,
if she'd been Crystal's most intimate friend, but as it wa
she was telling the simple truth. "I never met her. Hear(
she was new, didn't have a man yet."

"Now, I heard that, too," Alex said conversationally
"And I heard that Bobby wanted to make her one of hi
wives."

"Maybe. Bobby likes to start them young."

Alex struggled with his disgust. She'd been seventeen
he thought. A runaway who hadn't know the rules and
would never have a chance to learn them. "Did Bobb
roust her, put on the pressure?"

"Can't say."

"Can't say? Or won't?"

Rosalie opened the hand on her hip and began to drun
her fingers there. "Listen, I don't know what Bobby did.
I've been keeping out of his way lately."

Saying nothing, Alex studied her face. The bruising hac
faded. "Seems to me Bess is paying you enough that you
could stay out of his way altogether."

"That's my business."

"And hers," Alex said evenly. "I don't want him find-

ing out about this sideline of yours and going after her.''
His eyes were cold and passionless. "Then I'd have to kill
him.''

"You think I'd turn Bobby on to her?'' Arrogance was
sidelined as fury snapped into Rosalie's voice. "I *owe*
her.''

"What?''

"Respect,'' she said, with an innate and graceful dignity
that had Alex softening. "She had me eat at her table. She
even said I could stay in her extra bedroom. Like a guest.''
Her lips thinned at Alex's expression. "Don't sweat it,
honey. I didn't take her up on it. Sure, she's paying me,
and maybe you don't think that's any different than me
taking money from some slob off the street. But she treats
me like somebody. Not some *thing,* some*body.*'' Embarrassed by her own vehemence, she shrugged. "She doesn't
have the sense not to.''

"She's got sense, all right. Not all good.'' Alex's lips
twitched, even as Rosalie's did. "Maybe she hasn't gone
so wrong here. I just don't want her hurt.''

"Neither do I.'' Rosalie tapped a scarlet nail on his chest.
"You got a bad case, cop. Stars in your eyes.'' The little
wisp of envy came and went, almost unnoticed. "Make
sure you keep them in hers, or you'll answer to me.''

His grin flashed before he could prevent it. The charm
of it nearly had Rosalie changing her mind about cops.
"Yes, ma'am.'' Like Bess, he wanted to say something that
would stop her from going back on the streets. Unlike Bess,
he accepted that there was nothing that would do it.

"Maybe I see why she's so stuck on you.'' When he
moved his blocking arm, she stepped into the elevator,
turned. "You be good to her, Stanislaski. She deserves
good.''

The elevator doors clunked shut. Alex stood studying
them a moment before he turned and wandered down the
corridor to find Bess.

She was bent over the keys, rapping out a machine-gun fire of words onto the monitor. Her fingers moved like lightning, but her eyes were far away. In Millbrook, he thought, smiling to himself.

She had her legs crossed under her, up on the chair. The way her shoulders were hunched, he imagined her muscles would complain loudly the moment she came back to earth.

She was wearing a skirt again, a little leather number in bold blue that was hiked high up on her thighs. The hot-pink blouse she'd tucked into it should have clashed with her hair, but it didn't. The blouse looked like silk and was carelessly shoved up to her elbows. A half-dozen gold bracelets clanged at her wrist as she worked. Rings flashed on her fingers, and the big Gypsy hoops she wore at her ears peeked out of her tousled hair.

His heart ached with love for her. And his loins... Alex let out a little breath. He wanted, quite simply, to devour her. Inch by delicious inch.

What the hell was he going to do, he wondered, when she tried to slither out of his life? He was sure she would, as she'd done with others before. He could lock her up, carry her off. He could beg or threaten. He already knew he would do whatever he had to in order to keep her in his life.

What had ever made him think he would one day find some nice, pretty woman with simple tastes and a quiet style? Someone who would be content to sit home while he worked his crazy hours? Who would have and help him raise the houseful of children he so badly wanted?

With Bess, nothing was simple, nothing was quiet. She would never be content to sit home but would badger him incessantly, picking at him until he gave in and talked about the darker aspects of his work, those pieces of his life that he wanted to keep locked away from everyone who mattered. As for children... He didn't know how the devil to get and keep a ring on her finger, much less ask her to help make a family.

Being in love with her left him helpless, made him stupid, brought him a kind of fear he'd never faced as a cop. Not fear for his life. Fear for his heart.

He could only take his own advice and leave things as they were. Handle each day until she was so used to him she'd want to stay.

As he watched, she stopped typing, lifted a hand to her neck for a quick, impatient rub. Her skirt hiked higher as she shifted. It took all his control not to lick his lips. She punched a few buttons, had the machine clicking. A moment later, the printer beside her began to hum.

With a smile on his face and lust in his heart, Alex closed the door quietly at his back. Locked it.

She jumped like a rabbit when his hands came down on her shoulders. "Didn't anyone ever teach you to sit in a chair?"

"Alexi." She pressed a hand to her galloping heart. "You scared— Oh…" Her sigh was long and heartfelt as he massaged away the aches. "That's wonderful."

"You're going to do permanent damage if you keep sitting like that all day."

"I was planning on soaking in a hot tub for two or three days." She leaned into his hands.

"Where's Lori?"

"She wasn't feeling too terrific." As the printer continued to rattle, Bess closed her eyes. "I told her I was leaving, too. Then I snuck back. I wanted to make a few changes for tomorrow." She brought her hand up to one of his, skimming her fingers over it to the wrist. "You said you might have to work late."

"Lead fizzled. We'll work on tracing the heart necklace down, but that's better during business hours."

"Trace it down?"

"Hit the jewelers," he explained, "see if we can track down to when it was bought. Long shot, but…"

"Do you think the heart has a personal meaning for him?"

"Like some woman broke his heart, so he gives them a symbol of it before he whacks them?" He gave a little grunt as he continued to knead her muscles. "It's a little too obvious to dismiss. Psychiatric profile figures him as sexually inadequate on a normal level, so he pays for women to perform. He wants them and detests himself for that, as much as he detests them for being available. The fact that he goes through a short courtship routine shows that—" He broke off as she reached for a pad. "Hold on, McNee." He gave her shoulders a hard squeeze. "I don't know how you do it. One minute I'm thinking about getting you out of these clothes and the next you've got me talking about a case." He pressed a kiss to the top of her head. "No notes."

Her fingers retreated from the pad, but with obvious reluctance. "I like hearing you talk about your work. I want you to be able to talk to me about anything."

"Apparently I can. Even the stuff I don't want you to hear. I've got a problem with you, Bess. You won't let me tuck you into that nice safe corner where I want you to be."

"You only think that's where you want me to be." Smiling, she tugged his hand around so that she could kiss it. "You like me right where I am." Turning his hand over, she pressed her lips to his palm. "I'm going to stay there."

She felt his fingers tense, then relax slowly as he spread them over her cheek. "I was watching you while you worked."

A rippling thrill raced through her at the words and at the shimmer of desire she heard in them. "Were you?"

"And thinking." His hands slid down over her breasts, sampled their weight, molded them. "Fantasizing."

Her head fell back against the chair. Her breathing quickened. "About?"

"The things I'd like to do with you." Through layers of silk, he caught her nipples, tugging gently. "To you."

When she tried to shift in the chair to face him, he increased the pressure, held her still. Her dazzled eyes focused on the monitor. She could still see the ghost of herself there, and his hands moving. Sliding. Stroking.

Impossibly erotic to see, and to feel. Dry-mouthed, she watched his fingers undo her buttons and saw the dark shadow of his hair as he pressed a hot mouth to her throat. She lifted a hand, hooked it around his neck as she tilted her head to offer more.

"I can shut down in thirty seconds."

He bit her lightly, just above the collarbone. "I'm not going to give you a chance to shut down."

She laughed shakily, even as she lifted her other arm to capture him in a reverse embrace. "I meant the computer."

He would have laughed himself, but he'd stopped breathing. "I know what you meant."

"But I—" He slipped a hand under her skirt, and it was so sudden, so searing. Before she could gasp out in shock, he had driven her ruthlessly to the peak.

"I watched you." Each word burned his throat as she poured into his hand. "I wanted you." Half demented, he whipped her up again, pressing his face into her neck as her body shuddered, shuddered. "Do you remember the first time I found you here?"

"What?" She couldn't remember her own name. There was only this need he was ruthlessly building inside her again. "Alexi, please. Come home with me. I need—" This time she cried out as the third high, hard wave swamped her.

"I wanted you then." In one violent move, he spun her chair around and dragged her to her feet, and her already weakened system went limp at what she read in his face. "Let me show you exactly what I wanted."

This wasn't the smooth and patient lover of the night before. This man with the fierce eyes and bruising hands wouldn't cuddle her and whisper exotic endearments. This was the warrior she'd only glimpsed. He would plunder. Whether or not she was ready, he was showing her that dark, reckless side of him that he kept so tightly controlled.

In the moment when he stared at her, the look in his eyes hot and concentrated, she understood that excitement took a twist into the primitive when it carried a touch of fear.

He fisted a hand in her hair and yanked her against him. His body was like rock, vibrating from deep within, as if from an erupting volcano. For that moment, there was only the strength and the fury of the inevitable.

His mouth burned over hers, his tongue diving deep, while his free hand tugged the snap of her skirt free. He wanted her flesh, craved it. That heated silk, those alluring curves and taut muscles. Time and place had lost all impact. There was only here. Only now. Only her.

Shivery fingers of fear ran up her spine. She hadn't known what it was to be wanted this way. It was so huge, so violent, so glorious. Before, he had given her more than she had ever dreamed of. Now, he seemed compelled to give her more than she had ever *dared* dream.

Beside them, the printer stopped its practical clatter and dropped into a hum. The low, waiting sound was drowned out by the thundering of her heart. The bright working lights overhead seemed to dim as he took her hips and pressed her hard against him.

"You make a war inside me," he muttered as his teeth scraped roughly down her throat. "There's no end to it. No peace from it. Say my name. I want to hear you say my name."

"Alexi." When his lips crushed down on hers again, he felt her breathe it, warm, into his mouth. "Take me. Now."

The wild need slammed into her so that her mouth was as turbulent, her hands as frantic. Dozens of tiny explosions burst inside her body, merging into one huge tumult of sensation that battered, bruised and bewitched. She was all but sobbing with it as she tugged and pulled at his clothes.

She was quivering for him. Couldn't stop. The power and pressure growing inside her was all but unbearable. And the heat, the furnace blast of heat, had her skin slicked and her head spinning. Glorying in it, she brought her mouth to his bare shoulder, savoring the taste of flesh. His busy, bruising hands had her bearing down with teeth and nails. His breath hissed in her ear as she reached down to curl impatient fingers around him.

Confused and tangled phrases whirled in his mind. He heard them burst from his lips to hang on the thick air as he fought to catch his breath. On an oath, he gripped her shoulders and hauled her back.

Her face was flushed, her eyes were glowing. He'd marked that ivory skin. He could see where his fingers had pressed, where his roughened cheeks had scraped. But the part of him that would have been shocked by his lack of care was far overshadowed by a dark and desperate desire to conquer, to consume. To mate.

He saw them now as brands, signs that made her his. Only his.

With a jerk of his head, he tossed his hair back. The way it swayed and settled had new emotion burning her throat. Naked, muscles bunched as if to fight, he looked so magnificent he dazzled her eyes.

Then he looked at her, and the smile that had nearly formed on her face froze into wonder.

"No one makes you feel like this but me."

His accent had thickened, and the sound of it sent chills along her heated skin. She could only shake her head.

"No one touches you like me." He took his hands from

her shoulders and gripped the bodice of her chemise. "No one has you, ever again, but me."

"Alexi—"

But he shook his head. He could feel her heart pounding under his hands, and his own chest was heaving. "Understand me. You're mine now." Her eyes widened with shock as he jerked his hands and ripped the chemise in half. "All of you."

He pushed her back against the table, watching the play of stunned excitement over her face. Yes, he wanted to excite her. And shock her. Stagger her.

His fingers dug into her hips as he lifted her. He was braced, straining like a stallion at the bit. "Hold on to me," he demanded, but her fluttering hands slid off his sweat-slick arms. His breath heaved out, his fingers dug into her smooth, taut flesh. "Hold!"

She met his eyes then, and felt that wild whip of power. Drunk on it, she gripped his hair and wrapped her legs around him. When he plunged inside her, her body arched back, absorbing that first rocketing flash of heat. It was like being consumed from the inside out.

She felt the cool surface of the table against her back first, then his weight on her. Greedy for more, she tightened around him, matching his fast, frantic rhythm, dragging his mouth back to hers so that they could echo the intimacy with their tongues.

He lost himself. There was only her now, and the need to possess her. The desperate craving to be possessed by her. Images reeled through his brain, all dark and sharp-edged, until he thought he would go mad.

And went mad.

In a frenzy of movement, he dragged her farther onto the table, crushing papers, knocking aside empty cups, scattering pencils. He couldn't take his eyes from her face, the way her eyes clouded, like fog over moss, the way her lips trembled with each gasping breath. There was a bloom on her skin now, a rose under glass. He was hammering himself into her, empowered by a rabid fury of emotion that had its razor-tipped fingers around his throat.

Too much, she thought frantically. Never enough. The harsh overhead lights fractured into rainbows that blinded her eyes. They seemed to arch around his head, but she didn't think of angels. His eyes were so dark, so fiercely focused. Even as her own grew leaden, she refused to close them.

Oh, to watch him wanting her. Taking her.

She couldn't understand the words he murmured, over and over again. But she understood what was in those eyes. They were tearing each other apart, and they couldn't stop. The animal had taken over, and it had diamond-sharp claws and jagged teeth.

There was nothing left but the sound of their mixed labored breathing, the solid slap of flesh against flesh, and the heady scent of hot, desperate sex.

She felt his body go rigid, felt the rippling muscles in the arms she gripped turn to stone. He groaned out her name as his eyes sharpened like daggers. When he poured himself into her, she cried out in triumph, then again in wonder as he drove her over that crumbling edge with him.

The strength that had screamed through him switched off like a light, and he collapsed, panting, his full weight on her. Fighting for breath, he wallowed in her hair, drawing in the scent of it and the fragrance they'd made together. He couldn't find his center, the focus that was so vital for survival. He no longer had one without her.

God, he could feel her vibrating beneath him, shuddering from the aftershocks. And there were tears mixed with the dew of sweat on her face.

With breath still burning his lungs, he levered himself on his elbows and shook his head to try to clear it. At the movement, she made a small, whimpering sound in her throat that both aroused and dismayed. Trying to find the gentleness that had always been so easy for him, he shifted their positions and began to stroke her hair, her shoulders, her back.

Murmuring apologies, he cradled her like a child. "*Milaya*, I'm sorry. I hurt you. I must have hurt you. Don't cry."

"I'm not crying." But, of course, she was. He could feel the tears fall even as she ran kisses over his face and throat. "Just tell me you love me. Please tell me you love me."

"I love you. Shh." He covered her mouth tenderly with his. "You know I love you."

"I love you." She pressed those wet, shaky kisses to his cheeks, to his jaw. "You have to believe that I love you."

A hot fist clenched in his gut, but he kept his hands gentle. "Just let me hold you."

Tearing up again, she pressed her face to his shoulder. "Even now you don't believe me. Alexi, what more can I do?"

"I believe you." But they both knew he said it only to comfort. "You belong to me. I believe that."

"You're everything I want." She relaxed against him, satisfied that he would take that much.

"No more tears?"

"No."

He tilted her chin up to search her face. "How badly did I hurt you?"

"I don't think the results will be in for days." She smiled a little. "How badly did I hurt you?"

His eyes narrowed, and her smile widened. "You're not...upset?"

"About what?"

"I was an animal." With a hand that had yet to steady, he brushed her tumbled hair out of her face. "I took you on a table like a lunatic."

"I know." After one long, satisfied sigh, she slid her body lazily over his. "It was wonderful."

"Yes?" Guilt began to turn to pride. "You liked it?"

After being so thoroughly ravished, it wasn't difficult to stroke his ego. "It was like being dragged off by some barbarian. I couldn't even understand what you were saying. It was exciting." She kissed his cheek. "Frightening." And the other. "It was also the most erotic experience of my life."

"You were crying."

"Alexi." She touched a hand to his face. "You didn't just overpower me. You overwhelmed me. No one's ever made me feel more wanted. More irresistible."

"I can't resist you, but I'm sorry I put bruises on you."

"I don't mind—under the circumstances." After another luxurious sigh, she glanced around the room. "I don't know how I'll ever work in here again, though."

Now he grinned, wickedly. "Maybe it'll inspire you."

"There is that." She shifted to straddle him and watched his sleepy eyes skim down to her breasts and back. Possibilities, she thought. There were definite possibilities in that look. "Being a cop, I imagine you've been through arduous physical training."

The possibilities had occurred to him, as well. "Absolutely."

"And you'd probably have amazing recuperative powers."

His brow lifted. "Under the right conditions."

"Good." To be certain she created them, she ran her hands over his still-gleaming chest.

With a half laugh, he caught her wrists. "McNee, wouldn't you rather pick this up in bed?"

For an answer, she leaned over, letting her lips hover a breath away from his. The tip of her tongue darted out to trace the shape of his mouth, to dip teasingly inside, then retreat. Slowly, she tilted her head. Softly, she tasted his lips. Achingly, achingly, she deepened the kiss.

"Does that give you a clue, Detective?"

Chapter Eleven

"I can't believe you want to spend the best part of a Saturday morning in a sweaty gym." Alex was stalling, even as he walked with Bess up the iron steps that led to Rocky's.

"It's your sweaty gym," Bess said, and kissed him.

The past few days had been almost like a honeymoon, she thought. If she took out the hours they'd both been at work. But they'd made the most of what time they'd had together, snuggling on the couch in her place, cooking a meal in his, wrestling in bed in both.

She was starting to hope that he believed she loved him. And, once he did, she wanted nothing more than for them to take that next step. The step that would lead to an authentic honeymoon, with all the trimmings.

"You picked me up at my gym yesterday," she pointed out.

"That wasn't a gym." There was the faintest trace of a masculine sneer in his voice. "That was an exercise palace. Fancy lighting, piped-in music. All those mirrors."

"At least I'll be able to see when my butt starts to drop."
He gave it a friendly pat. "I'll let you know."

"Do, and die," she said smartly, and pushed through the frosted glass doors.

She immediately thought of every bad boxing film she'd ever seen. The huge room echoed with grunts and slaps and thumps. It smelled of mildew and sweat and... She took a testing sniff and decided she didn't want to know what else. There were exposed pipes along the ceilings and walls, and there was a hardwood floor that looked as though it had been gouged by spikes. The boxing ring that was set up in one corner was already occupied by two compact, dancing men in tiny shorts who were trying to pop each other in the eye.

A trio of punching bags hung at strategic points. A half-naked man with a body like a cement truck was currently trying to whip the tar out of one of them.

Weights were being employed as well. She watched tendons bulge and muscles bunch.

They didn't worry about mirrors and lighting here. Nor did she spot any of the high-tech equipment she was accustomed to. This was down-and-dirty—squat, sweat and punch. She sincerely doubted there would be a juice bar in the vicinity, either.

"Had enough?" Alex asked. He was obviously amused at the thought of her stripping down to her leotard and having a go with the boys.

Bess closed her mouth, then answered his grin with a cool stare. "I haven't even started yet."

It was his turn to drop his jaw when she peeled off her sweatshirt. Beneath she wore a snug, low-cut crop top in zigzagging stripes of green and purple. As she shimmied out of her baggy street shorts, he shoved the discarded shirt in front of her.

"Come on, Bess, put your clothes on. Sweet Lord." The bottom half was worse. Over formfitting tights she had on a teeny strip of spandex that covered little more than a G-string. "You can't wear that in here."

"Is it illegal?" She bent over to stuff her sweats into her gym bag and heard the heavy thump of weights as they were dropped. Maintaining position, she turned her head and smiled at the pop-eyed man staring at her.

The catcalls and whistles started immediately, the sound swelling and bouncing off the cinder-block walls. Alex was very much afraid there would be a riot—one he was likely to incite himself. "Damn it, put something on before I have to kill somebody."

"They look harmless." She straightened again and lifted her arms to tie the short curls at the nape of her neck into a stubby ponytail. "Anyway, I came to work out." With a challenging grin, she flexed a muscle. "How much can you bench-press?"

"McNee, don't you dare—" He broke off with an oath as she blithely strolled across the room to chat with the weight lifter. The two hundred pounds of muscle began to babble like a teenager. Alex had no choice but to send out a warning snarl, much as a guard dog might to a pack of encroaching wolves, before he went after her.

She pulled it off, of course. He should have known she would. The men started out drooling, kicked over into laughing and finally wound up competing with each other to show her the proper way to perform squat lifts, chin-ups and leg curls.

Before an hour was over, she'd been shown pictures of wives and children, listened to sob stories over sweethearts and stopped being ogled—unless it was at a discreet distance.

"You sure you want to do this?" Alex asked again, tapping his gloved hands together.

"Absolutely." She smiled at Rocky as he himself laced up her gloves. "I couldn't leave without one sparring match."

"You watch out for his left—it's a good one," Rocky advised her. "Kid could've been a contender if he hadn't wanted to be a cop."

She winked at Rocky. "I've got fast feet. He won't lay a glove on me."

Two of her new admirers held open the ropes for her so that she could step into the ring. Enjoying the sensation, she adjusted her padded helmet. "Aren't we supposed to wear those funny retainers?"

"The what— Oh, mouth guards?" He couldn't resist, and he leaned over and kissed her to an accompaniment of hoots. "Baby, I'm not going to hit you." In a friendly gesture, he tapped his gloves to hers. "Okay, put your hands up." When she did, lifting them toward the ceiling, he rolled his eyes. "It's not an arrest, McNee." Patiently he adjusted her hands until they were in a defensive position.

"Now, you want to guard, see? Keep your left up, keep it up. If I come in like this—" he did a slow-motion jab at her jaw "—you block, jab back. That's it."

"And I fake with my left," she said, and did so.

"If you want." Lord, she was sweet. "Now try for here." He tapped his own chin. "Go ahead, you don't have to pull it." When she punched halfheartedly, he shook his head. "No, you punch like a girl. Put your body behind it. Pretend I'm Dawn Gallagher."

Her eyes lit, and she swung full-out, only to come up solidly against his block. "Hey, that's good." Impressed, she swung again. "But I've got to move around, right? Fake you out with my grace and fancy footwork."

She did a quick boogie that had the onlookers clapping and Alex grinning at her. "You got style. Let's work on it."

He was enjoying himself, showing her the moves. And it certainly didn't hurt for a woman living in the city to

learn how to defend herself with something more than an
ammonia-filled water pistol.

"It's fun." She ducked her head as he'd shown her and
tried two quick jabs with her left.

"Always room for another flyweight," Rocky called out
to her. "Come on, Bess, body blow."

Chuckling, she aimed for Alex's midsection and dodged
his light tap toward her chin. "You look so cute in gym
shorts," she murmured.

"Don't try to distract me."

"Well, you do." She danced around him again, and,
laughing, he turned toward her.

"Okay, that ought to—" He ended on a grunt when she
connected hard with his jaw and set him down on his butt.

"Oh, God." She crouched instantly, battering his face
with her gloves as she tried to stroke it. "Oh, Alexi, I'm
sorry. Did I hurt you?"

He wiggled his jaw, sending her a dark look. "Right
cross," he muttered as men climbed through the ropes to
cheer and hold Bess's arms in the air.

"I'm really sorry," Bess said again as they started down
the iron steps. But she was fingering the little bit of tar-
nished metal Rocky had pinned—with some ceremony—to
her sweatshirt. "You said not to pull my punches."

"I know what I said." He'd be lucky if he didn't have
a bruise, Alex thought. And how the hell would he explain
that? "You only got through because I was finished."

She ran her tongue over her teeth and stepped outside.
"Uh-huh."

"Don't get smart with me, McNee." He snatched her up
and swung her around. "Or I'll demand a rematch."

Wildly in love, she tossed her arms around his neck.
"Anytime."

"Oh, yeah? How about…" He trailed off with a grimace
as his beeper sounded. "Sorry."

"It's all right." She only sighed a little as he tracked down a phone and called in. As she stood beside him, watching his face, listening to his terse comments, she realized that their plans for a picnic in the park and some casual shopping were about to go bust.

"You have your cop's face on," she said when he hung up. "Do you have to go in?"

"Yeah." But he didn't tell her they'd found another victim. It was bad enough that he was spoiling their plans for the day. "It's probably going to take a while. I'm really sorry, Bess."

"Look." She framed his face with her hands. "I understand. This is part of it."

He brought those hands to his lips. "I…" But he didn't tell her he loved her, because she would echo the words, and it made him nervous to hear them. "I appreciate it," he said instead. "And I'll make it up to you."

"Tell you what—why don't I finish up what I have to do, then stop by the market? I'll make dinner. Something that won't spoil if it has to be warmed up a couple of times."

Though his mind was already drifting away from her, he managed a pained smile. "You're going to cook."

"I'm not that bad. I'm not," she insisted with a bit of a huff when he grinned. "I only burned the potatoes the other night because you kept distracting me."

"I guess it's the least I can do." He kissed her lightly once, then again, longer. "I'll try to call."

"If you can." She waved him off, then stood watching while he jogged down into the subway. With a quick laugh, she spun around, hugging herself.

She felt just like a cop's wife.

"I hope you don't mind me dropping by."

"Of course not." Rachel took a look at the bulging shopping bags in Bess's hands. "Been busy?"

"Whenever I get started with that little plastic card, I can't seem to stop." She dumped her purchases inside the apartment door. "You look wonderful. How can you look wonderful less than a week after going through childbirth?"

"Strong genes." Pleased in general, and with Bess in particular, Rachel kissed her on both cheeks. "Come sit down."

"Thanks. I— Oops." She dipped into the bag and pulled out a gold foiled candy box. "For Mom."

"Oh." Rachel's eyes took on the glow a woman's get when she looks at a lover—or a five-pound box of exclusive chocolates. "I think you just became my best friend."

Chuckling, Bess dug into the bags again. "Well, I know that people tend to drop by with baby gifts." She held out a box wrapped in snowy white with bright red lollipops scattered over it. "And, though I couldn't resist the tradition, I figured you deserved something really sinful for yourself."

"I do." Rachel tucked the baby box under her other arm. "It's really sweet of you, Bess, and unnecessary. You and Alex already brought Brenna that wonderful stuffed dragon."

"That was from us. This is from me. It's a girl thing. I saw this tiny little white organdy dress with all these flounces and little pink bows and I couldn't resist."

Rachel's new-mother's heart melted. "Really?"

"I figure in another year she might want to wear motorcycle boots, so this may be your only chance to play dress-up."

"I swore that whatever I had, I wouldn't make sexist decisions in dress or attitude." She sighed over the box. "White organdy?"

"Six flounces. I counted."

"I can't wait to put her in it."

"Ah, company." Mikhail strode out of the bedroom with

Brenna tucked in his arm. "Hello, Aunt Bess." He kissed both of her cheeks, then her mouth.

"You said you wouldn't wake her up." This from Rachel, who was already leaning over to coo.

"I didn't. Exactly. What's this?" Recognizing the gold foil box, he flipped it open and dived in.

"Mine," Rachel said in a huff. "If you eat more than one, I'll break your fingers."

"She was always greedy," he said over the first piece. "Where's Alexi?"

"He got called in."

"Good. Now you have time to sit down. I'll sketch you."

"Now?" Womanlike, Bess lifted a hand to her hair. "I'm not exactly dressed for it."

"I want your face." Obviously well used to making himself at home, he opened the drawer on an end table and rummaged for a pad. "Perhaps I'll do your body later. It's a good one."

Her laugh was quick. "Thanks."

"You might as well cooperate," Rachel told her, and crossed over to take the baby. "Once the artist in him takes over, you haven't got a chance."

"I'm flattered, really."

"There's no reason to be," he said absently as he unearthed a suitable pencil. "You have the face you were born with."

"Thank God that's not always true."

That caught his interest. "You had it fixed?"

"No. I just sort of grew into it."

"Not there," he told her before Bess could sit. "Over there, closer to the window in the light. Rachel, when do I get the drink you promised me?"

"On its way." She stopped nuzzling Brenna long enough to look up. "What can I get you, Bess?"

"Anything cold—and a shot at holding the baby."

"I can accommodate you on both counts." Rachel laid her daughter gently in Bess's arms. "She hardly ever cries. And I think her eyes may stay blue. Like Zack's."

"She's a beauty." Bess leaned down to brush her lips over the curling dark hair and to draw in the indescribably sweet scent of baby. "Like all of you."

"Move," Mikhail ordered his sister. "You're in my way."

Shooting off a mild Ukrainian insult, she headed for the kitchen.

"Talk if you like." Mikhail gestured with his pencil, and began to sketch.

"It's one of my best things." She'd already forgotten to be self-conscious. "Where's Sydney and Griff?"

"Griff has the sniffles." The pencil was moving with quick, deft strokes over the pad. "Sydney fusses over him, but she says *I'm* fussing over him and sends me out on errands."

"Which he does by coming by and plaguing me," Rachel called out.

"She's happy to see me," Mikhail said. "Because she's lonely, with Zack and Nick over checking on the progress of the new apartment."

"Oh, that's right, you're moving." Comfortable, Bess tucked up her legs. "Alexi mentioned it."

"We need a bigger place. Of course, it was supposed to be ready a month ago, but things never run on time. I'll miss this one," she said, coming back in with a tray of cold drinks. "And having Nick underfoot. But I imagine he'll like having this place to himself."

Bess reached for her drink with her free hand, gently jiggling the baby with the other. "I guess he had as big a crush on you as Freddie has on him."

For a moment, Rachel only stared. Then she let out her breath in a quiet laugh. "Alex said you saw things."

"Just part of the job."

Rachel didn't consider herself a slouch in the reading-people department. "So, how big a crush do you have on Alexi?"

"The biggest." Bess smiled and rubbed her cheek over Brenna's. "He thinks I'm flighty. Fickle. But I'm not. Not with him."

"Why would he think that?"

"I have a varied track record. But it's different with him." When Bess lowered her head to murmur to the baby, Rachel glanced at her brother. They exchanged a great deal without uttering a word. "It makes me envy people like your sister, Natasha," Bess went on. "Those three beautiful children, a husband who after years together still looks at her as if he can't believe she belongs to him. Work she loves. I envy all that."

"You'd like a family?"

"I never had one."

Rachel knew it was the lawyer in her, but she couldn't help moving along the line of questioning. "Does it bother you that he's a cop?"

"Bother me?" Bess's brows lifted in surprise. "No. Do you mean, will I worry? I suppose I will. But it's not something I could change, or that I want to change. I love who he is."

"He's making you sad," Mikhail said quietly.

"No." Bess's denial was quick enough to startle the dozing baby. She soothed her automatically as she shook her head. "No, of course he isn't."

"I see what's in your eyes."

He would, she realized, and felt the warmth creep into her cheeks. "It's only that I know he doesn't trust me—my feelings. Or, I suppose, the endurance of my feelings. It's not his fault."

"He was always one to pick things apart." There was brotherly disgust in Mikhail's voice. "Never one to take anything on faith. I'll speak to him."

"Oh, no." This time, she laughed. "He'd be furious with both of us. All that Slavic pride and male ego."

Instantly Mikhail's eyes narrowed. "What's wrong with that?"

"Nothing." She grinned at Rachel. "Not a thing. I'll just wear him down in my own way. In fact, I'm going to start tonight. I'm cooking dinner. I thought maybe I could call your mother, find out if he has a favorite dish."

"I can tell you that," Rachel offered. "Anything."

"Well, that certainly widens my choices. Do you think she'd mind if I called her, asked for some pointers? My kitchen skills are moderate at best."

"She'd love it." Rachel smiled to herself, knowing her mother would hang up the phone and immediately start planning the wedding.

It was after midnight when Alex let himself into Bess's apartment with the key she'd given him. He was punchy with fatigue, and his head was buzzing from too much coffee. Those were usual things, as much a part of his work as filing reports or following a lead. But the sick weight in his stomach was something new.

He would have to tell her.

She'd left the television on. In an old black-and-white movie a woman screamed in abject terror and fled down a moonlit beach. As he shrugged out of his jacket, Alex moved across the room to switch it off. Before he reached the set, he saw her, curled on the couch.

She'd waited for him. The sweetness of that speared through him as he crouched beside her. For so many years now, he'd come home alone, to no one. Gently he brushed the dark red curls from her cheek and replaced them with his lips. She stirred, murmuring. Her eyes fluttered open.

"I'm just going to carry you into bed," he whispered. "Go back to sleep."

"Alexi." She lifted a hand to rub over the cheek he

adn't shaved that morning. Her voice was thick with sleep, er eyes glazed with it. "What time is it?"

"It's late. You should have gone to bed."

She made a vague sound of disagreement and pushed up n one elbow. "I was waiting up, but the movie was so ad." Her laugh was groggy, and she rubbed her eyes like child. "It zapped me." She circled her shoulders before aning forward to kiss him. "You had a long day, Detec- ve."

"Yeah." And maybe, because she was half-asleep, he ould put off the rest. "So have you. I'll cart you in."

"No, I'm okay." She sat up, yawning. "Did you eat omething?"

"I caught a sandwich. I'm really sorry, I tried to call."

"And got the machine," she said with a rueful nod. 'Because I'd forgotten the paprika and had to run back out o the market."

"You cooked?" The idea both touched him and accented ais guilt.

"I amazed myself." It felt good to settle against him when he joined her on the couch and slipped an arm around ier. Cozy, right, and wonderfully simple. "Your mother's ecipe for chicken and dumplings—Hungarian-style."

"Csirke paprikas?" Normally it would have made his mouth water. "That's a lot of work."

"It was a culinary adventure—and the cleaning lady will probably quit on Monday, after one look at the kitchen." She laughed up at him, then scrubbed her knuckles over his cheek when she caught the look in his eyes. "Don't worry. It'll heat up just fine for tomorrow's lunch. Then again…" She snuggled closer. "If you're feeling really guilty, I'll take you up on that ride to the bedroom—and whatever else you can think of."

But instead of chuckling and scooping her up, he pushed away to pace to the television and snap it off. "We have to talk."

His tone had nerves skittering in her stomach, but sh
nodded. "All right."

He thought it might be best—for both of them—if the
had some of the brandy she had offered him during a
earlier crisis. Trying out the words in his head, he walke
to the lacquered cabinet.

"It's bad," she murmured, and pressed her lips togethe
hard. Her first thought was that he had changed his min
about her. That he had finally taken that good look she'
been afraid of and realized his mistake.

"It's bad," he concurred, then brought the snifters to th
couch. "Here. Drink a little."

"It's all right. I don't make scenes."

He tilted the brandy toward her lips himself. "Just
little, *milaya*."

She closed her eyes and did as he asked. He couldn't sa
that sweet word to her in that loving tone if he'd change
his mind. "Okay." A deep breath, and she opened her eye
again.

"There was another murder last night."

"Oh, Alexi." Instantly the image of Crystal LaRue'
mangled body flashed behind her eyes. "Oh, God." Sh
caught his hand in hers and squeezed. "Last night?"

"The desk clerk found her this morning. They had ar
arrangement. She only used that room for work, and he wa
ticked that she hadn't checked out and slipped him his usua
tip." He was taking it slow, deliberately, so that the genera
horror would pass before he hit her with the specifics
Again he tipped the brandy up to her lips. "She'd rented
the room three times last night. He caught a glimpse of the
third john when they went up, so we've had him looking
over mug shots most of the day."

"You'll catch him."

"Oh, yeah. There's no doubt about it this time. He didn'
find the guy in the books, but he gave the police artist a
fair description. We'll be broadcasting it. This time we

should have his blood type, too. DNA. Couple of other things.''

''You'll have him soon.''

''Not soon enough. Bess, the woman...'' His fingers tightened on hers, but he told her the worst as gently as he knew how. ''It was Rosalie.''

She only stared, and he watched, helpless, as the color simply slid out of her face. ''No.'' She was tugging her hand from his, but he only held tighter. ''You're wrong. You made a mistake. I just saw her. I just talked to her a couple of days ago.''

''There's no mistake.'' His voice toughened, for her sake. ''I ID'd her myself. Rechecked that with prints, and the desk clerk's ID. Bess, it was Rosalie.''

The moan came out brokenly as she wrapped her arms around herself and began to rock. ''Don't,'' she said when he tried to gather her close. ''Don't, don't, don't.''

She sprang up, needing the distance, desperate to find something to do with the helpless rage that was building inside her. ''She didn't have to die. It isn't right. It isn't right for her to die like that.''

''It's never right.''

It was his tone, the cool detachment of it, that had her whirling on him. ''But she was just a hooker. Don't get involved, right? Don't feel anything. Isn't that what you told me?''

He went very still, as if she'd pulled a gun and taken aim. ''I guess I did.''

''I wanted to help her, but you told me I couldn't. You told me it was a waste of my time and energy. And you were right, weren't you, Alexi? How fine it must be to always be so right.''

He took the blow. What else could he do? ''Why don't you sit down, Bess? You'll make yourself sick.''

She wanted to break something, to smash it—but nothing was precious enough. ''I *cared,* damn you. I cared about her. She wasn't just a story line to me. She was a person All she wanted was to go south, buy a trailer." When he breath began to hitch, she covered her mouth with he hands. "She shouldn't have died like that."

"I wish I could change it." The bitter sense of failur turned his voice to ice. "I wish to God I could." Befor he realized the glass was leaving his hand, he was heavin; the snifter against the wall. "How do you know what I fel when I walked into that filthy room and found her like that How the hell do you know what it's like to face it an(know you couldn't stop it? She was a person to me, too.'

"I'm sorry." The tears that spilled over now spilled fo all of them. "Alexi, I'm sorry."

"For what?" He tossed back. "It was the truth."

"Facts. Not truth." He'd tried to soften the blow, t(cushion her when his own emotions were raw. He'd needec to comfort. His eyes had been dazed with fatigue and pair and the kind of grief she might never understand, but he'(needed to shield her. And she hadn't allowed it. "Hold me please. I need you to hold me."

For a moment she was afraid he wouldn't move. Then he crossed to her. Though his arms were rigid with tension, they came around her.

"I didn't mean to hurt you," she murmured, but he only shook his head and stroked her hair. Grieving, she turned her face into his throat. "I wanted to make it a lie some-how. To make you wrong so it could all be wrong." She squeezed her eyes closed and held tight. "She was some-body."

He stared blankly over her shoulder as he remembered one of the last things Rosalie had said to him. *She treats me like somebody.* "I know."

"You'll catch him," she said fiercely.

"We'll catch him. We'll put him away. He won't hurt anybody else." Though her words still scraped against him,

e rocked her. He would tell her the rest and hoped it
elped. "She had a knife."

"I saw it. She showed me."

"She used it. I don't know how bad she hurt him, but
he put up a hell of a fight. It's recorded."

"Recorded?" Eyes dull with shock, she leaned back.
'My God. The tape. I gave her my mini recorder."

"I figured as much. For whatever consolation it is, the
act that you did give it to her, and she decided to use it,
s going to make a difference. A big one."

"You heard them," she said through dry lips. "You
eard—"

"We got everything, from the deal on the street un-
il…the end. Don't ask me, Bess." He lifted a hand to cup
er face. "Even if I could tell you what was on the tape, I
vouldn't."

"I wasn't going to ask. I don't think I could bear to know
what happened in that room."

Calmer now, he searched her face. "I've only got a few
hours. I have to go in first thing in the morning. Do you
want me to stay with you tonight, or would you rather I
go?"

She'd hurt him more than she'd realized. Perhaps the
only way she could heal the wound was to admit, and to
show him, that she needed comfort. Needed it from him.
Drawing him close, she laid her head on his shoulder.

"I want you with me, Alexi. Always. And tonight—I
don't think I'd make it through tonight without you."

She began to cry then. Alex picked her up and carried
her to the couch, where they could lie down and grieve
together.

Chapter Twelve

Judd flexed his hand on the steering wheel as he turned on West Seventy-sixth. He wasn't nervous this time. He was eager. The idea of bringing Wilson J. Tremayne III— a U.S. senator's grandson—in for questioning in the murders of four women had him chafing at the bit.

They had him, Judd thought. He knew they had the creep. The artist's sketch, the blood type, the voiceprint. It had been quick work on that, he mused. Flavored with luck, Bess's tape had been one of those twisted aspects of police work that never failed to fascinate him.

It was Trilwalter who'd identified Tremayne from the sketch. Judd remembered that the boss had taken a long, hard look at the artist's rendering and then ordered Alex to the newspaper morgue. The desk clerk had picked the reprint of Tremayne's newspaper picture from a choice of five.

From there, Alex had used a connection at one of the local television stations and had finessed a videotape of Tremayne campaigning for his grandfather. The lab boys had jumped right on it, and had matched the voice to the one on Bess's tape.

It still made him queasy to think about what had been on that tape, but that was something he didn't want to show to Alex. Just as he knew better than to let Alex spot his eagerness now.

"So," he said casually, "you think the Yankees have got a shot this year?"

Alex didn't even glance over. He could all but taste his partner's excitement. "When a cop starts licking his lips, he forgets things. Miranda rights, probable cause, makes all kinds of little procedural mistakes that help slime ooze out of courtrooms and back onto the street."

Judd clenched his jaw. "I'm not licking my lips."

"Malloy, you'll be drooling any minute." Alex looked over at the beautiful old building while Judd hunted up a parking space. The Gothic touches appealed to him, as did the tall, narrow windows and the scattering of terrace gardens. Tremayne lived on the top floor, in a plush two-level condo with a view of the park and a uniformed doorman downstairs.

He came and went as he pleased, wearing his Italian suits and his Swiss watch.

And four women were dead.

"Don't take it personally," Alex said when they got out of the car. "Stanislaski's rule number five."

But Judd was getting good, very good, at reading his partner. "You want him as bad as I do."

Alex looked over, his eyes meeting, then locking on Judd's. There wasn't eagerness in them or excitement or even satisfaction. They were all cold fury. "So let's go get the bastard."

They flashed their badges for the doorman, then rode partway up in the elevator with a plump middle-aged woman and her yipping schnauzer. Alex glanced up and spotted the security camera in the corner. It might come in

handy, he thought. The DA would have to subpoena th
tapes for the nights of the murders. If they were dated an
timed, so much the better. But, if not, they would still shov
Tremayne going and coming.

The schnauzer got off at four. They continued on t
eight. Side by side, they approached 8B.

Though the door was thick, Alex could hear the strain:
of an aria from *Aida* coming from the apartment. He'
never cared much for opera, but he'd liked this particula
one. He wondered if it would be spoiled for him now. H
rang the buzzer.

He had to ring it a second time before Tremayne an
swered. Alex recognized him. It was almost as though the
were old friends now that Alex had pored over the news
paper shots and stories, the videotape. And, of course, he
knew his voice. Knew it when it was calm, when it wa
amused and when it was darkly, sickly, thrilled.

Dressed in a thick velour robe that matched his china-
blue eyes, Tremayne stood dripping, rubbing a thick monogrammed towel over his fair hair.

"Wilson J. Tremayne?"

"That's right." Tremayne glanced pleasantly from face
to face. He didn't have the street sense to smell cop. "I'm
afraid you've caught me at a bad time."

"Yes, sir." Never taking his eyes off Tremayne's, Alex
took out his badge. "Detectives Stanislaski and Malloy."

"Detectives?" Tremayne's voice was bland, only mildly
curious, but Alex saw the flicker. "Don't tell me my secretary forgot to pay my parking tickets again."

"You'll have to get dressed, Mr. Tremayne." Still
watching, Alex replaced his shield. "We'd like you to
come with us."

"With you?" Tremayne eased backward a step. Judd
noted that his hand eased down toward the doorknob,
closed over it. Knuckles whitened. "I'm afraid that would
be very inconvenient. I have a dinner engagement."

"You'll want to cancel that," Alex said. "This may take a while."

"Detective—?"

"Stanislaski."

"Ah, Stanislaski. Do you know who I am?"

Because it suited him, because he wanted it, Alex let Tremayne see the knowledge. "I know exactly who you are, Jack." Alex allowed himself one quick flash of pleasure at the fear that leaped into Tremayne's eyes. "We're going downtown, Mr. Tremayne. Your presence is requested for questioning on the murders of four women. Mary Rodell." His voice grew quieter, more dangerous, on each name. "Angie Horowitz, Crystal LaRue and Rosalie Hood. You're free to call your attorney."

"This is absurd."

Alex slapped a hand on the door before Tremayne could slam it shut. "We can take you in as you are—and give your neighbors a thrill. Or you can get dressed."

Alex saw the quick panic and was braced even as Tremayne turned to run. He knew better—sure he did—but it felt so damn good to body-slam the man up against that silk-papered wall. A small, delicate statue tipped from its niche and bounced on the carpet. When he hauled Tremayne up by the lapels, he saw the gold chain, the dangling heart with a crack running through it that was the twin of the one they had in evidence. And he saw the fresh white bandage that neatly covered the wounds Rosalie had inflicted as she fought for her life.

"Give me a reason." Alex leaned in close. "I'd love it."

"I'll have your badges." Tears began to leak out of Tremayne's eyes as he slid to the floor. "My grandfather will have your badges."

In disgust, Alex stood over him. "Go find him some pants," he said to Judd. "I'll read him his rights."

With a nod, Judd started for the bedroom. "Don't take it personally, Stanislaski."

Alex glanced over with something that was almost a smile. "Kiss off, Malloy."

They had him cold, Alex thought as he turned into Bess's building. They could call out every fancy lawyer on the East Coast, and it wouldn't mean a damn thing. The physical evidence was overwhelming—particularly since they'd found the murder weapon in the nightstand drawer.

Opportunity was unlikely to be a problem, and as for motive—he'd leave that up to the shrinks. Undoubtedly they'd cop an insanity plea. Maybe they'd even pull it off. One way or the other, he was off the streets.

It went a long way toward easing the bitterness he'd felt over Rosalie's death. He hoped it helped Bess with her grief.

He'd nearly called her from the station, but he'd wanted to tell her face-to-face. As he waited for the elevator, he shifted the bunch of lilacs he held. Maybe it was a weird time to bring her flowers, but he thought she needed them.

Stepping into the car, he tucked a hand in his pocket and felt the jeweler's box. It was even a weirder time to propose marriage. But he knew he needed it.

It scared him just how much he'd come to depend on having her with him. To talk to him, to listen to him, to make him laugh. To make love with him. He knew he was rushing things, but he justified it by assuring himself that if he got her to marry him quickly enough, she wouldn't have time to change her mind.

She believed she was in love with him. After they were committed, emotionally and legally, he would take as much time as necessary to make certain it was true.

The elevator opened, and Alex dug for his keys. They'd order in tonight, he decided. Put on some music, light some candles. He grimaced as he fit the key into the lock. No, she'd probably had that routine before, and he'd be damned if he'd follow someone else's pattern. He'd have to think of something else.

He opened the door with his arms full of nodding lilacs, his mind racing to think of some clever, innovative way to ask Bess to be his wife. The color went out of his face and turned his eyes to midnight. He felt something slam into his chest. It was like being shot.

She was standing in the center of the room, her laughter just fading away. In another man's arms, her mouth just retreating from another man's lips.

"Charlie, I—" She heard the sound of the door and turned. The bright, beaming smile on her face froze, then faded away like the laughter. "Alexi."

"I guess I should have knocked." His voice was dead calm. Viciously calm.

"No, of course not." There were butterflies in her stomach, and their wings were razor-sharp. "Charlie, this is Alexi. I've told you about him."

"Sure. Think I met you at Bess's last party." Lanky, long-haired and obviously oblivious to the tension throbbing in the air, he gave Bess's shoulders a squeeze. "She gives the best."

Alex set the flowers aside. One fragile bloom fell from the table and was ignored. "So I've heard."

"Well, I've got to be going." Charlie bent to give Bess another kiss. Alex's hands clenched. "You won't let me down?"

"Of course not." She worked up a smile, grateful that Charlie was too preoccupied to sense the falseness of it. "You know how happy I am for you, Charlie. I'll be in touch."

He went out cheerfully, calling out a last farewell before he shut the door. In the silence, Alex noticed the music for the first time. Violins and flutes whispered out of her stereo.

Very romantic, he thought, and his teeth clenched like his fists.

"Well." Her eyes were burning dry, though her heart was weeping. "I can see I should explain." She walked over to the wine she'd poured for Charlie and topped off her glass. "I can also see that you've already made up your mind, so explanations would be pointless."

"You move fast, Bess."

She was glad she had her back to him for a moment. Very glad, because her hand trembled as she lifted the wine. "Do you think so, Alexi?"

"Or maybe you've been seeing him all along."

"You can say that?" Now she turned, and the first flashes of anger burst through her. "You can stand there and say that to me?"

"What the hell do you expect me to say?" he shot back. He didn't go near her. Didn't dare. "I walk in here and find you with him. A little music, a nice bottle of wine." He wished he had been shot. It couldn't possibly hurt more than this bite of betrayal. "Do you think I'm an idiot?"

"No. No, I don't." She needed to sit, but she locked her knees straight. "But I must be to have been so careless as to have an assignation here when you were bound to find me out." Her eyes were like glass as she toasted him. "Caught me."

He took a step forward, stopped himself. "Are you going to tell me you didn't sleep with him?"

In the thrum of silence, the flutes sang. "No, I'm not going to tell you that. I'm not ashamed that I once cared enough for a very good man to be intimate with him. I'd tell you that I haven't been with Charlie or anyone else since I met you, but the evidence is against me, isn't it, Detective?"

She was so tired, Bess thought, so terribly tired, and the scent of the lilacs made her want to weep. Rosalie's funeral had been that morning, and she'd quietly made the arrangements herself. She'd gone alone, without mentioning it to Alex. But she'd needed him.

"You let him kiss you."

"Yes, I let him kiss me. I've let lots of men kiss me. Isn't that the problem?" She set down the wine before she could do something rash, like tossing it to the floor. "You didn't come to me a virgin, Alexi, nor did I expect you to. That's one of the big differences between us."

"There's a bigger difference between a virgin and a—"

He broke off, appalled with himself. He wouldn't have meant it. Stumbling, horrified apologies whirled through his head. But he could see by the way her head jerked up, the way her color drained, that there would be no taking back even the unsaid.

"I think," she said in an odd voice, "you'd better go."

"We haven't finished."

"I don't want you here. Even a whore can choose."

His face was as pale as hers. "Bess, I didn't mean that. I could never mean that. I want to understand—"

"No, you don't." She cut him off, her voice so thick with tears that she had to fight for every word. "You never wanted to understand, Alexi. You never wanted to hear the one thing I needed you to believe. Now the only thing you need to understand is that I don't want to see you again."

He felt something rip apart in his gut. "You can't have that."

"If you don't leave now, I'll call Security. I'll call your captain, I'll call the mayor." Desperation was rising like a flood. "Whatever it takes to keep you away from me."

His eyes narrowed, sharpened. "You can call God Almighty. It won't stop me."

"Maybe this will." She gripped her hands tightly together and looked just over his shoulder. "I don't love you, I don't want you, I don't need you. It was fun while it lasted, but the game's over. You can let yourself out."

She turned away and walked quickly up the stairs. There

had been hurt in his eyes. If there had been anger, she knew, he would have come after her, but there had been hurt, and she made it to the bedroom alone. With her hands over her face, she waited, biting back sobs, until she heard the door close downstairs. With a sound of mourning, she lowered herself to the floor and tasted her own tears. They were bitter.

Impatient and unsympathetic, Mikhail paced the floor of Alex's sparsely furnished apartment. "You don't answer your phone," he was saying. "You don't return messages." He kicked a discarded shirt aside. The apartment was a shambles. "Lucky for you I came instead of Mama. She'd box your ears for living like a pig."

"I gave the staff the month off." With the concentrated care of the nearly drunk, Alex poured another glass of vodka from the half-empty bottle on the table.

"And drinking alone in the middle of the day."

"So, join me." Alex gestured carelessly toward the kitchen, where dishes were piled high. "Bound to be a clean glass somewhere."

Mikhail washed one out before coming back to the table. He sat, poured. "What is this, Alexi?"

"Celebration. My day off." Alex took a swallow and waited for the vodka to join the rest swimming through his system. "I caught the bad guy." With a half laugh, he toasted himself. "And lost the girl."

Mikhail drummed his fingers on the table as he drank. It was no less than he'd expected. "You fought with Bess?"

"Fought?" Lips pursed, Alex studied the clear, potent liquid in his glass. "I don't know that's the term, exactly. Found her with another man."

Mikhail's glass froze halfway to his lips. "You're wrong."

"Nope." Alex reached for the bottle with an almost steady hand. "Walked in and found her lip-locked to this guy she used to be engaged to. Bess has this hobby of getting engaged.''

Mikhail merely shook his head. Something was not quite right with this picture. "Did you kill him?"

"Thought about it." Before he drank again, Alex ran his tongue over his teeth. Good, he thought. They were nearly numb. The rest would follow. "Too damn bad I'm a cop."

"What was her explanation?"

"Didn't give me one. Got pissed, is all." He set the glass down so that he could use both hands to rub his face.

"Because you accused without trusting."

"I didn't accuse," Alex shot back, then pressed his fingers to his burning eyes. "I didn't have to. What I didn't say was unforgivable. She tossed me out on my ear, but not before she told me she didn't love me anyway."

"She lies." Before Alex could lift his glass again, Mikhail grabbed his wrist. "I tell you, she lies. A few days ago she visited Rachel and the baby. I made her sit for me and sketched her while she talked of you. There's no mistaking what I saw in her eyes, Alexi. You're blind if you haven't seen it yourself."

He had seen it, and the pain of remembering what he'd seen clawed through him so that he stumbled to his feet as if to escape it. "She falls in love easily."

"So? There is love, and love. How many times have you taken the fall?"

"This is the first."

"For this kind, yes. There were others."

"They were different."

"Ah." Patient and amused, Mikhail held up a finger. "So it's okay for you to play with love until you find the truth, but it's not okay for Bess."

"It's—" Put that way, it was tough to argue with. Especially when his head was reeling. "Damn it, I was jealous. I have a right to be jealous."

"You have a right to make an ass of yourself, too."

Pleased, now that he knew it could be fixed, Mikhail kicked back and crossed his booted feet. "Did you?"

"Big-time." Alex swayed, then sat down heavily. "I was going to ask her to marry me, Mik. I had the ring in my pocket and these stupid lilacs. I was scared to death she'd say yes. More scared that she'd say no." He propped his spinning head in his hands. "What the hell was she doing kissing that son of a bitch?"

"Maybe if you had asked nicely, she would have told you."

With a lopsided grin, Alex turned his bleary eyes on his brother. "Would you have asked nicely?"

"No, I would have broken his arms, maybe his legs, too. Then I would have asked." With a sigh, Mikhail patted Alex's shoulder. "But that is me. You were always more impulsive."

"We could go find him." Alex considered and, warming to the idea, leaned over to give Mikhail a sloppy hug. "We'll go beat him up together. Like old times."

"We'll try something different." Rising, Mikhail hauled Alex to his feet.

"Where we going?"

"I'm going to put you in a cold shower until your head's clear."

Alex staggered and linked an arm around his brother's neck. "What for?"

"So you can go find your woman and grovel."

Unsure of his footing, Alex stared at the tilting floor. "I don't wanna grovel."

"Yes, you do. It's best to get used to it before you marry her. I have more experience in this."

"Oh, yeah?" Enjoying the idea of his big brother crawling at Sydney's feet, he grinned as Mikhail thrust him, fully clothed, into the shower. "Can I watch next time?"

"No." With immense satisfaction, Mikhail turned the cold water on full and listened to his brother's pained shout bounce viciously on the tiles. "This is a very good start," he decided.

"You son of a bitch." They were both laughing when Alex grabbed Mikhail in a headlock and dragged him under the spray.

He was nearly sober by the time he walked into Bess's office, but he wasn't laughing. It was hard to laugh when your throat was thick with nerves.

He was going to be reasonable, he promised himself. They would discuss the entire matter like civilized adults. And if she didn't give him the right answers, he'd strangle her. He could always arrest himself afterward.

But he only saw Lori sitting at the keyboard, frantically typing. "I'll have the damn changes by six," she called out. Her brow was furrowed in concentration as she glanced up. Her eyes frosted over.

"What the hell do you want?"

"I need to see Bess."

"You're out of luck." Nobody hurt her friend and got away with it. Nobody. "She's not here."

"Where?"

She offered an anatomically impossible suggestion, offered it so coolly he nearly smiled. But it wasn't enough. She leapt up and slammed the door shut. Locked it. "Sit down, buster, I've got an earful for you."

"Tell me where she is."

"When hell freezes over. Do you know what you did to her?" She took the flat of her hand to push him back. "Why didn't you just cut her heart and slice it into little pieces while you were at it?"

"What *I* did?" He jammed his hands into his pockets so he wouldn't shove her back. "I'm the one who walked in and found her snuggled up to that pretty-faced playwright."

"You don't know what you found."

"Then why don't you tell me?"

She'd die first. "You don't know her at all, do you? You didn't have a clue how lucky you were. She's the most loving, most generous, most unselfish person I've ever known. She'd have crawled through broken glass for you." Afraid she'd do something violent if she didn't move, Lori began to pace. "I was so happy when she told me about you. I could see how much in love she was. Really in love. She wasn't just taking you under her wing until she could find someone for you."

"Find someone for me?"

"What do you think she did with all those other men who were dazzled by her?" Lori tossed back. "Oh, she'd try to talk herself into being in love, and thinking they loved her back, and the whole time she'd listen to their problems like some den mother. Then she'd steer them in the direction of some woman she'd decided was perfect for them. She was usually right."

"She was going to marry—"

"She was never going to marry anyone. Whenever she said yes, it was because she couldn't bear to hurt anyone's feelings. And, okay, because she always wanted to have someone she could count on. But however loyal, however sensitive, she is to other people's feelings, she's not stupid. She'd tell herself she was going to get married, then she'd go into overdrive finding the guy a substitute."

"Substitute? Why—?" But Lori wasn't ready to let him get a word in.

"Not that she ever calculated it that way. But after you watched it happen a couple of times, you saw the pattern. But you…" She whirled back to him. "You broke the pattern. She needed you. You made her cry." Angry tears glazed Lori's own eyes. "Not once did I ever see her cry over any man. She'd just slip seamlessly into the my-pal-Bess category, and everyone was happy. But she's cried buckets over you."

He felt sick, and small, and he was beginning to understand a great deal about groveling. "Tell me where she is. Please."

"Why the hell should I?"

"I love her."

She wanted to snarl at him for daring to say so, but she recognized the same misery in his eyes she'd seen in her friend's. "Charlie was—"

"No." He shook his head quickly. "It doesn't matter." What did matter was trust, and it was time he gave it. "I don't need to know. I just need her."

With a sigh, Lori fingered the square-cut diamond on her left hand. Bess had pushed her into taking the right step with Steven. She could only hope she was doing the same in return. "If you hurt her again, Alex—"

"I won't." Then he sighed. "I don't want to hurt her again, but I probably will."

She weakened, because it was exactly the thing a man in love would say. "I sent her home. She wasn't in any shape to work."

"Dyakuyu."

"What?"

"Thanks."

She hated feeling this way. The only way Bess could get from one day to the next was by telling herself it would get better. It had to get better.

But she didn't believe it.

She hadn't had the heart to throw out the lilacs. She'd tried to. She'd even stood holding them over the trash can, weeping like a fool. But the thought of parting with them had been too much. Now she tormented herself with the fragile scent whenever she came downstairs.

She thought about taking a trip—anywhere. She certainly had the vacation time coming, but it didn't seem fair to leave Lori in the lurch, especially since Lori had added wedding plans to her work load.

A lot of good she was doing Lori, or the show, this way, she thought. But the problem of the people in Millbrook seemed terribly petty when compared to hers. Too bad she couldn't write herself out of this one, she thought, as she stood in the kitchen, trying to talk herself into fixing something to eat.

Well, she'd certainly made the grade, Bess told herself, and pressed her fingers against her swollen eyes. She'd fallen in love and had her heart broken. Great research for the next troubled relationship she invented for the television audience.

The hell with food. She was going to go up to bed and will herself to sleep. Tomorrow she would find some way to put her life back together.

When she stepped out of the kitchen, what was left of her life shattered at her feet.

He was standing by the table, one hand brushing over the lilacs. All he did was look at her, turn his head and look, and she nearly crumpled to her knees.

"What are you doing here?" The pain made her voice razor-sharp.

"I still have my key." He lowered his hand slowly. Her eyes were still puffy from her last bout of tears, and there were smudges of fatigue under them. Nothing that had been said to him, nothing he'd said to himself, had lashed more sharply.

"You didn't have to bring it by." If composure was all she had left, she would cling to it. "You could have dropped it in the mail. But thanks." Her smile was so cold it hurt her jaw. "If that's all, I'm in a hurry. I was just on my way up to change before I go out."

"You can't look at me when you lie." He said it half to himself, remembering how her eyes had drifted away from his face when she said she didn't love him.

She forced her gaze back to his, held it steady. "What do you want, Alexi?"

"A great many things. Maybe too many things. But first, for you to forgive me."

Her face crumpled at that. She put a hand up to cover it, knowing it was too late. "Leave me alone."

"*Milaya,* let me—"

"Don't." She cringed away, crossing her arms over herself in self-defense, and his hands stopped an inch away. There was an odd catch in his breath as he drew them back and let them fall to his sides.

"I won't touch you." His voice was quiet and strained. "Please, let me say what I've come to say."

"What else could there be?" She turned away. "I know what you think of me. You made that clear."

"What I did was hurt you and make a fool of myself."

"Oh, yes, you hurt me." She was still trembling from it. "But not just that last time. You hurt me every time you pulled back when I needed to tell you how much I loved you. I thought, I won't let it matter, because he'll have to see it. God, he'll have to see it, because it's right there every time I look at him. Every time I think about him. And he loves me. He wants me. In my whole life, no one wanted me. Not really."

"Bess."

She jerked away from his hands. "My parents," she began, turning back. "How many times I heard them say to each other, 'Where did she come from?' As if I was some stray pet that had wandered in by mistake."

When she began to roam the room, her shoulders still hunched protectively, he said nothing. How could he tell her he was sorry he'd opened up old wounds, and sorry, as well, that it had taken that to have her reveal those smothered feelings to him?

"I handled it." Those stiff shoulders jerked as she tried to shrug it off. "What else could I do? It wasn't their fault, really. They've always been so perfect, in their way, and I could never be. Not for them. Not even for you."

"Do you think that's what I want?"

She glanced back then. The tears had dried up. There was no point in them. "I don't know what you want, Alexi. I only know it keeps circling around. I went from my parents into school. Those awful teenage years, when all the girls were so bright and pretty, and falling in and out of love. No one wanted me. Oh, I had friends. Somewhere along the line I'd learned that if you didn't try so hard, if you just relaxed and acted naturally, that there were a lot of people who'd like you for what you were. But there was never anyone to love. There has never been anybody to love until you."

"There's never going to be anyone else." He waited until she turned back. "I love you, Bess. Please, give me another chance."

"It won't work." She rubbed at her drying tears with the heel of her hand. "I thought it would, I wanted it to. I was so sure love would be enough. But it's not. Not without hope. Certainly not without faith."

The calm way she said it had panic streaking through him. "Do you want me to crawl?" He ignored her defensive retreat and gripped her arms. "Then I will. You're not going to push me out of your life because I was stupid, because I was afraid. I won't let you."

Was this how a man crawled? she wondered. With his eyes flashing fire and his voice booming? "And the next time you see me kissing an old friend?"

"I won't care." With a sound of disgust, he released her to stalk the room. "I will care. I'll kill the next one who touches you."

"Then New York would be littered with bodies." It should be funny, she thought. Why wasn't it funny? "I can't change what I am for you, Alexi. I wouldn't ask you to change for me."

"No, you wouldn't." He scrubbed his hands over his face and struggled to find some balance. "I know a kiss between friends is harmless, Bess. I'm not quite that big a fool. But the other night, when I walked in—''

''You assumed I was betraying you.''

''I don't know what I assumed.'' It was as honest as he could get. ''When I saw you, I felt… It was all feeling,'' he said carefully. ''So I didn't think. In my heart, in my head, I know better than to assume anything. One of my own rules that I broke. There were reasons.'' Calmer now, he walked back and took her hands. ''We'd just finished the bust, and I was wired from it. I knew I'd tell you about it, all about it. I'd gone beyond trying to separate that part of my life—any part of it—from you. It was going to upset you to think about it, because of Rosalie. I knew that, too. Damn it, I knew you'd gone to that funeral alone, and I felt like the lowest kind of creep for letting you.''

He was prying her heart open again, inch by inch. ''I didn't think you knew.''

''I knew.'' His voice was flat. All he could think was how desperately he wanted to hold her. ''You leave notes everywhere. All these pieces of paper scattered around, with scribbling on them about dry-cleaning and dialogue and appointments. I saw the one about the flowers you'd ordered for her, and the directions to the cemetery.'' He looked down at their hands. ''If things hadn't been moving so fast in the investigation, I would have taken the time. I would have tried to.''

That she didn't doubt. ''It was more important to me that you catch the man who killed her than that you go stand over her grave.''

''I wasn't with you,'' he said, more slowly. ''And I wanted to be. And when I got here, I wanted to…'' This was hardly the time to bring up the ring in his pocket. ''I was churned up about a lot of things, Bess. My response was way out of line, and I'll apologize for it as often as you like. But I'd like you to hear me out.''

''It's all right.'' She gave his hands a squeeze, hoping

he'd release hers. He didn't. "Alexi, Charlie was here be-cause—"

"I don't need to know." Now he let her hands go to bring his own to her face. He wanted her to see what was in his eyes. "You don't have to explain yourself to me. You don't have to change yourself for me."

She felt something move inside her heart and was afraid to believe it was healing. "I'd rather clear the air. I was too angry to do it before. He came by to tell me that Gabrielle was expecting. He was like a little boy at Christmas, and he wanted to share his good news with a friend. And to ask me if I'd be godmother—even though it's seven and a half months down the road."

He lowered his brow to hers. "You should have slugged me, McNee." When he moved his mouth toward hers, he felt her retreat. Patiently he stroked his thumbs over her temples. "Just once," he murmured and tasted her lips.

He didn't mean to deepen the kiss, didn't mean to crush her against him and hold her so tightly neither of them could breathe. But he couldn't stop himself until he felt her body shake with a fresh bout of tears.

"Don't. Please don't." He pressed his face into her hair and rocked her. "I'll break apart."

Turning her face into his shoulder, she fought back the worst of the tears. "I didn't want you to come back. I didn't want to feel this again."

He deserved that, he thought as he squeezed his eyes tight. "You were right to send me away. I want a chance to prove to you that you're right to let me back in." He brushed a hand through her hair. "You're so good at lis-tening, Bess. I have to ask you to listen to me now."

"You don't need to apologize again." She could do nothing but love him, she realized, and, drawing back, she managed a smile. "And I can't let you back in, because you were always here."

Her words brought a pressure to his chest. He pressed

their joined hands against it to try to ease it away. "Just that easy?"

"It's not easy." She supposed it would never be easy. "It's just the way it is."

"Mikhail said I would grovel," he murmured. "Bess, you humble me."

"Let's put it behind us." She drew a deep breath, then kissed both his cheeks as a sign of peace. "I'm good at fresh starts."

"No." Taking her hand, he pulled her to the couch. "I like our other start. We don't need a new one, only to play this one out. Sit." He pulled her down with him, keeping her hand close to his heart. "You explained, now I will. I was afraid to believe in you. No woman has ever meant what you mean, and I let myself imagine that you'd be with me forever. Just as I let myself imagine that you'd turn away. And because I was more afraid of the second, it seemed more real."

"It's hard to be afraid." She turned her cheek to her hand. "I know."

"You don't know all." He glanced away, toward the flowers subtly scenting the room. "You kept the lilacs."

"I tried not to." She smiled again. "But they were so beautiful."

"I brought you something besides lilacs that day." He reached into his pocket and drew out the box. Her hand went limp in his. He watched her lips tremble apart. "I don't think it's ostentatious." When she only continued to stare, he shifted. "That was a joke."

"Okay." The two syllables came out in a whisper. "Are you—are you going to let me see it?"

For an answer, he opened the box himself. Inside was a gold band set with a rainbow of gems. He knew what they were only because he'd asked the jeweler to identify each of them. The amethyst, the peridot, the blue topaz, the citrine.

"I know it's not traditional," he said when she remained silent. "But it reminded me of you, and I wanted—hell, I wanted something no one else would have thought to give you."

"No one has," she managed, barely breathing. "No one would."

"If you don't like it, we can look for something else."

She was afraid she would cry again and knew it would do neither of them any good. "It's lovely. Beautiful." She managed to tear her gaze from it. "You bought me this before? You had it with you the other night? You were going to give it to me, then you walked in and saw me with Charlie." Laughing, she lifted a hand to her cheek. "I'm surprised you didn't gun us both down. I couldn't have written it better myself."

"Then you forgive me?"

She already had, but since he was looking so nervous, she nodded. "Anyone with such good taste deserves a second chance."

"I bought this days ago, but it took me a while to work up the nerve. Facing a junkie with an Uzi seemed easier." But he was into it now, and he was going to finish. "My idea was to pressure you to accept it, then push for a quick wedding so you wouldn't change your mind. But that was wrong." He closed the box, and was encouraged by Bess's quick gasp of dismay. "It was stupid, and it showed a lack of faith in both of us. I'm sorry."

"I— You—" She let out a frustrated breath. "I don't mind."

"Of course you do," he said. "It was calculating, even devious, when a proposal of marriage should be romantic. So, when we're both ready, I'll ask you properly."

Her face fell. "When we're both ready?"

"I don't want to push you when you might be feeling a little vulnerable. Especially since a long engagement is out. So I'll give you time."

"Time," she echoed, ready to scream.

"It's fair." He waited a beat. "Okay, I'm ready."

Before she could laugh, he was down on one knee. "What are you doing?"

"A proper proposal of marriage." He nearly launched into his humble little speech. Instead, his eyes darkened when she continued to laugh. "You don't want one."

"Damn right I want one. But I want you up here." She took his hand to tug him back to the couch so that they were at eye level with each other. "I want you to look me right in the eye."

"Okay, then I get something I want, too."

"Name it."

"I want to hear you say it." He caught her hand, brought it to his cheek. "I want very much to hear you say it. I need to hear the words from you."

"I love you, Alexi." For the first time, she said the words smiling, knowing they would be taken as they were meant. "I'm going to love you forever."

He turned his face so that his lips pressed into her palm. Taking the ring out of the box, he slipped it onto her finger. It shot out a rainbow of color. As he linked his fingers with hers, he lifted his head. "Be my family." He shook his head before she could speak and felt himself stumble. "I meant to be romantic. Let me—"

"No." Overwhelmed, she laid a hand over his lips. "That was perfect. Don't change it. Don't change anything."

"Then say yes."

"Yes." She threw her arms around him and laughed. "Oh, yes...."

* * * * *

If you enjoyed reading about
the Stanislaski brothers, look for

**THE STANISLASKI SISTERS:
NATASHA AND RACHEL**

2 complete novels available in one
fabulous volume, from Silhouette Books and
CONSIDERING KATE,
a brand-new book
in the Stanislaski saga,
available from Special Edition.

Only from
#1 *New York Times* bestselling author

**NORA
ROBERTS**

Both books on sale in February 2001,
at your favorite retail outlets.

Here's a sneak preview of
TAMING NATASHA, the first story
in The Stanislaski Sisters: Natasha and Rachel.

It was only dinner, Natasha told herself as she walked to the door. And he was only a man, she added, pulling the door open.

An outrageously attractive man.

He looked wonderful, was all she could think, with his hair swept back from his face, and that half smile in his eyes.

"Hi." He held out another red rose.

Natasha nearly sighed. Giving in a little, she tapped the blossom against her cheek. "It wasn't the roses that changed my mind," she said.

"About what?"

"About having dinner with you."

He smiled then, fully, and exasperated her by looking charming and cocky all at the same time. "What did?"

"I'm hungry." She set her short velvet jacket on the arm of the sofa. "I'll put this in water...."

The restaurant he'd chosen was only a short drive away. Over her first glass of wine, she told herself to relax and enjoy. Over dinner, she was careful to steer the conversation toward subjects they had touched on in his class. But Spence was equally determined to explore more personal areas.

"Tell me about your family."

Natasha slipped a hot, butter-drenched morsel of lobster into her mouth. "I'm the oldest of four," she began, then became abruptly aware that his fingertips were playing casually with hers on the tablecloth. She slid her hand out of reach.

Her maneuver had him lifting his glass to hide a smile. "Are you all spies?"

A flicker of temper joined the lights that the candle brought to her eyes. "Certainly not."

"I wondered, since you seem so reluctant to talk about them." His face sober, he leaned toward her. "Say 'Get moose and squirrel.'"

Her mouth quivered before she gave up and laughed. "I have two brothers and a sister. My parents still live in Brooklyn."

"You said you were about five when you came to the States. Do you remember much about your life before that?"

"Of course."

He ran a fingertip down her wrist and surprised a shiver out of her. Before she moved her hand away, he felt her pulse scramble. "What do you remember?"

Because her reaction annoyed her, she was determined to show him nothing. She only shrugged. "My father bringing in wood for the fire, his hair and coat all covered with snow. The baby crying—my youngest brother. The smell of the bread my mother baked. Pretending to be asleep when I listened to Papa talk to her about escape."

"Were you afraid?"

"Yes." Her eyes blurred with the memory. She didn't often look back, didn't often need to. But when she did, it came not with the watery look of dreams, but clear as glass. "Oh, yes. Very afraid. More than I will ever be again."

"Will you tell me?"

She started to pass it off, but the memory remained too vivid. "We waited until spring and took only what we could carry. We told no one, no one at all, and set off in the wagon. Papa said we were going to visit my mother's sister who lived in the west. But I think there were some who knew, who watched us go with tired faces and big eyes. Papa had papers, badly forged, but he had a map and hoped we would avoid border guards."

"And you were only five?"

"Nearly six by then." Thinking, she ran a fingertip around and around the rim of her glass. "Mikhail was between four and five, Alex just two. At night, if we could risk a fire, we would sit around it and Papa would tell stories. Those were the good nights. We would fall asleep listening to his voice and smelling the smoke from the fire. We went over the mountains and into Hungary. It took us ninety-three days."

He couldn't imagine it, not even when he could see it reflected so clearly in her eyes. Thinking of the little girl, he took her hand and waited for her to go on.

"My father planned for years. Perhaps he had dreamed of it all his life. He had names, people who would help defectors. There was war, the cold one, but I was too young to understand. I understood the fear in my parents, in the others who helped us. We were smuggled out of Hungary into Austria. The church sponsored us, brought us to America. It was a long time before I stopped waiting for the police to come and take my father away."

"That's a lot for a child to deal with."

"I also remember eating my first hot dog." She smiled and picked up her wine. She never spoke of that time, never. Not even with family. Now that she had, with him she felt a desperate need to change the subject. "No childhood is ever completely secure. But we grow up. I'm a businesswoman, and you're a respected composer. Why don't you write?" She felt his fingers tense on hers. "I'm sorry," she said quickly. "I had no business asking that."

"It's all right." His fingers relaxed again. "I don't write because I can't."

"I know your music. Something that intense doesn't fade."

"It hasn't mattered a great deal in the past couple of years. Just lately it's begun to matter again."

"Don't be patient."

When he smiled, she shook her head. "No, I mean it. People always say when the time is right, when the mood is right, when the place is right. Years are wasted that way. If my father had waited until we were older, until the trip was safer, we might still be in the Ukraine. There are some things that should be grabbed with both hands and taken. Life can be very, very short."

He could feel the urgency in the way her hands gripped his. And he could see the shadow of regret in her eyes. The reason for both intrigued him as much as her words.

"You may be right," he said slowly, then brought the palm of her hand to his lips. "Waiting isn't always the best answer."

"It's getting late." Natasha pulled her hand free, then balled it into a fist on her lap. But that didn't stop the heat from spearing her arm....

ATTENTION **JOAN JOHNSTON FANS!**

Silhouette Books is proud to present

HAWK'S WAY
BACHELORS

The first three novels in
the bestselling Hawk's Way series
now in one fabulous collection!

On Sale December 2000

THE RANCHER AND THE RUNAWAY BRIDE
Brawny rancher Adam Phillips has his hands full when
Tate Whitelaw's overprotective, bossy brothers show up with
shotguns in hand!

THE COWBOY AND THE PRINCESS
Ornery cowboy Faron Whitelaw is caught off-guard
when breathtakingly beautiful Belinda Prescott proves to be
more than a gold digger!

THE WRANGLER AND THE RICH GIRL
Sparks fly when Texas debutante Candy Baylor makes handsome
horse breeder Garth Whitelaw an offer he can't refuse!

**HAWK'S WAY: Where the Whitelaws of Texas
run free…till passion brands their hearts.**

"Joan Johnston does contemporary Westerns to perfection."
—Publishers Weekly

Available at your favorite retail outlet.

Where love comes alive™

USA Today Bestselling Author

SHARON SALA

has won readers' hearts with thrilling tales
of romantic suspense. Now Silhouette Books
is proud to present five passionate stories from
this beloved author.

Available in August 2000:
ALWAYS A LADY
A beauty queen whose dreams have been dashed in a
tragic twist of fate seeks shelter for her wounded spirit
in the arms of a rough-edged cowboy....

Available in September 2000:
GENTLE PERSUASION
A brooding detective risks everything to protect the
woman he once let walk away from him....

Available in October 2000:
SARA'S ANGEL
A woman on the run searches desperately for a reclusive
Native American secret agent—the only man who can save
her from the danger that stalks her!

Available in November 2000:
HONOR'S PROMISE
A struggling waitress discovers she is really a rich heiress—
and must enter a powerful new world of wealth and
privilege on the arm of a handsome stranger....

Available in December 2000:
KING'S RANSOM
A lone woman returns home to the ranch where she was
raised, and discovers danger—as well as the man she once
loved with all her heart....

You're not going to believe this offer!

In October and November 2000, buy any two Harlequin or Silhouette books and save $10.00 off future purchases, or buy any three and save $20.00 off future purchases!

Just fill out this form and attach 2 proofs of purchase (cash register receipts) from October and November 2000 books and Harlequin will send you a coupon booklet worth a total savings of $10.00 off future purchases of Harlequin and Silhouette books in 2001. Send us 3 proofs of purchase and we will send you a coupon booklet worth a total savings of $20.00 off future purchases.

Saving money has never been this easy.

I accept your offer! Please send me a coupon booklet:

Name: _____

Address: _____ City: _____

State/Prov.: _____ Zip/Postal Code: _____

Optional Survey!

In a typical month, how many Harlequin or Silhouette books would you buy <u>new</u> at retail stores?

☐ Less than 1   ☐ 1   ☐ 2   ☐ 3 to 4   ☐ 5+

Which of the following statements best describes how you <u>buy</u> Harlequin or Silhouette books? Choose one answer only that <u>best</u> describes you.

☐ I am a regular buyer and reader
☐ I am a regular reader but buy only occasionally
☐ I only buy and read for specific times of the year, e.g. vacations
☐ I subscribe through Reader Service but also buy at retail stores
☐ I mainly borrow and buy only occasionally
☐ I am an occasional buyer and reader

Which of the following statements best describes how you <u>choose</u> the Harlequin and Silhouette series books you buy <u>new</u> at retail stores? By "series," we mean books within a particular line, such as *Harlequin PRESENTS* or *Silhouette SPECIAL EDITION*. Choose one answer only that <u>best</u> describes you.

☐ I only buy books from my favorite series
☐ I generally buy books from my favorite series but also buy books from other series on occasion
☐ I buy some books from my favorite series but also buy from many other series regularly
☐ I buy all types of books depending on my mood and what I find interesting and have no favorite series

---

Please send this form, along with your cash register receipts as proofs of purchase, to:
In the U.S.: Harlequin Books, P.O. Box 9057, Buffalo, NY 14269
In Canada: Harlequin Books, P.O. Box 622, Fort Erie, Ontario L2A 5X3
(Allow 4-6 weeks for delivery) Offer expires December 31, 2000.

PHQ4002

Silhouette®—

where love comes alive—online...

eHARLEQUIN.com

your romantic books

💜 Shop online! Visit Shop eHarlequin and discover a wide selection of new releases and classic favorites at great discounted prices.

💜 Read our daily and weekly Internet exclusive serials, and participate in our interactive novel in the reading room.

💜 Ever dreamed of being a writer? Enter your chapter for a chance to become a featured author in our Writing Round Robin novel.

• • • • • •

your romantic life

💜 Check out our feature articles on dating, flirting and other important romance topics and get your daily love dose with tips on how to keep the romance alive every day.

• • • • • •

your community

💜 Have a Heart-to-Heart with other members about the latest books and meet your favorite authors.

💜 Discuss your romantic dilemma in the Tales from the Heart message board.

your romantic escapes

💜 Learn what the stars have in store for you with our daily Passionscopes and weekly Erotiscopes.

💜 Get the latest scoop on your favorite royals in Royal Romance.

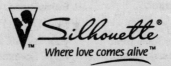